THE SOCIETY

For a Restored America

CG ABBOT

Blazing Sword
Publishing Ltd.

CG Abbot/Blazing Sword Publishing, Ltd.

Colorado Springs, CO 80907

www.blazingswordpub.com

Publisher's Note: This is a work of fiction. Names, characters, places, and incidents are products of the author's imagination or are used fictitiously. Locales and public names are sometimes used for atmospheric purposes. Any resemblance to actual people, living or dead, or to businesses, companies, events, institutions, or locales is entirely coincidental.

© Cover Art, Layout, and Design by Cora Graphics

Ordering Information:

Quantity sales. Special discounts are available on quantity purchases by corporations, associations, and others. For details, contact Ingram.

The Society/ C.G. Abbot -- 1st ed.

ISBN 978-0-9990318-7-2

❀ Created with Vellum

*Dedicated to the next generation charged
with carrying the torch for civil rights, equality, and
ensuring justice and liberty for all.*

Those who manipulate this unseen mechanism of society constitute an invisible government which is the true ruling power of our country
—Edward Bernays, "Propaganda" 1928, The Father of Modern PR

- - - - - - - - - - -

"I think today there might be a much
better chance of success of moving
attention away from the story."
-Carl Bernstein, Co-author of All the President's Men, Watergate Journalist

CHAPTER ONE

June Recent Past-Elizabeth Grant

In the kitchen, Elizabeth grabbed the teakettle before its shrill whistle could disturb the early morning quiet that lay like a shroud over the house. Hopefully, some tea would help to calm her nerves and her nausea, the physical results of her nightmares. She poured the water over her waiting tea bag in a mug.

She rubbed her sore thigh and then rotated her aching shoulder as the tea steeped. They were sore from falling out of bed in the grip of her dream. Her long chestnut hair was still disheveled and her pallor made the sprinkling of freckles across her face and cheeks stand out. Her heart was approaching a normal rate now.

She settled into a worn chair in Grandma's living room, last decorated a few decades ago when brown and gold country-patterned fabric with heavy oak touches were all the rage. The scent of lemon furniture polish clung in the air. She breathed deeply the steam from the tea and let her breath out slowly. The subdued light from the one lamp created a cocoon of safety and comfort. Now that the adrenaline rush was fading maybe she could get another hour or two of sleep after all.

The nightmares would pass, she had to face them head-on like you would a bully.

She took in the room, each knick-knack and crocheted doily. She used to spend every summer with her grandma and grandpa. It had been like a second home. Her first summer spent here was lonely, until she met Loralie, a local girl, in the park. She was only six and Loralie barely five, and they had been like sisters from that moment. They were both raised by single moms and didn't know their dads. Elizabeth's life had changed in that instant in the park.

Until seven years ago when it all changed again, all because she didn't come to visit over the summer. Her world shifted because of that simple decision. Loralie, the closest thing to a sister she ever had, disappeared that summer she didn't come to visit, and worse – they had fought terribly only weeks before she vanished.

Digging up bones.

Her life was moving along fine on a predictable path of school, and eventually college. When they had fought over Loralie's brother, Jeremiah, she couldn't have known that would be the last time they would speak, the last memory of her would be words of anger.

She took a sip of tea. Why had she started having the nightmares again? It had been over a year since the last one. But, this was her first visit to Mississippi since the night Loralie had gone missing.

Maybe just returning was enough to start her night terrors again. Shouldn't it be ancient history and the nightmares long gone? Okay, she still felt guilty for not visiting that summer, as if she could have prevented whatever happened to Loralie.

She held out hope that her dearest friend had left town touring with a band or something and got out of Cyprus. One day her friend would call and share her adventures..

Nightmares were one thing and even understandable, but seeing things – visions or hallucinations – was a whole different matter.

The night Loralie went missing was *the night* she swore she saw a vision of Loralie in her bedroom in Denver, Colorado. An image of a beaten and bloody Loralie, who was physically in Cyprus hundreds of miles away, appeared right there in her bedroom, frantically reaching out to her. Then Elizabeth passed out. When she regained consciousness her mother was holding her in her arms and dabbing her face with a cold washcloth.

It was on Elizabeth's insistent pleading that her mother called Mississippi in the middle of the night to ask a groggy Mrs. Carter to put Loralie on the phone. She remembered taking the phone, waiting for Loralie to talk to her so she could get that image out of her mind, only for Mrs. Carter to come back with ragged breaths and exclaim; "She's not here. I can't find her!"

It was the instant that she had that vision of Loralie that really changed her life. But she *had* seen her and was inconsolable for hours, so she was labeled "fragile", "over-sensitive", and "over-wrought". Being at grandma's was bringing it all back.

Digging up bones.

No physical trace was ever found of Loralie. Then the nightmares had started – and hallucinations of Loralie regularly over the last seven years. The nightmares terrified her, but the hallucinations… visions… whatever you called them – they left her doubting herself.

She made the mistake of researching what could cause hallucinations and was convinced she had a brain tumor or something for the first year. Still, she told nobody about her continued visions. As far as everybody else knew, her mother included, the night Loralie disappeared was the only time she experienced such a visual aberration, rather than the continual problem that plagued her still.

She shook her head to dismiss such serious thoughts. It was disconcerting to be here again. She wasn't the same person who had last run happily through the house, long ago.

She rubbed her eyes and sipped at her tea, clearing her mind. She stiffened when she heard a car pull into the driveway. Every cell in her body listened.

This wasn't Denver. People in rural little Cyprus were asleep at this hour. Maybe some were doing chores on the surrounding farms, but nobody was out visiting in the wee hours of the morning.

Barely audible footfalls on the veranda floorboards and a soft knocking at the door made her heart race. Just that quickly the feeling of a secure cocoon vanished – replaced by dread. She scanned the shadows and saw Loralie, forever sixteen, like an animated photograph, motioning with a degree of urgency for her to go answer the door. She swallowed, shakily set her tea down, and stood up.

Surely it's nothing. It'll be innocent, you'll see. But, she felt like she was on the very edge of a cliff and everything in her life was about to change, again.

She took a deep breath to calm herself and rolled her shoulders back, crossed the living room to the door and slowly opened it.

On the wide white-painted veranda was an elderly black woman with her hand poised to knock again. She lowered her hand and smiled. It was a wide genuine smile that made her eyes sparkle. In the illumination of the porch light, her coifed white hair looked more like a halo. She wore a turquoise cotton dress, was of average height, but stood proudly and with composure. Another time and place one might think she was Egyptian royalty.

"Hello dear, I'm Madame Antoinette of Shreveport, Louisiana. You must be Elizabeth. I've been driving all night to talk to you, hon." Her voice was melodic with a reserved southern drawl. She watched expectantly as Elizabeth blinked a few times.

"Ma'am, you're here to see me? At 4:30 in the morning? Are you sure you have the right house?" Elizabeth whispered because she instinctively felt the need to be quiet. A dog barked in the distance, then howled – a long mournful baying filled the air.

Madame looked around at the other houses on the street. All were dark and quiet. Returning her attention to Elizabeth she whispered, "I must speak with you about Loralie." Looking around again she added, "I had to visit when I was least likely to be seen."

CHAPTER TWO

The General

Somewhere in a sprawling Greek-Revival style plantation home in Louisiana, a chiming phone was breaking the quiet early morning hours. His hand reached in the dark to grab the cell phone on his bedside table, answering in the middle of the third ring.

"Hold on a moment." He eased into his leather slippers and grabbed his robe as he left his wife to her dreams. He closed the bedroom door softly and walked down the curved grand staircase making his way to the ground floor and his home office. He closed and locked his office door then plopped into his luxuriant tan leather desk chair.

"Okay, go." He listened for a moment.

His face transformed from sleepy to suspicious, "She hasn't been in town twelve hours and she's got visitors in the middle of the night? Who was it? How can you not know, it's a small town! I don't like this. Find out exactly who that woman was. I want to know why she visited. NOW!" He pushed the disconnect button. He missed the old phones you could slam down.

But, unfocused anger was only good if it spurred action, blind rage had to be harnessed and directed as fuel. His mentor and benefactor, Elijah Wiltshire, had taught him that lesson among many others.

The General of The Society for a Restored America sat at his hand-carved cherry-wood desk drumming his manicured fingers. The top of his head was bald, but a row of light brown hair ringed his head. His sturdy six-foot build was covered in Egyptian cotton pajamas of royal blue and a matching robe.

"I reckon the long waiting game may just be drawing to a close, now," he said aloud. His voice seemed ordinary but violence lurked under the surface like a cobra waiting to strike.

The General had always suspected that something had been passed along to Elizabeth. He would finally find out just how much Elizabeth knew. If there was anything that could actually incriminate The Society, it would be destroyed and anybody who knew about it would simply disappear – gator bait.

He lovingly picked up the antique looking dagger with an eight-inch serpentine blade and rosewood handle embedded with rubies. He toyed with it, deep in thought. His field man there in Cyprus was competent and he had a vested interest since he had overseen the killing of that nuisance black girl years ago.

Elizabeth had known too quickly that Loralie was missing; she had known too definitely that something was wrong. He damn well bet that turncoat, Noah Aarons, had already started documenting and collecting evidence before his men executed him. He tossed the knife up in the air, flipping and catching it with familiarity.

He was so thankful he had Society members in key positions of the FBI, so the instant Noah contacted the Bureau he was as good as dead. What they hadn't planned on was he had somehow passed some documents of some sort to that Loralie creature. Never finding those documents was a nagging loose end that made the General uneasy, which made him mad.

It seemed Elizabeth knew about the documents Noah had passed to Loralie. It was obvious she had been in contact with Loralie, how else could Elizabeth know she was in trouble? He never believed her wild tale of seeing Loralie's ghost. How gullible did she think people were?

He was fairly certain she didn't have possession of whatever documents or evidence Noah had secreted away, but she had to know where they were. Her visit to Cyprus was probably to retrieve them if Loralie had squirreled them away somewhere and told Elizabeth by phone before his men had snatched her. He had to ensure those documents could not cause The Society any problems now.

"That little bitch's timing is mighty inconvenient," he growled. The violence more evident in his voice as his hand clenched around the dagger handle, the red rubies pressed against his palm, cold and hard.

Now, of all times, was not when he would have picked to play their little game out. They finally had members in all the power positions within the federal government, the military branches, FBI, CIA, NSA, banking and finance, media, and all major city police forces as well as all major city governments.

He had built the basic secret society turned over to him by Elijah Wiltshire into a bona fide clandestine organization ready to shape the country to its prior glory. In a few more months, it wouldn't matter what Noah Aarons may have passed to anybody. In a very short time nobody could stop The Society!

And the beauty of the plan was how the people would gladly accept everything and never suspect they'd been led by the hand, deceived, until it was too late – if ever.

It was amazing how susceptible the majority of people were to propaganda – cattle wanting to be herded so long as it fed their anger or insecurity. The General and his leadership had taken Edward Bernays' engineering of consent concepts from his book "Propaganda" to heart. It provided a blueprint for their takeover, and it worked perfectly, and quietly too.

"Those who manipulate this unseen mechanism of society constitute an invisible government which is the true ruling power of our country." He spoke in reverent tones Bernays' words to the office walls.

The General raised the knife and with a flick of his wrist lodged it in a photo on the opposite wall. The knife wiggled in the right eye of the President of the United States, rubies glistening in the low light like drops of blood.

CHAPTER THREE

Elizabeth

Elizabeth snapped out of her confusion at the mention of Loralie, "Oh, please come in, pardon my bad manners." As she opened the screen door for her visitor to enter, she looked around the neighborhood, too. Nobody was in sight. The same trucks were parked along the street with their "Guns and God, Now More Than Ever," and "Insured by Smith and Wesson" bumper stickers. The hair on the back of her neck tingled and she could have sworn she was being watched.

"Please have a seat….Mrs…eh…Madame ….can I get you some tea or coffee?"

Her visitor sat down and patted the cushion next to her on the couch, "No my dear, we haven't time. I wish this were more of a social call so I could get to know you better, but there just isn't time."

Elizabeth stiffly walked to the couch and sat down. She wondered if she was still dreaming, it felt surreal. Madame Antoinette took a breath as if she had a lot to get out quickly.

"Loralie's mighty agitated and worried about you. She nagged me until I promised to drive up here and help you." Madame's silvery hair seemed to brighten the subdued lighting of the room.

Elizabeth's eyes grew large. "Where is she, is she all right? Why hasn't she contacted me? Or her mother at least?" Elizabeth's voice cracked, "I'd given up hope."

Maybe those visions of Loralie were just her guilt over the fight or wanting to see her so badly. Maybe Loralie had escaped the poverty and oppression in these parts. Maybe…

"Oh goodness me, I thought you understood. Well Loralie is, that is to say she – well surely you knew? Loralie's dead, Darlin'. But, she hasn't passed over to the other side yet." Eyes filled with concern stared at Elizabeth. She placed her hand over Elizabeth's and patted it.

"You… you're sure she's dead? I hoped someday she would contact me." It sounded ridiculous, even to herself, but there had never been any proof Loralie was anything other than missing. There never had been a *body*.

Loralie's image separated from the shadows of the room and came closer. Elizabeth looked away. She got control of her runaway mouth too; she suspected she was sharing far too much with a stranger.

"You knew, you just didn't want to accept it. Well, it's been years, you're all grown up and started your career. Time to get on with your life." She gently patted Elizabeth's folded hands again and squared her shoulders as if bracing herself for what was next.

Dead? There was a part of her, deep down and long buried that had suspected it. Nobody could have seen the horrific vision of Loralie those many years ago, brutally beaten, and not considered the possibility she was dead. That might mean the visions…

She glanced briefly at the vision of Loralie anxiously watching her every move. This vision was not bloody like the first time; she looked like she did that last summer they spent together.

Guilt assaulted her again. If she had just spent the summer here in Mississippi rather than taking that damned summer college-credit class, Loralie might be okay. They would have patched their friendship.

Digging up bones.

"I guess, maybe." She managed. "But didn't you say she's been nagging you?" Understanding reached Elizabeth's sleep deprived mind.

"Are you telling me you talk with the dead – a psychic or something?" She couldn't keep the slight edge from her voice. This was ridiculous. How could this seemingly intelligent woman believe such nonsense?

"Oh, now don't give me that skeptical tone when you've seen her with your very own eyes. I know she appeared to you when she died, but you couldn't accept it." Madame Antoinette nodded her head as if that settled the matter. "She says you continue to resist her. It seems the only way you're open to her is in your dreams. She just can't get you to understand... or accept her."

Elizabeth raised her right eyebrow. "My dreams, huh?" Not ready to admit to anything, Elizabeth didn't want to just swallow this lady's story hook, line, and sinker. She wasn't giving anything away to a stranger, nice as she seemed. But having just fallen out of bed from just such a dream, she couldn't deny it with much zeal.

"Now, I really can't be here long, apparently you're watched. Have been since Loralie died. Now she doesn't want you worryin' about her – she's just fine," Madame Antoinette's eyes softened, "you're the one in danger and really must be careful. The danger surrounding you is why she still tries to connect with you – her love for you never died."

Tears welled up in Elizabeth's eyes and she blinked them away. Was this a cruel joke? *Her love for you never died.* How could she believe what this woman was saying?

But, she had often wondered if her nightmares were somehow glimpses into Loralie's last moments. *Don't ask how that could be possible, because logically it just couldn't.* But that was a different matter from believing this stranger was in contact with Loralie's spirit, which was just impossible. Wasn't it?

Surrounded by danger? How could she be in any danger? This simply didn't make any sense.

"Begging your pardon Ma'am, but I just don't see how I could be in any danger. I mean, there's no reason for it. I'm an architectural engineer. I live a pretty boring life focused on my career. I'm not a threat to anybody. No offense ma'am, but I think you've got the wrong person."

She may have been out of practice with the southern propensity for manners, but Elizabeth didn't want to hurt this woman's feelings either. She liked her in spite of her fanciful ideas. *Constantly watched? That clearly wasn't her. She was a nobody, struggling with experiencing visual* aberrations *and scary dreams, granted, but still a nobody.* She stood and started to move toward the door.

"I'm not leaving just yet, Sugah. There's more; and as I've already mentioned, I need to leave soon enough as it is. Now sit back down right here and before you know it, I'll be gone. But not before I tell you what needs to be said." Madame Antoinette pursed her lips and settled into the couch.

Elizabeth felt the lack of sleep and her inclination to like this lady was clouding her mind. Like a child obeying her mother, she sat down next to her visitor.

"Now for the important part. Stay with me now. Loralie's been dead all these years. But why she was killed has put you in a bushel of danger. Worse, your coming back has put you in even a bigger mess. You need to get on home as soon as you can zip your suitcase and jump in your car." Her eyes bore into Elizabeth seemingly willing her to listen.

She didn't believe in the psychic thing, nor the notion of talking to the dead, even if she herself saw Loralie in the shadows. But this stranger seemed to genuinely believe she was in danger.

"I'm just watching the house for my grandmother. I'm not doing anything and I really can't see how I'm in any danger." She smiled to give no offense. *Really, she was no threat to anybody.*

"Loralie said you wouldn't leave." Madame Antoinette let out a sigh. "You must've realized continually seeing Loralie's spirit is extraordinary." She continued to gaze directly into Elizabeth's eyes until Elizabeth looked away.

"You have a gift, my dear, that you've been denying. Believe me when I say, if you won't go directly home, then your very life depends on you embracing your gift as quickly and totally as you can." Madame Antoinette stopped with that.

Elizabeth realized her mouth was gaping open. She quickly shut it and swallowed several times. It was just too ludicrous to comprehend.

"It's not a gift when you're sent to a psychiatrist, or have pastors praying the devil will leave you alone, or when your mother and uncle watch you as if you'll suddenly snap in front of them. It isn't a gift to see your best friend's face all swollen, bloodied, and her dress in shreds. That's no gift, but a problem I'm dealing with." Her shaky voice finished.

"My dear child, neither you nor your family understands these matters." Her voice was soothing. "Now I understand why Loralie was so desperate that I help you. But, your family simply isn't equipped to guide you in this area." She caressed Elizabeth's cheek with a soft yet strong hand and continued.

"I need to prepare you as much as I can in a few minutes. Take this." She shoved a CD that appeared created on a home computer into her hands. "That's instructions on how to meditate. Don't even think of giving it back to me. This is vital, whether you believe it or not, you've gotta start meditating daily. Daily, you got that? Oh, I almost forgot this." She handed Elizabeth an old portable CD player and a pack of batteries. *How did she find this old tech stuff?*

"Was...was she...murdered?" Her mind seemed to be lagging behind, like one of those foreign movies where the mouth talking is out of synch with the voice. She had finally realized her visitor hadn't said how Loralie had supposedly died.

"Now don't focus on that, it was a long time ago and you need to move on. Don't be dragging up old problems or borrowing trouble." Madame Antoinette reached into her tidy purse and withdrew a handful of something.

"Here. You must wear this at all times!" She quickly slipped a small flannel pouch at the end of a big loop of leather around Elizabeth's neck. "Gris-gris, or Mojo, you know. I made it special for you – it's for protection." Her eyes showed tenderness and maybe a hint of fear.

Elizabeth stared at the small flannel bag dangling around her neck. She sniffed it and found it to smell of herbs. "What...?" *What was gris-*

gris and how was it supposed to protect her? She surmised it was likely more superstition, but it couldn't hurt she supposed.

"Oh, I just wish I'd more time with you dear," she took a breath and looked directly into Elizabeth's eyes, holding her captive with her gaze. "You've got the sight, no denyin' that. I know you're afraid of it, don't understand it or even like it, but you've got to embrace who you are or you'll never find peace. You've got to learn to quiet your mind, to meditate." She blinked and Elizabeth looked away, seemingly breaking the hold that had kept her focus locked on this unusual woman.

"You aren't imbalanced because of this gift. It isn't wrong or a sign you're in the grip of Satan, nor any other fool idea. " She paused when Elizabeth sucked in her breath. "You've gotta believe and trust your-self, dear. I know it troubles you when you sense Loralie around you, see her, or have the dreams," Madame Antoinette's voice was commanding and forceful. "You're stronger than you can imagine."

How could this stranger know her biggest fears? Once it was clear she didn't have a brain tumor, she succumbed to fear of the alternatives along with her family. She'd never had anyone tell her this was special, only a bad sign. All that aside, seeing her missing dearest friend in visions repeatedly didn't feel special at all.

Madame Antoinette stood up. "It's gotten late, I really need to leave before it gets any lighter out."

Elizabeth followed her to the door, unable to make a coherent sentence from the lack of sleep, the emotions of the nightmare, and then this strange visit. What do you say to a stranger who appears in the early morning hours dropping a few bombshells on you and then just as suddenly rushes off? Once they reached the door Madame Antoinette turned.

"One final thing, let me give you the name and number you can call for help. It's important you don't trust just anybody," she gently touched Elizabeth's arm. "Do you understand? She's very clear. I got Loralie's okay to give this name and number. This is the only person I know you can trust." Madame Antoinette handed her a card of FBI agent Malcom Alexander.

Elizabeth shook her head, "The FBI? I'm sure I won't be needing this, but thank you all the same." *The FBI?* But Madame wouldn't take the card back.

"Goodbye dear, I doubt we'll see each other again." For a brief moment Elizabeth knew that was true and felt very sad for knowing it.

Madame Antoinette opened the door, letting weak dawn light in and the barking of that dog in the distance. She turned and was out the door. She was backing her car out of the driveway and was gone just as quickly as she had arrived.

Elizabeth looked around again. Was that a neighbor's curtain swinging closed? She slowly closed the door and locked it out of habit. She belatedly wished she had hugged Madame, to have that solid contact to prove to herself this had all been real. It already felt like she had just dreamt the whole visit.

Loralie was dead and she was in danger?

CHAPTER FOUR

Jake Craig

The sun had just risen and Sheriff Jake Craig sat at his compact red Formica kitchen table. He stared into his black and bitter coffee, thinking. Elizabeth had actually come back to Cyprus! It had been seven years since she had last spent the summer.

Of course, he had taken a trip a few times to check up on her; not that she knew anything about his visits. He took his wallet out of his back pocket and rummaged until he pulled out the photo he kept of her at her college graduation. This way he always knew what she looked like all grown up.

She was pretty as a peach, not that fake glamour stuff; rather, what used to be called the girl next door. Her light brown eyes were sad even though she had a full smile. He remembered her graduation and noticed how she seemed alone, solitary. She chatted with several people but clearly wasn't close with anyone.

Well, he would figure out how to stay close to her or as close as he could without her wondering why. He ran a hand through his salt-and-pepper crew cut. How the years had slipped by. This was an important summer and he better get a move on. He tucked the photo back into its secure place in his wallet.

Sheriff Craig stood up, unfolding his burly no-necked barrel-chested frame with few signs of age affecting him, slipped his hat on, shined his badge with his sleeve, and checked his revolver before heading out the door.

CHAPTER FIVE

Elizabeth Grant

Elizabeth attempted to go back to sleep, but it was out of the question after Madame Antoinette's visit. She sat staring, thinking, and processing for a few hours.

Questions kept running through her head. *How did a stranger know where to find her?*

Loralie's ghost was not really possible. Get real.

Why was she called Madame? Maybe she was a television psychic like on those late night commercials.

She couldn't really expect her to believe that a dead Loralie was worried about her safety. Inconceivable.

Perhaps hardest to grasp was that she was truly in danger. She was kicking herself for not asking what danger and from whom? She really had botched that whole chat, she blamed the nightmare for her poor handling of the whole bizarre visit.

Could somebody just be pulling a prank on her? Had she been punked? She was reluctant to believe that of the charming woman she had met just hours ago. No, she was perhaps a little delusional with the spirit communication thing, maybe she was actually from around here and heard folks talk about her visit and her imagination cooked up the rest.

She sat in the same worn chair she had sipped tea in earlier. She looked at the flannel pouch still hanging around her neck. She hadn't taken it off. *It wasn't hurting anything.* Gris-Gris she had said. It sounded familiar. *Where had she heard it before?*

It all seemed fantastic. A total stranger drives from Shreveport, Louisiana because her dead friend is worried about her. The pre-dawn visit had been improbable from the first knock to Madame Antoinette's sudden exit.

She shook her head vigorously. *Stop this! This will drive you crazy.* She walked to the kitchen and decided she needed some strong coffee; tea wouldn't cut it this morning.

You have to face your fears as grandpa had always said. Face it square-on without flinching – that's what he would have told her. That was the point to her watching the place for Gran while she went on a cruise, facing her past and what lurked there. Don't make your-self crazy second-guessing yourself.

The kitchen was dated with gold appliances and Formica counter-tops with matching yellow-checkered half curtains over the sink. She looked through the refrigerator and cupboards. She would have to get a few groceries that were more to her tastes, pickled pig's feet and ears weren't in her diet. Getting out of the house was sounding like a good idea, maybe go out for breakfast too. Stay active. She prepared the old tin stovetop percolator that Gran had used for decades that you only saw for camping anymore. It brewed a wicked strong cup of java, and she needed it.

She stood in the middle of the kitchen waiting for the water to boil.

Believe that you are a good person and you aren't crazy. Madame's words echoed in her head. What if she at least verified in her own mind what happened the night Loralie disappeared? She would be facing her fears and what happened to Loralie.

Elizabeth felt better having a plan, a place to start, even if it was just a step at a time. She poured the dark coffee into her cup and doctored it with sweetener and milk. She nearly choked on the strong and bitter concoction but drank it anyway. She could kill for her corner coffee shop and their divine Cappuccino back in Denver.

She wasn't ready to just accept Loralie being dead, but it lurked in the back of her mind. The nightmares were what really worried her. If they were somehow a glimpse into her last moments, as she sometimes considered, then Loralie was chased down with dogs by men with guns through the woods in the dark, caught, beaten, and even raped, then to have one vicious blow too many until Elizabeth would wake up screaming with waves of nausea overcoming her. It was a terrible thought that it could've really happened that way.

Elizabeth shivered and pushed those thoughts further to the back of her mind. She wrapped her hands around the coffee mug and forced a few sips down.

She began to blame herself for not doing something to find out what had happened sooner. But, Elizabeth had raised the alarm that dreadful night to find Loralie. Afterward, her mother would only tell her that Loralie was never found. Surely the police were called? Could they have found something and she was just never told since she was so distraught?

Tears welled up in her eyes. Elizabeth knew in her very being that her dearest friend in the world was likely dead and might have died a horrible death. It seemed holding onto the hope that somehow she was out in the world somewhere these past years was more and more a fantasy.

Digging up bones.

More than just a friend, they'd been sisters. Elizabeth tearfully remembered the summer they camped in the backyard and pricked their fingers and made themselves sisters. For the last seven years, Elizabeth had felt like she was just going through the motions without her sister, always anticipating Loralie to reappear in her life and pick up where they left off. She wiped her tears away and took another sip, her hands shaking.

Elizabeth had been sending money to Mrs. Carter, Loralie's mother, and wrote regularly to her little brother, Jeremiah. She had tried to be available to lend support to Jeremiah, like a surrogate sister. She had even gone to the same college Loralie and she planned on attending together.

The entire time she was in college she thought how much better it would've been if only Loralie were there...not the lurking vision of Loralie. She felt like she was stuck, like the past wouldn't let her go and had her tied up, immobile, or unable to move forward.

She was facing her personal fears of hallucinating for all those years, and it was time to establish the facts in her mind. Facts were comforting amidst all her emotions.

What had the police done or found? Was a missing person's investigation done? She didn't know, yet. Loralie's photo could have gone out in an Amber Alert or she was a statistic of runaways. Her mother and uncle kept her in the dark and wouldn't talk about it.

She would just have to get some answers for her inner peace, and for Loralie's family as well. She could at least do that. It might not excuse her inaction all these years, but maybe she could bring something good out of it.

She downed the last of her rock gut coffee and rinsed out the cup, leaving it in the sink. She grabbed her purse and extracted her keys. She would stop at the café she saw in town for a little breakfast.

She stepped out onto the front veranda that just hours before had Madame Antoinette standing there. The day was sticky-hot and humid, but a shiver ran up her spine. She looked around carefully, unable to shake a feeling of being watched.

On the porch, she picked up the paper. The Cyprus Sentinel's headline, Philadelphia Family Massacred By Gang, reported the news of a suspected racially motivated brutal slaughter of a white family by the Black Apostles gang. Five people killed, yet it barely registered in her brain. She tossed the paper inside and shut the door.

She still didn't know what to make of Madame Antoinette; somebody out there knew she had the hallucination of Loralie, somebody besides her barely visited psychiatrist. She doubted her family had shared it with any others since they did everything possible to avoid ever mentioning the incident. So many questions, she needed answers.

As she got into her Mustang, a shiver ran down her spine and she had the overwhelming sensation her every move was being scrutinized. Didn't Madame Antoinette believe she was watched?

CHAPTER SIX

The General

The General of the Society for a Restored America was drinking his morning cup of Kopi Luwak coffee from Indonesia. He enjoyed his morning ritual with his $600.00 a pound brew of caffeine while reading the paper. The Washington Post was the third paper this morning. All of them had extensive coverage about the murdered family in Philadelphia.

He was pleased and a little excited as his plan unfolded on the national scene. He sat on his patio in his plush red cedar outdoor furniture, relaxed while preparations for his son's ninth birthday began around him.

The large canopy tent was being set up first because of the unmerciful sun and heat. The catering staff would have the tables ready to set out a spread of food from lobster and steak to a variety of pasta just prior to the diner portion. White clad dark skinned servants scurried about, darting glances sideways at him.

His brother-in-law, Mark, strode across the lush lawn to join him. Mark had married the sister of the General's wife, Charlotte. Mark was his second in the Society's hierarchy until the time that his young son, Caleb, was ready and able to take the reins. He was tanned from hours on golf courses, and his sandy brown hair was perfectly clipped.

Mark poured himself some coffee from the carafe and leaned back against plump cushions. "I see you're enjoyin' the news. It's everywhere I look, and online it's even more prevalent. Everyone jumped on the Black Apostles gang bein' behind the murders as we intended." His slight accent carried a hint of his South Carolina roots.

"Yes, our media members were primed, and so far they're on schedule. Everythin' is going as planned." The murdered family had become martyrs for The Society, and he would remember them as such. "To the Johnson family and their sacrifice." The General raised his coffee cup.

"Is that all you can say? I feel like celebratin'. This is the kickoff of The Society's move to restore this nation. It's what you and Elijah, may he rest in peace, have been buildin' for decades." Mark's eyes were bright and he couldn't stop smiling.

Elijah Wiltshire was the man who recruited him into The Society. Elijah was also the prior General and had mentored him and shaped him to be his successor as the next General of the organization. It was Elijah's vision to take The Society further than could have been conceived of at its founding in 1869, only four short years after the War of Northern Aggression had ended and the Ku Klux Klan had begun.

"I'm excited, but we must keep our eyes on the end game with the President. We mustn't celebrate prematurely. We're still in the openin' moves." The General tamped down his jubilation, no time to get cocky.

He continued, "I spoke to the police chief in Philly this mornin'. He has lined up police retaliation lookin' for the killers, and thanks to the war on drugs, he has arranged no-knock raids complete with flash-bang grenades to occur tonight all over Philadelphia's black community. Particularly where the Black Apostles live." He allowed himself a small smile.

"That should blow up a storm. Will we get riots sooner than later?" Mark was trying to understand how the strategy in a long game was played.

"He reckons demonstrations or riots should start overnight and our White House member is pushin' for the National Guard to be called in. So far, it's goin' like clockwork."

The General poured another cup of coffee for himself from the carafe, added a splash of creamer, and stirred with a gold-plated spoon.

"Where are we with Rance Hunter?" Mark leaned forward in anticipation.

The general hesitated to answer, watching the preparations at the tent to stall and pick his words carefully. "Green light there, guards are set to execute the escape as planned, we have Bret Howard ready to do his investigative report on Rance and his *breakout*, leveragin' the fear." He rose to go inside, signaling this talk was over.

All celebration left Mark's eyes, replaced with a challenge. "Now, when you goin' to tell me who our White House member is? I'm your backup and second in command after all. A trouble shared is a trouble halved."

The General jerked to a stop and slowly pivoted to face his brother-in-law. "Now, I don't plan on tellin' you. We're utilizing a cell structure to keep information compartmentalized and I figure you don't need to know." Besides, he just didn't trust Mark that much. Their White House insider was their most highly-placed asset, and he was keeping that man's identity to himself.

The General turned his back on Mark and left the birthday party preparations behind him until later.

CHAPTER SEVEN

Madame Antoinette

Madame Antoinette stopped briefly for breakfast at a truck stop with dirty windows and red-checkered vinyl table coverings. She chose a table by the window to keep an eye on the truck. The smell of bacon grease and maple syrup permeated the warm diner and a spring in her vinyl booth seat dug into her thigh.

The rusted army-green truck with monster tires and two occupants that began tailing her just outside of Cyprus was parked down the road apiece. She hadn't seen anybody leave the truck, so they must be sitting watching her, too.

She wasn't really hungry, this was a test and it was telling her a few things. The most important information was how they seemed prepared to follow her a long distance, maybe all the way home.

That was a problem. Her fingers stroked an envelope in her lap she had brought in from the car. It was addressed to Malcolm Alexander and stamped, ready to be posted. But, how to get it posted without her tail knowing was the trick, because she sensed they mustn't know about this envelope.

The waitress, a skinny wisp of a thing, sauntered over with pen and pad ready to take her order. She hadn't even looked at the menu, just stared out the window at that green truck. How could she eat at a time like this? She supposed it was best to keep up appearances for now.

"You have grits?"

"We surely do, ma'am. One order of grits. Will you be wantin' any eggs or toast with that?"

"Coffee. Some coffee would be good." The waitress, Cora from her name tag, spun on her heel and sped off.

Antoinette tapped the envelope in her lap with one fingernail. The realization struck her that this letter would reach Malcolm after she was dead. It didn't seem fair to put him through that. Her eyes clouded up, her throat tightened, and she blinked rapidly.

Malcolm had always been her favorite nephew. He was smart and brave and she knew he wasn't corrupt. She had to get somebody who could actually do something to help in this madness that Elizabeth was caught in the middle of. He was the only person she knew in law enforcement. Maybe, as an FBI agent, he could save Elizabeth's life. It was too late for her now – she was as good as dead. What was that saying, dead man walking?

The waitress dropped the coffee off with a handful of half & half packets and smiled at her as she bustled past the table.

Antoinette returned to staring out at the truck that sat there. Nobody got out, even for a bathroom break. And then she saw a slight glint of light from inside it. Now she knew, they had binoculars and were scrutinizing her. She tapped the envelope in her lap again. How to do this?

Antoinette sat in the diner and fretted through her grits. She would glance out the window every few minutes. She couldn't seem to stop. She had to get the envelope mailed without whoever was in that truck seeing it. She knew on a cellular level in her being that if they saw her mail it - it would never reach Malcolm. She had to get this letter to Malcolm – it was imperative.

She began to think philosophically about it. Faced with a matter of hours before her death she was worried about getting help for a stranger. But she could not – no, would not, have it any other way.

She sensed that she would have just enough time to make her will, insurance policy, deed, prepaid funeral plan and other important papers easy to find.

Once she mailed the letter to Malcolm, she would make a goodbye call or two on her drive back. She just wanted to tell a few people how much she loved them while she had time.

She continued contemplating her preparations for her impending death while watching a few people at the register paying their bills. It was time for her to check out from life. She was grateful she had enough warning to prepare. Yes, she was blessed in that respect.

The next person in line stepped up and chatted pleasantly, his arm bumping a basket in front of the register. Her eyes grew wide and her heart quickened. The basket!

The basket was for outgoing mail. She surveyed the angles and the possible view from the truck outside. She could do it. She could block the view with her body and slip the envelope in with the others. Nobody would ever know. It looked like locals used it as a convenient drop box. She closed her eyes and said a little prayer of thanks.

She grabbed her bill and strode toward the register, her envelope hidden from the watchers on the other side of her body. In what Antoinette hoped was an unnoticed move, she placed the letter in the basket face down and smiled brightly at the waitress ringing her up.

CHAPTER EIGHT

Jake Craig

Jake Craig had driven past Estelle Grant's house thinking he could drop in and visit with Elizabeth, but her Mustang wasn't in the driveway. It would be simple enough to locate her. Her royal blue mustang was the only one in town and he could go through the majority of town in all of fifteen minutes.

He spent, a few minutes of driving up and down streets lined with Southern Colonial two and three story frame houses in white with various colors of trim and large colonnades for shade. He found her car downtown in front of Momma Mae's Diner. Momma Mae's could be featured in a fifties movie and always conjured images of poodle skirts just looking at it. It stood in the middle of rows of red brick squat buildings.

He figured he needed breakfast and this was the best for the coin and it might be easier to catch Elizabeth in a neutral place. He parked his police cruiser around the block.

The instant he entered the clean and bright diner, the longtime hostess, Vida waved to him. She was built sturdy and for hard work.

"Hey there, big fella! You gonna let us cook you up a proper breakfast?" Her smile was one of the few sure things in this world that was guaranteed to start your day off on a happier note. "I see you runnin' into the Kwik Stop all the time and grabbin' nothin' more 'n coffee and a cardboard pastry."

"Mornin' Vida. I got a hankerin' for some of Amos' famous corned beef hash that I couldn't shake." He spotted Elizabeth sitting in the back. "Now say Vida, is that gal back there Estelle's grandchild? I think I'll just stop by and welcome her to town." Vida raised a penciled eyebrow. She slowly smiled and winked at him. "Sure is Shuga, but you surely knew that."

He stopped next to the table, his hat in his hand and a smile on his face. "G'mornin' to you miss Elizabeth. It has been a coon's age since I saw you last."

Elizabeth Grant's long brown hair fell gently over her shoulders like a silken fan and her brown eyes appeared troubled. He'd like to know why she looked like she had a terrible burden weighing her down.

"I'm sorry, do I know you?" Her brows bunched together. He rarely heard anything other than the various southern accents, so her voice was a bit jarring.

"Why I reckon I've known you since you were no bigger than a minnow in a fishin' pond and came to visit each summer. I'd often have dinners with your grand folks. I wanted to stop and say how glad I am you're back with us." He made no move to shuffle on, for he was going to have breakfast with her if he had to be rude and invite himself.

She blinked a few times as if trying to recall. "Did you have an old hound dog that waited for you on the porch while we had dinner?" She finally asked hesitantly.

She wasn't going to invite him to sit from all indications. Guess he was just going to have to be rude. "Yes, and I've never had another hound as good as that un. Am I too late to join you for breakfast?"

"Oh," she slowly smiled "please, have a seat." She motioned to the seat across from her. "I can't help but notice you're a local policeman."

He placed his uniform western hat on the vinyl booth seat next to him and faced her. "Yes, that I am. Now, that doesn't bother a big city gal, does it?" He offered up his warmest grin.

"Contrary to popular belief, big cities aren't filled with immoral people or hardened criminals. No, it doesn't bother me Mr, --?" Her smile beamed to soften her words.

"My manners! Jake Craig at your service. I'm a long-standin' friend of your family."

"Jake, I'm sorry I don't remember much about you from those childhood summers." She paused for a fraction of a second. "How long have you been on the force here in town?"

"I reckon seventeen, no closer to eighteen years coming up. As soon as I came back from servin' in the Army, I joined the Sheriff's department."

"You probably know most everything that happens around here. Could you catch me up on the events I've missed in the last few years?"

His eyebrows twitched the slightest bit. "Now Miss Elizabeth, I don't believe for a minute you care about Temperance Wiley gettin' Alzheimer's and sneakin' out of the house causin' a three-county search only to find her in the old drive-in for a triple feature." He watched her closely.

He did indeed know most everything that went on in town and he also had seen many youngins grow up and could tell what they were thinking, sometimes before they knew it themselves. It made his job easier. He had not gotten to watch this gal growing up every day, but he suspected what she was after.

"Why don't you save us both some dancin' 'round and tell me what you're anglin' for, huh?"

To her credit, she blushed and her smile lost some of its zeal. "Yes, well. I hear there are no secrets in a small town." She took a breath. "So what can you tell me about that summer seven years ago?"

So that's where she was headed. Could she just be curious or is she on dangerous ground?

"There are damn few secrets in this town, that's a fact. And I'm fully aware of that summer and how you might be interested in catchin' up on what you missed."

At that inconvenient moment, Vida arrived with Elizabeth's fruit and yogurt bowl and Jake's corned beef hash and eggs. He stared at her bowl.

"Well, I declare, what in the blazes…?"

"It's just yogurt and fruit." Her voice was a touch defensive. He coughed then dug into his nice normal breakfast of corned beef hash with three eggs scrambled and sausage links.

Apparently, she wasn't very hungry or her momma hadn't taught her one lick of manners, because she insisted on talking through breakfast. He knew her momma quite well and doubted she had failed in this area.

"You were going to tell me about the summer seven years ago."

"I don't believe I ever agreed to such a thing," he countered after carefully swallowing a mouthful of sausage and taking a generous gulp of his coffee. Vida made about the meanest coffee in town – it made your hair stand up and vibrate. He loved it.

"Look, Miss Elizabeth, I know full well what you're after, but for the life of me I can't figure out why you want to dig up old bones."

Her smile faded and her jaw muscle worked. She licked her lips and swallowed while holding her spoon midway to her mouth. It was several heartbeats before that spoon with a dab of yogurt-smeared fruit was gradually lowered to rest in the bowl.

"I don't know much of what happened. I only know Loralie was reported missing. I hoped the police could tell me if anything was ever concluded." Elizabeth's voice was calm, measured, and he would bet a month's pay she damn well knew more than she was letting on.

"Now, I don't know if I should be encouragin' you down this path." He took a slow swallow of more coffee as he regarded her. "You should just let the past stay in the past. But, I'll tell you that I was the investigatin' officer and everythin' pointed to her run-in' off. You know, livin' in that rat hole south of town she weren't ever gonna be more than the rest of um. A witness came forward sayin' he saw her hitch a ride at a truck stop with some big-rig driver." He reached over and patted her hand.

He hoped she would realize there was nothing to chase after and her childhood friend escaping life in Cyprus was some comfort. The sooner she accepted her friend was long gone, the sooner she could move on.

He saw her eyes contract just a little and an eyebrow slightly raise. A knowing crept into her eyes. He had seen this before but usually, when he was confronting some drunk in a bar. It was a signal that the person had just decided on an action -- for better or worse, and usually it was for the worse. He didn't like the looks of this. Whatever could be in the head of Elizabeth Grant? Nope, he didn't like it. He was gonna have to keep a careful watch on her.

CHAPTER NINE

Elizabeth Grant

Elizabeth returned to gran's house after breakfast and some grocery shopping. It wasn't for lack of food in the house, just a lack of food that she was used to or wanted to eat. She was more of an herbal tea drinker and lots of vegetables and less on the gravy-smothered everything. She had put away the groceries in a daze.

She was considering what the Sheriff had said about Loralie. Sure, she had hoped Loralie had escaped town, even dreamt up the wild idea of her touring with a band. But for *responsible* Loralie to suddenly take off with a trucker without even saying goodbye to her mom or brother... well it was utterly inconceivable.

It made her furious at herself. She had been so concerned about being sent to a shrink and how people viewed her that she didn't question or push for answers. She let them keep her in the dark.

The more she considered the notion that Loralie would just run off suddenly, hitching a ride with a trucker, the more it was absolutely ludicrous. With the groceries all put away, Elizabeth paced the living room like a caged animal, energy building with no place to vent. The swamp cooler blew her hair around gently but didn't cool the fire lit inside. She subconsciously fished the gris-gris bag out from under her shirt where it was discreetly hanging and held it. *What could she really do about it now?*

She had already decided after Madame Antoinette's visit to find what had been done about her disappearance. It appeared not a damned thing was done. If Loralie had actually turned her back on her mother, brother, and best friend, and that was a damned big IF, then Elizabeth's recurring hallucinations were probably just the subconscious issues she suspected they were and facing them might be the cure. But, if she was dead, which seemed the only real possibility in her opinion, her family deserved closure... she didn't know what that really meant about her visions in that case, and she didn't want to think too hard on it either.

She stopped pacing and grabbed her compact purse from the couch. She extracted her cell phone from a side pocket and looked up the phone number of Loralie's younger brother Jeremiah in Meridian, the closest town to Cyprus. They had kept in touch over the years, Elizabeth regularly sent money to help Mrs. Carter out since she was still waitressing.

The cell phone had no signal. *Figures, too rural out here.* She dialed the house phone. It was like stepping back in time with the old black Bakelite rotary dial style.

"Jeremiah, it's Elizabeth. Am I interrupting anything?"

"Hey Liza girl, how is Cyprus? Was your trip uneventful? I'm guessin' you're settled in and wondering what to do with your time." His voice was cheerful and melodic.

"I have some questions for you and I don't want to bother your momma with them." She continued pacing, but the old phone had a cord that limited her range. The connection had a high-pitched hum in the background that was irritating.

"Oh. I thought we'd talked that out. I was a stupid kid and I stopped, never did it again and I won't ever again." His voice was weary.

"No, I didn't mean you're dealing. I believe you stopped when Loralie went missing." She took a deep breath.

Digging up bones.

Jeremiah had fallen in with the wrong crowd back then, a drug and criminal crowd, and for once Elizabeth and Loralie didn't agree on what to do, which sparked their argument.

After the dust settled from Loralie's disappearance and she reconnected with Jeremiah, he swore he went clean and never went down that road again. He now worked as a teacher and was afraid his youthful stupidity would rear its head and hurt his career.

"I just found out that the police dismissed her case because somebody claims she left with a trucker. Do you know who said that?"

"I remember it clearly. It was that buck-toothed bully Calvin Morrison, he wouldn't shut up about it. I got suspended from school for two weeks for givin' him a bloody nose over the crap he was sayin'. That was the highlight of High School for me. The town's folk never would've stopped with the nasty things to say, they just loved to drag her name through the slime with the rumor mill. It was best we moved away."

She was trying to understand, but it felt like she had been in another world this whole time. "Nobody told me. Mom said she just disappeared into thin air. Why didn't you tell me?" She had stayed in touch with Jeremiah through letters and eventually emails, but he never said anything about the supposed trucker.

"Your family all said not to tell you, it would upset you too much. I thought that was a load of crap, but it wasn't my place."

"And?"... She could tell there was more. The humming on the line continued as Elizabeth paced back and forth within the cord's reach.

"I guess I was ashamed. Thought maybe she'd left us because of me; because I'd let her down so bad. Sometimes I thought she might've confronted one of the guys I was runnin' with and they hurt her or something. I just couldn't tell you and have you blame me."

Digging up bones.

Talking should make her feel better, but it was bringing up her self-doubts. "Well, I was treated like a fragile piece of glass that might shatter. I was pretty ashamed myself, I think I believed it... just a little at the beginning. So, I avoided asking too many questions." She could feel the weight of the old low self esteem like a cement block pulling her down.

"Jer, I just don't believe she ran off. Think back for me. Tell me about that summer, what was she doing? I know she was taking a summer class so I didn't come to visit as usual."

"Not just any class, she got that special college course over the summer as a special student at Jackson State University. It was gonna help her get scholarships for college. She had to commute into Jackson twice a week."

"I had forgotten that. Jer, how could she possibly hop a ride with a strange trucker when she had such a burning drive and had already sacrificed so much to just up and throw it all away?"

"I didn't think so - but come on Liza, it's been seven years."

"Exactly my point. She'd have contacted us. I know she would've contacted you at least."

"Liza, what're you saying? That she didn't grab a ride out of town with a trucker? Then where the hell has she been?"

Elizabeth didn't speak. It really did all make sense. Loralie had to be dead just as Madame Antoinette had said. Her silence was the evidence that could not be ignored. If Loralie were alive she would have contacted her brother and mother at least.

"Jeremiah, what's the only thing that would've really stopped your sister from contacting you? From suddenly - with no warning, stopping in the middle of that college class?" He had to come to the realization himself, she wasn't going to say it.

"I know where you're goin' with this. Don't think it hasn't crossed my mind a time or two. But I'll be honest, I'd rather think she ran off and made a life for herself away from Cyprus than she was. . . " His voice was strained and trailed off.

"I think I convinced myself of that too. I'm sorry I didn't really ask before, I guess I couldn't face it either. After I talked to the sheriff this morning and he told me the official report was she ran away, I couldn't ignore it anymore. I know that just can't be true." It was time to face the truth.

"Don't you be trustin' that sheriff now, I remember him. There are stories 'bout him and he's no friend of the village." The village was the run down segregated part of town where most of the blacks lived. Electricity was not reliable, water and sewage often didn't work, and the police didn't care to investigate much of anything there. Loralie was hell-bent to get her mother and brother out of there by getting college scholarships and getting a good job. The phone started clicking, just a few clicks amidst the humming background. Elizabeth's brow creased. Was it just rural phone line problems or was it somebody listening in? What would somebody listening in sound like? She found she was holding the protection gris-gris bag in her hand as if it really could help in some way.

"We should at least meetup while you're here." Jeremiah's voice was kind.

"Love to Jer, how would tomorrow be? I can drive down to Meridian." They decided where to meet for lunch and she got directions.

Elizabeth hung up but stared at the phone. The hair on her arms and on the back of her neck prickled. Something didn't feel right. Were those noises on the phone just a coincidence?

The hazy image of Loralie appeared in front of her and tried to knock the phone off the little stand but her ethereal hand couldn't make solid contact. If Elizabeth were to take that as a sign, she probably shouldn't trust the landline phone again.

She talked herself into listening to the meditation CD that Madame Antoinette had made for her. Out of curiosity only, just to see what it was. But first, she felt oddly compelled to go check the backyard. It was illogical since she had just tended to Gran's prize flowers this morning. It was as if an invisible hand was pressing against her back propelling her to the back door.

Dread crept over her as she looked at the back door lock. She had locked it when she came in after watering this morning like she habitually did. She lived in the lower downtown section of Denver, known as LoDo. She always locked doors. It was an ingrained practice. But the door was clearly unlocked now. Her stomach clenched and a trickle of fear crept up her spine.

Only somebody who knew Gran didn't lock doors would leave it that way thinking it was normal. But, Elizabeth always locked doors, always. She examined the door handle and deadbolt. She was no expert, but it didn't appear like there were any signs of forcing the lock. It seemed somebody either had a key or could pick a lock. A chill ran through her core.

She was going to have to think of something to alarm the door like stacked cans, or she wouldn't be getting any sleep. She wanted to stay calm, she had no real evidence of somebody in the house.

Besides, she reasoned, small towns had different rules. Her neighbors may come and go as they please and that might be acceptable to Gran. *That was possible, wasn't it?* She took several deep breaths and steadied herself.

She forced herself to calmly search the modest house. Elizabeth was particular about where she placed things on her bedside table, but things were slightly different, the few things she had unpacked and placed in drawers had been shifted and rumpled, her suitcase had been moved too.

She sat down on the bed in her old room, her shoulders slunk forward and her head drooped. She didn't think this was a case of an overactive imagination. Somebody had been in the house and looked through her personal items while she was out, but taken nothing as far as she could tell.

Was the humming and clicking she heard on the phone just normal line problems or did it mean somebody listening to her calls?

Could a friend of Gran really have come by to check on the place and was curious about her? Nothing was missing from her stuff, so a snoopy neighbor was possible... *right?* She was shaking in the core of her being, and deep breathing wasn't helping. She mentally outlined how she was going to booby trap the doors.

She had stuck her head in the sand for too long, but she wasn't going to let minor things stop her now. She just had to be logical and keep her emotions in check. She hugged herself to ward off the sense of isolation... of being so totally alone. Seeing Loralie out of the corner of her eye standing in the corner with her arms crossed and worry in her eyes was not comforting.

CHAPTER TEN

Madame Antoinette

Madame Antoinette, affectionately known as Netty to her family, knew her death was approaching but not the exact when or even how. It was an incomplete foreknowledge, just enough for her to prepare herself emotionally but too little to stop it. At best, she could have called the police and attempt some story of a prowler in hopes they would drive by a few times, but they were stretched thin and the report would likely go unaddressed until a day or two later.

Of course, she had locked all the doors and windows, no need to make it easy for whoever would be invading her home. She walked through her modest home in Shreveport, located in an older neighborhood with trees lining the street and populated with folks her age.

She ran a shaking hand along the door molding with pencil marks of Cecilia's height and age as a child and sighed. She was exhausted from being up all night and then the drive back, but when time is short, as she sensed, you don't take a nap.

Her home had been an achievement her late husband had worked hard and saved a long time to acquire. She still remembered the day they moved in and her Clive had carried her in the front door. A tear slid down her right cheek at the memory. There were many good memories in this home, tempered with sadness.

Her breath caught, and she choked down a sob. The premature death of Clive due to cancer had been a heavy blow to her. Cecilia, her only child, would likely sell the house since few could afford the property taxes in town any longer. Cecilia lived in neighboring Bossier City, anyway.

She placed both hands on the door to her altar room where she kept her spiritual practice tucked away. She never practiced publicly like some folks in New Orleans do for the tourists, but people who needed her always found her through friends and family. The pocket door Clive installed looked like a part of the corner.

She had left directions in this private sanctuary for her family to find along with her will, insurance papers, and letters to specific relatives expressing her love. She was hoping that only a family member would find them. But, there was always a chance that her unknown, but expected, murderer could find this space, which was why she had to mail that package to Malcolm rather than leave it here.

She had decided against cleaning one last time and just roamed from room to room, caressing a photo here, holding a sentimental knick-knack there. She had lived a good life with few regrets. She had sowed a few wild oats, loved and been loved, raised a child, and gave back to the community.

She barely heard the floorboard squeak behind her before strong arms encircled her and a second man quickly thrust a gag in her mouth. They had to be the men who had followed her from Cyprus in the truck. The smell of body sweat overwhelmed her. She still wasn't going to make this easy and kneed the pale blond man who had gagged her. He sucked in his breath. "God damn bitch." He raised his fist to hit her.

"No! Remember our orders now. Don't leave no evidence of an attack, stand down." The man holding her in a vise-like grip growled.

To Netty's surprise the blond man lowered his fist but continued to glare.

The man holding her didn't flinch when she tried to kick his shins.

The blond man held his groin with one hand as he closed the curtains in the living room. He then took a plastic case out of his pocket and held up a syringe that he tapped a few times and squirted a few drops.

She noticed he wore gloves and realized that they would probably get away with this. Blondie with the syringe avoided her feet and approached from her left side. He poked her arm and refrained from jabbing the needle, apparently remembering his orders. For once in her life, it really was "just a pinch." Was she to die by injection?

But Madame Antoinette could not know the shot was intended to lower a person's inhibitions, making them chatty. This particular shot was a cocktail built upon the standard Amobarbital with a few added CIA experimental psychoactive drugs.

"Why did you go and visit Cyprus this mornin'?"

She found she didn't have the energy to evade or lie. "I visited that poor Elizabeth."

"How do you know Elizabeth Grant?"

"Loralie's restless spirit pleaded and begged that I get her to leave and go back to Denver." The two men smirked at each other. Still, the blond man looked around the room with big eyes and swallowed loudly.

She had never been a spiteful soul, but in this moment she wished she would've placed a curse on them. They were low-lifes and hurt people without a second thought. It was pervasive in their auras. But, she wouldn't know how without looking in some resources. *That's what she should've been doing in the last hour.*

"What did she tell you? What does she know about The Society?" His voice was strong, despite the slight quiver.

"What society? I told her she needs to go home, but she doesn't know me, or have a reason to listen to me." She said in a breathy voice.

"What information, what proof does she have on The Society?"

"Who're you people?" Her abilities of foreknowledge were rarely a complete picture, mostly key pieces to a puzzle. She began to realize Elizabeth was involved in something far bigger and more dangerous than even Loralie had feared.

"What do ya know of The Society for a Restored America?"

She was still held tight by the man behind her and she couldn't give much of a struggle anymore.

Blondie took a plastic ziplock baggie out of his other pocket and removed a cloth. He held it in his hand and grabbed her face by the jaws, then held the sweet smelling cloth over her nose and mouth.

Her gaze was fixed on the framed family photos on her white wall, particularly her wedding picture with Clive in his borrowed suit.

She drifted in darkness aware of being carried and lifted. There was a sensation of falling and then an explosion of sharp pain ricocheting through her entire body. But she was still in darkness. The pain finally stopped and a light that blazed ahead slowly drew closer. When it reached her, she saw Loralie standing next to Clive with light streaming behind them. Clive held his arms out to her. Her sweet Clive, at last.

CHAPTER ELEVEN

The General

The General was in his corporate office, having just finished with the last meeting of the day with all his direct report managers for his media empire. He had to come into the office for a few hours and take care of a few things before the birthday party for his son.

He sat behind his cherry wood desk with the sole adornment being the photo of his Charlotte and little Caleb. He drummed his fingers on the arms of his Italian leather ergonomic chair.

What to do about Elizabeth? Could he have been fooled all these years? He was sure that she didn't know anything about the details of Loralie's death or where the bitch had hidden the evidence Noah had passed to her.

But, Elizabeth hadn't been in Cyprus for a full twenty-four hours and she was having odd visitors in the wee hours of the morning. Something wasn't right. Well, from all appearances Elizabeth was not involved and did not possess the smuggled evidence. But it had to be somewhere. So the cat-and-mouse game would continue.

Perhaps he should have killed her long ago... but then there would always be the risk that Noah's proof of The Society, whatever that might be, would surface. He felt strongly that the evidence Noah had collected absolutely must be recovered at all costs. Elizabeth was the best chance of reclaiming it and destroying it for good.

His cell phone buzzed. He hated interruptions to his workday with Society business; but honestly, he was not getting much done churning over the complication Elizabeth presented.

It was a text message, cryptic but meaningful: "Subject told us nothing. Problem eliminated." He blew out a breath. Elizabeth's early morning visitor hadn't told his operatives what he needed to know about Elizabeth. It didn't matter now, she was dead.

He began to pace to the door and back to the window. Again and again. It was like the month before competing in the Olympic Games, he theorized, all the planning and working hard for the gold. Now it was waiting for the moment and taking the prize.

His phone vibrated in his hand. Yet another text message. "Searching for anything. Nothing yet." He didn't bother to reply. They had searched Elizabeth's apartment in Denver as well as the house in Cyprus and still nothing. He had lost count of how many times over the years her belongings had been tossed and searched. Her early morning visitor would now have her place searched as well.

He took his cell phone and dialed. Time to focus on other matters now.

"Henrietta, it's me again. I'm checkin' in for any last minute updates. Did the cake arrive?" He listened to the assurances of perfection guaranteed while he gazed upon the photo on his desk. It would be easy to spoil Caleb, their only child and future general of The Society.

"Now, the face painter and balloon artist will be there, right? I know they aren't as popular as pony rides and circus acts, but I want to keep it simple... Yes, I'm still leadin' the children in the traditional games!... What the Krenshaw's did for their girl don't amount to a hill of beans, you just make sure everythin' I asked for is there." With that, he hung up.

She might be the premier children's party planner for the country club set, but she expected him to compete with the other parents for the most lavish items. That upset him. If he were going to compete, he'd just hire Cirque du Soleil to set up in the backyard.

He was going to lead the children at the party in games like Pin the Tail on the Donkey, a three-legged race, and others. Money wasn't everything, after all. Which was why none of the guests were to bring anything more than a greeting card.

He made sure his only child never wanted for anything every day of his life. Particularly, after all the miscarriages Charlotte had endured until their miracle child was born, premature but healthy. So Caleb's present today was enjoying his family and friends.

He had a phone call with the president of his mid-west operations regarding some organizational restructuring before he could go home and prepare for his son's birthday party.

He twirled his leather chair around, strode over to his in-office snack bar to get a shot of Espresso before his last phone call of the day. All thought of the woman somewhere in Shreveport that his men killed left his mind after the last text message. She was unimportant, nothing.

CHAPTER TWELVE

Rance Hunter

The gray walls of the 9x9 room contained a gray metal table with matching gray metal chairs and smelled of sweat and piss. The overhead fluorescent lights flickered non-stop.

Rance Hunter hadn't gotten used to prison life. He never would. He hated the enforced celibacy, hated not being in control, hated the food, and he hated the depressing environment. He'd been in prison throughout the long trial and was transferred here, Corcoran, California – small town nowhere, awaiting a more permanent assignment in a few weeks.

He knew he broke the law and knew why laws were important to a civilization. He wasn't stupid. He even had a college degree. But laws weren't equally applied and people born into poverty surrounded by drugs, pimps, prostitutes, and murderers weren't afforded the same treatment or opportunities as people raised with nannies, gold-plated dinnerware, yachts, and trust funds.

The "one percent country club set" could bilk paying their taxes, rob retirement funds from their employees, take out life insurance on the same employees to get paid when they died, and then seriously break laws right and left without much more than a slap on the wrist.

But let a slum dog do the same and he's a dangerous thug, a career criminal. He sighed and focused on the matter at hand.

The shuffling around from prison to prison didn't stop him from conducting business. It was best he continue to run the gang rather than the power struggle that would likely take place, even though his co-leader should, by all rights, become the leader.

Rance sat opposite his lawyer, one he hadn't previously met from the law firm, in a private room so legal matters would not be all over the visitor room. There were two security guards stationed, one inside the room and one directly outside.

"Mr. Hunter, I'm Michael James." They shook hands across the table. "I realize you normally deal with Mr. Cummings from the Los Angeles offices, but your business in Philadelphia warranted a visit from me to ensure your interests are protected." The expensive suited lawyer looked pointedly at the guard at the door. Rance Hunter folded his heavily tattooed arms across his chest, the orange prison jumpsuit strained at the bulk of his muscles.

"I've been worried 'bout my music label there. What can you tell me? How're we doing?" He had hired a large law firm with offices in most of the cities he operated in long before he got convicted under RICO charges. They were more than accommodating despite his being in the middle of rural California where the prison he temporarily lived at was located. Who in the hell had ever heard of Corcoran California for Christ's sake?

In reality, he was secretly talking with his lawyer about plans for the gang, since his legal case didn't have much hope of springing him.

"Here is a summary of the recording studio's outlook. We need to go over the contracts of some of the talent. It appears some competition may be stirring up trouble for you."

Rance was reading the papers Mr. James had handed him. It was more of a situation report on the violence in Philadelphia. The problem was spiraling out of control since that family had been butchered and the Apostles fingered for it. It seems that his local man-in-charge in Philly was shitting bricks about it and desperately wanted to ensure Rance didn't think he was so reckless as to kill that family.

The Apostles were just as violent as any gang, but that family had been slaughtered in a scandalous and headline-making way, which he didn't go for. Plus, his gang didn't kill innocents who had nothing to do with Apostles' business. It was that simple.

Rance slammed his fist on the metal table making the polished Mr. James blink. This was when being stuck in the middle of nowhere behind bars was the most aggravating. He should be out there among his people, figuring out who did this and fucking them up but good. He figured it was either a rival gang or the police to justify a bloody round up of gang members.

"I don't want to lose any of my business to a competitor or somebody with a grudge. What do you suggest?" All code. Especially now the Apostles were implicated for the murders in Philadelphia. No doubt this visit was being taped and the authorities would scour every word said looking for anything to connect him with the murders.

Mr. James paused for a moment, but when he spoke he stared into Rance's eyes. "I believe things may be more... complicated. I suggest we bring in a consultant to help turn the business around."

Rance had been watching the news reports and listening to the radio so he wasn't completely unaware. This was serious shit going down and fancy lawyer here was advising him to bring in help. He had never needed help outside of his second-in-command before, but he couldn't take care of business the same while in lock-up. Rance took a deep breath and thought for a moment.

"I've never turned to a consultant before. Are we talking an expert in the industry who can turn the business around?" He wasn't sure who or what Mr. James might be thinking. Who could help with something like this?

Mr. James leaned forward slightly. "I was thinking of somebody who can dig deeper, who is unbiased, trained in researching and uncovering problems, and who can then assist with your public image." Rance was still trying to grasp exactly what he meant.

Unbiased, digging, researching, and helping their public image? That wasn't any enforcer or muscle he ever heard of, that sounded more like a librarian, a publicist, or... a reporter? His eyes widened as he stared into Mr. James' eyes.

Use some eager reporter looking to score a big story and let that reporter take all the risks and blow the frame job, while he and his gang sat back and watched the shit storm. Genius. That's why he paid the legal firm's extravagant retainer fees. Keep his hands clean, but get the attention off his organization.

"I get you, this consultant could *report* findings and get our righteous business back on track. If I'm understanding you?" Mr. James nodded once slowly without loosing eye contact.

Rance remained seated while Mr. James packed up his papers and quietly left. The guard looked Rance over, sizing him up, calculating. He knew this guard, McKenzie, would be the first to shove a shiv between his ribs if he had a chance. But no matter, he could take care of himself, which was why they would transfer him to a maximum-security prison in a few weeks, for everybody's safety.

Come to think of it, he wasn't sure how he got this side trip to backwater California in the first place.

CHAPTER THIRTEEN

FBI Agent Malcom Alexander

Jackson, Mississippi, the "City with Soul," was named after Confederate General Andrew Jackson and proudly mixed the legacy of the past with modern culture. For much of its history it was a small town in spite of being the capitol, but eventually grew into its big shoes to be the largest city in the state. It's known for its overall affordability and its music. Jackson was now proudly the home of Braves Baseball, Showboats Basketball, and the Maddogs Football team. It is the only capitol city in the U.S. to sit on top of a volcano—the Jackson Volcano. The city also has an FBI field office located on Echelon Parkway and Watkins Drive.

FBI Special Agent Malcom Alexander grabbed his cell phone from his belt and noticed it was his mother calling. *Odd.* She didn't believe in bothering him at work.

"Momma, I'm surprised you're callin' me. Somethin' wrong?"

"Baby, I... it's your Aunt Netty. Honey, she's dead. She was on a ladder fixing her gutters and fell off. Why would she do it herself? I just don't understand how this can happen." His mother's voice broke, and he heard a sob.

"Aunt Netty fell?" As if in slow motion, he slowly sat down in this desk chair, staring directly ahead. He dealt with life and death situations and snap decisions daily as an FBI agent. Jackson had big-city crime too. But, all his experience and training vanished into thin air when it came to his family.

"How... How did she... where?" He managed to stammer out. Instead of questions coming to mind he was blank.

"Malcolm, I just don't understand. Netty was finally doing well after Clive's death. This just can't be happening." Then the floodgates started to crack and she let out a few more sobs.

"Mom, I'll get off work and be right there. Just don't drive or anything. I'm on my way." He hung up, but sat limply at his desk as his aunt's death took hold of him. He held his head in his hands as his elbows rested on his light gray metal desk in a room full of gray metal desks.

This was going to be hard for his mom. His parent's divorce was bad enough but now Momma's only sibling suddenly dying was a crushing blow. Maybe after the funeral he could take some time off and spend it with her.

But Aunt Netty! He ran his hands through his short-cropped hair. He licked his lips, it seemed so inconceivable. Netty had helped raise him; she was always so strong, so resilient.

As he got up from his desk, intending to ask for grievance leave, he had a feeling sock his solar plexus that Netty's death was not an accident. It was a feeling that took over fast and had his scalp tingling and his stomach turning. Something was very wrong here.

Aunt Netty was fixing her gutters? He covered his mouth with his hand. She was afraid of heights, so there was nothing that would get her higher than one step on a kitchen stool.

He broke out in a sweat and his hands began to shake. Oh shit! What had Aunt Netty got in the middle of that got her killed? He was going to ask for more time off than just the funeral. He wanted to go to Shreveport and have a look around her home. He made a quick call to the Shreveport police department.

"Yes, Special Agent Malcom Alexander. Can you give me the results thus far from the death of Madame Antionette...?" Apparently they didn't need her last name. He listened as they ran through what sounded like a one page report. "Thank you, Sergeant." He hung up.

He could go through Aunt Netty's home all he wanted. He didn't have to clear anything with the local police, since it was already being called an accidental death. He bit on his thumbnail.

The knowledge that he must keep this to himself swept over him with equal certainty. Aunt Netty had taught him to follow his intuition, it had saved his life a few times, and right now it was screaming that he had to step carefully.

CHAPTER FOURTEEN

Elizabeth Grant

Elizabeth fidgeted the afternoon away, and by late afternoon she was searching for calm. Some sort of escape for her frayed nerves. Figures Gran didn't have any liquor in the house, she could really use a stiff drink. She rarely drank, but a Scotch and water might help her relax a little.

At first Gran's house was like finding a favorite old pair of jeans – cozy, comfortable, and cocoon-like. But the very same old house offered no balm from the troubles plaguing Elizabeth now.

The simple white two-story with dark green trim and ample front veranda had been a loving shelter for her grandparents and her mother, even herself during the summers. The house hadn't changed, it still had the same peace, embracing the occupants in its warmth and comfort, as if that was its sole mission.

But Elizabeth could not be soothed. The past was restless and needed appeased – thoughts of danger invaded her mind, stripping any false security and leaving her feeling exposed.

Even now the house beckoned her to stay within and shut out the world, to hide within the illusion of safety. It was tempting, but the bliss of ignorance had been shattered, never to be reconstructed. She couldn't pretend or willfully ignore the situation any longer.

So she gathered up the CD player and homemade CD that Madame Antoinette had made for her and resolutely strode into the backyard. Time to see what the CD had on it. She settled into a lawn chair under the large weeping willow tree. In the early evening shade of the willow, it was a sticky ninety-six degrees with colorful flowers all along the wooden fence. Gran was in the local garden club and she had an impressive collection of exotic flowers and aromatic scents.

She closed her eyes and listened. The recorded voice of Madame Antoinette reached out to Elizabeth. *"Find a quiet place where you won't be interrupted and sit comfortably. Close your eyes."*

Elizabeth settled into the chair and closed her eyes. A smile perked her lips as the voice brought back a vision of her early morning visitor. That was only a matter of hours ago.

"Take deep breaths through your nose and exhale through your mouth. Breathe into your belly, letting it expand into your chest and slowly exhale."

Elizabeth focused on her breathing for several minutes. She took in deep breaths perfumed with strong honeysuckle and magnolia from the garden surrounding her.

"Imagine before you there are stairs leading down with forty steps. Imagine stepping down to 39, down to 38, 37, 36..."

Elizabeth visualized walking down stairs, then through a door. Madame's voice continued to lead her as she found a wooded mountain landscape through the doorway. She saw butterflies floating around in the shade from a circle of massive trees. It was cool with the hint of wild flowers in the air.

She carefully looked around and saw a red fox hiding behind the trunks of several aspen trees. The fox's furry ears didn't stop moving – always alert and rotating like plush little satellite dishes. She observed the fox. He seemed afraid of something and ducked further behind the tree trunks.

Elizabeth wanted to go to the skittish animal when Madame Antoinette appeared a few hundred feet away in a patch of sunshine. She had blood on her shimmering image and her head was cocked at a startling angle. That couldn't be right; at least she hoped it was only her subconscious anxiety and not reality. She looked back at the fox to observe him slinking away, all stealth and quiet. She got the distinct feeling the fox was telling her to get away and lay low – hide.

Her eyes snapped open only to find herself still in the backyard in the shade of the weeping willow tree, but her heart was hammering. Without thinking, she held the gris-gris bag in her hand.

CHAPTER FIFTEEN

Juanita Alvarez

Philadelphia, the city of Brotherly Love, was known for more than the Liberty Bell or Independence Hall where the Declaration of Independence and U.S. Constitution were signed. Those are just two among the sixty-seven nationally significant historical landmarks in Philly. But the city also has many highly regarded museums, including one of the largest in the world, the Philadelphia Museum of Art, with its long flight of entry steps that were featured in the movie Rocky. The city has several major national companies headquartered there, and a vibrant arts, culture, and sports scene. The "Philadelphia Sound" was legendary in the early rock scene too.

But, the city of Brotherly Love was the site of the supposed gang killing, or as the newspapers referred to it, "Slaughter of a White Middle-Class Family". The city was about to be the historic center of a much different historical happening.

Juanita Alvarez sat in a seedy bar and grill, the Red, White, and Brew a mile or so from downtown Philadelphia. She was a freelance reporter currently covering the horrific murder of the Olsen family. She wiped the tabletop with her napkin again.

When is this guy going to show up? She looked at her watch and up at the door again. The dive had large grimy windows with faded cotton fabric scraps hanging across the top that might have been blue at one point. The linoleum was worn and just as dirty as the windows and the smell of cigarettes and grease clung to every surface. She was fairly certain she saw a cockroach scurry down the hall towards the bathrooms.

The man behind the counter informed her to order before the after-work crowd arrived, which was still an hour or so away. She found it doubtful this place ever saw a rush. Somehow, she couldn't manage more than a soda. Shit, she was already thinking of the shower she was going to race home to once she hit the door.

A tall black man, maybe late teens or early twenties, in sagging baggy jeans and a black sleeveless undershirt strutted in looking around. He spotted her and slightly nodded but sat down at the table next to her booth, both facing the door and nobody behind them.

"Ya Alvarez?" he said just loud enough for her to catch.

"Yep. And you would be Mr...?"

"Ya don't need to know my name. Give me ya number where I can call ya."

"No. I don't know what information you have for me to just give you my phone number."

"Ya got ta understand this family getting sliced and diced was not part of the Black Apostles." He said using his finger to hammer the point into the table.

The waiter who tended the counter approached slowly with a slice of pie and soda, set them down at the boy's table and scurried off. Interesting, he was a regular with a standing order.

"The police tell me that they have evidence, graffiti and such, at the... the scene." She swallowed. She shouldn't have thought about the crime scene photos a police contact had let her peek at. Such horror.

"I'm telling ya, it ain't the gang. I don't care what the cops think they know. They're wrong, lyin' even." He whispered between sips of soda. The man behind the counter dropped a cup and mister sagging jeans jumped.

"Why are you being so careful if you're innocent?" His secret-agent act was getting to her.

"It ain't the Apostles I'm 'fraid of seeing me talk wit you. The people that whacked that family want everybody thinking it's the gang. I'm a dead man if they think I know anything. I've survived many things cuz I'm careful and I ain't dying for this bull shit." Sweat began to roll down his cheek.

"Do you have proof, something solid? You know, more than your word I can work from? I need more that I can follow up on."

This could be a huge tip, or nothing at all. It could go either way. There was a slim chance this might lead to something that could catapult her career. She wasn't out for the cheap sensationalist crap. She wanted to be recognized as an investigative journalist, like fellow Philadelphians Barbara Laker and Wendy Ruderman, or Chris Hedges.

She believed hard-hitting journalism was disappearing from the "news" and being replaced with corporate sponsored messaging. Most serious reporters tried to cover a war on foreign soil, but she had a war building right here at home with no need to get extra vaccination shots.

She understood just how dangerous this could get, if this guy had honest information she could be risking her life just as surely as standing in the middle of Syria or Afghanistan. Her eyes were wide open.

"I can slip ya something, but not here or now. That'll give ya a start, ya know." He shoveled a big piece of pie into his mouth while scanning the street out the front window.

"I need more than just something. If this is as dangerous as you say, I'm not risking my ass for just anything. This had better be the truth. I want facts the Black Apostles aren't behind this."

"You'll have your facts. I ain't doing your job for you bitch, you'll have to do a little digging, but I got the goods."

She stood up and dropped a slip of paper with her cell phone number next to his glass of soda, paid her bill, and left quickly. The phone number was to the pre-paid cell phone she had just bought to be on the safe side. *Eyes wide open and all that jazz.*

CHAPTER SIXTEEN

Malcom Alexander

Shreveport, Louisiana had its big city attractions, like Louisiana Downs racetrack for Thoroughbred horse and exotic animal races, regular casinos and riverboat casinos, and a thriving craft beer scene. But cheaper neighboring Bossier was where Aunt Netty's only child Cecilia lived.

Malcolm had gotten his mother settled at cousin Cecilia's house after the three-and-a-half-hour drive. It was a fairly direct route from Jackson west on Interstate 20. His mother hadn't spoken much during the drive, which concerned him. While he had the time, he wanted to look over Aunt Netty's home without anybody else. He wasn't planning to grieve or look at what material possessions had to be sorted through, rather to investigate. So, it was best done alone to not worry family.

Right now he was in Aunt Netty's tidy backyard, having parked in the alley-access driveway. He wanted to look through the house for anything that might have been missed. Since the police never considered her death anything but an accident, tragic and sad, but still an accident, they had not combed the property for evidence. There was no reason why he couldn't use the key cousin Cecilia gave him and do his own investigation of the house.

He stood at the periphery of the backyard. He ran shaking hands over his short-cropped hair and took a deep breath. The last time he had been here was for Aunt Netty's birthday, he had given her a single diamond pendant on a gold chain. He pushed the memory away. No time for that now, he forced himself to be detached. *Just another crime scene.*

The first order of business was the backyard, so he started from the rear of the property and took out his powerful flashlight and began walking the grid. Although he was not a forensic tech, he knew the standard procedure of dividing the crime scene into a grid for methodical evidence collection. If he actually found any evidence, he wasn't sure how he would get it analyzed, since this wasn't an actual case. He would figure that out later.

Although he was starting this search in daylight, he had purchased an industrial strength flashlight with the highest lumen value he could afford. You can't collect evidence if you can't see it. He was painfully aware that his solution was a cheap hack. He wished he had access to the powerful lights that the forensic techs used.

He found a few distorted footprints, a collection of wrappers in various stages of decomposing, and a few blond hairs lodged around a bolt on the ladder from which Aunt Netty had fallen.

He methodically photographed the evidence, bagged, tagged, and documented his findings, all the while recording detailed notes in a pocket notebook. He also made a sketch of the yard and the position of the ladder. His back was aching now, and he had several hours yet to go through the house.

After he finished the backyard, he climbed the ladder and checked the gutters to see if there was any reason at all for Aunt Netty to have defied her fear of heights for the unlikely chore that supposedly caused her death. He couldn't find any problem. In fact, the gutters looked new – not more than a year old he suspected. So, there was no apparent reason for her to be compelled to climb a ladder and check the gutters.

The back door opened into the compact laundry room off the kitchen. No forced entry evident, perhaps it had been picked. He couldn't tell. He began the same process over again by walking a grid with all the lights on and using the flashlight. He took photos of the rooms in general.

The going was slow because he was collecting fingerprints using talcum powder for dark surfaces and cocoa powder for light surfaces applied with extra care using a big bushy makeup brush. It was another improvised substitute, but it was better than feeling he didn't do everything possible to uncover what happened. He transferred any prints to a contrasting light or dark sheet of construction paper using clear cellophane tape and noted where they were found. He was sure that the most common print he was finding were Netty's.

Occasionally, he stretched to get the kinks out of his back and glanced around at the family photographs scattered on bookshelves with knick-knacks or hung on walls. It was surreal that he was processing a crime scene in Netty's house. Her death was still inconceivable to him. He felt she would come home any moment and scold him for making a mess with powder everywhere.

He finally found something on the carpet in the living room, two more blond hairs. He took photos of the hairs with rulers for scale reference and Post-its to make ID markers. Under the couch tucked back next to the living room drapes skirting the carpet was a ring. The style was similar to a man's signet ring or college class ring. He used another Post-it note for a marker again, photographed, bagged, and tagged it.

Otherwise, the home seemed orderly, with no signs of a struggle, but empty and depressing. Perhaps the hairs he had found would have the follicle intact for a DNA test. He finished processing the rest of the house without much other than the blond hairs he considered helpful.

He found the letters to family members in Aunt Netty's altar room where she practiced Hoodoo, not Haitian type but more the New Orleans variety. He noticed one addressed to himself, but pushed down his emotions and pocketed the letters for later.

Then he allowed himself a few moments to think. He stood in the middle of the living room, his mind attempting to find reason while his heart ached. He was positive it was no accident. The lack of a struggle or a smoking gun of some sort was a setback, but not unexpected.

If his intuition was correct, Aunt Netty's death was not what it seemed. Then what could it possibly have been? A break-in or burglary would have left signs of a struggle. No evidence of either.

An argument turned deadly seemed unlikely with Netty, she was rarely angered and was usually the calm influence. And, an argument would likely have had neighbors noticing a commotion, but neighbors said all was quiet. According to the emergency response personnel nobody even heard Netty cry out. Somebody stopping by for a fertility charm had discovered her crumpled body.

Could somebody have a grudge against Netty? He wanted to say no, but he knew his aunt was a powerful Hoodoo practitioner. He grew up with incomprehensible events commonplace around Netty. Could somebody have taken offense at her power? Could she have lifted somebody's curse and made an enemy? Curses weren't as common as Hollywood depicted, but it did happen.

He had found everything he was likely to discover. He stood up and looked at the family photos clustered on the wall. He sucked in his breath when he saw Aunt Netty in the reflection of a photo's glass. He whirled around to find nothing behind him. His heart hammering, he turned back to the wedding photo of his aunt and uncle to see her reflection still there. She looked directly into the picture. Then she was gone. *Did he just imagine seeing her because he wanted to see her so badly, or was her spirit really in the room?* He had seen stranger things.

He shakily locked up and began the drive back to cousin Cecilia's. He would hand the letters over to the family members along with the Will and insurance papers he had found. He had a lot of thinking to do about what he was feeling – and seeing. Perhaps there would be some indication of what had happened in the letters. And, he had the strands of blond hair he found plus the ring.

CHAPTER SEVENTEEN

Elizabeth Grant

Elizabeth awoke to sunshine, heat, and humidity at 7:30 the next morning. The swamp cooler had been working hard all night, still her room remained the warmest in the house. The events of yesterday all seemed like a vague memory after a solid dreamless sleep. No nightmares.

She had tried the radio for some music, but the news of riots in Philadelphia overnight dominated the airwaves with only sporadic music. She quickly grew tired of hearing Hank Williams Jr.'s "A Country Boy Can Survive," "Song of the South," and "Drinkin' Beer Wastin' Bullets," and other odes to country living repeatedly between the shocking news reports. She had grown up listening to country music in the summers and pop music during the school year, but it didn't have the same appeal in light of the escalating events in Philadelphia plus her own quest for answers.

Elizabeth stepped out the front door to grab the newspaper sitting in the middle of the lawn. She idly watched two neighborhood ladies jog past with perfect hair that she speculated looked to be held in place with a bottle of hairspray each. One was in a turquoise running outfit, color coordinated from her headband down to her shoes while her running partner was all in pink. They had perfect makeup too. They stared at her as they jogged past.

She became acutely aware of how she had grown up between two worlds and no longer felt at home here. If it were Denver, they would wear an old T-shirt from a 5K run and a random pair of shorts or sweats with the hair quickly pulled back in an elastic band, like she wore.

She picked up the newspaper and saw the headline proclaiming "Police Retaliate Overnight" above the fold. She couldn't think about that right now, she had to finish watering the flowers in the backyard before she could leave for the library.

She dropped the newspaper on the dining table on her way out the back door to water Gran's flowers that bordered the yard along the fence. Her garden was colorful and lush with a mix of fragrances. It looked like a professional landscaper had designed the glorious site, but it had been Gran's vision and Gramp's labor.

In truth, the flower garden was probably the real reason she was house-sitting while her mother took Gran on a three-week cruise through Europe. This was the trip of Gran's life and she had been like a kid planning it, but she just couldn't stand for her flowers to perish with the Garden Show competition approaching. So Elizabeth took the time off from work in the middle of the busy season at her architectural firm to ensure Gran's garden would survive her absence.

Gran still had the old manual hoses with a gentle spray nozzle for watering, so Elizabeth tackled that task before the heat was oppressive, enjoying a little mist wafting on her occasionally.

"Ya must be Estelle's granddaughta." The voice came from an elderly neighbor man over the chain-link fence who was watering his lawn and flowers too. His comb-over was obvious and his smile restrained.

"Yes sir, I am."

"Welcome to ye Miss Elizabeth, I'm Hollis. Hollis Picket. I promised your Grandma to look out for ye, so ye give a holla if there is anythin' ye need." A polite smile accompanied the hospitality.

"Very kind of you, I'll call you if the need arises. Promise." She was quickly soaking the flowers while careful to follow Gran's written instructions.

"Ye gettin' on okay? If ye're feelin' like company, there's a dance at the Bingo hall tonight."

"Thank you, but I'm keeping busy. I don't really know anybody in town to show up at a dance."

Not that she was interested in meeting men. She was too busy with work and hadn't felt like dating since college. Even then, she was torn emotionally with her visions and couldn't open up or trust… at least that's what her boyfriends had all said. *Whatever.*

"Maybe ye'll run into ole friends. Your grandma said ye used to spend summers here. I'm sure ye have some friends waiting to get caught up with ye." His smile had not varied. The old geezer watched her every movement like a mongoose watching a cobra as she scurried among the flowers, dragging the water hose behind her. She felt his eyes follow her.

Elizabeth glanced over, ready to say something but hesitated when she saw the vision of Loralie standing at the fence between Mr. Picket and herself. Loralie held her hands out as if to signal stop while shaking her head "no". Elizabeth stared at Loralie.

Usually, she had seen the vision of Loralie when she was alone, never in public. Loralie was less transparent and more solid now too. Maybe her acknowledging that Loralie was probably dead was making the visions more real. Possibly all the thinking about her was just making the vision seem real, because her subconscious wanted to see her again so badly. *There was a very logical answer to it – really.*

"If ye like pie, my wife made a pecan pie. Come over anytime and have some coffee and a slice." His eyes didn't seem to blink but had narrowed.

Elizabeth mentally slapped herself. *Get a grip, it isn't the first time you've seen Loralie, so what if it's with other people around now? Maybe that was progress and the visions would go away soon.* She cleared her throat.

"Not at the moment, thank you. I have to make some phone calls, if you'll excuse me." She shut off the water and retreated inside. She wanted to call the office and see how the sprawling office complex she was assigned to was continuing without her. She was anxious over another architectural engineer handling the job. But, mostly she wanted away from Hollis, he gave her the creeps.

She grabbed a small spiral notebook to record what she was finding and tucked it in her purse. Earlier this morning she had documented her nightmares, noting details that had stuck out over the years in the notebook. If there was any message or truth in the dreams, then she should capture it now while still vivid in her mind. She already included the name "Calvin Morrison," the person who had claimed to witness Loralie leave the truck stop with a big rig driver.

She quickly dialed her office in Denver so she could be on her way to the library to research old newspapers. She kept her eyes studying the carpet rather than looking around, just in case Loralie was loitering. Sure, she was here to face what happened years ago, but seeing visions of her was still unnerving.

CHAPTER EIGHTEEN

Harlan Siesbolt

Special Agent in Charge Harlan Siesbolt sat in his office with a senior FBI agent sitting across from him. This visiting agent was a fellow Society member who came from the D.C. office and was taking an unusual interest in one of his officers. He was average with a few extra pounds that made him look puffy and soft and his comb-over didn't work. His eyes had the glint of a zealot.

"I just want you to call him. I know he's on grievance leave, but just check in on him. I want you to show concern for his well being." He had a sour look on his face like eating nails for breakfast would be a pleasant change. His voice was absent any accent and devoid of emotion as well.

Special Agent in Charge Siesbolt licked his lips, "I believe I can sound concerned for him; although I honestly thought you'd be asking why he hadn't left the Bureau yet." Malcolm was a rising star in the FBI and given enough experience and some mentoring he could climb up the ladder and one day run this state office. But, the Society was systematically weeding out blacks from law enforcement and federal positions as much as possible, Malcom wasn't easy to discourage or fire for cause.

He received only a stare in answer. The room seemed to grow

warmer as the seconds ticked past. Harlan picked up the phone and dialed Malcolm's cell phone number. He was no doubt with his mother and he wouldn't get much time for this call. The superior agent reached over and poked the "speaker" button.

"Alexander here." His voice was always a pleasant mix of rich smooth tones that witnesses loved to open up for.

"Malcolm, I'm sorry to bother you. I know you've a lot on your mind right at the moment."

"Yes, sir. What can I do for you?" He sounded tired to Harlan's ears.

"Now, I just wanted to reach out and see how you're doing. Several of the agents have been asking if they can help out in any way." It sounded insincere to his ears and hoped that Malcolm wouldn't see through this call.

"It'll just take some time, sir. The family's in shock, you know. It's just hard to believe it was an accident, it seems so unlikely."

"I can imagine it is very difficult to deal with your grief and be strong for your mother. Are you holding up okay?" The man across the desk from him leaned back into the guest chair and crossed his arms.

"I can't really say, sir. You know how it is. My mom is takin' it hard. I appreciate the call, sir. It means a lot to the family." Harlan thought he detected a bit of strain in his voice. At least it wasn't suspicion about motivation for the call. He raised his eyebrows in question to the D.C. agent who replied with the "keep it going" finger roll.

"Anythin' in specific that is troublin' you son? I called to be of support and I'd like to at least be a listening ear if you need it." That sounded nearly true. The Society's superior agent sitting in his guest chair wanted him to talk, so he was all ears. Harlan reminded himself of The Society's importance. It was taking Malcolm too long to answer.

"I know it's hard opening up to the agent in charge. Think of me as another agent wanting to help you out." He nearly believed it himself.

"Well... I'm just having a hard time believin' my aunt's death is an accident. I... I think it's suspect. It seems silly and insignificant, but she wouldn't have gotten on a ladder. She was afraid of heights more than one step up all her life." He stopped talking.

Now the ball was back in his court. Was this why The Society was interested in him, was his aunt's death important in some way? The way The Society was organized into cells, he wouldn't know if Malcolm's aunt was on the wrong side of The Society and been eliminated, but it was looking to be the case. Malcolm would likely have to die. But, it saved Harlan the trouble of getting him out of the Bureau.

"Give it time son, sudden tragedies like this are hard to accept. We can get you some counseling when you come back, help you through the grieving." Harlan hoped it sounded sincere and not like he was choking on the words.

The D.C. agent nodded his head and smiled a tight, grim little smile. He got up and left the office without a word. Harlan finished the call and said he would check back in with Malcom in the next couple of days. After hanging the office phone up, he took a deep breath. He was glad to have Mr. D.C. gone.

SAC Harlan Siesbolt was unaware of the phone call taking place on the sidewalk outside the front door of the FBI office building.

"Looks as though the accident didn't look probable. She was afraid of heights and they staged her falling off a ladder and breaking her neck." He listened for a moment.

"He thinks it was unlikely, but Siesbolt tried to assure him it was just the shock of the tragedy and all. Frankly, I'd be surprised if he didn't ask questions as an agent. For now it's normal, but let's monitor his phone calls and activities."

CHAPTER NINETEEN

The General

The Louisiana sun shone brightly overhead and a slight breeze rustled the trees countering the humidity. The backyard was resplendent with white linen-covered tables; one for his son's piled high gifts, another table weighted down with food for the late luncheon, and of course a table for the three-tier birthday cake. That didn't include all the games spread out across the lawn, from a beanbag toss and badminton to horseshoes and a sack race.

The clown he had hired to do balloon animals and face painting would arrive shortly. The party planner had gone with his concept of a more traditional birthday party, rather than trying to outdo his peers.

His wife, surrounded by children, was leading them in the games according to her detailed schedule. Another Society woman, who had a child attending the party, was assisting her. Blond-haired and blue-eyed Pastor Akron sauntered over carrying a small china dessert plate with chocolate birthday cake and sat next to him in a matching red cedar cushioned chair.

"What a beautiful day for your son's birthday. As if God is smilin' down on him, a sort of anointin' of the next General." Pastor Akron beamed brightly and dabbed chocolate frosting from the corner of his mouth with a napkin.

"It is a glorious day to be sure. Our long awaited moment is approachin' to restore the nation to Godly order." The General reclined back into the cushions of the patio chair and steepled his fingers, "A lot of work has preceded this historic moment we're on the precipice of initiatin'."

He tolerated the good pastor, mostly because so many members of The Society loved feelin' they were on a righteous crusade. He didn't need anybody to validate his plans were sealed with approval, he knew in his core he was righteous.

"I'm glad that you invited me here today. I'd very much like to say a prayer and blessing over the beginnin' of this critical move to bring the nation back to a blessed path." His eyes looked expectantly at the General and a glint of excitement, perhaps even zeal shone brightly.

"Why don't we go to the privacy of my office; where we can discuss and pray over the impendin' battle to bring the nation back to its former glory." The General stood and walked towards the large antebellum mansion he called his home. Pastor Akron followed in his wake, the plate of chocolate cake left sitting on the table – forgotten.

Pastor Akron had never been in the General's home office before and from the look on his face, he regarded it as an honor. He didn't flinch or even blink at the picture of the American eugenics researcher Harry Laughlin holding his Nazi Germany honorary doctorate for his work on the "Science of Racial Cleansing" nor at the picture portrait of the President with a knife stuck in an eye.

The General sat in his plush office chair, the closest to an official chair he had, and allowed Pastor Akron to place his hands on his head.

The pastor's voice began in a sing-song cadence, "Lord God, we pray today for your blessin' on The Society for a Restored America and its guidin' light, the General. We ask that you bless their critical work, their reachin' children in schools combatin' the lies that all are equal and the willful disobeyin' of God's plan for mankind and the races.

Bless their reaching the young and impressionable of our nation through the many teachers they have placed, the movies, the technology of social media they utilize, and the books they have published

proclaimin' your ordainin' of the white race as culturally and morally superior.

Bless their work as they move this nation into alignment with your holy plan and elevate the white culture that has been under attack for decades; protect them as they march forth as your sanctified soldiers. We pray that you hand them victory over your enemies and their rebellion against your ordained order that has torn down our nation and brought violence, disharmony, and drugs.

Bless all The Society soldiers as they go into battle against the Great Deceiver and the evil message of equality among races and among genders. They have denounced Noah's curse *"A servant of servants shall he be unto his brethren"*, they have spit on your wise and righteous order of the races. In Jesus' most holy name we pray. Amen."

The General had sat still through the long prayer. He believed that a man made his own destiny, but he was all for covering his bases. After all, it couldn't hurt. He knew that many of the members of The Society validated their feelings towards blacks, Jews, or Mexicans with the Bible. He had no such need to justify his beliefs to anybody.

As soon as the pastor was done with the prayer, the General's eyes flew open and zeroed in on Pastor Akron. "Thank you, pastor, that was most inspirational. If you'll excuse me, I've a few issues I should check into regardin' our plans and their moving forward." He smiled a tight little grimace at the man of God before him. He had never truly liked the man, but he served a purpose, that of keeping his membership happy.

"Of course General, I'm just honored to offer the blessing on Operation Cancer Eradication. Thank you so much for inviting me to the festivities of your son's birthday. I'll get out of your way. He slowly turned as if taking in every detail of the General's historical artifacts from the white supremacist and nationalist movements and similar organizations decorating the office. He halted in front of a framed Confederate flag, a historic piece of cloth. You could still see singe marks and a few bullet holes. Pastor Akron seemed to stand a little taller in front of the flag until the General reminded him that he was waiting for him to leave.

The General turned on the window air-conditioning unit since the room got intolerably hot and stuffy with the door closed. Its chilled air fighting against the heat and sounding like jet engines laboring for takeoff. He made himself a mint julep, more for nostalgia than actual preference, and added a few ice cubes from his bar fridge. He was now ready for his meeting.

He sat at his desk and woke his laptop from its sleep. He logged into an online virtual world, something that he never would have done for personal use, considering it a true waste of time. But, for the sake of The Society, it was useful for quick communications and went under the radar and undetected. Which is why, he supposed, terrorists used such online arenas as well.

In this virtual world they had created an invitation-only meeting space for members and fashioned it after the Old South and his computer representation, or avatar of himself, was a Confederate General.

He fancied himself as a modern-day Confederate as he spread the truth about the war of Northern Aggression being over the South's material rich industries instead of its servitude practices and thus were valiantly defending their way of life rather than traitors. But, it was no longer a southern issue because those who were ready to rise up and take the nation back under white control were all over the nation.

Thus, technology to communicate all across the country efficiently was instrumental. There was only one other member currently in the virtual space reserved for The Society, and that was his textbook publisher who was responsible for assisting in providing a myriad of history and social science textbooks from elementary to high school that had the correct version of the war of Northern Aggression represented.

This publisher had also done a wonderful job of creating a magazine targeted solely to teachers and provided stealthy ways to teach children the truths about servitude and the genetic inferiority of certain races as well as the true reason for the war, Northern greed. It also showed how America, in spite of what the hypocrites said, was built on servitude or base rate labor – from the blacks building the early economic engine, to the Chinese building the railroads for expansion westward, and the current Mexican agricultural servitude.

He turned his speakers on so that their computer avatars could actually speak to one another. "I'm fixin' to get back to my other responsibilities, so give me your report and we can be on our way." He tended to lean into the spot where the microphone was.

A rather scratchy and gruff voice replied back, "We're on schedule and can provide new teaching materials to roughly 75% of all high schools immediately and within the following month have the rest covered. The elementary schools will only have 50% coverage until about a month out. But, after the first month of the new president's term, all the U.S. schools should have their accurate new History and Social Studies books."

"What about the teacher's guides?"

"We're 100% ready for all elementary and high school teachers on those new guides, I'm including middle schools in that tally." The little computer representation of the publisher did a little dance.

"Excellent job. I anticipate within the first few weeks of the new President's term you'll be in full distribution mode. Be sure to have enough in stock or production to handle the load. Contact me if any further fundin' is needed and I can funnel it to you."

"I hate to even bring it up, but when will cabinet positions be decided?"

"Don't worry, the new President will appoint you as head of the Department of Education within the first month. So, please take that into account and don't let it hold up distribution of books." He had the cabinet picks already lined up for the new POTUS.

He finished up with his publisher and waited for his next appointment to meet him in the same virtual world. It was barely 2 minutes before his media coordinator joined him. His avatar looked like a 1940s reporter.

"How's your assignment comin' along?" He didn't care that his voice was abrupt as he leaned towards the computer's microphone again.

"We have two thirds of the major news channels on board to follow your station's lead reporting that Middle East terrorists have recruited the vast majority of the black citizens of the nation." This particular avatar stayed still, very still. As if the man himself were waiting for the verdict on his report, or he wasn't comfortable in this virtual world.

"Only two thirds, huh?" He was silent for a moment before answering. "I'd hoped for ninety to a hundred percent. We have to run with what you've got, but keep workin' on the remainin' news channels. Use whatever means necessary to ensure nobody contradicts the reports." The general realized that his media coordinator might not be fully up to the task of doing *whatever* it took. He would gladly send someone to reinforce the message. He cut the meeting short and disconnected from the virtual meeting world.

Now it was time to get back to his son's birthday party. He had been gone too long already, and he was looking forward to videotaping the children's antics. His son needed to enjoy his carefree youth while he could.

Besides, he was excited to give his present, a framed large movie poster for his room of the original movie "The Birth of a Nation" that sported a huge heroic Klansman on horseback, plus the film title and actors, and the words from the movie, "The former enemies of North and South are united again in defense of their Aryan birthright." They had watched the historic movie, credited with resurrecting the dead KKK that was used for recruitment by the Klan as well as The Society, together as a father and son bonding time.

Next summer they would visit Stone Mountain to see the huge bas-relief depiction of the three heroes Jefferson Davis, Robert E. Lee, and Stonewall Jackson. They will be among the four million visitors paying homage a year.

CHAPTER TWENTY

Elizabeth Grant

E lizabeth felt like she was back in college hunkered at the library doing research, only she was in a smallish building circa 1920s from all appearances. The newly added Greek Revival touches were understated, but the original hardwood floors glowed with pride.

Next to the ancient microfiche readers, one with an "out of order" sign taped to the screen, sat clunky old computers with the bulky monitors allowing internet access. She had never appreciated the library system in Denver more. She took a few minutes to get the hang of the microfiche reader since she had been in elementary school the last time she saw one. Somehow they kept two in working order when there weren't any replacement parts available for the last twenty or more years.

She had been scanning through the Cyprus Sentinel for the year Loralie disappeared, which wasn't as big a task as she originally feared because the paper only published twice a week. She started in April and was moving through the year so she could get a full picture of the town at that time. She was into the month of June and noticed a murder. The odd part was the coverage was not on the front page, but rather buried among coverage of club meetings, a square dance, and plans for the Fourth of July celebration.

Murder in this rural town should be front-page news. Why bury it? She carefully read the sparse report and took notes. Noah Aaron was the victim, in his forties, lived here most of his life, found by the railroad tracks outside of town to the East, shot in the head and left there in the weeds. The police decided the killer had to be a vagrant or a drifter and closed the case.

Elizabeth sat back. No real investigation – just blew it off. It didn't even sound like they looked for the phantom drifter who shot a life-time resident. Just like in a horror movie where your car breaks down in some backwater town and the next thing you know *there is something wrong with the town*. A chill ran down her spine and reverberated through her legs. She had not quite reached the date she was looking for. Noah Aaron's article was the day before Loralie disappeared.

The next issue of the paper had a small notice of Loralie reported missing. Barely two sentences, as if she didn't warrant more attention. The lack of attention given Loralie's sudden disappearance and Noah Aaron's murder made her wonder.

She looked around the small library and its patrons suspiciously. A feeling of dread settled into her bones.

The next edition of the paper dated a few days later said a witness, no name, from Doug's Truck Stop and Diner out on State 19 between Okati-bbee Lake and Meridian reported seeing Loralie loitering and eventually leave with a trucker. She remembered Okatibbee Lake well. During the summers she would go to the water park there, and a few times Gramps had taken her camping and fishing on the lake. But she didn't know of any truck stop out there, although it had been a long time ago. If Jeremiah was correct, the witness was Calvin Morrison. *Wonder if he's still around?*

She stretched her arms and legs and looked away from the microfiche reader to catch a muscular man among the stacks with a John Deere baseball cap and a gray T-shirt watching her. He appeared to be in his thirties. He didn't look away when she stared into his eyes. She raised an eyebrow.

Perhaps news had circulated who she was and people were just curious. Sure, that's it. *Just like somebody looked around the house out of curiosity yesterday when she was out?* She wished she could take out the gris-gris bag tucked under her shirt and hold it.

Suddenly, the man broke his glare directed at her, turned and stomped away. Elizabeth exhaled. *Now is not the time to let your imagination run wild.* He probably didn't like strangers and was suspicious of her. Nothing more than the small town sensitivity to outsiders.

She found nothing more of note to note from June and July. By then, she was famished and decided to get something to eat at the little diner, actually the only diner where she had eaten breakfast yesterday.

CHAPTER TWENTY-ONE

Malcom Alexander

Malcom sat in the funeral home's office with its soothing wood tones and soft blue fabrics listening to elevator music. He was there to assist his mother and cousin with the funeral arrangements, but his mind was replaying the phone call with his superior.

Aunt Netty's death had shaken him up, his search of her house and finding blond hairs had him suspicious, so it was no wonder he was questioning Special Agent in Charge Harlan Siesbolt's phone call checking up on him. He felt he was on the fringes of something happening much larger than himself and he was clueless and powerless.

"Malcom, please tell your momma she needn't spend her money on this fancy casket. We're payin' for this." Cousin Cecilia demanded with a no-nonsense air of finality. Cecilia and her husband were financially sound, not well-off mind you, and insisted on paying for the funeral, knowing his mother was on social security and would go broke to give her sister the best. He agreed with his cousin in this case.

He rested his hand on his mother's arm and looked into her red, swollen eyes. "Momma, let Cecilia do this for Netty. Netty knows you love her and always will. That'll never change, Momma."

His mother's soul-sick look eased, and she sniffed. She leaned over and kissed him on the cheek then turned to Cecilia and smiled. "You're a good daughter Cecilia. Who am I to stand in the way of you honoring your mother?"

He excused himself when they began with details for the funeral itself. Once outside and away from any windows where somebody might overhear and punched a number into his cell phone.

"Rick my man, Malcolm. Can I get lab work done for me personally but with a rush on it? I'm payin' for this one... A few hairs and fingerprints... tomorrow mornin' it is."

CHAPTER TWENTY-TWO

Juanita Alvarez

Juanita received a text on her pre-paid phone. It provided a time and place, presumably to meet, nice and simple and no hint of what to expect. Before she had left for the meeting, she wrote a note at her home with just a few details in case she never returned. She would burn the note if she returned, but it was there just in case.

Riots had begun in several parts of town in response to police raids overnight. Those raids were a lit match on the bone-dry kindling of long-held injustices. She couldn't believe the police didn't know their actions, particularly the widespread distribution of the raids, would only produce rioting in the streets. They couldn't have planned it better if they intentionally tried to set a match to the city.

Her hands shook occasionally, and she jumped at loud noises as if the tension in town was wound extra-tight and subconsciously impacting her.

The text message gave the address of an abandoned factory. North Philadelphia still had pockets of urban decay and higher crime, despite the Mayor's efforts. Some older and poor areas had seen rejuvenation, but this one remained untouched by such influences.

The factory, with the long-forgotten company name faded on the red brick north wall, was four stories tall and covered nearly a city block. Many of these empty warehouses or factories were torn down, but this one had escaped the notice of city officials or it was somebody's tax write off.

She parked in what seemed was the old visitor parking where the main business door once had been, now covered with plywood. She sat in her car, not venturing around to the more secluded areas of the property. The neighboring buildings were low brick structures, hunkered down to weather the economic storms; an automotive glass and window shop, a plumbing supply warehouse, and a semi tractor-trailer repair shop lined the road. All of which had grimy windows and minimal people in evidence.

Juanita looked at the license plates to her car sitting in the passenger side floorboard. She considered it a sensible precaution, but paranoid was paranoid. How much information could you really keep private in this day and age? Still, something small like her plates just might make a difference if this was as big as she sensed.

They don't teach this in journalism courses... *How to Stay Alive 101: Introduction to protecting your life and family when investigating volatile stories.* She sure wished they taught such a class. She arrived a few minutes early and kept looking around slowly, taking in every slight shadow in the high noon sun. Then she saw the kid from the café, to the right side of the building.

He appeared to be loitering, leaning against the building and lighting up a cigarette. She slowly got out of her car and walked in his direction, scanning the area, her heart pounding, and her palms suddenly sweating. She took a deep breath to steady her quivering hands. There was nobody else in sight, but she wouldn't know if there was an army inside the building watching.

She stopped next to him and leaned her shoulder against the building, facing him. In the bright sunlight, she could see he was older than she first thought; maybe early twenties.

He spoke first, "Let's make this quick before lunch is over and the people down the street are around. I got ya some evidence to start." He handed her a paper with two names on it. "Those are the first cops on the scene." He held his hand up to stop her protest before she argued that was nothing.

"Just listen. Those cops were seen in the area already. People ain't blind and there's a neighborhood watch lady who seen those guys sitting down the street 'bout an hour before they pulled up with lights all flashin'. Sudden-like, these guys have new cars and shit like they hit the fuckin' lottery." He took a deep drag from his cigarette.

Juanita waited because there had to be more. He took something out of his pocket and quickly slipped it into her hand. It was a memory flash card about the size of a quarter. She slipped it into her purse where she kept her business cards for the moment.

"That's a cell phone video from a neighbor that night. Pay attention to the activity in the backyard of the Olsen's house." He stopped and scanned the area before continuing, "Nobody knows about this video. When this person was questioned later if he had seen or heard anything, he was told those policemen couldn't have been sitting down the street. He was told he was wrong and not to go spreading lies, not to talk to reporters or anybody." He paused and stared at her.

"The police didn't listen? You're saying the police ignored what a witness was telling them? Was this person high or drunk or something like that?"

"What fucking bullshit is that? No, this is a regular working Joe, keeps his nose clean." He took another drag from the cigarette.

"Then how did you get it?"

"Not everybody related to a gang member is part of the gang, ya know. When this working person heard about the gang tags in the house, he turned it over to his relative for protection from the police. Ya see, this working person has been getting, ya know, some attention from the cops now."

"The person who took this video is being harassed? Just because he said he saw cops hanging out down the street? Is this what you have for me?" This was not real evidence; there was no smoking gun here. The cops could have been taking a break.

"You got the video and names of the cops. Follow their money; I can't do that for you. The video is more for you to know we're levelin' wit you. Both those pigs have badge bunnies and working girls they use. I don't know the names of their current holster humpers, but Belle works the Packer Avenue dock area. She has one as a regular. You'll get no trouble from her manager if you talk with her, but you don't want to be seen wit her." He flicked the cigarette butt down and shuffled his feet like he was anxious to leave.

"How am I supposed to talk with her then? She isn't a truck stop connection or a call girl I can meet somewhere? She could just tell me what you want her to say. Hell, you could be her pimp for all I know. How do I know I'm not being lied to?" Maybe she shouldn't push so hard, but she wasn't the gang's little reporter bitch and she needed to set that boundary now.

It was likely these cops had badge bunnies, or the cruder but equally common term holster humpers; essentially, cop groupies who gave sexual favors. It wasn't unheard of for a cop to frequent a hooker either, and the double standard was a major pet peeve of hers.

"I can arrange something and text you where you can meet her more private like. What you believe is up to you. But, I think you'll want to hear what she has to say. She has nothing to do with the Apostles, pure white bread honey that one."

"Okay, I'll talk to her. I'll watch the video and look into those cops. I just hope this isn't a waste of my time."

"It ain't. Ya got yourself a gun – least a stun gun, don't ya? This is the real deal and ya gotta stay alive to tell the truth of it." With that, he walked off toward the back of the factory building.

Juanita looked around and noticed a grease monkey at the semi-truck garage climbing into the engine compartment of a big rig. Lunch break was over apparently.

She wiped her shaking sweaty hands on her jeans and headed for her car. She was going to be busy trying to get private bank records of two cops. If it wasn't serious before, it sure as hell just got real. She was between a serious gang and alleged dirty cops. One misstep and she'd never be heard from again.

CHAPTER TWENTY-THREE

Elizabeth Grant

Elizabeth had intended to return to Gran's house and journal her thoughts on what she had discovered in her research before driving to Meridian to visit Jeremiah. Instead, she felt compelled to find Loralie's old house, if it was still standing. She visited the house a few times briefly in the past. She remembered it as drafty around the windows, dimly lit, and scrubbed clean despite the ever-present dust from the dirt roads in the neighborhood.

Like the rest of Cyprus, modernization was not a priority, so she could navigate by memories and guesswork into Loralie's part of town.

The dilapidated state of the homes struck her. One roof was visibly sagging, one porch was barely standing, screens were missing from most windows, exterior paint was worn off exposing weathered wood in most cases. The rest of Cyprus had at least been maintained, but not here. The dirt road had ruts and holes she hoped would not swallow her car whole.

She finally recognized Loralie's old home by the rosebush climbing a trellis that her mother had planted one summer. The trellis was no longer white, leaned to the right and appeared tied up to secure it. The peach-colored roses were in full bloom. Mrs. Carter had heard peach roses expressed gratitude and appreciation, so she insisted on saving up to buy a starter bush.

Elizabeth got out of her car and stared at the sagging, dust-covered roses. Sadness overwhelmed her, as if the gratitude Mrs. Carter felt for what blessings she had was forever tainted by Loralie's disappearance.

Elizabeth looked around, unsure what she expected or why she felt compelled to drive here. Her memories of the place were far sunnier since nostalgia can often gloss over details with the emotions associated with the people or place.

She reminded herself that some people never experienced friendship as close as those two unsuspecting girls of her childhood. She was fortunate to have known Loralie and been so close.

She slowly turned, surveying the reality of her friend's life. A few preschool-age children played in a mud puddle like it was clay to sculpt. One child watched her, wary of her every move. No doubt this child was an effective neighborhood watch. There were a few elderly folks sitting or rocking on their shady porches.

Directly across the street sat an elderly black man, his white hair cropped short and glasses on the tip of his nose, openly staring at her. He nodded to the empty chair next to him.

There was something about him that compelled her to join him. She crossed the dirt road, trudged up his three porch steps, and eased herself into the rocker. She felt older just seeing the sad conditions.

They sat beside each other with the view predominately of Loralie's former home before them. After several minutes he broke the silence with a strong, vibrant voice.

"Never thought I would see you again, Pigtails."

She looked at his dark crinkled face with surprise. Somewhere in the back corners of her mind sprang forth the memory of an energetic man who told jokes and gave hard candy to the children. That was before such kindness would be suspect. He had always called her Pigtails as he would gently tug on one.

"Mr....Jackson, right?"

"That's right, Pigtails. Didn't think you'd remember me either."

"You're part of my happiest memories. I don't want to forget any of those days." This was an unexpected tonic and she would forever be grateful to Mr. Jackson for helping her to revisit the joy of her summers here.

"If you're lookin' for her family, they moved right after the home was vandalized. I hear they went to Meridian ifin you wantta look 'em up."

"Thank you, I plan to see them again here soon, but what vandalism?" This was news to her.

"Oh, I reckon it was a day or two after Loralie went missin', the house was ransacked. The beds and couch slashed. Scared poor Mrs. Carter near to death. They packed up what they had left that was still in one piece and were gone the next day. I hated to see Mrs. Carter go."

"Did break-ins happen often then?"

"Every once in a while a TV or stereo got stolen. Folks here don't have much. But I never heard of tearin' a place apart like that before or since. Then their movin' away in a rush . . . ." He stared across the street, leaving the statement go unfinished.

"Mr. Jackson, you probably see a lot of what goes on here. Do *you* think she ran off?" She held her breath.

"No, can't-never-could believe that. Loralie was determined. Never seen such dogged determination in someone so young, and she was hell bent on goin' to college and givin' her momma and brother a better life. Mind ya, I could understand runnin' away from this hole of a place, but it just wasn't in her to give up like that. I just don't see it." He looked into her eyes.

"Me neither, sir. Me neither." They stared at the peach roses.

CHAPTER TWENTY-FOUR

Sheriff Craig

Sheriff Jake Craig sat ramrod straight in his rickety chair behind his dented and abused tan metal desk surrounded by tan walls. The Sheriff's station occupied one space in a building built in the 1960s. A television and small appliance store had formally leased the space. The cheap tile floors were chipped and gouged over the years, and it was obvious where the traffic flow had been when it was a store by the dark trails on the tan tiles.

At least he had an office with a door for privacy; the rest of the small staff worked in an open space with equally battered beige desks crowded around a multitude of tan metal filing cabinets and dilapidated chairs for visitors or those being processed. The back of the station consisted of five holding cells and a supply room that was barely a closet, and the evidence room that was roughly the size of two closets.

There were many thoughts swirling through his mind about what Elizabeth's visit might mean. She hadn't visited for seven years. Did this mean she would begin visiting regularly, or was she here for another reason?

He reached into his back pocket and withdrew his billfold, withdrawing the worn photo of Elizabeth taken at her college graduation.

He stared at the photo while considering the other morning with her in the diner. Her mother had done well, raising an independent and shrewd young woman. But she had a big city mentality and only a whisper of proper southern manners. Her momma had told him before she left Cyprus, "What good is southern charm if you scratch the surface to find it covered less virtuous qualities?"

He let out a long, sad sigh and his shoulders seemed to slump minutely. The shrill clanging bell of the tan Bakelite telephone with a large rotary dial jerked him from his contemplation of Elizabeth Grant and her visit to town. He kept requisitioning and requesting more modern telephones that would allow one person to direct calls, but there was never the budget for it in this little stop-in-the-road on the way to better things.

"Sheriff Jake Craig, how may I help ya?" He grabbed a pencil and paper to write any pertinent information.

The voice on the other end didn't bother identifying himself, "That little granddaughter of Estelle's was seen around town askin' questions. She showed a total lack of all sense when she went into the Bottoms by herself and was even seen sittin' and chattin' on a black man's porch. Disgraceful!"

"I'll have a talk with her, but you can't expect her to act like the rest of us. She was raised with different ideas. I'll try to rein her in." He was impatient with the caller since this really wasn't his job.

"I suggest you start keepin' better tabs on her, or she may find out the hard way about the proper way of things here." Dial tone.

CHAPTER TWENTY-FIVE

Juanita Alvarez

Juanita sat in her car parked outside a pleasant suburban home. This was the address that Heath had told her where to meet him. It was nondescript and blended in with the other muted-color homes with standard lawns. Heath had barely got off with a year in jail and probation after his identity theft charges.

She had already questioned the hooker, Scarlett, that the gang contact had provided her. It didn't get her any closer to a final story. She hadn't been sure where to turn until she remembered this miscreant.

Who do you call when you need to dig into a cop's personal finances and you aren't Internal Affairs? There isn't a hacker's association that advertises, "Suspect your husband, we can find out all his dirty little secrets".

She had met this twenty-something crook when she covered his trial and reported on the financial toll of identity theft, including the personal angle of the perpetrator. She had sold that article to a police association magazine for a pittance, but at least she had sold it. Now it might pay off towards a much bigger story.

She needed to know if the cops implicated by her informant

received money as she was told. She had no authority to subpoena those records; it wasn't under public domain such as a publicly held corporation's financial reports, so she was left with no other choice than use a resource such as this. If the cops had no obvious payments made to them, then she need not go any further.

She quietly got out of her car, glanced around, and prayed nobody would ever know she made this visit. She raised her hand to knock on the gray-green door when it opened, and before her stood the digital degenerate. She reminded herself he was a thief because it would be easy to believe he was a young professional. He wore a button-up stripped dress shirt with the cuffs rolled up to his elbows, designer jeans that neither sagged nor were skin-tight. He had diamond studs in his ears and a Vacheron Constantin watch on his tanned wrist that somebody else probably paid for with their life savings. He had exquisite taste, expensive and beyond his means, but exquisite.

"Juanita, I didn't expect to hear from you ever again after you used me, then tossed me aside like yesterday's news." He flashed his professionally whitened smile that was intended to melt any woman – and some men. He had perfected his charm, but she believed herself immune because she knew he was a criminal.

Besides, he wasn't that attractive. He had one of those faces where the individual components were unremarkable, but the whole was a pleasant mix without being stunning. He just really knew how to charm people.

"I need your expertise on a story." She felt the direct approach was best in this case.

"I have other talents you haven't explored." His eyebrows danced a little jig.

"Heath, let's keep this strictly business." She focused on his eyebrows rather than look into his eyes, it was safer that way.

"But dear, what's in it for me if not you? We both know you can't afford to actually hire me." One eyebrow arrogantly arched.

"Have you no sense of civic duty in the least? The city is facing a crisis and you expect a roll in the hay." She huffed.

"How is you showing up on my doorstep, expecting free expert services going to help the city, Nita?"

She licked her lips. She didn't dare tell him what she was working on, but if he agreed to hack the banking information, he deserved to know that crooked cops might be onto him.

"If you agree to help, I can tell you what I know. But not before."

"Civic duty and city in crisis? Is this your way of telling me your story has something to do with that home invasion and murdered family?" He scanned his neighborhood with cold evaluation. "This is my safe-house where the cops and feds haven't traced me. I hope you haven't brought them right to my doorstep."

"As far as I know I'm not being followed. I don't think I'm on the radar yet since I've only begun. That'll probably change if you help me."

"I have a bad feeling about this, chickadee." He scowled at her.

"I haven't actually said anything. But I have to be honest that it could be very dangerous." She began to believe this was a bad idea. She quaked at the realization of just how dangerous messing with crooked cops could be.

Heath seemed to notice her slight shiver, grabbed her by the wrist and jerked her inside, slamming the door behind her.

CHAPTER TWENTY-SIX

Elizabeth Grant

Elizabeth was on State 19, headed towards Meridian to visit with Jeremiah. This visit was long overdue, and she hoped to ease her conscience about that last argument with Loralie besides finding out what he knew about her last days.

Her royal blue vintage Mustang zoomed past thickets of trees with scattered wildflowers and patches of blackberries here and there bordering the road broken by an occasional dirt side road with no signage. Her air conditioner cranking out cool air barely pushed the sweltering heat to the back.

She kept glancing in her rearview mirror. The rusty green truck was still behind her, hanging back far enough she lost sight of it for a few seconds. It was the same truck she swore followed her since she left her visit with Mr. Jackson. This was the main road in and out of Cyprus, so it was probably just a coincidence.

The image of the man glaring at her in the library sprang to her mind. Then there was the intruder who waltzed into Gran's home and went through her luggage and personal items. It didn't matter much if small town folks didn't like an outsider; it felt like there was an unnatural interest in her that couldn't be explained away when you considered a truck was following her.

She fished in her purse with one hand and dug out her cell phone. No reception. Perfect. Her inner voice screamed she was being followed. For several miles it had hung back, but no longer. Out of the corner of her eye, she could see Loralie in the passenger seat fidgeting, which seemed incongruous for a spirit to be sitting, let alone nervous.

She tapped a fingernail against the steering wheel as the truck came closer. Maybe the distance was no longer an issue, as if the driver didn't care if she realized she was being followed. She was grasping for some ideas of what to do before the truck got much closer. She had to take advantage of the distance while she still could.

She was approaching a curve in the road where the truck would lose sight of her for a few moments. She scanned for a dirt road to pull off while she had the opportunity. She might have missed the turnoff, it was so overgrown with weeds and brush if it weren't for Loralie appearing in the middle of the road wildly pointing. Elizabeth quickly braked and dove her car onto the neglected trail.

She crawled along so she didn't leave a trail of dust to follow. She pulled off the trail and spun the car around so it was in the weeds on the other side facing State 19. If the truck's driver realized she had taken this road, she wanted to get back onto the main road rather than get lost on this rutted side trail.

She wasn't completely hidden, but this way she could view enough of the road to see the truck when it passed. One hand gripped the wheel in a white-knuckle vise-grip and the other held onto the gris-gris bag from around her neck as she waited. She let a breath out as the truck zoomed past the side road.

Okay, now what? Should she run back to Cyprus with her tail between her legs or try to make it to Meridian to see Jeremiah? She wanted to ask Jeremiah about the home vandalism after Loralie disappeared, but was it worth the risk? Maybe she was over reacting, the truck might just be headed out of town on the only road going that direction.

She crept the Mustang up to State 19 for a peek. If the truck kept going, then it probably had not been following her. She could see the green truck trying to turn around in the road. That was a blinking neon sign she'd been correct. Loralie, back in the passenger seat, appeared to chew her nails. Elizabeth accelerated and turned towards the truck and Meridian, regretting it as soon as she did.

The truck had barely finished turning around in the road and was facing her when she blasted past it doing seventy. She looked in the rearview and saw the truck sitting there with a man in the passenger seat watching her through the truck's rear window. All she could see was he had blond hair. They didn't have time to turn around again and catch up with her at the speed she was going. She shook all over.

CHAPTER TWENTY-SEVEN

Juanita Alvarez

Juanita sat in Heath's basement full of computer technology. There were two metal server racks about six feet tall sitting off the floor on pallets full of computer servers, Cisco routers, switches, and various other electronic components she couldn't guess their function. His long desk held four monitors. In the far corner of the oblong room was an area rug with a couch, coffee table, and a television mounted to the wall. It smelled of a woodsy plug-in air freshener with a hint of mint and an undercurrent of coffee permeated the space.

Heath had swiftly broken down her resistance, and she had divulged what her story involved.

"You're telling me that the Black Apostles are feeding you information on dirty cops. If you don't find anything on the cops, what're they going to do to you? What if they're right and you're putting yourself in the cops' gun-sights? This is a no win for you, Nita." He dug his hands through his sandy blond hair, mussing it.

"I know this is beyond anything I've investigated or reported on before. It's already scaring the *mierda* out of me." She took a deep breath. "I think I'm already too far in to just quit. I don't think the gang will take that graciously. So, I have to find out as much as I can, or plan on leaving the country fast." She attempted a laugh but knew it was flat.

"You thought of me to get you out of this mess! Don't you have a boyfriend to torment for this? Some guy to play your white knight?" She slowly shook her head no with wide eyes.

"Finally, no boyfriend. That's like the sixth time I've asked." He stared at her with a lopsided grin. "I guess it's time to play the hero for once." He didn't move. "I'm going to save your sweet neck or get us both killed." He strode to his desk and sat, surrounded by monitors, and began typing.

Juanita released her breath. He had taken it all rather well. His blunt assessment of her predicament had ratcheted up her nerves. She shook her head and wondered how she got in the middle of this mess. She was a good girl, went to Mass *almost* regularly, confession once a year, she said the Rosary... okay, she believed in birth control and abortion, so she was a casual Catholic.

But even so, she was a good person, and she believed an independent press to be an indispensable part to a free society and had the responsibility to uncover corruption and injustice. That was why she chose this career. Anything worth having was worth fighting for, right? So this good girl would fight with everything she could.

"So, what're you doing? Are you looking into their bank records already?" She was confused. He had software up she had never seen before, but it didn't look like a web browser or a bank's website.

"No, I'm contacting people on the Dark Net who specialize in this and can actually remain anonymous. This is out of my league and I don't want to get myself killed, but I also know you won't let this go. You need people who are cunning and can do more to keep you safe than I ever could."

"I'm tired of anonymous contacts already. I'd like to know who I'm dealing with."

"They stay anonymous for everyone's safety. It's why they can do what they do." He stared at her as if she should understand.

"This all sounds too criminal. Maybe this wasn't a good idea. Sure you can't do it?" She didn't need to get involved with rogue hackers, she was already skirting danger with this story.

"You need these people more than you can ever realize. And no, you need skills beyond what I can do." At least he had not told her to "trust" him, she might have run if he had. Sure, he had charisma and that clean-cut boyish charm rather than genetic good looks, but he was still a thief when you got right down to the core of him.

He turned on his computer speakers for talking over the internet with various hackers. Juanita was wide-eyed and dry-mouthed next to Heath.

The hair on the back of her neck stood up as she realized she wasn't Woodward or Bernstein, but then neither of them had worked such a story before and Woodward took risks meeting Deep Throat late at night. Was she up for this scale of investigation and danger? Was she out of her depth before she had really begun?

Only one way to find out.

CHAPTER TWENTY-EIGHT

The General

The General was in Washington D.C. for an important visit with his inside person in the White House. Nobody knew he was here, not even his brother-in-law, for it was better that only he knew the identity of the inside man.

He flew into the capitol on his private airplane and was met at the airport by a rented limousine service. They were now pulling up in front of the Watergate Hotel and office building. He maintained a cooperative apartment in the Watergate East building. He also kept a small office in the Watergate office building, the infamous site of the burglary and scandal of the Nixon era.

His luggage would be dropped off and taken to his apartment while he went to his office for his meeting with the Vice President of the United States. He was about ten minutes early, but that was necessary to ensure his visitor did not wait in the hallway and risk being seen.

He had barely sat down in the ultra-modern office and poured himself a twenty-five-year-old single malt Scotch out of a cut crystal decanter when there was a staccato knock on the door and the vice president quickly entered the room.

The man was tall and lanky, built like the cowboy from Texas that he was, except for his "perfect preacher" hair seen on most every television evangelist. Perhaps the most striking characteristic of the man before him was his ability to project sincerity and wholesomeness while underneath he was secretly a Society member who lied to everyone around him about his political leanings.

"Let's make this as fast as possible, I'm due back on the Hill and my absence will be noticed." There was no smile on his face, and for once his serious and calculating eyes were truthful.

The General purposely took his time by strolling over to the Bose stereo system, turning on some classical music, and then poured a Scotch for his visitor. The cowboy took a big gulp of the drink as if it were milk and sat down facing the General across the sleek minimalist desk with a glass top.

The general took a deep breath and began, "I've been mappin' out what our post-victory moves should be. There are several pieces of legislation and executive orders that are goin' to need quickly passed. Do you think that will be a problem once you've taken the helm?" He scrutinized this career politician before him with open skepticism before continuing.

"I've been forgin' many alliances and workin' relationships in anticipation of needing' a coalition that'll back us. I believe most any legislation we deem necessary can be presented in the context of the national crisis and get passed with little opposition." The General took a hearty swig of scotch. It went down smooth.

The Vice President sat forward in the streamlined ergonomic chair like an eager student, "I've had a few thoughts on that. I believe our first move should be to begin the repeal process for constitutional amendments thirteen, fourteen, fifteen, and nineteen." *Oh, out of the mouths of babes.*

"That's very ambitious to begin with as our first major push. Do you really believe you have adequate support to pull it off?" The general knew several people had floated repeal of those particular amendments, the abolition of slavery and civil rights as well as women's vote, over the last few decades. It was never an idea that got enough traction.

The General took another sip of his scotch and leaned back in his chair, "I was thinkin' of tightenin' immigration to allow white European countries only, and sanction more for-profit prisons to bring back servitude and manual labor for the inferior races. We've been successful with buildin' up this program already and I believe people won't question this move."

The cowboy politician smiled, "By the time we've secured the presidency, all of the media coverage that you'll have generated tying the majority of niggers to Middle East terrorist groups will make repealing the amendments rather easy, even downright patriotic to all remaining citizens . . . even the liberals." He let out a gruff laugh.

"If we can push the media onslaught fast and hard enough tyin' blacks to terrorists and radical Muslims, it may be easy to push both pieces of legislation plus even more simultaneously. We'll need to have all the legislation and executive orders written up and waitin' for the first few days of your presidency – while everythin' is in flux and the nation is still in shock from the crisis." The General smiled inwardly. *Yes, that's the way to go. That'll do the trick.*

Save up so there is an onslaught of bills and executive orders and legislative moves making it near impossible to keep up with the sheer volume, let alone fight each measure. While everyone is still reeling from the assassination of the president and the nation is in turmoil with violence in the streets, it is the perfect time to slip all of their plans for a restored America through. If people do eventually realize the extent of what was done, it would be too late.

The vice president, or should he refer to him as the next president, had a gleam in his eye. "Then we have a lot of work ahead of us. I want to include a mandate for history books to be rewritten with the proper view of our nation's history..."

CHAPTER TWENTY-NINE

Elizabeth Grant

Elizabeth had met with Jeremiah and was back in Cyprus at Gran's house by late afternoon. For her own peace of mind, she took a longer route to return, one that swung her around to enter Cyprus from the opposite direction. She had allowed herself to cry a few tears as she drove back, pulling over occasionally.

Spending time with Jeremiah had brought long-buried emotions to the surface more than staying at Gran's house or the visit with Madam Antoinette. Emotions she had buried deep, particularly when she thought her visions of Loralie were signs she was losing her mind.

Watching Loralie's *spirit* kiss and smooth Jeremiah's hair chipped away at her locked away grief.

She sat in the living room with the afternoon sun streaming in the front windows through the sheers. She wrote the events of her day in her notebook. Everything from her library research, meeting with Mr. Jackson, being followed on the road to Meridian, and what she learned from Jeremiah (which wasn't much). She sipped on some pink lemonade as she scribbled her notes. Jeremiah added little to what Mr. Jackson had told her.

Yes, their house had been vandalized. Mrs. Carter had read some note left on the refrigerator and started packing up immediately. Jeremiah never saw the note, and his mom never told him what it said. But it seemed clear to him it was some sort of threat. Jeremiah suspected his mom believed Loralie was dead from that point since she acted like she would never see Loralie again. His mom had told him not to contact Elizabeth because she was in a *delicate* state, so he wrote her secretly and kept their continued contact hush-hush.

Heavy footsteps on the porch and a loud rap on the door sent her heart thudding. She closed her notebook and placed a book on top of it before going to the door. Her eyebrows rose in surprise upon opening the door.

"Sheriff, to what do I owe the pleasure?" He was clearly off duty now from the jeans and plaid western shirt he wore. No polo shirts for this guy.

"Now I'm just stoppin' by seein' how you're doin'." He glanced inside.

Elizabeth sighed inwardly, "Won't you come in. Can I get you something to drink?"

"Thank you, mighty kind, but no." He settled on the couch and she sat on the edge of the nearby chair as silence blanketed them. After a few moments, Jake Craig cleared his throat.

"I reckon your visit's goin' well?" Not much of an icebreaker, but he had made an attempt.

"Yes, it's going fine. I could only ask for internet and better cell phone reception to check in with work easier." All true, as far as it went.

He took a deep breath before saying, "Now, I understand you've been askin' around about your friend's disappearance. Perhaps you shouldn't stress yourself, dear. Consider this a vacation."

"Really? Is this just small town gossip or are my movements monitored?" Any attempt at working on her southern manners and subtext were left in the dust after being followed out of town.

"Monitored? Now of course not, bless your heart. People just notice things and they find you a break from the monotony. Don't read anythin' into it now." He leaned forward and looked directly into her eyes. "But, I reckon feathers do get ruffled easily round here by strangers stirrin' up old ghosts." Elizabeth shivered at the word choice.

Digging up old bones.

"Is this the sole purpose of your visit? To tell me to stop my natural curiosity?" A slow burn of anger pushed aside caution.

"Now what's that old saying? Curiosity killed the cat, dear. I'm just suggestin' you might want to let people get to know you again. You haven't been around for so long, it's the same as a stranger poking their nose into people's business."

"I seem to recall I was never considered part of the Cyprus family, even with all the summers I spent here. I don't think I've the time to waste waiting for them to hopefully, maybe, someday warm to me."

"Now darlin', all your questions aren't goin' to amount to a hill 'o beans. Now, you might just save yourself the trouble and try to enjoy your time here." He rubbed a hand across his jaw. "Surely you can relax the few days remainin' of your time. Maybe take a day trip or two and visit Southern historical sites. Get out a little, dear."

She searched his eyes and her hand went to her throat. She wanted to grab the gris-gris, but resisted.

"I seem to recall Gran saying Cyprus was getting some tourist interest with the remodeling of Whispering Oaks Plantation. Maybe I should go visit it again."

"Now dear, the remodel has barely begun. Whispering Oaks, like the town in general, can be dangerous to outsiders. You should think about doin' some site seein' away from town for a bit. Surely, I can watch after the house."

I bet you can. Probably have a key too. Hmmmm.

CHAPTER THIRTY

Juanita Alvarez

J uanita was still sitting in Heath's safe house basement. The remnants of delivered Philly Steak sandwiches scattered around and empty Yards Pale Ale bottles in the trash. The subdued lighting and a full stomach helped her relax.

Was it terrible that she felt more comfortable with Heath than most people she knew? That she trusted Heath to help her on this story bothered her, nagged and picked at her, as if she were a criminal by association.

Since she didn't have a publisher to foot the bill for a lawyer and a court order for bank records, she convinced herself this was the only way to get the truth without having goons follow her or break into her house. Corrupt cops could do a lot of damage and she turned to Heath in her fear mixed with determination.

They had talked with a few experts about the problem of getting the bank records of the two cops, and it was possible. But they rarely liked to go into actual financial accounts. They liked to make statements and provide a warning when they hacked as part of their activism. They were specifically looking for a member who liked the challenge and felt it was worth the risk.

They were using voice over IP with yet another member of the loosely organized hacking group. It was surreal discussing this with a stranger on a back-lit screen. Heath assured her this was how he connected with hacktivists around the world.

"Let me see if I understand you. Probably crooked cops involved in that family's murder and you want me to hack into their bank accounts for proof because nobody else has risen to the challenge. Is that about it?" From her voice, Juanita was estimating a middle-aged woman, maybe from the mid-west. She said to call her Betty.

"Yep, that sums it up. We're leveling with you, this is likely dangerous, and will probably bring a ton of trouble on your trail unless we can do it without detection." Heath glanced in Juanita's direction, a spark of hope showing in his eyes. This was their sixth person and even Heath seemed less enthusiastic with each new contact until now – until Betty, the hacker extraordinaire.

"If I take this on and these cops are involved, what then? I don't want to risk so much hard work only to have it dropped. I'm just saying, follow through is the key." The back-lit image of "Betty" sounded adamant. Juanita knew she had a point. Once Betty did the electronic and illegal digging; it was up to her to shine the light on the bad cops. She had to have as much at risk, too.

"I promise you, I'll do everything in my ability to bring them to justice. Any evidence will be used to stop them. I don't know what else I can do." She was hoping the small reporting jobs she had done with a few online news sources had built her reputation and one of the sites would break the story. She couldn't imagine them not running with it considering the media frenzy over the murders and the riots.

"Give me the information; I need their names and which bank in particular." She became animated, tapping away on her keyboard as Heath relayed the information to her.

"Slick, listen up so you do this next time. I'm gonna use an IP forwarding algorithm to cover my tracks, hit them with a distributed denial of service to distract them while my script searches and downloads these dirty cops' banking transactions. This might take me a while. I'll get back with you in an hour or two to give you an idea of how this is going. I make no promises though." The screen went blank as she disconnected.

"Don't worry 'Nita, I don't plan on ever hacking a bank. I've already forgotten what she said."

Juanita turned to Heath. "Do you think she can do this and really not get in trouble?" She wanted to stay on task. She also didn't want to endanger others to get a story. Yeah, she had the killer instinct all right.

His promising her good behavior felt too much like he thought... well, like he thought there was something between them, or might be something, like he cared what she thought. She wasn't comfortable with that.

"I know she's good. She's one of the best and doesn't like to leave any trace of her intrusion. If anybody can get the bank records without attracting notice, she can."

"She doesn't strike me as a digital hacking ninja type."

"Oh, you'd be surprised. We aren't all slackers or live in virtual game worlds as an escape from real life. Hacktivists are computer professionals, by and large, who take their role seriously." He reclined back in his desk chair and put his feet up.

"How long do you think it will take before we hear back on her progress?" She grabbed the last potato chip.

"This might be a long night, so we should get comfortable." His eyebrows danced.

She threw a wadded up napkin at his head, but he caught it effortlessly. She had been eyeing the small couch against the far wall and figured she could at least get a nap in. She suppressed a yawn.

"I don't want to brag, but I'm not so bad. You might just enjoy yourself if you put yourself in my hands." His lopsided grin oozed boyish charm.

"Here I thought computer geeks were socially inept. Who would've thought a tech nerd would be a lecherous Don Juan?"

"A Don Juan geek, I like it. Can I use that? I'm not lecherous, however. I can't help it if I enjoy women." He was giving her the soulful look now. "I act a gentleman when introduced to the family, and I even open doors and pay for dinner."

Juanita chuckled. "You wouldn't survive with my family, you are culturally challenged and too slick. My mother would chew you up and spit you out before you made it to the meal." She could see in her mind's eye, it wouldn't be pleasant or amiable.

"Is your mother why you're so... uptight?"

"I know what you're doing. I'm not telling you about my family or personal life so you can weave this illusion of familiarity to increase your chances with me. Not happening." Even though she ached to have someone to share with, it wouln't be Heath.

"You really believe I've only one thing on my mind?"

"You're a guy, right? You freely admit you're a man-slut. How did I misread that?" The verbal jousting game was standard with Heath. She was too on-edge to enjoy it this time around.

"Seriously, we've never just talked, it's always been your job. Let's start with something basic, okay? My favorite movie is the *Thomas Crown Affair*, both the Steve McQueen and Pierce Brosnan versions. Your turn." He motioned for her to answer.

"I have more than one. *All the President's Men*, of course. Then would be *The Post*, *Goodnight and Good Luck*, and *Spotlight*." His reaction was predictable, every guy she met didn't like how serious she was, how she was dedicated to reporting.

He nodded his head, "Ahh, now we're getting somewhere. I can see how all of those would inspire you, maybe even motivate your career choice, ignite that fire for truth and justice."

"Superman was the first superhero, and it's significant he was a reporter for his cover so he could dedicate his life to protecting the nation by bringing the truth to light too." It had slipped out before she could filter, before she could stop herself. She turned her back to him. He probably thought that was cheesy or childish.

"So, my dad and I are always butting heads, no matter what it's about. We can argue over the weather. Is it that way with your mom?" His voice was hesitant, unsure.

She let out a long, exaggerated sigh. "My mother thinks I don't know my place." She had already let out her journalist nerdy self, why not complete the humiliation?

Heath raised his eyebrows in surprise.

Juanita twisted a strand of hair. "My mother thinks I should get married and pop out babies. She hates that I went to community college and that I'm working and single. It's a cultural thing. There you have it." She had never shared that with anybody.

"Okaaaaay, she wants grandkids and all that. But college is a good thing, at least my family was always talking about it when I was a kid. There was no option, I was to go—no questions asked." He swung his feet off the desk and down to the floor.

"You wouldn't understand." She licked her lips and swallowed. "My parents, they… they're undocumented." She glanced at him quickly to see his reaction and held her breath.

"Oh. Well I sure won't tell anybody. What does that have to do with your going to college or being happy?"

"We're not welcome, we're not equal, we're not to strive for better, make no waves, draw no attention to ourselves." Her heart was hammering, she forced an inhale, "I want more for my life, but I might draw attention to them. Plus, I'm turning my back on my family, even my heritage by not getting married and having kids. I'm a disappointment all around to my mother." She focused on the wall. Sure, she had friends whose families weren't so dogmatic about the getting married or career issues, but not her mother.

Shit, she hadn't intended to share so much. She did what she said she wouldn't do. Let him get familiar with her life, let a sense of closeness develop.

Heath was quiet for a few moments as Juanita continued twisting that strand of hair. He seemed to be thinking, that wasn't good. Maybe this would be the end of his flirting.

"I guess it doesn't matter what culture or country you come from, parents think they know what's best and children fight to be their own person and make their own way." He looked her in the eyes. "Look at us, we aren't as different as you think."

"We have more differences than things in common." She bit out, not willing to let the closeness take root.

"You're growing fond of me though, I can see it. The ice is melting." He smiled, soft and genuine.

She let her breath out. Focus on the assignment, that's what she had to do. Juanita realized she still had the cell phone video to view. She might as well get that done and see what was in the video while they waited. Besides, he might be helpful with the tech side of the video.

"I also have a cell phone video taken the night of the attacks. Do you think we could watch it?" She held out the small memory card the gang contact gave her.

Within a few minutes they were watching the video, without the popcorn Heath had offered to pop. It did indeed show a cop car parked down the block at dusk with a time and date stamp. Then the video changed to the now infamous house where the family was slaughtered and the gang graffiti and tags were spray-painted inside the house. The angle wasn't directly in front, but rather to the side so you could see into the backyard that had a weak porch light on.

"The shadows at the front window are all over the place." Heath noticed. The curtains were drawn but rough shadows played across it, too distorted to tell what was happening. "There are more than two people is all you can really tell." He stated the obvious.

"How do we know it is really from that night?"

"I checked the metadata attached to the files. It was that night, and the times coincide. Hell, it even has GPS data included. This is the real deal 'Nita." He looked pale in the glow of the monitors.

A chill shot down her core as the mood shifted to knife-edge danger. They were watching a video of the family being killed and it was eerie quiet, no blood-curdling screams. She felt the walls of the basement closing in on her.

The shadows changed, the motions seemed more forceful. Juanita couldn't help but conjure the crime scene photos she had gotten a peek at and realized this had to be the violent spree after the family was dead. She swallowed loudly, her breathing sped up, and her hand covered her mouth.

The back door opened and three men were briefly caught in the porch light. They all wore black, but the dark sprays and splatters on their Caucasian faces was clear. They disappeared into the alley with barely a full second in the light. The next scene showed the same cop car that had originally been down the street, gradually pull up in front of the house with the lights flashing and siren screaming.

The two cops walked up to the door, without drawing their guns for safety, kicked in the front door and then stood in the doorway talking on their shoulder radios. After a minute had passed, another police car came zooming up. The video stopped.

"Holy shit 'Nita, we have proof it wasn't the gang but white guys. Holy mother-of-god, it was a setup."

They sat starring at each. Heath's eyes were wide and Juanita shook from the inside out.

CHAPTER THIRTY-ONE

The General

The General sat at the dinner table with his wife and son. The ten foot long antique table was grand for entertaining. The dining room walls were dark gold with white baseboards and cove base. A golden light emanating from the elegant European styled chandelier bathed the room with warmth.

"The golf tournament at the club will be a nice opportunity for me to chat with Beatrice about the Ladies Auxiliary and see if she'll sponsor my application."

"I'm sure she'll jump at the chance to bring you on board, who wouldn't? Besides, you are very persuasive, dear. I should know." He reached over and squeezed her hand. Charlotte was a petite brunette with an iron determination. She smiled her thousand watt-smile at him as a reward for his support.

A young serving woman dressed in a crisp white and black uniform nudged through the swinging kitchen door with the plates of dessert, Crème brûlée with a berry topping. She moved carefully, placing the plates gently at each place setting, and quickly moved to the next.

"Mother, you said we could have my birthday cake and ice cream." Caleb stuck his lower lip out and glared.

"Caleb, I never promised to my recollection. I said we'd see, and I decided against it. If you don't want to eat this, you'll sit and wait for us to finish before we dismiss you." She snapped out.

The General barely noticed, he was preoccupied with the situation in Philadelphia and the next stages of his plan. It was progressing as he had planned. His cable-news networks were picking up the theme that there were racial tensions that were turning deadly and using his prepared talking points.

There were widespread riots last night that helped to fuel the tensions. He had strategically placed agitators on the streets and also in the police force to keep the violence going. All of which served his purpose to accentuate and create an uprising, or the appearance of one, to justify the takeover he envisioned. The white populace was getting fearful, and he would keep the pressure on so everyone felt afraid for their lives.

Caleb threw his cloth napkin in the middle of the table and stood up, his hands on his hips. "You lied to me and I hate you."

The air instantly filled with tension, not because of his words but the anger the General felt for his son's outburst.

"What did you say to your mother?" The General turned his thoughts away from strategies to elevate racial animosity and assessed the heir to The Society, who just celebrated his eighth birthday. He stood up and gave his son a searing look.

Just as he was about to rain down an attitude adjustment, his cell phone chirped indicating a text. *His man at the White House wanted to talk... insisted on talking.* He was the only person in The Society that interacted with this man, the only one who knew exactly who he was and gave him orders.

He wanted to take his son to task, his hand itched to swat his little behind. He looked his lovely wife in the eyes. She shooed him away with her hands and stood from the table with a determined look in her eyes as she approached Caleb who stood defiant, hands on his hips.

"Now dearest, let me handle this phone call and I'll take care of Caleb."

"Don't worry. It's time Caleb and I have ourselves a serious little talk."

"I'll be right back."

He briskly strode to his sound proof home office. After he closed and locked the door, he setup his secure phone, the Data STE with the government enhanced crypto card. Within a few minutes he was on the phone to his inside person at the White House, the Vice President.

"I was in the middle of dinner." He snarled, "What is so urgent you couldn't wait?"

"The President plans on sending representatives to Philadelphia."

"That's all? We expected sending a few stand-ins for a good will tour. Now, if he were to personally visit we could easily arrange a hit there. You should emphasize to him how his presence is needed. Only contact me if he's goin' so you can relay details." This was the simplest contingency they had planned for. The President would essentially be delivered into their hands if he went anywhere near Philadelphia.

"I... I wanted to know how the prison break was going?"

"Right on schedule." His voice was still tight with displeasure at being interrupted.

"How long before I can take office? Each day playing second fiddle to this man is torture." His voice was tinged with disgust.

"Patience now. When we're done, the people will be downright beggin' for our reforms and sweepin' changes."

He disconnected unceremoniously. While he was here, he made another short call to the man who liaised with both Federal and state prisons across the country.

"Surprised to hear from you today, didn't you tell me you were busy today?" The baritone voice was friendly like a bear.

"I wanted to check in. How is your schedule for both Federal and State prison readiness?"

"Well, I'd like to go over this in more detail, but we're on schedule with a few exceptions. Those are mostly within the Federal Bureau of Prisons. We don't have a Society member in a high enough position to push through the funding as fast as we need for those prisons."

"What about the private prisons? I want the majority placed in private prisons so we get free labor."

"I have worked out phased implementation of private prisons that will take five years once we're in control of the White House."

He finished the call and hung up. He wasn't happy with the arrangement, but this had been one of the last pieces geared up, so he couldn't expect fast results where most of the other programs had been in process when he became General over a decade ago.

Now to deal with his strong-willed son who he found in his bedroom sulking. He shut the door and his son swallowed.

"You were disrespectful to your parents and impatient. Your behavior was unacceptable." He studied his son sitting with arms crossed but eyes bulging and a little quake of fear shaking him. Good.

"What's your punishment?"

"Mom says I can't go out for two days and one week without video games or television." His lower lip trembled.

"You're lucky, do you know how I would've punished you?"

"Yes sir, the switch." He swallowed again.

"I expect better from you. Why is that?"

"Because I'm the next General of The Society for a Restored America and I must live up to my superior genes." He recited the answer.

The General stood and faced The Society's flag on a pole standing in the corner, "Let's say the pledge, son."

His son stood by his side and they recited the pledge in unison, the child's voice grew stronger with enthusiasm.

I pledge allegiance to: The God given intellectual and moral superiority of the White race. I vow to: Fight to uphold the White culture, and win the nation to economic prosperity, justice, and Christian charity by providing servitude where inferior races find contentment.

CHAPTER THIRTY-TWO

Lukas MacKenzie

I t was early morning along California State Highway 43 and the Correctional Officers were just getting the prisoners out of the van and organized for a day of hot backbreaking cleanup.

Highway 43 is a modest two-lane that runs North-South alongside the BNSF Railway tracks. Farmland on both sides of the long, isolated stretch of road was more reminiscent of the Midwest rather than the Golden State.

Lukas MacKenzie jumped out of the prison van that stopped on the shoulder of the highway with his automatic weapon ready. The smells of freshly mowed hay and rich soil greeted him and brought memories of his family's farm to mind.

Johnson and Murphy got out from the front seats and helped check the roster as each prisoner exited the van in leg shackles and chains. The last man in the van, Rance Hunter, towered over the guards.

A jagged scar down his left cheek stood out in the bright, blistering sun beating down. "It's already a hundred out here, few hours it'll be even higher and we sweating our fucking asses off. You trying to kill us?" Hunter's voice challenged.

"We got to be here with you too, so I ain't inclined to feel any sympathy," Lukas tossed back at him. *Hunter was a lippy one.* He didn't voice the myriad of things he wanted to say, which all boiled down to how he hoped some of these blacks would die here. But that would be a loss of cheap labor, can't have that.

Hunter wouldn't let it go, though. "I don't see water. We'll need water, or you'll be killing us for sure." He was observant too. Guess that's why he was a leader and not just any little gang puke.

"We got water, but mostly equipment. Sooner we're done, sooner we all get out of the sun. Move." Lukas motioned with his gun to join the others.

Hunter looked him over, starting at his feet, lingering on the gun, and finally up to his eyes. Lukas swallowed and raised his gun slightly. Hunter's eyes swung over to Murphy, then Johnson with the same appraising scan. He finally hopped out of the van and strolled, like he was a king in his own goddamned castle, over to the other prisoners. Several shrank away as if they could smell the men he'd killed like a cheap cologne.

Once Hunter arrived at the prison after his long strung-out trial, there was a short window of a few weeks before he was processed and transferred to a Supermax prison that handled the more violent and dangerous of prisoners. Today was quickly pulled together to take advantage of this window of opportunity.

Lukas had gotten the job as a guard at California State Prison in Corcoran with help from The Society. After getting hired by the prison system, MacKenzie and several others got their jobs specifically with the breakout of Rance Hunter in mind.

The plan had depended upon getting Hunter on this low security road crew, and it was the part he had bet would fail. Yet, here the man was, ready to clear thigh-high grass with petty criminals. Now was the moment of truth – it was go-time. It all came down to the next few minutes.

Lukas looked around, taking in a full three hundred sixty degree scan. He saw some kid on a red bicycle pedaling on a path through the fields to his right, in the general direction he would have to head soon. The kid should be long gone by the time the breakout was in swing. Lukas' mission was to get Hunter to a waiting helicopter when it was time.

In order for Hunter to get on this low security detail, O'Neil in the Admin's clerk office must have changed Hunter's score from 180 to 18, making his classification minimum security rather than maximum while looking like an innocent typo. That was the most likely way Lukas could imagine for Hunter to find his way on the road crew.

Or maybe the prison labor crews got less scrutiny. Prison labor was the modern slave labor and was highly profitable, and much was overlooked to meet demands. Things had come full circle and the inferior low bred races were back to cheap manual labor; benefiting, profiting, and serving their betters. It was what God intended for the lesser races.

Lukas watched as Johnson lit up a cigarette, the silver smoke hanging, lingering, and clinging in the hot thick air. His mind wandered again. They had to get Hunter out alive and without The Society implicated. Fortunately, they only had ten prisoners in this crew. *God was smiling on them.*

The van typically followed the work crew alongside the road with flashing caution lights while the guards supervised with guns, but today they needed to stay in this area. The Society promised an interruption of traffic so there wouldn't be any witnesses to the abduction. But cars were still zooming past, so basic equipment was unloaded and distributed as if this was a typical work crew.

Before long, traffic from both directions slowed to a trickle and then stopped. He didn't know how, but they shut down the roads. *Whew! They didn't need commuters with cell phones videotaping Hunter's abduction.*

Hunter noticed the change in traffic, his head swiveled looking at the road and the dissipating cars. He shot a glance at Lukas and his gun with suspicion. Guess that's why he's stayed alive this long in the gangs.

Murphy and Johnson by the van looked at each other and nodded then looked his way. Slipping on their gas masks, they withdrew canisters with their gloved hands and tossed them among the prison crew. The canisters spewed a gas that lowered visibility and rendered anyone breathing it unconscious. So, in a few seconds each of the prisoners slumped to the ground unconscious. The gas hung low in the air, creating a thick, potent cloud. It was Lukas' turn now, time to take his place in history as a patriot.

He smiled. He was instrumental in the plan to restore America to greatness. They could not fail, *must not fail*. The nation's future depended on them, on him. He would deliver Hunter to The Society. When the history books wrote about how the nation was pulled from the brink of ruin and put back on the righteous path, surely he would be remembered for his critical role!

Lukas stepped over bodies and knelt by Rance Hunter's massive form. Jesus, he was a big man with bulky muscles from all the gym time. This brute favored a punching and kicking bag to practice his mixed martial arts during exercise time.

He swiped away some sweat from his brow and took a shaky breath. His heart was beating fast in anticipation. *Sweet Jesus, he was really doing it, really breaking a dangerous gang leader out of prison to fuel a race war.*

He wrangled the muscle-bound man, now dead weight, but couldn't get a solid grip on him. He continued wrestling with the body, finally getting him over a shoulder and holding his shackled legs. He had to take a few moments to get him balanced.

He strained under the weight, moving as fast as he could without tripping. His legs burned and he felt sluggish. He was plowing towards the designated spot for the helicopter to meet him, the tall grass grasping at his legs like hundreds of wispy fingers. It was roughly a quarter mile from the road into the middle of the field.

He barely heard the helicopter approach, skimming the fields, over his pounding heart and labored breathing. It hovered just above hay, doors open and two men waving him to hurry. It wasn't just any helicopter, it resembled the B-2 Stealth Bomber with its sharp lines.

It had to be the HAL Light Combat Helicopter he had read about. Rumor from Soldier of Fortune magazine said it was built from advanced composite material on the frame to reduce its radar detection and used a cutting edge digital camouflage system.

He suspected it had adapted features from the Eurocopter Tiger to minimize sight and sound signatures too. That would explain why he could barely hear it above his heavy breathing.

Hot damn, The Society had a stealth helicopter for this mission. How and where they could secure such a restricted helo MacKenzie was clueless, but he was excited to see it in action.

It could fly under the radar undetected and follow irrigation ditches towards the ocean and then be lost among other recreational flights, literally go anywhere from there.

His legs nearly collapsed by the time he reached the runners of the high-tech helo hanging in the air. Hands reached down and lifted Hunter from his shoulders, relieving him of the weight. He took his mask off and tossed it to them, no need for that to be found. His clothes were soaked with sweat from his exertion and the wind from the rotors provided some slight refreshment.

He wanted to do an end zone dance from the adrenaline and elation of successfully heisting Hunter, but his legs were trembling after his efforts. He sank to the ground in slow motion, spent. Hit the wall of exhaustion. But, they had done it. *He had done it.*

Now, he had to get back to the road crew and act like he had been gassed with the others, but he needed a moment to recuperate before running back. He had to proceed under the assumption that everything went according to plan. He smiled bright; they had done the hardest part, surely they could not, would not, be stopped now.

He was on his knees before the helicopter when he saw it. The red bicycle peeking out from tall grass along a dirt path about thirty yards over. A puff of smoke rose from the grass then dispersed as it was caught in the helo's wind. The kid.

Where was the kid? But he would never find out. He never heard the shot to the head that ended his life. He never suspected he was a loose end.

CHAPTER THIRTY-THREE

Elizabeth Grant

Elizabeth had not slept well, every time she reached deep sleep she plunged into strange and terrifying dreams. Loralie and Madame Antoinette would frantically grab at her, trying to pull and drag her away. Loralie was crying and pleading, but Elizabeth felt an equal pull to stay where she was, to fight, to stand her ground.

At one point, she had the sensation that there were other people on the edges of her awareness, waiting for their turn onstage. One was a massive black man, his arms large and his face indistinct except for a prominent scar on his left cheek and an overall aura of anger and lethal power. Another man she never saw, but sensed authority and calming energy projecting from him. It was all jumbled together with little sense in the way dreams go.

Once the sky started to turn a soft gray, she was exhausted. She could have run a marathon through the night and felt better. Her usual herbal teas she had purchased just would not do the trick this morning, so she boiled coffee in Gran's old stove-top percolator until it was black. She had never been a fan of coffee, but she felt so sluggish from the turbulent dreams and she wanted to be as awake and sharp as possible.

Sitting on the front porch veranda, she sipped her second cup while watching the sunrise hues of bright salmon orange and coral red blended into early morning sunshine. She remembered the CD Madame Antoinette had given her to use for meditation as she drained the last drop of coffee. She needed to do the meditation again; she needed to immerse herself in the quiet, peaceful place and maybe she would relax.

Elizabeth sat on the couch with the CD player and earphones rather than meditate in the backyard. She took much longer to focus on her breathing and to visualize the stairway leading down to the door opening to the lush garden this time.

The skittish fox from her last visit greeted her and led her deep into the center of the garden. She no longer heard the recorded voice guiding her. The fox stopped next to a large circular stone fountain, and the splashing water seemed to calm and soothe her. Elizabeth sat on the fountain rim and drank from the splashing water using a cup left on the rim. The water was cool and refreshing. Looking around, there was more detail than her last visit, the garden lusher and the air more fragrant.

"I know you're scared, dear." It was Madame Antoinette's steady voice.

Elizabeth turned her head. She was sitting next to Madame on the rim of the fountain. The sight of her brought relief to her soul; and yet Elizabeth was sad because she could not hug this woman.

"You're in the midst of schemes, plots, and plans you know nothin' about. We're with you to guide you the best we can, but you must be open to hearin' us now. Trust your gifts, child."

Elizabeth's skepticism must have shown because Madame frowned. There had to be a logical explanation, she didn't understand what it was. She needed to understand the reasons she thought she saw Loralie and why she felt watched and followed. She struggled to ask questions, there was so much she didn't understand. But she couldn't seem to speak. Nothing came out. This meditation was no doubt her imagination, so that was logical to an extent.

"Now, I understand you fine, dear. We're here and fixin' to help you." Loralie was suddenly in front of her and took her hand, like so many years ago. She felt herself tear up. Obviously her imagination was getting out of hand and she couldn't see any good coming from this.

Digging up old bones.

"Now, you refuse to leave, no matter how hard I try to convince you. I wish I could've prepared you better, dear." Madame shook her head slightly.

Loralie's youthful voice brought a flood of emotion choking her throat, "I'm fine, Lizzy. You don't have to do anythin' for me. You're in danger now, be takin care of yourself."

"Your life is now intertwined with others' lives," Madame Antoinette continued. "Some might not seem like the best allies, but together you're stronger than you think. You must rely on your gifts to know who you can trust." Antoinette's eyes bore into her.

Elizabeth shouted in her mind. *What danger? From who? Why me?* It made no sense, and it must make sense. Even this meditation exercise that allowed her emotions and desires to drive her imagination wasn't helping, wasn't bringing understanding. *What about the strangers in her dream? What was that about?*

"In your dream there is one you'll help and the other will help you. You're intertwined now. Remember, we're here with you, don't forget, now. Look for us dear, be open to us." Madame Antoinette's voice rang in her mind.

Loralie turned as if to leave and Elizabeth rushed out her thought, *Please forgive me Lora. For not being here that summer, for our argument. But most of all, for not looking for you.*

Loralie turned and shook her head, "I forgave you long ago for that argument, and the rest don't amount to a hill of beans. You couldn't have stopped what happened and you couldn't have found me." Loralie reached out and squeezed her hand, then turned.

Madame Antoinette and Loralie walked off into the lush growth encircling the garden and fountain. The fox had sat nearby waiting. He cocked his head as if to ask, "What now?"

Elizabeth's eyes sprang open to find herself sitting on the couch, relaxed and calm but with just as many questions as before, if not more.

She wasn't entirely sure the meditation had helped other than to calm down. She couldn't dwell on that disturbing dream any longer, so she retrieved the Cyprus Sentinel from the front porch. She had forgotten what the old-school newspapers were like with the black ink on her hands and the fighting with folding the pages. She found she missed the tactile experience of the print news, except for the messy ink smears on anything she touched.

Elizabeth sat at the kitchen table with a fresh cup of coffee close by her hand and unfurled the paper. The headline screamed "Gang Leader Breaks Out of Prison" and in front of her was a mug shot photo of the man from her dream. The man with the scar on his left cheek and a tattoo on his arm and an aura of lethal danger was from her dream, his angry eyes staring at her from the page. She gasped loudly and felt a wave of nausea hit the pit of her stomach. She dashed to the kitchen sink and hurled the coffee that had become roiling acid in her stomach.

How could this be? How could this man be in her dreams?

She returned to the table after rinsing her mouth and splashing her face with water. The closer she came to picking the paper up again, the more the pit of her stomach protested. She forced herself to read the lead story.

Three guards, Murphy, Johnson, and MacKenzie had died during an early morning prison break. The article claimed there were fears that the leader was joining up with his gang, who were implicated in the massacre in Philadelphia, to enact a domestic terror agenda. It also speculated that Al Qaeda recruited Rance Hunter specifically to unleash a reign of terror upon the nation. The claims were wild and could only lead to fear. She was surprised the paper had printed such unsubstantiated conjecture.

She studied the photo. *I've never met this man and never heard of him either. I'm sure of it.* She thought maybe she had heard about him somewhere, or seen a news report before. Any logical explanation. But that was the problem, there was no explanation of why he was in her dream. He was a complete stranger in every aspect. *Why dream about a gang leader and possible terrorist? None of it made any sense.*

It was hard for her to make sense of much since Madame Antoinette's initial visit. She suspected someone had been in the house, then there was the angry man at the library, she was followed by the truck on the road to Meridian, the sheriff's strange warnings to leave town, and then a night of horrific dreams featuring a man that appears on the front page of the paper all left her feeling adrift in a storm, tossed about with no control. *What the hell was it all about?*

CHAPTER THIRTY-FOUR

Juanita Alvarez

J uanita slowly woke. Her first sensation was that her neck was kinked, then that she was half sitting up and uncomfortable. She was pleasantly warm, though. Her eyes sprang open, and she glanced around without moving. She wasn't in her compact bedroom, but in a darkened basement. Heath's geek cave. She must have fallen asleep.

Her pulse spiked when the couch she was propped up on moved under her and the warm spot on her back moved. She had fallen asleep in Heath's arms. She could feel her bra and jeans constricting her. *Whew!* How could she have let her guard down and gotten cozy with a criminal? She vaguely remembered being asleep and Heath joining her on the couch, apparently she was too tired to protest. Her cell phone rang, the cell phone she was using for communication on this story.

She quickly got up and answered the call from the other side of the room, away from the warm comfy couch with Heath stretching. It was her informant, that's how she viewed him, probably wanting to know about her progress. She felt as though she had to answer to an employer.

"I'm here."

"I'm sure you've heard the news. I'm telling you we know nothing about it."

"I don't know what you're talking about." Her imagination ran wild with images of another home invasion and massacre.

"Hunter was broke out of jail in California early this morning."

"What! Holy shitballs." Her mind whirled. She got Heath's attention with her outburst.

Hunter was a hardened criminal but also a stabilizing factor in the gangs. Without him leading, the Black Apostles be far more brutal and vicious. Even in prison he kept the balance of power equalized among the major gangs on the outside. He wasn't a Boy Scout, but he was better than many of the alternatives.

"I swear we had nothing to do with it. I don't care what you hear, it ain't us. And let me tell you, that has us shitting bricks, reporter girl." He sounded out of breath.

"50 Cent, you've got to be upfront with me." Her voice didn't betray how shook up she was as she raked a hand through her bed-head hair.

"Don't call me that, I ain't called that."

"Well, you never gave me a name, so live with it or give me a name." While she talked on the phone, she locked eyes with Heath and she held onto the connection as if he kept her grounded.

"Tito. I like the Jacksons." That was not what she had expected at all.

"Okay *Tito*, I watched the video and I believe you as far as that goes. But, if you guys broke Rance Hunter out of prison, I don't think I should get involved past the dirty cops." This situation seemed to be spiraling out of control and she wasn't sure she should be in the middle.

Heath had seemed groggy and sluggish, but he was alert at the mention of Hunter's jailbreak.

"God damn it girl, it wasn't us. Somebody else busted him out. We have no idea what's happening to our boss, he could be dead for all we know. Do ya think this is a coincidence right after framing our gang for a multiple murder? Now think about this, do ya think we won't avenge Hunter?"

A thought made its way to the forefront of her mind, this was looking much larger than it initially appeared. Targeting Rance Hunter ensured gangs across the nation would rise up since the Black Apostles operated in almost every major city and Hunter helped to keep a shaky peace in place among the gangs whether out of fear or back-room-deals nobody was sure. Add to that, over the last several decades the gangs had strategically enlisted members into the military branches for training, but also as an outlet to funnel military grade weapons to inner cities.

These large and highly organized gangs had progressively become militaristic in their strategies and tactics. If the gangs began open war because of accusations of abducting Rance Hunter, a gang leader renowned for stabilizing inter-gang relations, the police – even as militarized as they had become – wouldn't be capable of controlling the fallout.

But, maybe the family's murder was part or a bigger agenda, to set the stage for Hunter's jailbreak and spark violence in the streets? But nobody really won in that scenario. Her mind focused on the phone call.

"Why are you calling me, I can't help. I don't know anything about Hunter. I didn't even know until you called. This is far outside my scope and experience."

"Called you 'cause this is beyond the local pissant cops blaming us for that family's murder. We want you to find out who the hell has Hunter, and we want him back. You're already on the trail and you know we didn't kill that family." Tito's voice was getting raw, like he'd been talking for hours.

Her mouth had fallen open and her mind locked. No, this couldn't be happening. Sure, this was a huge story, but she felt completely beyond her depth. She didn't want this. Heath was up and flitting around the basement.

"We'll pay your expenses, whatever you need. Just find him."

"I thought you said the Apostles would avenge this? Why get me involved?" She didn't want in the middle of this powder keg waiting to blow up. Her stomach was churning and cold desperate fear had settled in her core.

"Look, the second-in-command backed you to find him. That's our first aim, to get him recovered safely. If he's dead... we still wanta know who was behind it."

"You do realize, I've never done an investigation of this scale. Right? I don't want to fear for my life because I'm in deeper water than I've ever been before." There, she said it. She held her breath.

"Ya think we don't know that? We got the cops crawling up our asses, hauling us in for questioning and shit. We can barely handle business as it is. But the cops aren't watching you and you believe us about that family's murder." He paused for a moment as if deciding whether to say what came next.

"Plus, I wouldn't advise turning your back on us now reporter girl. 'Specially after our number two guy has backed you. That would be a slap in the face, and we ain't in the fucking mood for that shit right now. Keep this phone, let us know if you need to travel 'cause we can take care of it and we'll have somebody in town you can call if you need backup. You should have a platinum credit card waiting for you at your home to cover costs – within reason of course."

She sucked in her breath. *So much for keeping where she lived a secret from the gang. Shit and damn it.*

"You really didn't think you could keep where you lived from us, did you?"

This was happening too fast. She looked around the basement at Heath, the racks of servers and various electronic equipment, and the bank of computer monitors. She would need help, lots of it.

"I may need to hire help, hackers and stuff."

"Use the credit card. I don't think you can exceed the limit, and we will pay it off as soon as charges appear. Just dig, dig deep, and tell us everything you find."

"I still want to publish the story." Yes, she was a reporter in her soul. She couldn't help it.

"After you give us whatever you uncover, we don't give a shit what you do. If it gets you an award, good for you. We have other things to worry about."

"I'm probably going to really regret this, but I'll do what I can. I'll have to fly to the prison and investigate."

"You bet your *life* you'll do everything you can. We'll get you a ride on a jet. How soon can you leave?"

Apparently the gang's rap recording label had a small jet for use with the artists and executives. Tito was commandeering its use, which told her he was more than a small time member like she first thought.

She had two hours to pack and get to the small airport that handled private traffic. She hung up and looked around, shell-shocked. She scrubbed her face with hands. Heath had been packing up computer equipment while she talked.

"We got the bank accounts on those cops, plus a little more information Betty thought would help us. I have it on a memory card." He patted his shirt pocket. "I'm coming with you."

That stopped her cold. She stared at him still gathering items and packing two computer cases.

"Why the hell would you do that? I signed up for this crap when I wanted to do this for a living and I'm petrified. They aren't asking any longer and the danger level has sky-rocketed."

"Look, I don't fully understand why I feel so strongly about this, but I do. I'm not letting you go by yourself and I'll just run a scam and drain somebody's account somewhere and follow you. Do you want that on your head?" His hands were on his hips, his jaw was set, and his eyes blazed.

She had to think fast. She didn't want to endanger anybody else, and he probably knew the risks as well as she did. He was right; she didn't want anybody loosing their savings either, if he came with her the Apostles were willing paying the bill. She was going to doubly regret this. She nodded her head.

"Besides, you'll need me and my shady friends. We can cut through obstacles you don't even know about yet. I think time is definitely not on our side and you need answers sooner than later." He had a point there.

Another thought struck her, and she stopped in mid-stride to her purse. If nobody knew who had Hunter, what if it wasn't a rival gang? What if somebody else was engineering the potential gang war?

Hunter had folded in a few other ethnic gangs into his Black Apostles, an unheard of move which upset many. The Asian and Latinos gangs would likely be in the thick of the turmoil. It was probable the National Guard would be out in full force in every major city in the nation if the gangs began an open war, perhaps even martial law would be instituted. It had not been since the Civil War that battles had raged in our cities, but it could easily come to that and the violence would escalate, innocent deaths would be epidemic, while large cities would look like bombs had hit.

With the nation suffering such internal turmoil, whoever was behind this was positioned to get whatever they wanted while the nation was dealing with bloodshed in the streets, widespread panic, and innocent collateral damage. That opened up the pool of potential kidnappers to a myriad of opportunistic and influential people or even anti-government groups who would use such an opportunity to strike. There must be a simpler motive behind this, but she knew this was equally feasible.

CHAPTER THIRTY-FIVE

The General

The General of The Society for a Restored America was euphoric. He sat in his home office in his leather chair at his hand-carved cherry-wood desk enjoying his third cup of certified Kopi Luwak coffee as usual, but today was electric. Operation "Cancer Eradication" was well on its way, and the successful prison break of Rance Hunter this morning made him feel like he had won an election.

He had been on his secure encrypted phone, courtesy of his CIA and NSA members, talking with the Vice President about the continuing details of the operation at this point.

Classified technology wasn't all his Society members had garnered for his use. He had paid close attention to his FBI members on how to hide or launder money and set up dummy corporations to funnel money to several shell businesses that surreptitiously carried out the public aspects of their agenda.

He set his coffee cup down and jumped up, energy pinging through his muscles. He threw his raw silk curtains back and surveyed the back lawn. It was a glorious day, sun shining down like a blessing from God and a strong breeze, like the winds of change. He would have to call Pastor Akron and tell him his prayers were being

THE SOCIETY • 133

answered. He was nearly giddy and wanted to skip around. But he couldn't lollygag about when he had business to attend to and keep the momentum going.

He had two more Society officers to contact about the next steps in their plan. He sat down and forced himself to focus on the task. He was using a video-messaging service for these quick communications rather than the classified phone. He wanted to look these men in the eye and felt it was a trade-off worth the video capability despite the lower security.

When he got the video connection, a military man in an army uniform appeared on the monitor, his graying temples and handsome features fooled people that he was approachable. He was a ruthless son-of-a-bitch and one of the most fervent members. If the General didn't have a son to pass leadership of The Society over to, he would install this man when he retired. His brother-in-law Mark wasn't leader material.

Other than the Vice President, his recruiting of Lieutenant General Louis Garrett was a big feather in the General's cap. He was the Chief of the National Guard Bureau, which meant he sat on the Joint Chiefs of Staff as well.

"Louis, I hope you have good news for me," He sang out.

General Garrett was upbeat, and it came through in his voice. "The National Guard is on full alert. I used the violence in Philadelphia as a springboard to emphasize the dangers. I've briefed the Joint Chiefs of Staff that there is a domestic terrorism warning since the prison-break. They are ready and will be the first line of defense when the President gives the order."

"How is the President's attitude regarding the situation and your recommendations?"

"He's listening. I think he'll follow my ideas, especially since I have the other Joint Chiefs agreeing with me." Louis had a tight smile; any smile on him was rare.

They covered a few minor points and ended their conversation quickly. The less time spent on these calls, the better.

He set up for the next call regarding the news coverage on the growing situation. The video connected and a clean-shaven man with perfect-coifed hair and a boyish look, except for his eyes that could penetrate steel, was waiting for him. This man was his director over his various media channels and helped him maneuver the owners of the other media conglomerates.

"Chuck, tell me how it's shapin' up."

"I've firmed up details with Bret Howard to do the exposé on VOX, claiming widespread terrorist links to all black gangs in the nation. Once the story is airs on VOX, VNN News is ready to pick it up and run with it. From there it should be all over the media. Bret Howard was a good choice, his reputation as a top investigative reporter is intact and will jump-start this. Bret will add a tale of his personal safety being in danger for reporting on it."

"No other reporters will contradict his account?"

"My contacts at the other networks are all going with what we feed them. They've no intention of wasting their time fighting Bret's story or the media push, they're jumping on the bandwagon like we planned. There may be an independent small paper or news broadcast here or there that question a few aspects, but they won't amount to anything." His youthful face was all business.

"I don't want some hotshot reporter thinkin' he's goin' to win a Pulitzer and shed any doubt on this operation. I want to know if you get anybody who looks like they're goin' to break ranks and have a snowball's chance of diggin' anythin' of substance up. They won't live long." He wasn't about to tolerate any meddling in this operation now. He rubbed his hand along the leather armrest.

"We have several media outlets spreading fear of large-scale attacks from the Black Apostles and they are producing results. Nobody suspects the reports were written before the murders ever took place, waiting to be used." They wrapped up the call with a few short items to discuss.

He leaned back and looked up at the large gold-gilt portrait of Elijah Wiltshire, the man who made him into the youngest Society General since its founding in 1869. He raised his cup of coffee in a silent salute. Old man Wiltshire would be proud.

The prior Generals had limited their thinking in how to accomplish The Society's goal. They limited their growth to ensure secrecy but that kept them from achieving their vision for the nation. Elijah Wiltshire had selected him to continue the legacy because of his unique approach. It was simple, convert the country slowly through manipulation, and hide the true agendas behind "necessity", "public safety", "Founding Values" and "National Security," even the "War on Drugs" and "War on Terror" played into his plans.

He recruited more aggressively than any of his predecessors and placed thousands of Society members into influential key positions. He had even started a "scholarship program" of sorts to pay for tuition at top colleges if a young member had potential.

Prior to his taking over, recruiting had been limited to scouring a few groups such as the Sons of Confederate Veterans, the Order of the Confederate Rose, and the Military Order of the Stars and Bars, Confederate memorabilia stores, even the Confederate Air Force for potential members. It wasn't easy and the vetting process was slow and careful to find true kindred spirits.

But, he had aggressively branched out across the nation into the radical Christian territory and home schooling arenas, recruiting from those who felt angry at the nation's direction. Like-minded people were everywhere across the nation from Alaska to Florida, Hawaii to New York. He also developed an aggressive social media presence. This had allowed him to establish major bases in every large city in the US. He had maintained the stealth and secrecy of The Society along the way.

He had become an expert in peeling back the layers of a person to find their fear over the world today. It was a frightening time to live and he knew how to expose buried feelings of fear and loathing over changes in society. For some it was the rap music and gangs to get them to expose their true feelings hidden behind civility and "everybody should get along".

White people are done with getting along; tired of being pushed to the back of the line for jobs or consideration, and with some careful nudging many took up the cause to put the inferior races back in their place.

Don't even get him started on the "Black Lives Matter" movement when he knew dogs that were smarter, hell more dogs were employed with bomb and drug sniffing canine units than welfare sucking blacks. White privilege was another term that made his blood boil. He planned on reinstalling true white privilege. They hadn't seen anything yet.

He stood and prepared to go into his downtown office and run his corporation. He had a bit more pep in his step and he was whistling a lively tune. Some days he felt he bore the weight of the world, but today he felt as though it wasn't such a burden. He was about to set his nation on the right track. Today, life was good.

CHAPTER THIRTY-SIX

Elizabeth Grant

lizabeth was restless and unsettled after her recognition of
Rance Hunter, the gang leader who appeared in her dream,
and she couldn't sit still. She needed to get out of the house
and move. She thought about taking a drive; something that usually
helped her to think. But after being followed the other day, she didn't
feel comfortable driving far since she didn't know the area very well.

Part of her anxious energy came from the growing feeling that
something was about to happen, a tension waiting for the lurking
threat to materialize.

She had considered looking up Calvin Morrison who claimed to
see Loralie take up with a trucker, but it was clear in her mind he was
lying. He wouldn't open up to her just because a few years had passed
since he covered for a murder. No, following that lead was a waste of
time.

She didn't seem to have many more options. If she were a cop, she
would say her leads had all dried up. She sighed, so much for finding
the truth and bringing closure to Loralie's mother and Jeremiah or
resolution to herself. Instead, she felt like she had stirred a hornet's
nest and was about to get stung. Plus, she hadn't seen Loralie yet
today. For as much as her visions worried her, this too wasn't normal.

She remembered the sheriff's visit and how she had mentioned the remodeling of Whispering Oaks Plantation. He seemed to steer her away from checking out the antebellum plantation house and instead wanted her out of town. Recalling the strange visit made her want to feed her professional curiosity as an Architectural Engineer and see the renovations herself.

She was already driving before she realized she had decided to visit Whispering Oaks.

She knew right where the property was on the edge of town since she had played on the grounds with Loralie many summers. It had sat empty and boarded up for many years and the grounds had grown wild, but it was a great place to play Hide-and-Seek, Red-Rover games, and tell scary stories in the summer dusk for the town's children... away from adults.

News of the renovations had reached her via professional journals, and she had hoped to see the plantation house during her stay. Why not now? She could focus a little on architectural issues rather than Loralie, gang leaders, and dreams.

She parked in the small gravel lot and stood at the end of a long tree-lined hundred-yard long path leading directly to the front steps. It was more like a grand processional route with silent sentinels lining the way. The massive old oaks with their branches intertwined overhead formed a dense canopy displaying wisps of Spanish Moss dangling down like thick spider webs with the sun peeking through in spots.

Standing there, a sense of history washed over her and touched her psyche with echoes of lives once lived. Whispering Oaks was the ultimate romanticized image of the American South.

The lush green grounds looked like plush velvet draped luxuriously around the house. It was improved from the bedraggled image in her memory. There was much about the South of her childhood she remembered fondly. Growing up with such grand examples of architecture had definitely spurred an appreciation that developed into her career and love of classic building styles.

At the end of the wide entry drive sat the white two-story house that was the classic Greek-Revival mansion that typified the South's plantation era, complete with a wide front veranda lined with large fluted carved columns that provided shade to sit in the hot summer afternoons with a cool drink.

She walked down the wide path under the leafy canopy when she spotted a coyote peering at her from around a tree trunk half way down. It reminded her of the coyote in her meditations. It strode to the middle of the path and sat. He stared at her. *As if he was blocking her way. But, that was ridiculous. Could he be dangerous?* She continued walking and eventually the coyote loped away, watching her over his shoulder with wary eyes as she advanced.

The front doors were open and there were a couple of shadowy figures moving inside that she guessed were men working on the renovation. The closer she got, the more "aged" the house appeared. There wasn't anything indicating major problems from the cursory look she could get.

The white paint was cracked and peeling in many spots, one of the ornate columns to the side had separated from the veranda ceiling and needed securing, while a few of the boards on the wide front porch showed signs of rot and might not support a person. She probably wouldn't get inside for a tour, but she could at least talk with a representative and get an idea of the scope of the project out of professional courtesy. She realized she was excited to see the iconic structure restored, the craftsmanship in such older buildings fascinated her.

Standing before the few stairs to the veranda, she saw a plaque on one of the columns to the right proclaiming, "The Whispering Oaks Plantation Home is being renovated by Restoration America" along with their logo. The logo was unusual with a bricklayer's trowel crossed with a sword over an outline of the nation. The trowel was easy to relate to renovations, but the sword was an odd choice.

"Can I help you?" A tanned, well-muscled blond man in jeans stood on the veranda, arms crossed, looking down at her from the shadows. He seemed to just appear as she had not seen him come through the door.

"I've heard about the renovation in trade magazines and thought I would stop by and see how it's going." She was hoping to present herself as a colleague so he could talk technically with her. But the instant he spoke the hairs at the nape of her neck stood on end.

"Now you can just turn around. We aren't open for gawkers, lady."

"I'm an architectural engineer and I'm interested in the challenges with such a historic house…"

Then, Loralie was back. She popped into the scene like the genie on an old television show. She was in the man's face, studying him, then the oddest thing happened. A hand went to her throat, and she backed away, her eyes filled with terror and she gasped for air. Then she was gone again. The fine little hairs on Elizabeth's arms were all standing tall.

"Lady, I can't allow you being here. My boss has put a stop to tours. After those magazine notices, we got flooded with too many people to keep our schedule." His words were slightly apologetic, but his face and body language yelled he was laying down the law.

Elizabeth had been to several job sites and had always been treated with professional courtesy, she expected the legendary Southern welcome would have applied here. There was no scaffolding, and she wasn't in a dangerous area with potential risk of injury or accident. She couldn't understand why they wouldn't want to show off the work they were accomplishing on such a prestigious renovation.

"I'm sorry I dropped in without any notice. Can I speak to your foreman about a good time to return? I'm from Colorado and truly wanted to see the work here." But, there wasn't any construction noise, no hammering, no boots stomping around, nothing to indicate work of any kind. There hadn't been any noise as she approached from the parking lot either. *What about that important schedule?*

"Well, that is somethin'. Colorado, huh? I'll be honest wit you, I don't believe the foreman's gonna change his mind. In fact, I haven't and I'm gonna insist that you leave now. I'd hate for this to become a trespassin' charge." Still the same rock-hard expression.

She didn't want to have another "chat" with Chief Jake Craig after his attempt to get her out of town. No doubt he would chastise her for not listening to him. After Loralie's reaction to the *foreman*, she had lost her interest anyway.

She turned and walked back down the wide processional of massive oaks. About halfway, she glanced back and found the man stood watching her, presumably to make sure she indeed left.

The coyote joined her again, trotting along on the other side of the oaks, slowing when she slowed. Once in the car and his chaperone duties concluded, the coyote eventually wandered out of sight.

She couldn't dismiss that the foreman's attitude wasn't a typical reaction for a high profile historic renovation. If she didn't know better, she would think they were hiding something. *No, that couldn't be it. All the strange things happening since she arrived had her creating a bogeyman in every shadow, that's all.* But Loralie's reaction wasn't her imagination.

She turned her car around and took one last look down the oak-lined lane. A shiver shot down her back.

Upon arriving back at Gran's house, she was greeted with the house phone ringing and rushed to answer it.

"You sound out of breath. Did I catch you at a bad time Liza?" Uncle Jairus's voice created the sense of being a child once again and never quite measuring up.

"Just getting in and ran to catch the phone is all." She took a deep breath and sat her purse down. Without a conscious thought, she took the gris-gris bag out from under her shirt where she hung it each day since Madame Antoinette gave it to her. She held it tight as she talked.

"I'm sorry I took so long to call and see how your stay is going."

"Everything is just fine, no need to worry." No need to check up on her either she wanted to add, but refrained.

"But I do worry about my favorite niece." She knew he was trying to be supportive and fill the gap left from having no father growing up, but she never forgot his insistence that she see a psychiatrist. He no doubt thought he was doing the best for her, but she would have preferred a family that just went into denial, to be honest.

"I'm fine, really. Nothing to report." *Nothing to see here, move along.*

"Don't be like that. I'm just makin' sure you aren't havin' a difficult time, considerin' everythin'."

He was tapping his ring against something, which always annoyed her. She took a deep breath and put her attitude in check.

"I'm rearrangin' my schedule to come visit. If it's a bother, I'll stay at the Inn outside of town." This took her by surprise.

"That's really not necessary Uncle Jairus, I'm fine. I was thinking of taking a little trip, see some local sights for a day or two. You really don't have to rearrange anything on my account." She was probably being transparent in her evasion, but she didn't care. She had a lot on her mind and having him in the house would be more strained than usual without her mother to referee.

"Now, I insist darlin'. I want to be there, even for just a day or two. We can bond."

Yeah, right. *I'd rather French kiss a barracuda than spend an hour bonding with you.* Okay, maybe she hadn't gotten over the forced psychiatrist visits, or the way he talked down to her mother either.

She never liked him, and contrary to what her mother drilled into her that you forgave family because they are the most important thing in life, she didn't have to like him or forgive him if he didn't change. She gritted her teeth and commenced to dissuade him.

CHAPTER THIRTY-SEVEN

Malcom Alexander

Malcom had gotten up early and drove to Jackson. He had talked to his buddy, Kevin, at the Forensic DNA Center the very next day after he had searched Aunt Netty's home. This was the lab that the FBI office outsourced their backlogged evidence testing to occasionally, so he felt confident in their discretion and their competence.

He had no choice but to pay for the testing out of his own pocket. A credit card was taking the hit. They would do DNA specimen match testing, but getting DNA to match the hair he had found for identification was the hard part since he didn't have any suspects nor the databases and resources of the agency.

He would owe Kevin for a long time since they met in the predawn hours and Kevin was labeling the tests as sensitive to minimize other lab personnel from peeking into the work.

Driving back in his black SUV, he had his lights flashing and would shave about a half hour off his travel time from Jackson to Shreveport zooming down Interstate 20. He hoped to get back shortly after his cousin's family woke up and before they worried where he had gone.

He was wondering just how he would investigate, let alone determine potential suspects to match with the hairs he had found if he didn't have a starting point? He had no idea what had really happened, nor what his aunt could have gotten in the middle of leading to her murder. He knew she had been murdered with every fiber of his being, but he was at a dead end unless he received a lead to investigate.

He was discouraged at the chances of finding the truth. At least he hadn't shared what he knew had really happened to Aunt Netty. If he couldn't find the person or persons responsible, then he would be the only one to live with that unresolved weight.

The funeral was scheduled for tomorrow. Cousin Cecilia and his mother had done the planning while he was consumed with how Netty died. He was hoping to talk with those attending the services to pay their final respects and get an inkling of what she had been doing or people she had spent time with the last week or so prior to her death. Just maybe that would give him a direction to investigate.

He arrived at Cousin Cecilia's home to find members of her church visiting and delivering meals. He found his way to Cecilia's husband, Tom, hiding in the kitchen away from the invaded living room.

"Wondered where you'd gotten off to," Tom smiled as understanding warmed his eyes. "This must wear on a bachelor to live with a full house and children underfoot. Did you get some time to breathe?"

"Yea, I took a long drive. It helped to get time to think and clear my head." He poured himself some sweet tea with ice, then drank a few gulps. "I know this hasn't been easy for you and Cecilia either." They stood in silence, watching the women in the living room chat and commiserate from their safe distance.

"Cecilia doesn't show it, but she's right devastated. I figure she's tryin' to make her mother proud. Do ya think she feels guilty she didn't follow in Netty's practice and beliefs?" Tom studied the kitchen tile. The murmur of the visiting church ladies seemed to accentuate Tom's words.

Malcom blew out a breath. He wasn't good at this. "Damn Tom, you live with her. I couldn't tell you about Ceec. I never understood her growin' up, and I don't imagine that's changed now." He ran a hand over his unshaved chin. "But Ceec knows as well as I do that Netty didn't care what faith you had, so long as you had compassion."

"I think she's tryin' to step into Netty's shoes, helpin' folks in her own way. Like she couldn't stand for you guys stayin' anywhere but here durin' the funeral." He turned and looked out the window to the small backyard. "Oh, you just missed the mailman, he starts his day on our street. There was a large envelope for you. It's on the table."

Malcom retrieved the curious mail and took sanctuary in the backyard at the well-used picnic table. He had to be careful he didn't sit in finger paint remnants or other hazards. There was no return address on the envelope. *Strange, only a few people knew the address or that he would be here.*

He removed several sheets of paper, but the familiar handwriting of the letter caused him to gasp and his hand to shake. It was Netty's graceful cursive he had always loved. A lump formed in his throat. He quickly scanned the letter before his emotions swept him away.

My dearest Mal,

I know this is likely a shock to receive this letter. I'm probably dead when you read this, so I knew you would be at Cecilia's. I want you to know you have always been dear to me, like the son Clive and I never had. I've been honored to see you grow from a curious and mischievous boy into the valiant man you have become. It is your sense of justice and protecting those who can't protect themselves from forces that are stronger that causes me to reach out with a special request.

I knew my death was a possibility, probable even when I decided to help Elizabeth. I have had a young spirit frantic to help Elizabeth, who feels responsible for the peril she is surrounded by on every side. The young spirit, Loralie, died about seven years ago.

Men were looking for some papers a man had, but he had given them to Loralie to pass to the FBI and she found herself hunted until they caught her. Loralie doesn't quite understand what happened or why. When she didn't give them the location of where she hid the book and papers, they brutalized her until she died. But these desperate men think Loralie somehow sent the evidence to Elizabeth Grant, or at least she knows where it may be hidden.

My death was at the same hands that killed Loralie and are now watching Elizabeth, expecting her to retrieve or unveil the evidence that will expose them. I tried to warn Elizabeth, but she is unaware of the danger she is in, but I felt I could persuade her, at least warn her. This letter means I have failed to convince her to leave and failed in any attempt at keeping my visit a secret. She is watched carefully.

She needs help... and guidance. She has the sight but has repressed it for years. I don't know what the outcome will be, that is still in shadow and still being written. It is bigger than some small town drama since the FBI was involved those years back. I shouldn't ask for you to intervene, but I have failed and you are the only option available to me now. I researched the best I could to give you any advantage, and I include my efforts with this letter.

You don't have to go to Cyprus, but if you do, I must warn you to trust only yourself as you aid her. I love you dear boy; you are the best of our family with nobility in your soul. I will be with you, never doubt it.

With my eternal love, Netty

After reading the note, it was stained with fresh tears. He could smell her perfume, White Shoulders, that he got her every Christmas, which made him feel she was close and yet miss her with an ache in his heart.

He read it twice more and then sat and stared at the fence. Netty had just given him the lead he needed, the reason for her death, and proof she was murdered. Maybe not proof a judge and jury would accept, but it was ironclad to him. He couldn't help but feel as though Netty was speaking to him from the grave.

As a child he grew up with Netty counseling the grieving to pay attention to their dreams and the dearly departed would visit them to let them know they were okay. But Netty hadn't visited him. Now he understood why. She wasn't ready to move on yet, and he had work to do. Apparently, she had plans for him.

He studied the few other items in the envelope. There was a Business Journal notice of Elizabeth Grant's hiring at a Denver Architectural firm with her picture, apparently printed from the internet. She had straight brown hair that framed her face, brown eyes and a smattering of freckles across her nose. He studied the photo. He would describe her as a pretty girl, the type who didn't know she was, yet her eyes were those of somebody who had survived tragedy. He had seen that look in the eyes of people who had been hurt physically in abusive marriages, sometimes in robbery victims. But there was a slight glint of steel within those rich brown eyes.

A few other mentions about this Elizabeth such as graduation from college and an old engagement notice. No wedding announcement though. Netty's letter and the photo were the important parts. The employment notice provided him with what Elizabeth looked like, and the letter gave Netty's involvement with her. The rest he didn't need.

He put everything back in the envelope and stood up. He would make a trip to some rural town called Cyprus right after the funeral, and he had a lot of preparations to complete. *You don't have to go to Cyprus, but if you do, I must warn you to trust only yourself as you aid her,* reverberated through his mind.

Tom was at the open backdoor, concern wrinkling his forehead. "Everythin' all right? Didn't expect you'd be getting' mail after only a couple days."

"Nothin' to worry about. Say, do you think I can swap cars with you for a few days? I really need to get away after the funeral. You know, *away* from everythin' a bit, and I need a four-wheel drive so I can do some camping and clear my head." He wasn't taking any chances after SSA Siesbolt's phone call checking up on him. He was about to investigate what got his aunt killed. He no longer knew who he could trust, and he needed to cover his tracks as best he could in a few hours.

CHAPTER THIRTY-EIGHT

Elizabeth Grant

After the phone call with Uncle Jairus, Elizabeth was on edge and felt caged. She decided to enjoy "down-town" Cyprus and went back out. Downtown consisted of three blocks along Lee Street, lined with squat red brick buildings dating from the 1950s.

Elizabeth had been walking, soaking in the snatches of conversation with various degrees of accent and the occasional pungent odor of the meat processing plant a few miles east of town spoiled the fresh air and made the hot muggy air more stifling. Seeing Loralie in the meditation had resurrected childhood memories that she relived as she strolled.

She snapped photos of the park in the center of town that had the same bronze statue of the town's founder where she and Loralie had spent many afternoons flying a kite, throwing Frisbees, and celebrating the Fourth of July with the rest of the town. It was where they had initially met, playing dolls in the lush green grass. The park had expanded their flowerbeds, thus attracting many buzzing bees.

She left the park and walked back to Gran's house. She noticed the woods that butted up to the back of the homes on Gran's street and smiled as more memories returned.

She remembered playing in those woods with Loralie. It didn't look as though they had changed much. *Wonder if the tree house Gramps built for them was still there?* She cut through a backyard, feeling a powerful need to find that tree house and maybe climb into it one last time.

She scouted around among the trees, trying to remember the exact location. The desire to find the tree was stronger now, a compulsion or a drive. Out of the corner of her eye, there was movement in a clump of trees and a brief flash of movement. But when she looked directly at the spot, it was gone. *The coyote again?*

She walked to the clearing where she had glimpsed something. There was the coyote, sitting a few yards away, regarding her. The animal shook its head from side to side as if saying no, then turned and trotted off.

Standing there, she realized she was next to the tree that harbored their old tree house. But she didn't see the planks of wood nailed to the tree trunk as she remembered.

Up close, Elizabeth inspected for any signs of the old makeshift plank steps, but only found a rusty nail still embedded in the tree. Looking up, she could just make out a few boards beyond the Kudzu growth higher up. *Damn Kudzu*, it would eventually kill the tree that had been their base in many adventures.

With the handy plank steps removed it wouldn't be easy to climb up since there were no low hanging limbs even if she jumped. Careful study provided one option. She would have to get a little run and scramble up the trunk just enough to get a hold of the lowest branch juncture. Fortunately, she had worn her sturdy athletic shoes.

As she began a short run at the tree she was surprised at her own determination to climb it. She planted one foot on the bark and leaped. She missed the branch and tumbled to the ground. *Just a few scrapes. She received worse on a few hikes.* She got up and tried it again… and hit the ground. Lying on her back looking up at the tree, she was positive this was the site of their old tree house.

She decided to give it one more try before coming back with a better plan another time. She allowed herself more room to run and hit the trunk with a bone-rattling jar, pushed off on what traction the bark allowed and grabbed the rough branch near its juncture with the trunk.

The momentum from the run had caused her to swing while clinging to the branch. Her legs hadn't slowed yet, but her hands were already feeling raw. She shifted her legs on a swing and hoisted herself up. It wasn't pretty and she wouldn't get any points for style or grace, but she finally clawed her way to straddling the branch. She had gained several more scrapes and a few bruises, no doubt.

It was slow going climbing up, but not as strenuous as the running leaps. She found the tree house hidden beneath the vines. Only a few boards appeared to be missing from the structure, but she was on the wrong side and had to maneuver around to the entrance, fighting the coiling Kudzu vines. The Kudzu had just taken hold or she wouldn't have been able to get through at all. She had forgotten how invasive Kudzu infestations could be, completely blanketing everything in its path and blocking all light and killing whatever it covered.

She crawled into the basic box structure, testing each board. Heavy shadows lived here with only subdued sunlight reaching inside thanks to the vine coverage. It was smaller than she remembered, much smaller. There was a large, thick spider web in one ceiling corner that she gave a wide berth. Most of the posters they had hung were in tatters and faded. Now that she was here, her compulsion to see it again seemed silly.

She had stirred up the years of dust and pollen. She sneezed several times before continuing to look around.

One tattered paper pinned to the plank wall fluttered. The crayon writing was still legible. It was the blood pact they had signed when they pricked their fingers and became sisters, forever joined in this world and the next. *Wonder if kids still did that? Wonder if that's why Loralie was with her still?*

She could remember when they did the pact like it had just happened. Her eyes were swimming as she eased it from the pushpin and held it to her chest. An ache – emptiness grew, and she attempted to swallow the lump in her throat. She wiped away a few tears and sniffed from the dust and her emotions, then rolled it up and held on to it.

Loralie appeared by her side, her translucent image biting her thumbnail and shifting her illusionary weight from side to side. She looked at Elizabeth and shooed her with her hands. Elizabeth gulped several times.

She had never seen Loralie in such a state before. First, her reaction to the man at the plantation home and now this made her more anxious than all the other things that had happened. Loralie darted a glance to a darkened area.

Elizabeth remembered Gramps had built a little cubbyhole for them to pass secret messages to one another. They had used it often, even if the messages were nothing much. She gazed around in the half-light and found it. She had the silly thought that maybe there was one last note left for her. It had a small door with the hinge placed inside so it was invisible; the knothole was the only way to open it. She eyed it warily. Somehow sticking her fingers through the opening gave her visions from some cheesy late night horror movie.

She took a deep breath and stuck two fingers through and pulled. Nothing. She yanked. And yanked again. It opened with a shriek from the warped wood and a spider scurried out. She squealed and jumped, heart pounding.

Shit, no bug spray or fly swatter. She was reconsidering this whole adventure. *What was she doing in this old playpen? Crap, that spider was big.*

"They just don't grow that big in Colorado." Another deep breath. "I guess it's official, I'm a city girl." She declared to the universe as if it was news. She looked around, but Loralie was already gone.

The spider had already disappeared between some boards. Her skin was crawling as her imagination had bugs on her. She looked in the cubbyhole quickly. There was something crammed in diagonally to fit in the tiny space. She grabbed the item and wrestled it loose, stopping several times to fling imaginary bugs off while her feet did a dance on the creaking floor. The item suddenly gave way, and she landed on her butt, the boards bent under her weight but held.

That was enough for her. She slowly stood up. *Time to get out while the house held together.* As she turned to leave, she looked at what she had pried loose. It was a book of some sort, caked with layers of dirt. Surprisingly, there was no water damage, but evidence of a few bugs having damaged the hard binding. Gramps had built a secure little hiding place. She flipped a few pages and saw Loralie's fat, swirling cursive handwriting. But towards the back it looked like a small notebook tucked inside. She would look it over in better light... after a shower.

CHAPTER THIRTY-NINE

Juanita Alvarez

Corcoran, California is a small rural agricultural based town, barely more than a gas stop on the way to other parts. But, it has a state prison holding the infamous cult leader and murderer Charles Manson plus, for a short time, the gang leader Rance Hunter, and the lesser-known California Substance Abuse Treatment Facility.

The inmates are included in the population totals from censuses, thus estimates claim roughly forty-nine percent of the population consists of inmates, and twenty-seven percent of residents are below the poverty line. You can still pick cotton there, but it isn't king after the Great Recession hit and farming suffered in general from the recent drought. Thus, the prison is one of the biggest employers in town, so people aren't too happy about all the media attention making their biggest source of jobs look bad.

Heath tossed Juanita's large suitcase onto the hotel room bed. He swung around light on his feet.

"I know it's gang money and all, but we could save a little by sharing the room." He raised an eyebrow.

"Since when are you so conscientious?" She stood in the doorway with her hands on her hips. "Do you feel obligated to make propositions because you know I'm gonna turn you down?"

"I keep hoping you'll take me up on one someday." He moved away from the bed and studied her. "You've been unusually... bitchy since we left Philly. That phone call with your mother put you in this mood?" He crossed his arms.

"Let's talk about who Channing Nielson is?" Her eyes glinted. "Imagine my surprise when you used fake identification at the airport."

"That's all it is, fake. I didn't steal an identity. Look, since my specialty became known, I'm now monitored. That's why I met you at a home that has no official connection to me. This investigation doesn't need any scrutiny because my name was flagged. Okay?"

She continued to glare at him, eventually lowering her arms.

"Okay, fine." She looked around her room. The Corcoran Country Inn was one of only two places renting rooms in the small town. She had done some initial research while on the plane and found Rance Hunter was still loose, with no official leads as to what happened. Thus, the two hotels were doing a booming business as reporters flooded to the area to report on his prison break.

"So, what's eating you?"

Her head whipped around from looking out the window at the parking lot view to regard him. She let out a huff. "Yeah, okay, my mother just... just... I don't want to talk about it. Really."

"Okaaaay, do you want to go over what I noticed in those cops' finances now? It might mean something." He watched as she paced the worn carpet a few times before nodding.

"Yeah, but let me call the prison one more time." She dialed from the hotel room's phone the number she memorized after a few calls from the plane and asked for the Warden by name. The local number might help as he would see she was in town now.

"Sir, Juanita Alvarez again to make an appointment to speak with you or someone in your office... I realize you're very busy... Could I be included in any press conferences then, please?" She gave her contact one more time. "I will be there in the morning... National

Gazette News. Will there be a Q and A? Okay, thank you." She hung up slowly. She had sold a few pieces to National Gazette and convinced them to back her story on the prison break without knowing her particular angle.

"The morning, huh? Is that a good thing?" He leaned back against a wall that had a poorly patched square about the size of a fist.

"It's not a one-on-one interview, so everything will be sanitized and Public Relations approved. I had hoped for access to their records and some interviews with a few correctional officers." She rubbed her temples.

It had been a long-assed day, and she needed rest. But, rest would have to wait. Where to begin when she didn't have time to foster contacts in this small town?

"I have an idea." He sat down in the one stuffed side chair and motioned for her to sit on the bed. "We can learn the names of the guards involved and what others may have seen, at least what is being talked about."

Her eyebrows rose, and she motioned for him to keep talking.

"We go to the popular hangout, likely a bar, and we make friendly with the locals. I can charm a few local gals and you can use that city girl allure on the local guys who'll be falling at your feet. We can get the unsanitized scuttlebutt and get something to eat at the same time."

She looked at her watch but avoided his eyes. Something about being with him in a room dominated by a bed made her uncomfortable. "We can meet with the guy that Tito sent and see what he can tell us, then go. He should be here shortly, anyway. About those financials..." She looked over to find him smiling.

"Those financials, okay." His eyes were shining bright.

He grabbed his tablet computer, leaving the rest of his equipment packed, and plopped back down on the bed next to her. She put a little space between them. The hacked Philly cops' bank information showed a few suspicious deposits.

"But, they aren't large sums. If you were paying off a cop, you would think it would cost more." Her brow furrowed and her eyes remained on the laptop screen.

"It's the source of the payment that sticks out to me. I checked on this Restoration America and the website is old and doesn't appear to have changed in three years, besides the fact that it doesn't give any solid information about what they do." He shifted on the bed to face her.

"There was a phone number, so I called using my computer so it'd be hard to trace, but there was a standard voicemail picking up. When I dug for public financial information, what I found shows it's a subsidiary of a different company. It looks like a shell company of some sort to funnel money without leaving a significant trail. It's one of the oldest workarounds... well, you know." He flashed his lopsided grin.

"But a few thousand dollars each just doesn't scream payoff. The risk to their careers and reputations would warrant more than that." Juanita shook her head.

"What if it wasn't a payoff, but to cover expenses?" He jumped up from the bed and paced. "What if that was for smaller payoffs and various expenses? They could've been behind the cover-up willingly rather than bribed." He stopped and looked at her with one eyebrow raised.

"They'd have to be in on the murders, not just paid to look the other way though. Helping the perps to get away with it, knowing full well they would set up the gang for it." Her suspicions this morning regarding the bigger implications of Hunter's prison break leapt to mind.

She continued, "Combine that with Hunter's prison escape that his gang is getting blamed for, yet they're ready to retaliate against whoever nabbed him. What if this entire situation has been manufactured?" They stared at each other, their eyes widening as the possible implications grew in their minds.

"Worst case is bloodshed in the streets," she said as he ventured, "Widespread violence."

"But to what end?" He rubbed the back of his neck.

"Let's see, who would benefit from instigating gang violence?

Some Wallstreet investors who knew how it would play out in the stock market," she ventured.

"Well, off the top of my head, a rival gang is the obvious choice. Then there is anybody who has suffered at the hands of The Black Apostles." He turned and paced back again. "The outside bet would be on somebody wanting to strike when the nation is in turmoil. That list would have a few powerful countries or terrorist groups." He turned again.

She could almost see smoke coming out of his ears as the gears turned.

"If any of this is remotely close, then that company, Restoration America, that fronted the money to those cops would be connected and lead back to whatever person, gang, or outside group that's running this scenario." That seemed logical, and best of all it was a paper trail, actual evidence.

"Hey, didn't you say you talked to a hooker that serviced one of those cops? Did she mention if he was into any ideology like Timothy McVeigh or the Unabomber?" His face was hopeful.

Juanita took out her steno book she used for taking notes, ignoring Heath's laughter. She flipped through. "Okay, Mr. Techno-geek..."

"That's Don Juan Geek to you, remember?"

"Whatever. Scarlet claims he was a little rough but not any worse than others, he particularly hates how the nation is going in the wrong direction, was always preaching about how the blacks and illegals were destroying the country. You know, pretty standard fear-based rhetoric."

"Then why did Tito want you to talk to her? She had to know something."

"Yeah, I asked if she knew any reason he might know about the Anderson family's murder..." she turned a page, "all she could say was..." Juanita stopped and stared at Heath. She swallowed and wrapped her arms over her stomach that was now clenched.

Her voice was a harsh rasp, "He would talk about how there needed to be a catalyst, a spark to start the fire of change, and maybe this spark needed help from dedicated people to get the fire blazing." She shook her head. No, it couldn't really be some racist or extremist scheme, could it?

Holy Mother of God, why did she leave her rosary at home? She had a desire to start saying the rosary again.

Their individual thoughts were interrupted by a knock on the door that signaled the arrival of the gang contact in California to finalize on paper the exact nature of their arrangement to cover everyone involved.

CHAPTER FORTY

Elizabeth Grant

Elizabeth was sitting at the dining table with the book she retrieved from the treehouse. Her first priority had been a shower to remove all the dirt and stop her skin from crawling. She still brushed off imaginary spiders.

She held the simple-worded sisterhood pact in crayon and remembered the night they had camped out in the backyard here. They both had no father and shared how they wondered about who their dads were. Loralie had said if she had no father, she wanted me as a sister. They were only nine and ten at the time. She already packed it away, safe and secure in her suitcase so she didn't misplace it.

At the dining table, she cleaned up the outside of the journal with a damp dish towel, slowly removing years of caked-on dirt. Gently turning the pages, she skimmed through Loralie's life recorded on the pages. It was slow going because the writing was faded enough to make it hard to follow.

"Jasmine slapped me today in the bathroom cause I wouldn't let her look on my test in history. We never liked each other, but she tries to make my life hell..."

"Homecoming. Who cares? Momma won't let me date, so I'm not going..."

"*Going to Homecoming, hoping to see him there. If he dances with anybody else, I will just die...*"

Seems Loralie liked a guy, but she never wrote his name and she never mentioned a guy to her. Elizabeth never realized how much of each other's lives they had missed out on because of the miles between them.

She flipped through the pages to see how many were filled. Loralie's writing stopped about three-fourths into the journal. Tucked into the back of the book was a thin notebook, but it wasn't Loralie's writing. The notebook's inside cover said "Noah Aaron, Patriot."

It seemed to be another journal of some sort, stuck in Loralie's diary. This one wasn't your usual writing of life's trials and joys and disappointments, but details of some company or organization. Elizabeth's stomach soured as she read the first paragraph.

I know you want names of the hierarchy and structure of The Society. I only got a few names. They value secrecy above all else and keep information from getting out. Not like other groups who want you to know and recognize the other members. I know the people I deal with in my little piece. So I'll do my best to report names of those in charge. For now, I have Asa Larsen and Ezra Easton, both called Lieutenant (makes them higher in the structure than me, but not much.) I know the guy running the show is The General, but I haven't a clue as to his real name. Will work on that. I reckon I'll volunteer for increased responsibility and see if I can get a bigger role, learn more then. The persuasive carrot used in recruiting is that we have many, many key people throughout the government and important agencies, but no real proof of anything. I'd think it was all just a big snow job, but I think it's for real.

Elizabeth stopped reading. She wasn't sure what to make of the entry, but it made her nervous. Mostly, she was baffled why this was in Loralie's Diary.

I don't know how old this is, cause this is just a story told to us. But if it's real, that might be some proof to start with. The story is Quincy Blanchette's quick execution that is told to us all. This was a few years back but I don't know exactly when, seems he told his wife 'bout what he was involved in as a matter of pride. Nothing very specific like I'm doing. They shot him in the back of the head as he knelt and asked for forgiveness. They tell us this story in our first months and make clear there's no mercy when you betray them. So, maybe there is something to it. But that's a start.

She looked over her shoulder to make sure the back door was locked and then held the gris-gris bag from around her neck.

There was something at the edge of her mind, something that she came across that made reading this entry seem familiar. She dug out her notebook where she had written down her research and scanned her notes.

There it was. When she was at the library she had come across the brief account of Noah Aaron. He was shot in the head and left in the weeds along the railroad tracks east of town. The police chalked it up to a vagrant or drifter killing for money. That was the news item in the paper printed just before the edition with a short notice of Loralie missing. She remembered how strange it seemed his death had been buried among unrelated notices.

The execution death of Quincy Blanchette described in the journal entry was exactly like the brief notice in the paper of Noah Aaron's death. Blanchette was supposedly killed for telling his wife, so could they have found out this Aaron guy was recording details about The Society and shot him?

The hair on the back of her neck tingled. *What in the hell was Noah Aaron's journal doing in Loralie's diary?* It sounded like Noah was involved in something dangerous, maybe even illegal. Could he have gotten Loralie involved in his troubles, got her killed? Who was he writing these notes to, anyway?

CHAPTER FORTY-ONE

Tito/Doberman

Chicago was the birthplace of the Black Apostles and the centralized headquarters for its widespread operations. The first few times Tito traveled there for a meeting, he did the tourist stuff. But not this time. This was nothing but business and it couldn't get any more serious.

Tito, known in the gang as Doberman, was sitting in a spacious living room with ten others. The furnishings were primarily white with splashes of blood-red pillows and other accent pieces with gold plated ashtrays. This was a gathering of the heads of Black Apostles business operations and regional centers, and Tito was the Philadelphia top dog attending.

Daniel Baker, or Ice pick for his preferred weapon, was Hunter's right-hand man in charge while he was in jail, stood up and the room quieted. "We're here to discuss the situation of Hunter's kidnapping. We've had a serious attack against our organization, but we don't know who's behind it. It's been ten hours since he was snatched, what's the word on the streets?" He looked around the group of men.

"We heard Nuestra Familia was bragging on nabbing him. They've got some pieces of shit in the prison." The Los Angeles boss, Apache, crossed his muscular tattooed arms and sat back, having shared his news.

"Any signs they might be for real?" Daniel shot back.

"Nothing, far as I can tell. Seems a bit... ambitious for them, I'm thinking."

Daniel fisted his lethal hands and looked around again.

"We heard some rumblings that the Russian mafia been measuring us up for a takeover, thinking to expand their operations by taking over ours." Miami's boss, Shark-tooth, cracked his knuckles, one large gold and diamond ring glinting in the light when he talked. "Just rumor, but snuffing Hunter could be an opening move."

"That would be their style, too." Daniel's frown deepened.

"We can strike the Nuestra Familia while Shark-tooth takes care of the Russians. We can strike them hard with some men from other locations." Apache's arms flexed in anticipation of the proposed battle.

"We got gangs wanting to take us down all the time," Tito blurted. He couldn't hold back any longer. "If it ain't the Cuban Corporation or Mickey Cobras, it's the Vietnamese Born to Kill. But taking on the Ruskies is suicide. The others'll circle like sharks to pick the bones." Apache glared at him. Tito had discovered Sun Tzu's The Art of War and believed "avoid what is strong, and strike at what is weak" was sound advice when dealing with the Russians.

"True dat." Daniel punched his hand and looked around to the others.

"You saying we can't fight 'em? We can't defend ourselves against a takeover? What kind of pussies you think we are?" Apache snarled back. Shark-tooth nodded agreement.

"These gangs have challenged us. Even if they didn't take Hunter, they'll see us as weak and an easy target unless we show 'em we ain't taking no shit from anybody. I say strike 'em hard." The Dallas/Houston boss with his flattop and scar encircling his throat gave an emphatic nod of his head. He was called Hardin after the bloodthirsty old west outlaw.

Daniel paced back and forth. His hand occasionally rubbed his chin or ran through his short hair.

Tito stared directly at Apache, read the challenge in his eyes. He took his phone and texted his inside person to learn all of Apache's weaknesses pronto. Actually, his contact was Apache's sister, Cenisa, who he had been fucking every chance he got. They met when he was in Los Angeles for a meeting and she seemed to get aroused at how Apache would kill them if he found out. Just thinking about what she could do with her mouth made him hard.

Daniel stopped pacing.

"I don't want resources tied up on both coasts if we find somebody else snatched Hunter, we'll be spread too thin." Daniel ground a fist into his other hand.

Daniel looked directly at Tito. "Anybody else got anything to say?"

"I say wait a couple days. Somebody gotta know something. We meet with our contacts, shake some hands, tighten up our alliances. Find out what everybody knows." He rarely said much, but not this time. "We've got to be sure before making a move. Otherwise, other gangs'll think it's their chance while we strike out at everybody."

"You still betting on that little reporter girl to save the day?" Daniel asked while several chuckled and scoffed. Apache made some lewd comment about what Tito could do with his alliances.

"She's just one piece, but if she finds anything it'll have proof. We need proof. And she'll probably get it in the news. That'll keep us from fighting the cops and the Feds when we may be busy eliminating an enemy or challengers." A few heads were nodding. Damn few, though.

"We can't fight 'em all, true." Daniel, legs apart and hands on hips, had a murderous look. "I wanta find out who did this, bad. I wanta be ready to strike hot and heavy when we know." His eyes were lit up, near maniacal, and his voice grew louder. "You find me who the hell did this, and we'll be ready to rain Hell down on them. You understand me?"

They had their marching orders. Gentleman Jack whiskey, a favorite because it's rumored to be named after the mobster Gentleman Jack Diamond, was liberally poured into glasses and distributed.

Tito let out his breath. They had about two days before Miami and

Los Angeles became battlegrounds. Apache and Shark-tooth would jump at a chance to flex their muscle. He knew the other gangs would love to take over their drug operations and other businesses, and patience wasn't the cornerstone of any gang's makeup.

But the real danger, in his mind, was the Russian mafia with their ruthless military efficiency. They operated in many nations, including the U.S. A few years back an FBI director had said they posed the greatest threat to national security.

He had just taken the hand of one of the barely dressed girls that had strolled in now that the business was done. He was still hard and had to fuck some bitch till he couldn't move. He was about to pop a Viagra and grab another girl's hand, then find a room upstairs.

Daniel motioned him over and whispered, "I want to know everything little reporter girl finds as soon as you hear. She could be our best chance after all, but I hate waiting on a fucking girl."

CHAPTER FORTY-TWO

Rance Hunter

He felt hot, then cold. There were times he was aware of lying on a cold floor, though he could feel thick humid air holding him in a deceptive embrace. His mind fought to shake loose the heated siren arms, but the warmth would sink him down into the dark depths of oblivion.

He swam close to the surface once, clawing his way up, willing himself to break free of the weight dragging him under into inky black nothingness. He was strong, few men could survive his fists, or his stranglehold. But his strength did him no good in this battle. Snatches of voices drifted over him, barely touching.

"… double dose already and he's about to come to… weighs a god damn ton, two men probably….why's this piece of shit so important…" He couldn't quite make sense of the words, they floated in his mind, separate, with no context.

Rance hated going back into the darkness where he had visions of his childhood. The nightmare of his father beating him and his siblings, of his mother lying dead on the bedroom floor from too much booze, his gentle and kind sister on the tenant house stoop shot five times played like a movie before him. Was he crying?

Little Angelique had been his inspiration, his hope, the best of their family. Her words rang like a clanging bell, "Take my hand, we can do anything together." How could you slay such innocence?

Don't make me remember that day again, please. He could take physical pain, was used to it even, but not Angelique's dying in his arms again.

CHAPTER FORTY-THREE

Juanita Alvarez

Heath opened the door for Juanita. She wasn't thrilled about convening in his room to work on the case after their trip to the local watering hole.

The Brunswick had been your typical old bar on the main street that runs through town. But, considering the influx to town, they were quickly pegged as members of the press.

"So, did you get anywhere with that gaggle of local girls?" She had been subjected to watching him lavish his charm on a group of girl-friends, even two-step with a few on the tiny dance floor. She took off her quickly purchased high heels that Heath insisted would make the local men open up on their intel-gathering expedition. She rubbed her feet.

"Well, it wasn't easy. I got the names of the correctional officers who died in the prison break for starters." A smug look lit his face.

"All of them?" The official press release from the prison had named only one of the deceased.

"Yep, all of them. I figure we can get a look at their financials too." He removed his sports jacket that made him look like a young Dot-com owner.

"If they were killed during Hunter's escape, they were probably trying to stop it. Why would we investigate them?" She didn't want to waste time they likely didn't have.

"I wouldn't be too sure about that. Seems at least one of the correctional officers networked to be on that road crew. People thought it was ironic he tried so hard for a position that got him killed."

"So?" Her hands were on her hips, again.

"I find it curious, not ironic. What if he was maneuvering to be close to Hunter when the security was lowest on the road crew?" His voice was full of excitement.

"I talked to somebody..." She began.

"The old coot with the missing front tooth?" Heath supplied with a chuckle.

"I talked to *somebody* who claims Hunter never should've been on that road crew and that someone must've really screwed up. He figured they'd get fired over the paper snafu."

"But if somebody was paid to make that paper snafu happen..." He was nearly jumping up and down.

"And a few specially picked correctional officers to assist in the prison break got on the same road crew..." She continued the thought.

"Hunter is jumped, maybe drugged, or knocked unconscious and whisked away." Heath proceeded.

"No, passing cars would've seen that. The official press release says there were no witnesses. But I found out why the other prisoners didn't see a blasted thing."

He motioned for her to spit it out.

"The old coot said something knocked out the guards and prisoners. Said he drove by and they were laying down like they were all asleep."

"Well, I don't know when he drove past. State 43 had one end blocked just to the south by a jackknifed semi truck and to the North there was a large gasoline spill closing it down until it was cleaned up. No cars were zipping past the prison work crew, so there were conveniently no witnesses to say if or how they were all rendered unconscious."

"I think he works on the farm right there and maybe used a private dirt road to get on 43. Still, why did several correctional officers end up dead if all the others were unconscious? There are missing pieces that make this puzzle very confusing. Couldn't they have just knocked out the guards too?"

"For now we can contact Betty and give her some names to check their bank accounts." At least they had made that much progress.

"I found out there is one bank in town that most people use, then there are about six in Visalia, the neighboring town, where they have the Sequoias." He proudly shared.

"Do you think Betty could check prison records first for those guards and then check out any paperwork snafu?" Juanita was focused and barely registered Heath's excitement over his information.

"I thought you didn't like using hackers unless you had to?" He stared at her, then winked. "Wouldn't want you getting dependent on the services of such bad influences."

"Give it a rest. I don't like it, but official channels will only get me so far, which is looking like nowhere."

"I don't know if Betty can help, it's a state prison and if there should be any sort of terrorists at the prison, even domestic terrorists, their records would have classified information. I expect their firewalls are robust, the question is – are they more robust than a bank's?" He turned on the equipment he had brought.

There was one main laptop that seemed oversized, plus other equipment attached around the cramped hotel desk. She pulled up a chair as the screen came to life and he entered his password to the computer.

Before long he was in the chat room where they had originally connected with "Betty." He read a few messages and let out a whistle.

"Honey, you won't believe this…"

"What did you call…?"

"There are volunteers to work on this, a dozen at least. They got wind of the gang being framed in Philadelphia and are jumping on the bandwagon to break this wide open." He looked at her with a big smile. "With this kind of manpower, we can get whatever records you want." His expression softened.

He stood up and took her by the hand, pulling her up from her chair. He took her in his arms and led her in a two-step dance around the cramped room as he hummed a song. It felt nice, but she would never tell him that. His citrusy cologne lifted her spirits and if she were honest, his upbeat attitude was helping her stay positive.

"When this is over, do you think we could...?"

"Not a chance in hell...," she began.

"... see the Sequoias?" He finished.

She stared at him with her mouth open but snapped it shut at a sharp knock at the door. "Pizza delivery."

She pointed to him as he pointed to her, question in their eyes. They both shook their heads "no." Heath jerked the door open to find a boy with a red bicycle holding a pizza box.

"Let me in quick-like." The kid, maybe twelve, looked around the motel parking lot while holding the pizza box in Heath's face. Heath took the box and stepped back, allowing the boy to push his bicycle in then prop it against the door once it was closed and locked. He wore a baseball cap with his shaggy blond hair poking out.

"I saw something this morning." His eyes traveled between them. They both stood with his arms crossed, surveying the kid.

"I was there, you know. Well, not alongside the road, but in the field."

"In the field, but you saw something. How's that?" Heath took the lead, man-to-boy talk.

"Yeah, well, I was in the field, you know, having a joint in privacy, you know. There was this sci-fi looking helicopter appears and then one guard comes running up carrying a black dude. A prisoner with his legs chained." He stopped long enough to take a breath.

"The helicopter guys take the prisoner, then shoot that guard. The helicopter rose up in the air for just a few seconds and they fired several times... maybe four. Bam-bam, bam-bam. With a regular rifle – not a Rambo gun like I expected." He spoke fast, but sure about his facts, and used his hands to illustrate. "Then it dropped back down low over the field and flew west. When the helicopter was all gone, like, I went over to see and there's all the prisoners and the guards on the ground. I thought they's all dead. I ran." He swallowed.

"Why didn't you tell the police all this?" Heath spit out, like he was interrogating the kid. Juanita marveled at how he had adopted the persona of a parent.

"First, I saw a guard getting a prisoner to the helicopter. Second, I heard it was some badass gang lord that was busted out. Why would I trust anybody from around here? I may toke some, but I ain't stupid." The kid crossed his arms and stared at Heath.

"What's your name and how old are you?" Juanita didn't like dealing with minors on a story.

"I'm Max and I'm Thirteen. But that don't mean I didn't see it. I know what I saw."

He may have some idea he saw something important, but even she wasn't sure what it meant, yet.

"Did you talk to anybody else about this?" She was ignoring the smell of the pizza in spite of her stomach growling. The Brunswick's food options were limited, so she hadn't eaten but a snack.

"I tried to talk to the cool reporter who reports in Iraq and war zones, but he shut me down before I could tell him anything." Juanita knew who that was. He likely didn't think a kid could add anything to the official releases.

Heath looked at her and gestured it was her call. She didn't like this, a kid showing up with such a fantastic account of the events. But he had just corroborated that the prisoners were unconscious. Maybe if he had to tell his story in front of his parents, any lies would come out. Besides, if he was telling the truth, his parents needed to be on high alert sooner rather than later.

"We need your mom or dad, cause you're a minor... and you need to get out of town when we're done here. Maybe you can visit some relatives."

CHAPTER FORTY-FOUR

Elizabeth Grant

Elizabeth woke to find herself on the couch, scrunched in an awkward position. Noah Aaron's notebook was still in her hand. She moved her joints to relieve the stiffness. The couch was not made with overnight comfort in mind.

Noah's notes were confusing. She didn't understand what he was explaining and felt she was missing a big piece to the puzzle. Only Loralie could have hidden his notes in her diary and then in the tree house. It had to be important, so she had to read through it.

After a breakfast of eggs and bacon, a luxury for her, she tended to the flower garden in the backyard before it got too hot. She even called into her job to check in and answer questions on her part of a project. She finally sat down at the kitchen table with the journal and her own notebook.

Her thoughts were a jumble. She had to be honest with herself. *Time to face what you came to face.* She had the excuse for the trip here to help Gran out by watching her place. But the truth really came back to Loralie.

When Elizabeth saw the vision of Loralie seven years ago, she suspected deep down her friend was dead. She never told the full story, not even to her mother. She had seen more than just her dearest friend and soul sister bloody before her, fading in and out, beaten and defeated. Elizabeth had also glimpsed what she had been through, felt the terror, even had the sensation of the blinding blow to her head that knocked Loralie out at one point.

She was the only other person on the planet who knew what Loralie had endured. Sure, she had insisted her mother call Mrs. Carter; and that's when the search began. But she should have done more. Even then, she couldn't believe what she saw was real. It wasn't logical, measurable, or verifiable, so she had to be imagining things. Then Uncle Jairus had sent her to psychologists because of her excitement and claim of seeing Loralie. But she should have done more. She owed Loralie.

She was here to pay her debt, perhaps with interest for it taking her so long to get the spine to even return to Cyprus. The meditation yesterday with Loralie before her had brought it back onto her shoulders.

Loralie's presence over the years was a continual reminder that Elizabeth owed her, and she still felt that seeing Loralie was either this guilt eating at her mind or it was the manifestation of her wanting Loralie back so much she imagined her.

The various suspicions she had about the truck that followed her or the sheriff warning her off would stop her now. She was scared, terrified after finding Noah Aaron's journal that likely got him killed and maybe Loralie too. But she just couldn't stop, not now. She took a deep breath and read through her observations in her notebook. There must be something else she could do, somebody else to talk to.

It was there in her notes from the talk with Jeremiah. She had thought the trip to Meridian had produced no information. She had loved seeing Jerry again, but she had felt it was a bust... until now. He had mentioned Loralie had begun to date, even though their mother wasn't happy with any distractions from her studies.

Fortunately, she had written down the name, Cedric Jones. She looked, but there was no Cedric Jones in the small local phonebook. She would have to go to the library and search neighboring town's phone records and perhaps even an internet search and since she was restless and had to feel productive, now was a good time.

She wanted to hide the journals before leaving the house. She wrapped them both in plastic wrap and slid them into a cereal box. Maybe it wasn't the most creative solution, but she didn't feel safe carrying either in her purse and hoped nobody would take the time to go through all the food items in a search. She had no illusion of privacy in Gran's house any longer.

As an additional step, she placed cellophane tape across the back-door to signal if somebody had entered while she was gone. Okay, maybe she read that in a Nancy Drew mystery or something, but it was subtle and couldn't hurt. She tucked her notebook into her purse and headed out the front door, locking it and putting clear tape at the very bottom.

"Miss Elizabeth, I brought you some of my wife's pie." It was the neighbor man. Picket something or other.

"That's thoughtful. You didn't have to, really."

"Did I catch you on your way out?"

"Yes, actually I…"

"I don't mean to bother you. I can bring it back. How long you fixin' to be gone?"

"I don't know for sure. I wouldn't want to inconvenience you with bringing it back over. I can stop by later." She continued walking toward her car.

"Heavens to Betsy, it ain't no bother. I'll keep a watch and bring it over when you return." He stood on Gran's lawn with the pie in his hand, watched her back out and drive away. When she was down the street, she could see in her rearview mirror he was watching her car, still standing in the same spot.

CHAPTER FORTY-FIVE

Juanita Alvarez

The Corcoran State Prison is an all-male facility located on 942 acres of the old Tulare Lake site and ancient home of the Tachi Indians. Over a fifth of the inmates are classified as security threat group members and thus housed separately from the general population. Even yard time for security threat group members is in large cages outdoors as they are considered too dangerous to not be caged.

Juanita drove alongside the high chain-link fences and blue watch towers manned by rifle-bearing guards. She realized every move, even visitors made, was under scrutiny and the first thing surrendered was privacy.

She arrived early to the press conference since she didn't know what to expect for a security gauntlet and checks. She dressed in a dark blue pinstriped skirt suit to look as professional as possible among her more seasoned colleagues. Her hand shook a little as she prepared to take notes from where she was seated in the third row and went over her list of questions.

The press conference was held in a small room at the prison that looked like a grimy visitation room modified to accommodate the press. It smelled of bleach, sweat, and pent-up anger. She estimated fifty or sixty reporters, some international outlets like Al Jazeera and the BBC, attended. She was not called upon to ask a question, no matter how much she waved her hand. She recorded the statements and Q&A period on her phone. She asked the Public Relations spokesperson to interview somebody, anybody. But no luck.

She saw the large network news got an additional and separate session with a tour, but they were handed a sheet with acceptable questions to ask and they all agreed before entry. That was likely why she wasn't included. She was here to investigate and report the story, not be handed a pre-scripted report.

She asked a few questions of the local reporters who also weren't invited, figuring they'd been covering the prison for years. The local media didn't consider the road conveniently shut down in both directions at the time of Hunter's escape suspicious, nor that the prisoners had been knocked unconscious somehow while the guards had been shot the slightest bit puzzling, and they definitely hadn't heard anything about a helicopter in the area.

The local reporters provided a few tidbits to give a human-interest slant. She needed to submit a story, any story, to National Gazette this morning. If she didn't have Heath's back-door avenues to get information, she would be really discouraged by now.

Upon returning to the hotel, she made a beeline to Heath's technology-filled room. He let her in with a bleary-eyed look. She handed him a drive-through breakfast burrito and a large specialty coffee.

"I was starving, thanks." He snatched the food and drink and gave her a peck on the cheek before she could object.

"How'd the press thingy go?" He managed to say while unwrapping his breakfast. Good thing she brought him two burritos and herself a separate one. He nearly inhaled the first egg, bacon, sausage, potato, and cheese, one with a side of salsa.

"Other than some human interest stuff, the conference itself was PR central with no real information. No mention of a screw-up allowing Hunter to be in a road crew. The network reporters didn't even ask. No helicopter sightings either. I know the prison is doing damage control and is praying to keep that quiet, but I can't figure out why the rest of the press corp. hasn't jumped on the inconsistencies reported." She took a big bite out of her breakfast. A little moan escaped her. It was delicious.

"That doesn't seem right. I can't imagine experienced reporters wouldn't have considered a gang leader pulling minimum-security road crew as a big red flag. Then there's the gassing and shooting mix." They were silent as they ate.

She finished a mouthful, "Plus they have an entirely separate building for inmates exactly like Hunter – the most dangerous, so they can't instigate riots or kill others. Hunter wasn't in that facility, but somehow in the general population."

Silence settled as they both ate for a little while, eyes closed, enjoying the amazing flavors. Big fast-food chains couldn't duplicate this.

"What if," Heath proposed between bites, "news corporation heads are convinced it was the gang and they just ran with it?"

"Wish I could say that was outlandish. The news channels from radio, print, and television are run by a handful of corporations and the heads of those corporations determine what is reported and how." She found it hard to swallow. "That's why I have sought independent reporting outlets, sad for my bank account though."

"So it's feasible the reporters have been told how to cover the escape and to focus on the gang angle by their newspapers or networks?" He pushed.

"Sadly, yes. It's possible and probable." She had lost her appetite all together.

"That would tell us what?"

She put aside her pity party over her career choice to think about that question. What did that reveal, if anything?

"Well, it suggests people at influential and high levels in the news media were quickly convinced that the gang was behind Hunter's breakout. Maybe the murder in Philadelphia tainted their collective mindset?" She massaged her temples.

"Could one of them influence the others that the Black Apostles are guilty, who then force that down their programming channels? High-level gossip with a dose of peer pressure, maybe?" Heath had stopped eating in the middle of his second breakfast burrito.

"Well, General Electric owns NBC, Viacom owns CBS, and Disney has ABC." Juanita held up a finger for each.

"News Corp has Fox and the Wall Street Journal, and Clear Channel has a huge chunk of all radio." Heath jumped in, surprising her with his knowledge.

"Time Warner has CNN, Headline News, and Time magazine." Juanita was up to six fingers.

"What about the Washington Post and the New York Times?" His eyebrows rose in question.

"The Post and the New York Times are owned separately, Amazon's Jeff Bezos owns The Post, and the Times is owned by the Ochs-Sulzberger family although they are publicly traded." She was animated now. This was her area. "Newspapers are a mixed bag, Gannett Company owns USA Today plus something like eighty other significant papers, and Media News Group has the San Jose Mercury News and sixty some others. Even if they aren't owned by the same company, syndicated content blurs those lines."

"Is it a small world? Would they know their peers at other papers or news channels?"

"I can't say how much time they spend together to chat, but I guess it's feasible the CEOs run in the same circles, maybe play golf with the same people. I imagine they know who the main players at other stations or papers are to keep a finger on the pulse of the business." Juanita said.

"How much can they influence what is reported, isn't that up to the editors?" He was frowning now. She was probably the only female that made Heath frown.

She rubbed her temples. "Actually, that's a point of contention. Many journalists have left to publish their investigations in books, and now the Independent news agencies claim they don't report corporate messaging. There is supposedly a lot of favor trading and conflicts of interest among the news executives. It's the dirty little secret of the news media." She threw the rest of her breakfast away, no longer hungry, and paced the small room like a caged lion.

"So the answer is a big *maybe.* Maybe the top echelon at the news corporations have told their reporters to not waste time investigating and that the Black Apostles broke their leader out of jail so that's all they care about." Heath's appetite didn't seem fazed, just slowed from talking. He took a big bite now.

There was nothing else to gain down that line of questioning, so they needed to move on. Although, it might explain why there was no hardened journalist digging into the situation surrounding the prison break.

"I spent some time on the laptop you lent me researching helicopters that Max might have seen. I really thought he was exaggerating, but the military has exactly what he described." She paused to let the military angle sink in.

"Shit, I was afraid you'd say that," Heath said. Juanita felt like they were spinning their wheels and not making much headway.

"So what is going on here? Get me up to speed."

"Well, we have five solid hacktivists who are helping out. All of them are under the radar with nobody looking at them. They're wicked skilled and passionate about finding who's behind the Philly murders and Hunter's prison break. They're going through the local banks with Betty overseeing the team. It may take several more hours before we get any bank records."

"I have to write up a story and send it in, so I'm headed back to my room." She was half through their adjoining door when he stopped her cold.

"Maybe you should publish the story about the Philly cops? It might flush whoever is doing this out."

She turned slowly. Sure, she had thought about it, but the gang had been so focused on finding Hunter they had dropped the cops investigation.

The gang's lawyer met with them shortly after they arrived and said she could publish her findings, no matter what she revealed in her investigation. She even signed a legal agreement, so she knew exactly where she stood with Tito and his gang. But if Max really saw a high-tech or stealth military helicopter, this prison break had some powerful, influential people involved. Somebody who could get such a specialized *military* grade helicopter.

"And flushing them out would be a good thing how?" She really didn't mind remaining anonymous.

"You're in the perfect position to set a trap with minimal risk." His eyes were all business.

"I'm in a perfect position? How do you get that?" Her voice was a little high.

"They'll have a near impossible task to trace you since you are flying on a private plane and using somebody else's business credit card and cash. That gives you a few layers of protection." She closed the door and sat back down. This was definitely a sit-down conversation.

"Can they trace me through my email?"

"I can set you up with a less traceable email and more secure internet to use in an hour or so."

At least he hadn't assured her with "trust me". She sensed the minute she published her investigation of the Philly cops, she would be on somebody's radar… and that had her scared.

"You mentioned a trap. What trap?" She had to ask, even if she would probably regret it.

"When your piece gets published, and it makes a stir – which it will, the first thing the responsible parties will do is to search for you on Google." He motioned to his computer setup, "We create a dummy website with your profile that is waiting with a hidden downloadable piece of software from a few points like a PDF file and an auto-play video that will send information back from that computer – like a downloaded transmitter. We could find out some contacts, locations, and such." He watched her.

She wished she had her rosary, but could also go to confession and make peace with God. This wouldn't end well, she just knew it.

"Have the website and trap ready but hold off. The timing isn't right. I wish I had some fake identification while you're at." Did she really just say that?!

Heath looked at her with sultry eyes and winked. "I like how you think, babe."

CHAPTER FORTY-SIX

The General

The General was back at his antebellum home in his private office. It was hot as Hades out and the air conditioning rustled his hair gently. Sunlight streamed in through the window, glinting off crystal and gold furnishings and décor. The smell of leather was prevalent with only a hint of tobacco from a bygone era detected. As if the tobacco farmed on the property had cured the very walls and floors and no amount of scrubbing, varnish, or paint could remove the odor.

He sat staring at the gold gilt framed picture on his desk of Byron De La Beckwith, even though he wasn't a Society man, but rather a KKK member.

Beckwith was the sniper who shot Medgar Evers in the back in full view of his two children and wasn't tried until thirty years after the fact. He kept the black-and-white photo on his desk for two reasons, first it represented the lesson that sometimes you had to resort to extreme measures and violence, and second that with money you could tamper with juries and influence you can get away with almost anything. He liked to call it cheating to win.

The picture also represented to him Project Cancer Eradication that he had planned and set in motion. The cancer, of course, was the insidious myth that we were all equal. In reality, white men of America were sanctified as superior by God yet were now under attack.

Byron De La Beckwith said it best during his third and final trial at age seventy-three, "I'm proud of my enemies. They're every color but white, every creed but Christian."

The General sighed. He had work to do and couldn't indulge this sentimental reverie any longer. Besides, he would never have hidden in some honeysuckle bushes and shot the man in the back like Beckwith had. No, he would have faced him openly and shot him in the face like the mongrel dog they all are while forcing his children to watch as a lesson.

The phone rang and jarred him out of his pensive state.

He picked up the phone but said nothing, just listened. "Package is successfully relocated and we'll be ready with video and audio samples in the next day, maybe two. How are we to get the audio and video to the reporter for him to splice and interject his interview questions?" The voice on the other end was excited, not the out-of-breath type, but rather overflowing enthusiasm.

"I want one of you to drive it into DC, where you'll meet the reporter in a park to make the exchange. I want one of your men that can be absolutely trusted to make the meet-up time and not get diverted or sidetracked." He sounded angry, but it was more that he was being aggressively clear on this point. He would not have any direct contact with the fake interview in case it wasn't successful.

"No problem, General. I'll pick one of my best men to make the delivery and even give him my pickup truck so there'll be no breakdowns on the road." The man's voice had gone from the exuberant to sober after the General's stern tone.

"Are you sure you'll have enough video and audio for the interview to the manipulated? You got the list of words and phrases needed to accomplish this, didn't you?" The General may use computers and automation in his business, but he still wasn't sure he trusted how this interview would be completely manufactured from spliced video and audio to make it appear as though this gang leader was calling for racial war against the white populace.

It seemed like an impossible task. Yet, he was assured it would be done and wouldn't be detectable unless it was put under scrutiny. The Society was paying top dollar for special-effects and digital artist, plus an experienced film editor to pull this off. They were Society members, but the money also ensured their silence along with a clear promise they would regret ever sharing information about this job.

"Call me back in a few hours with the name of the person who'll make the delivery. Then I'll give you the details for the meet." He hung up the phone; cutting the man off before he could reply.

He turned to his computer and logged on to the virtual reality internet platform and the specific antebellum world The Society had created for passing information. It was time for a follow-up with the Vice President on drafting their post-victory legislation and executive orders.

He had several more ideas they needed to discuss. They planned on ramming through a slew of legislative bills in the first thirty days of the new President's term. Shock and awe, so many pieces of legislation that few could keep up with them, let alone mount any resistance. He wanted to ensure there were no loopholes and no way around this restoration he envisioned for the nation.

CHAPTER FORTY-SEVEN

Elizabeth Grant

E lizabeth was at the small old library doing research again. The more she was there, the more its hardwood floors and Greek Revival flourishes typical in the South appealed to her. Although it was built in the 1920s, the builder stayed with the revival style rather than the then popular Art Deco or Bauhaus boxy design. It smelled of wood, lemon polish, many books, and decades of minds being stretched.

She had searched the Cyprus and Meridian phone books, but Cedric Jones wasn't listed. A search of the large colleges in the state resulted in a Cedric Jones who graduated from a college in Jackson around the time estimated. But she wasn't sure it was the same guy Loralie had dated. She checked the Jackson phone book with the idea he stayed in the area and got a job after college. She found two listings under C. Jones in Jackson. It was a long shot, but she would take it.

Her cell phone still didn't work in town, but she remembered a pay phone in the library and one at the local Gas n' Guzzle station. At the little wall mounted pay phone in a corner of the library, she pumped change into the phone and looked around before dialing the first number and held her hand around the phone receiver.

"Hello, is Cedric available please." She sang out softly in her professional business voice to the woman who answered.

"Yes, who's calling?"

"Please tell him Elizabeth from Cyprus is calling." She crossed her fingers and whispered a little prayer.

She could hear a muted conversation but couldn't make out anything that was said. At least this phone had a clear connection. After what felt like five minutes, a disembodied voice spoke to her.

"I don't know any Elizabeth from Cyprus. I can't help you." A man informed her.

"Wait, please. Did you live in Cyprus or know Loralie Carter?" The silence on the other end stretched out until the man took a breath.

"I ain't thought about either for years. So, you're *her* Elizabeth? She talked about you all the time, said you were like sisters."

"Yes, we were close like sisters." She thought about the blood sister pact in crayon she had saved from the tree house, now secured in a plastic bag in her suitcase. "I have a few questions for you, if you don't mind Mr. Jones."

He was silent for several breaths and finally spoke, "I've put Cyprus behind me. Don't care to drag that time in my life back up."

"I won't take but a few minutes of your time. I want to understand what was going on that summer." She looked around again and kept her hand around the receiver to contain her voice to the phone. "I want to understand what happened."

"I don't know nothin'."

"You may know more than you think, really." A few people in the library glanced her way, but none seemed overly interested.

"Okay. Now, if I had my druthers, I wouldn't be revisitin' this." His voice was strained.

"I know she was taking an advanced class at Jackson State University that summer to bolster her status for grants and scholarships later. Did she mention anything strange happen when she was in class or on campus?" She gripped the phone receiver tight with white knuckles. *Please give me something to work with.*

"Naw, she was intense, serious about the class work. She always went into things with focus – driven, I guess, but this really sucked her time. We only saw each other for a few hours on the weekends. She was buried with homework." His voice was subdued, low.

"I know there was a murder of a guy, Noah Aaron, in town that summer. What can you tell me about him? Was his murder ever solved?"

"I forgot about that. Yeah, that's right. The town was in shock I think, we didn't get that kinda killin' round there. Maybe a barroom brawl or a husband beating his wife, but never a killin' like that. Guess that's why everybody figured a stranger did it."

"Anything else about Noah from that summer you can remember?" *Come on. There has to be something!* She glanced around again, still nobody gave her much attention. Then, the hairs on the back of her neck stood up and a shiver shot down her back.

"You know, I remember Loralie sayin' she saw him in Jackson a few times." Elizabeth stood taller, at attention, and looked around for anybody listening in yet again. She felt she was being watched.

"Did she know why he was there? What he was doing?" She held her breath.

"Hmmmm. Lemme think on that. I recollect she said he talked to her the last time she was in Jackson. She was real surprised seein' how he always talked down to her momma and her. You know, like they was dirt and stupid."

"Any idea why he would change or how? Did something happen to him, did he lose somebody?" She was trying to help him remember that summer as quickly as possible. The sensation she was watched remained, and she wanted to finish the call.

"No. Leastways I don't think so. It woulda had to be big, cause he couldn't stand us. You know the type. He wanted the old South back like that was paradise or something. Then he's talking to my girl like she was an old friend." He scoffed.

"Did this Noah ever give Loralie anything?" She heard him suck in his breath.

"Yeah, yeah. He had somethin' he wanted her to hand over to a friend when she went to Jackson for class next time. Don't know what, but she said it was strange 'cause she was to meet the guy in a park. See, I reckoned he shoulda done it hisself."

"Can you place when he gave her the package and when he died?" With her hand still muffling her voice, her gaze kept darting around the library, searching for who was watching.

"Now that's a stretch. Jeez, it coulda been the same day or maybe the day before he died, don't know for sure." He didn't think anything odd about the question and didn't connect it with Loralie's disappearance. No doubt he thought she had run off and left him behind. It wasn't her problem to set the record straight.

She tried a few different approaches, but that was the most she was getting from Cedric. She thanked him for his time and hung up. She quickly looked around again, but didn't see anybody paying her any attention.

She thought about Noah Aaron's journal, wrapped up and hidden in Gran's cereal box. She sat down and wrote in her notebook the details of her talk with Cedric before she lost any of the conversation.

Who was Noah trying to send the journal to, and why ask Loralie to deliver it? This probably got them both killed? She swallowed hard at the thought that she could have in her possession what got two people killed.

But she owed Loralie.

CHAPTER FORTY-EIGHT

Malcom Alexander

Madam Antoinette's funeral was held in a Baptist church. It didn't matter that she wasn't Baptist but a follower of the Hoodoo faith. Those who considered Netty their spiritual advisor and healer made the trip, regardless. The multitude of the people packed into the small church and well-worn pews, and a dozen or more standing in the back comforted Malcom and his momma.

How could he be nervous about giving a simple eulogy? He had been shot a few times and been in gun battles. Still, his hands were sweating. *He would do fine, he wouldn't bawl like a baby in front of everyone. He was tougher than that, right?* Just because he hadn't cried yet, didn't mean he would pick the most public time to let his grief out.

Malcom stood at the pulpit looking over the women fanning themselves and the men loosening their ties. Bright sunshine shot through the wall of stained glass windows and projected a kaleidoscope of colors across the crowd. The heavy air reeked with a sickening sweet smell from the many flowers lining the front and sides of the church. He took a breath and nodded to his momma.

"Good day and thank you for being here, I'm Malcolm. This beautiful lady we're remembering today was my aunt. I was very blessed to have her in my life. Netty was more of a 'bonus' mom to me growing up. I learned about life through a different set of eyes with her. She taught me service to my fellow man, whether it was dragging me to serve soup at the local food bank and shelter rather than shoot hoops in the park, bringing clothes to the women's shelter, or including me in her spiritual work. I can't recall a time visiting without her making at least one trip to help a person in need."

He cleared his throat and blinked away the moisture welling up in his eyes. Several tears rolled down his cheeks, no matter how much he fought it. *Don't cry now.*

He continued in a shaky voice, "I remember one Thanksgiving, when Cecelia was visiting from college – so it was a full house, when a total stranger phoned. Somebody told him Netty could help with his sick child in the hospital. There was no discussion about whether she should go. She simply loaded up her prayer and spell supplies and rushed to the hospital to help. We held back dinner and when she returned, she gave thanks for being able to comfort and aid others." He wiped tears from his cheeks. He could barely see his notes. "That was who she was, to the core. We all loved that. It may have been inconvenient for her family sometimes. Like when she patched up a boy I had fought comes to mind." He smiled at the memory and the crowd chuckled.

He paused, swallowed hard and looked at the crowd of people Netty had touched in her life and took another deep breath.

Then he saw them. He couldn't have missed them, two FBI agents among the standing-room-only group in the very back. Even at a funeral where the black suits didn't stick out, they were still obvious to him. Either he could pick them out so easily, or they wanted him to know the Bureau was watching.

Their faces showed they were on duty and not simply offering their sympathies. Besides, he didn't know them and couldn't think of any reason they should be at his aunt's funeral. He brought his mind back to his three-by-five cards with his scribbled notes. Where was he?

"But, she was a living example of what she believed. She taught me that faith, any faith, must have hands to help and feet to meet people where they are. When I graduated from the FBI Academy, she told me she was proud I was helping people with my hands and feet too. I'd like to share this bit of a poem that expresses how I see Netty now, in her own words.

Life Beyond the Veil
Look for me, but do not weep,
What's dear to you, you can keep
Close at heart, be strong of mind,
My friends and loved ones, you are kind
To bid me well beyond the veil
Yet I remain with you, a pale visage,
one you may not see,
A scent of flowers flows from me
To herald the touch upon your arm
A guide, protecting you from harm
Be strong for as your heart does swell
Remember me and share it well.
'Til next we meet, I remain
A spirit drifting, for though I deign
To pass beyond and leave your side,
I'll wait for you and be your guide.

There were sniffles, coughs, subdued sobbing, and tissues passed among the pews. One lady he didn't know was inconsolable, weeping with her head in her hands. He watched the agents as he pretended to make eye contact with the mourners. Any nervousness over giving the eulogy was gone. Now he needed to ditch the watchers, if his suspicions were correct.

"We have gathered for closure, not goodbye. Netty is with us still, but in spirit now. Still helping in every way she's able. You can still smell her perfume, sense her eyes on you, or perhaps feel her touch. She is alive in each of us, and we can honor what she gave us by helping others with the same compassion and spirit of love. Thank you for attending today; it is a great comfort to our family to witness this outpouring of respect and love."

Through the rest of the service, he could feel Netty there with him. He knew she was comforting Cecilia, his momma, and himself with her presence. He even felt her light touch on his arm, like a whispered pat from her hand reassuring him.

He talked with many of the people in attendance, but nobody could shed any more light on her last week or two than the package he had received from Netty herself.

He knew Netty was, even now, urging him to console those who had viewed her as their spiritual guide, for they were bereft. He moved as if through a dream where the people seemed foreign, while Netty's spirit felt more real. He knew what she wanted him to say to each person. It was disconcerting; calling on a part of himself he didn't know existed, deep inside some chamber of his spirit that must have opened to Netty's touch.

After the graveside internment where the pair of agents watched from a distance and after he said goodbye to his momma, and before the reception, he finally escaped in Tom's four-wheel drive Suburban with camping gear and several weapons. Positive he had eluded the agents, he faced what was before him.

He needed to be prepared, or so he felt, sensing an urgency to be cautious, hurry, and brace for surprises. He wasn't sure if it was Netty still leading him or his own instincts.

Either way, the camping gear he acquired was stowed in the rear of the Suburban. He was on the road quickly, still in his funeral clothes, speeding towards Cyprus and Elizabeth Grant. He would change clothes along the way.

CHAPTER FORTY-NINE

Juanita Alvarez

Juanita was in her hotel room, a mirror image of Heath's with duplicate faded drapes and old carpet. When it was first built it was probably cozy, now it was like a middle-aged man showing his years and mileage and attempting to look nice under the circumstances; a comb-over here or a girdle there.

Sitting at the small desk, her finger hovered over the laptop mouse. One click and her story about the dirty cops would upload to National Gazette for publication. There was something holding her back, a sense like an internal warning system insisting that remaining under the radar was better in the long run.

Sure, she could make a splash with the Philly cops story, maybe even garner a regular spot with National Gazette or another newspaper, but it would alert the people manipulating the developments. If her suspicions matched the reality, there was a much bigger plan in motion and tipping her hand about any evidence the gang didn't slaughter the Olsen family and the cops' involvement would result in paper trails quickly covered up across the board. She needed every trail she could find before they were aware of her.

Juanita removed her hand from the mouse and scrubbed her face with her hands. This was too big to be impatient. She wanted the truth on the bigger conspiracy story, if it really existed. She changed the story to a write up about all the guards killed and everything she had dug up on their lives, then concluded with a human-interest piece on one of the correctional officers and sent that before she could change her mind. She had bigger fish to catch, no need to rush things. She sent a short email to her National Gazette contact that she was working on a much bigger story related to this.

There was a knock on the door adjoining her room with Heath's.

"Enter at your own risk," she sang out.

Heath opened it enough to poke his head through. "We have some interesting results filtering in. Want to come on over and take a look?"

She sniffed. "Popcorn?"

"It's a snack and keeps this from becoming too… serious."

She grabbed her soda and joined him. He had the chair from her room pulled up to his desk that had cardboard underneath one leg to level it. She slowly sat in the creaking chair and had the popcorn bag in her hands before he closed the door.

"The bank statements on a few of the guards have come in. Seems they had accounts spread between a few banks so it took awhile to catch all of them." He avoided her eyes as he sat down and pulled up a few screens. He printed out a few pages on the portable printer he had brought and handed her two sheets.

"I correlated some of the information."

Juanita scanned the two pages, but the second time through she scrutinized more critically. "I don't see anything, do you?"

"Look on the second page. The hackers went back a few years."

The second page had regular payments with a notation saying college scholarship fund. There were payments to a local college for tuition, books, parking fees, etc. It was the name of the organization that was a surprise.

"Wait, this scholarship fund sounds familiar."

"Should, it's the same institution that made the payments to the Philly cops first on the scene to the home invasion. The cops who sauntered in without their guns even draw. The address listed is the same for the scholarships and the payments to the cops. It's the same organization."

"Why include these other payments listed on the first page, they are different companies and don't seem suspicious?" She suspected he had a reason.

"Because all of these companies list the same address for their business." His voice was serious and heavy.

"There are… seven different companies here and they all have the exact same address?"

"Exactly the same. No suite numbers, just a simple street address." He clarified.

"That's possible, isn't it?"

"Have you ever heard of the Delaware Loophole or 1209 N. Orange Street?" She shook her head no but knew he would share the significance to show his value added in their little partnership.

"Delaware has become known as a state-side tax haven. Businesses incorporate there to avoid paying their taxes because of Delaware's practically non-existent regulations and laws. 1209 N. Orange Street is one address in Delaware that has over 250,000 separate business entities using the same address."

"Why would three correctional officers be getting several thousand dollars a pop plus supposed scholarship funds from companies using this tactic?" Her eyes narrowed and a handful of popcorn stopped midway to her mouth.

"Corporations list the address in their articles of incorporation, and mail may even be received there. But it primarily works great for shell companies or for laundering money."

"Soooo, you think these are probably shell companies for laundering money or something else?"

"I think it's more than a coincidence."

Heath leaned forward with his elbows on his knees, his head down. "Have you ever heard of the Russian arms dealer known as the Merchant of Death?"

"I know he was charged with terrorism after a sting operation caught him. Why?"

"The Merchant of Death and international organized crime use Delaware's laws to incorporate shell companies expressly to launder money because they allow extreme secrecy. The corporations remain anonymous to the point that we don't know what country they operate from, with little or no information on who's behind them." He paused and looked directly into her eyes before continuing.

"I think it's a similar deal, in this case, maybe not to avoid corporate taxes, but to remain anonymous. This could mean our suspicions are on target about a bigger plan than setting up the Black Apostles for some crime or even trying to take them over. There isn't much we can do to track them, but we can see what we can find on them."

Juanita sent a prayer of thanks to the Virgin Mary that she didn't send the expose on the Philly cops yet. She would need all the facts and proof she could get before she called attention to herself.

"So, do we keep pressing forward?"

She took a deep breath. "Yes. Those companies must have other records somewhere if they're making payments. Keep digging. See if any of these companies linked to the correctional officers can be traced back to their respective banks and any records there passed our way."

Was she crazy? She was actually hunting what appeared to be powerful and ruthless people. She had this lurking sense, like a shadow relentlessly following her that this was bad all the way around and more people would get hurt. Maybe even Heath or herself. She had the urge to check the cars in the parking lot.

CHAPTER FIFTY

Malcom Alexander

Malcom left and was on the road out of Cyprus in a few short minutes. He continually checked in the rearview mirror. As a precaution, he doubled back around a few times to shake any tail. He didn't see any repeated vehicles, but there might be more than just the two agents he saw at the funeral. What if there was a team tailing him? He couldn't worry about that now; only do his best to avoid detection. Outside of town, he stopped to gas the four-wheel-drive SUV he borrowed from his cousin, and to get fast food to eat.

He continued his vigilance until he was alone on the rural roads for a stretch of a half hour. He had escaped the Bureau's agents rather too easily. Their presence was troubling, particularly after his superior's phone call. But he couldn't pin down why they were so interested in him suddenly.

Last night he had done internet research on the town, the only advance reconnaissance he could really do. He tried Google Earth, but the town was too small or too rural to be included. *Imagine that.* He found a teen's blog and Instagram photos of the town's various events, but it didn't help him with the layout of the town.

He finally found a church on the street where Elizabeth Grant was located and had been very helpful by supplying a town map on their website for folks coming from other towns for their Sunday services. Thanks to the church's basic town map, he knew exactly where he was going.

He arrived at the house in Cyprus, but there was no answer at the door. He slumped down in the ordinary appearing smoky-gray SUV parked across the street and waited. The gray blended in nicely with the many trucks in town. He was in no rush, and after Netty's warnings of Elizabeth being watched, some surveillance was a good idea.

As he waited he noticed the subtle signs of a lookout next door: the living room curtain's careful movement as somebody kept looking out and the occasional upstairs movement at a window to get a better view.

Roughly ten minutes passed when he observed a royal blue seventies era Mustang pull up and park in the gravel drive. He recognized Elizabeth from the newspaper clippings that Aunt Netty had included with her letter. He would give her a few minutes to get settled in before he went to the door again. Maybe he should avoid the lookout and approach the back door.

She was just getting out of the Mustang when a white passenger van barreled up behind her car and two men jumped out. They ran to her, clapped a hand over her mouth, and dragged her back to the van.

Malcom had to give her credit, she had gumption. She kicked one in the nuts and was about to pull the other's hair out when a rag, probably dosed with chloroform, was held over her nose and she went limp.

It was maybe twenty seconds from when the van pulled up until they sped away. He didn't have time to even get out of his truck. Malcom ducked down as the van sped off. Shock gripped him by the throat; the answer to Aunt Netty's murder had been abducted before his eyes.

He followed the van without a thought, allowing enough space to stay unobtrusive. Elizabeth was his connection to whatever got Aunt Netty killed and come hell or high water, he wasn't letting anything happen to her now.

Keeping his distance further back than usual because in small towns everybody's car was recognized, he followed the van into the rural outskirts. He was hyper-focused and all his training kicked into high gear. He only hoped he could contain the coil of lethal intent in his adrenaline, for these two had to be connected to Netty in some way.

After several minutes, they took a dirt road that meandered around in the woods. He hung back and proceeded slowly so they didn't see the dirt cloud from his vehicle. He leaned over, opened the glove box, and grabbed the .357 Magnum he had secured there and placed it on his lap.

He could see the ominous ruins of some old plantation through the foliage and parked. He quietly retrieved the FBI issue stun gun from behind the seat where he had stored it this morning before the funeral along with the gun holster and a forest camouflage jacket. The gun rested snug against his ribs on his left side and the stun gun tucked into a pocket of the jacket. The gun against his side was comforting as a backup if he needed it. It was stifling hot, but he would rather have the advantage of the camo than be cooler.

He took to the trees, moving carefully from the cover of one tree to the next. Drawing closer to the ruins, he could see three-story-tall fluted columns looming with heavily ornate Corinthian capitals, twenty of them, standing in a square like an Antebellum Stonehenge hidden in a mystical forest. A few of the looming columns still had decorative metal balustrades stretching across what was once the third story balcony.

There were the remains of an elegant wrought iron stair railing sweeping upward in a graceful curve, ending in open air. Closer to the ground, a few remnants of charred wood stairs were evidence of the fire that no doubt destroyed the home.

He was grateful for the daylight. By night this would be perfect for a vampire flick. It didn't bother him; he had faced scarier in his stint in the Green Beret Special Forces, but the daylight was still appreciated. There was no sign of others as he scanned the perimeter.

The men carried a groggy Elizabeth and propped her up against a

nine-foot-tall square base of one column. One man took out a hypodermic needle and quickly injected her, driving the plunger home
before Malcom knew what he was doing. He was still about fifteen
feet away, behind a large column facing the men's backs.

They slapped her and shook her, bringing her out of her sedated
haze enough to question her. He nearly forgot his training, for his
first reaction was to hit the man for treating a woman so roughly.
Malcom draped his extensive battle training around himself and
waited for them to tip their hand as to what this was all about, maybe
even what had gotten Aunt Netty murdered. He could use the stun
gun on one and disable the other quickly and efficiently, like he was
trained. But for now, he needed answers.

CHAPTER FIFTY-ONE

Elizabeth Grant

Elizabeth felt each slap and rough hands shaking her. Gulping air, she fought down a wave of panic. *What had happened to her?* She had been to the library and tracked down Cedric, Loralie's boyfriend.

She had sat in the park and mulled everything over, writing in her notebook, and then came back to Grans when… somebody grabbed her from behind. That was the last thing she remembered, and the sickeningly sweet odor she could still smell and taste.

Suddenly water was dumped on her head, she sputtered and coughed.

"Come on Princess, we ain't got all day."

"What… what do'ya want with me?" her weak voice a whisper as she forced her mouth to form the words.

"You're gonna talk, tell us what we wanna know and you can go back. Promise." His voice seemed familiar, but her mind wasn't working enough to pinpoint where she knew it from.

She opened her eyes a little, like looking through a slit. She saw two guys crowded around her, standing in scruffy weeds and grass. Her head drooped but was yanked up by her hair and she yelped in pain. The pain made it through the fog in her brain.

She could see a pockmarked face close to hers and smell his coffee laden breath. He seemed vaguely familiar, but she still couldn't wrap her mind around where.

Over the man's shoulder, she could see Loralie staring at her with fierce intensity. She wasn't transparent, but seemed solid, standing next to the base of a column. *Where the hell was she? Where had they taken her?*

Loralie flapped her hands, then bit down on a knuckle. She ran up and tried to pull the men away from her, but her hands went through them.

Elizabeth glanced around at the massive columns around her reaching to the sky, felt one against her back, cold and hard, and panic rose within her. She didn't have a clue where she was. She broke out in a cold sweat and her breathing sped up as a sliver of terror shot through her.

Even if she could somehow escape, she would be lost. She looked back at Loralie and realized she needed her. At that moment it didn't matter that seeing her wasn't logical, it was the only thing keeping her from losing her grip altogether.

Loralie signaled to watch her.

"We want it, no more playin' around. Where is it?"

She looked up into his sweating face, scrunched her eyebrows and shook her head. *Where is it... where is what? What would be valuable enough to do this?* Her mind couldn't seem to focus on more than a fleeting thought. If she didn't have an answer, would they kill her? She didn't want to die.

"We know about you. We know you came back for the information." He was so close she could see his nose hairs.

"What information? What do you know about me?" Her voice squeaked. She couldn't see Loralie, he was in the way. *Don't leave me, Loralie. Please don't leave me.* Loralie was the only *person* she knew here, and Elizabeth needed her.

"We know you have the traitor's information. We know it wasn't in Colorado, so it must be here. Tell me where it is, and this doesn't have to get ugly."

"What traitor? I don't know any traitor." Her mind was trying to catch up, wake up. *Can't. Focus.*

"It's no use, holdin' out on us." Anger crept into his voice.

Loralie replaced the man's face suddenly. She had never been this close before.

"Listen. Help is here. Hang on." Loralie pointed to a black man peeking around a large column. "I won't leave you. But don't shut me out anymore."

Then she had flashes of images in her mind, like little snippets of a memory. It was the nightmare, but more vivid. She could smell the night-blooming flowers and feel the sharp pain from a beating. There were men and a pock-marked teen boy. The images shifted to her visit of the plantation home and the man on the porch staring down at her. The images faded away and Loralie was still close. She tried to reach out and touch her, but she couldn't lift her hand.

Loralie moved to the second man, who was standing back a few feet. Her hands balled into fists, she took a deep breath and yelled into the man's ear, her face contorted with the effort.

Elizabeth couldn't hear it, but the man swatted at his ear like a fly tickled it. But he licked his lips and spoke.

"Heya, I think you drugged her too much. She don't look so good. Give her a chance to come around."

"What the hell would you know?" The pock-marked man stuck his head closer and starred into her half-open eyes. "Maybe she needs to get her blood pumping. I can help her with that." His hand grabbed her breast.

Oh dear God, no. Please not that. I'd rather die. Her eyes swept the area for Loralie, but found the dark-skinned man. He looked dangerous in his own right.

"Help me." Her scream had no fuel, barely louder than a sob.

The dark man raised his hand and shot something that struck her tormentor in the back. She registered it was a stun gun. Her questioner was no longer in her face but on the ground.

The other abductor was now fighting off an attack from what she hoped was a rescuer. She struggled to stand, maybe get in a kick or punch herself, only to land hard, face forward, legs weak. She dragged her head up to look at the two men fighting.

The second abductor was bulky and dressed with work boots and overalls, but moved fast and was swinging a vicious right hook at the newcomer's head. The black man barely dodged the fist, but in avoiding the blow he lost an angle to punch in return.

Her would-be rescuer swung around and landed a roundhouse kick to Farmer Joe's shoulder, followed by a few rabbit punches to his nose. The nose bled, but the guy ignored the potential gusher to tackle and wrestle her rescuer to the ground.

But, with a roll of his shoulder, the rescuer shifted and flipped Farmer Joe to the ground before Elizabeth or Farmer Joe could process how he had done it. In a smooth fluid motion of one hand, a zip-tie appeared and secured her second abductor's hands behind his back, then he zip-tied Mr. coffee-breath. He wasn't even breathing hard.

Then he advanced on Elizabeth, hands out to his side as if he were approaching a frightened dog that might bite. He carefully helped her to her wobbly knees and propped her against a column.

"How'd you find me?" Talking was getting easier, but her tongue felt too large for her mouth and slurred her words. Another glance at her two abductors on the ground and she blurted, "Who're you?" That was better than the sappy *my hero* that had threatened to escape her mouth.

She wanted to say how thankful she was, how he had saved her from every woman's worst nightmare, probably saved her life too. But as soon as she opened her mouth, tears threatened to spill over.

"FBI Agent Malcom Alexander. And you're Elizabeth Grant." He wiped his forehead with the back of his arm.

"Malcom Alex… How do I know that name?" She scrunched her forehead in thought. A motion caught her eye. Directly behind Agent Alexander stood Loralie and Madame Antoinette.

"I told you he could be trusted. He's a good man," said Antoinette, eyes sparkling. Flashes of a graduation appeared in her mind's eye, like a private movie. She saw the man standing before her, only younger, graduating in a suit with the FBI emblem on the wall behind the platform.

The image faded and Malcom stood before her. She knew it wasn't logical. Could the drug they gave her somehow heighten her visions?

She could see Loralie and Madame Antoinette as clearly as this man... plus about a dozen others with clothing dating from the plantation era to the 1950s.

For the first time, she could hear Loralie and Madam speaking to her, and somehow they could share memories directly to her mind.

Elizabeth looked into Malcom's eyes. "She's very proud of you, you're being an agent. Says you're a good man and I can trust you." The words just came tumbling out.

He smiled brightly.

"But who are all these other people?"

CHAPTER FIFTY-TWO

Rance Hunter

R ance slowly became conscious. He felt he was lying on a soft surface because he was comfortable. He had almost forgotten how that felt since his arrest and lockup through the trial. Then there was the smell of clean air with a hint of some exotic flower.

When that registered in his brain, he knew something was very wrong. He never smelled air so good in his life.

His eyes flew open. He was in a minimally furnished bedroom, no windows, overhead light, one wooden chair and his bed with a sheet and pillow. *How long had he been unconscious?*

The last thing he remembered was being on the prison work crew. He figured he could easily take the correctional officers guarding him before they could shoot him. At least it seemed like a good idea then. *What the fuck had happened? How the fucking hell did he end up here?*

This sure as hell wasn't the prison, and he vaguely remembered being in a vehicle of some sort. He moved to get up and found his hands and legs bound. He tested the knots in hopes he could muscle out of them, but not possible.

"Will we be ready in time? The General wants everything on schedule now that we got him." A nervous voice spoke. It sounded like it was on the other side of the bedroom door. Rance didn't recognize the voice.

"We got 'im under control, it's the other little problem running around that needs dealt with. My part is on track." *Younger guy from the voice, and cocky. Shouldn't be hard to take him out.*

He considered his situation, and he had only one course open; he had to get out of that door. On the other side of that door was probably a way to cut himself loose, at least. He could barely stand. He was wobbly on his feet beside the fact his feet were tied together. His legs were rubbery.

He hopped over to the door. To his surprise, the door flew open and in walked a muscled man, the cocky guy probably, in jeans and a tee shirt with a hypodermic needle. His eyes narrowed, and he leaped at Rance, but Rance was primed to get out.

He tried to lower his shoulder and ram the man who stood in the way of his freedom. His feet were tied too well, and he fell into the man. He felt the needle plunge hard into his bicep. *God damn it to fucking hell.*

His last conscious thought was of how he would kill Mister cocky with his bare hands, squeezing the breath out of him.

CHAPTER FIFTY-THREE

Juanita Alvarez

"Tell me you've some proof, that you know who has Hunter." Tito's voice had a tinge of urgency.

"Not exactly. We're tracking down leads, but I don't have a name or group yet." She tried to keep her voice steady despite her dreading this call.

Juanita was in her hotel room again after visiting more local spots and talking with residents. *Nothing new on that front.* It was up to the team following electronic crumbs to find out who or what was behind Hunter's prison break.

"This ain't no game and we're running outta time. You got maybe a day before retaliation could begin. That'll make getting people to talk harder." Restrained emotion crackled in his voice. That scared Juanita more than any words he said.

"We've got information, but mostly we're following computer trails that require time to access." She couldn't come right out and say they were hacking bank records in the off chance the phone call had uninvited listeners. No reason to give them something to exploit. Besides, she didn't want a gang of criminals to know she could arrange for that.

"You don't have much time, little missy. This blows up and we might not be so understanding. Get me a name, a who. Fast." Dial tone.

Juanita had a quaking deep inside. She now regretted ever meeting Tito in that café in Philly only a few days ago. What they had dug up suggested no rival gang involvement. It appeared to be somebody more sophisticated and structured from the information Max provided of a high-tech helicopter, which wasn't a good sign for the continued health of Heath and herself.

She focused on her notes from all the interviews she had done whether in the bar, at the press conference, at the local softball park with parents, and from scouring the local papers.

She still felt she needed to hold off reporting the real story – the meat she had, like proof that the Philadelphia home invasion and slaughter intentionally set up the gang and at least two local police officers colluded, that Rance Hunter should have been in high-security lockup but was on a low-security road clean-up crew instead and that there was a financial paper trail.

Nobody else had reported her stories. She even had how they were possibly all connected because of payments to the Philly cops and the prison correctional officers. She couldn't wait much longer to break the story.

Heath poked his head through the door between their rooms.

It slipped out before she could rein it in, "You look like hell. How much sleep've you gotten?" They had only been in town barely twenty hours and she had slept only an hour or two but suspected he had worked right through.

"I'm fine. I think we have something, maybe enough of a lead to follow."

"We need direction, some focus. I've run out of leads from interviews, and most of those came from that bar last night."

They settled into chairs. No popcorn this time.

"I've had two of our hacker volunteers following the money from both the correctional officer and the Philly cops."

"I thought that was a dead end along with thousands of other businesses using the same address." She rubbed her eyes.

"We found an associated address in Mississippi that has received mail and maintains a phone in the business name."

Maybe the people behind the shell company were too cocky believing their evasive tactics kept them protected, that they made a mistake, let their guard down – slipped up.

"You think we should go check this out?" She appreciated the layer of protection that the hacking provided.

"Nothing replaces footwork, getting out and talking to people face-to-face. Isn't that what you said?" He taunted.

"Of course, just verifying you think this is a solid lead." Was her voice a little high?

"We both know this is dangerous and we're walking the razor's edge. That's why we got the kid secured away from here. Caution is a good thing." Heath confirmed.

"But?" She held her breath.

"I've no skin in this game. If your spidey-senses are telling you we're in too deep, I'm okay with stopping the investigation." He reached over and held her hand in his, warm and comforting. For a fleeting moment, she wanted more comfort, wanted to let him kiss her and lose herself for a few moments. She gave his hand a squeeze and took her hand back.

"Honestly, we've been in too deep since we left Philly. I'm scared, but... I think we're the only ones who know as much as we do. The truth will be buried if we stop, and we don't even know how bad this can get."

Heath added, "We also don't know what the end game really is despite our theorizing, or how far the people involved will go to get their results."

Heath's computer pinged several times in a row. He rushed over and checked notices coming in, then turned, his brows furrowed.

"Things just got worse." His face paled.

"What? What is it? What happened?"

"Looks like the Los Angeles branch of the Black Apostles just made a hit against the Nuestra Familia. They killed twenty of them with a car bomb. Further violence is inevitable now."

"Tito thought we'd have another day. I just spoke to him and he hinted we didn't have much time, but not that anything was going down. Could be no patience, too trigger happy, or maybe a part of our suspected conspiracy is helping things along. How sure are they it really was the Black Apostles?"

Any doubts she had about continuing her investigation disappeared. They couldn't just walk away and let the violence escalate when they knew this was coordinated.

"Good question, but does it matter now? That train left the station and even proof it was a setup won't stop the backlash that is coming any moment from the other gang."

"God damn it," slipped out. She quickly made the sign of the cross. Now was probably a good time to get far away from Los Angeles.

CHAPTER FIFTY-FOUR

Malcom Alexander

Malcom joined Elizabeth in her little curtained space in the local clinic. There were only five beds in the emergency section, but it was probably plenty to handle farming or ranch accidents or the occasional bar-room brawl. It glinted with stainless steel and bright fluorescent lights everywhere, smelled of bleach, and the low roar of conversations shattered any rest. Elizabeth was still recovering from whatever her abductors had injected her with, although she seemed more aware now.

He had called the police to go collect the men he had tied up in the old plantation ruins. He felt getting Elizabeth medical attention was the priority.

She was still pale, her eyes occasionally unfocused. He wasn't related, so the nurses were reluctant to discuss her condition with him. So he waited and waited. The burnt orange visitor chair had to be a leftover from some torture practice, hard plastic that most certainly did not fit the body but rather caused back pain.

He sat in the torturous chair next to the bed, trying not to disturb Elizabeth whose eyes were closed. The privacy curtain was flung open. A law officer stood holding the curtain back, glanced his way then focused on the girl.

"Miss Elizabeth, I need to talk to you if you're up to it." For such a big man, his voice was gentle. He was reminiscent of a tough cowboy from old western reruns, only not as photogenic. His salt and pepper hair was in a severe crew cut that made the sharp planes of his face stand out.

Her eyes sprang open, wary with a hint of anxiety. Then she glanced around until she saw Malcom in the chair and took a breath, relaxing.

"Sheriff." She nodded her head once in acknowledgement.

"I… um. I got a call to pick up a couple hooligans who gave you a scare, but there was nobody out at the old Whitmore Plantation ruins." He looked at Malcom briefly again.

"It was no scare, they drugged me and I think they'd have killed me if it weren't for Mr. Alexander here helping me out." Her eyes stayed focused on the Sheriff.

He blinked a few times as if considering the validity of her statement, then looked Malcom over intensely before holding his hand out. Malcom had been scrutinizing the Sheriff just as blatantly since he walked in. "Much obliged for keeping my… our Miss Elizabeth safe. What can you tell me?"

"Two Caucasian men. One in his thirties wearing coveralls, about five-ten and one-ninety-five pounds, dark brown hair, and work boots. The second man was mid to late twenties, dark blonde hair, pockmarked face, about six foot, and two hundred pounds. No identification on either, no plates on the vehicle, no registration or insurance card in the glove box."

"Impressive description, you a cop?"

"Off duty FBI." Malcolm hadn't planned on being so visible, now he was under this sheriff's microscope.

"And you stepped in against two men for Miss Elizabeth here? Where're you from?"

"Jackson. Elizabeth's a friend of my aunt. I came to break the bad news of my aunt's death and witnessed her being abducted outside the house."

At the mention of Madame Antoinette's death, Elizabeth swallowed and tears welled in her eyes. Interesting. Malcom hadn't thought much about her seeing Aunt Netty's spirit and her asking about the other spirits she could see. But now he wondered if she understood or trusted her gift at all. Perhaps another reason Netty got involved. She had been a mentor to gifted young people all her life.

Sheriff Craig made a move toward Elizabeth but stopped. *There's a story here. Wonder what it is.*

"Now look, I appreciate your stepping in like you done. Really, I do. I'd like to get your statement and get you on your way." He was all business now.

"Can we speak outside?" Time to talk professional to professional.

"If it involves me, I should be included."

Malcom patted her hand, "Just need to develop a professional working relationship."

They met in the hallway outside the Emergency waiting area. The institutional gray walls cast a gloomy shadow over them. Malcom displayed his FBI shield, anticipating the request.

"Sheriff, I understand you wantin' to circle the wagons and deal with locals, not outsiders. But these men were locals; they knew those ruins, which aren't on a main drag or a tourist stop. They also had drugs to knock her out and then revive her. So your local boys have connections. I believe she's in danger, and I can help." He wasn't going soft on the Sheriff. Either he would work on the problem or sweep it under a rug.

Sheriff Craig's face paled as Malcom spoke. His brows furrowed together and his lips pressed tight and he slowly handed Malcom' badge back.

"Are you tellin' me I can't protect my own... citizens?" He swallowed hard.

"I'm sayin' I can assist. I can observe. I can be her personal protection." He didn't want to push too hard in case he needed this local badge or his knowledge, but he wasn't taking no for an answer.

"You know how that'll look round here? An... outsider hangin' around her?" He shuffled his feet and fiddled with his uniform cowboy hat.

Malcom recognized his attempts to dance around the real issue. Folks didn't want a black man spending so much time with her, no matter who that black man might be. "Does she have family who can stay with her? Father or brother maybe?"

"She's here from Denver, lookin' after her granny's place. Her mother kept who the father was to herself before runnin' off to the big city." He let out a sigh. "It isn't appropriate to have just anybody stayin' with her, the good folks would be livid." He took several breaths and rubbed his jaw. "I'll have the neighbors keep a watch and assign a patrol outside her house."

Sure, the good folk would be livid if *he* was too close to *her*. Anything more Malcom could say would likely insult the man. It was looking like he would use that camping gear he'd packed if he couldn't get through to the man.

"We both know that isn't enough. Two men abducted her in broad daylight, they got away, and they're locals from their knowin' an isolated place to take her. So they'll look like they belong and probably know most everybody in town. They won't raise any suspicions. If you want her safe, you need me."

He watched the Sheriff fret, concern etched his face. Malcom felt he was missing something; there was more between this man and Elizabeth Grant than a law officer's concern, even considering small town distrust of all outsiders or prejudice.

Could the sheriff have helped Elizabeth's abductors get away? He was the investigating officer from his own account. Was he displaying concern for Elizabeth, or for an unexpected snag in his plans in the form of FBI involvement?

He really was off duty, as he'd said. But his presence alone could be problematic if this man was involved in the abduction, or Netty's death. Even off duty, the FBI carried clout because they were never fully off duty.

"I have a huntin' cabin tucked away in the woods. Few know it exists. Just for a night or two, keep her safe while I investigate," he ground out, clearly hating the compromise.

"I'll take it."

CHAPTER FIFTY-FIVE

Rance Hunter

R ance Hunter came back to consciousness in a stark white room with bright lights in his face. The lights were in front of him, on stands, in a semi-circle, as if he were on a movie set and ready for his close-up. Wouldn't that be fucking unbelievable? But he doubted that would be the answer to this ordeal.

His wrists were strapped to the wooden chair he sat in, his feet similarly strapped to the chair legs. He couldn't distinguish much around him with the lights blinding him. How long had it been since his last meal? He was so hungry he wanted to eat anything, just anything.

"Why did your gang break you out of prison?" a voice behind one light in shadow asked in a monotone, as if he were reading a script.

"I don't know what the hell you're talking about. You know who broke me out? You did. I've been kidnapped and you sure as hell can't blame this on me or mine."

He recognized this was bad, maybe not the worst circumstances he'd ever been in, but sure as shit close. Maybe he could figure out what was happening and where in the goddamn hell he was, even what they wanted from him, if he kept them talking. He needed to know what he was up against.

What is your agenda towards the government?" Still reading from the script. If only he could cram that script down the guy's throat. He tried to look around at the room, but it was all murky shadows beyond the light stands, so he was lit up like Vegas at night, but he couldn't see them.

"You got this all wrong. I got nothing to do with the government, I got no agenda. I'm serving my time like I was sentenced when all hell breaks loose and I'm knocked out. Where the fucking hell have you taken me?" He was trying to keep cool, but he was woozy, hungry, and losing his limited patience.

"Why did your gang slaughter the family in Philadelphia?" Voice still monotone.

"What kind of shit talk is that? We didn't do that, had nothing to do with that family. We wouldn't do that to an innocent family. They were nothing to us. I'm telling you, we're innocent of that bull shit rap." He wanted to slam his fist, but couldn't even feel his fingers with his hands tied so tight.

"What is your agenda against the white people of this country?"

"You fucking shithead, clean out your ears. I'm a businessman making money. I don't give a shit about you unless you're trying to keep me down or cheat me. You want to talk about the white agenda against my people? How about against the Indians you all stole this land from? How about the other people of color you whites keep under your boot! You don't like I made money, that I can sit in the same country club or restaurant next to your daughter, do you?" He struggled against his restraints, wanted to get his hands on the man behind the voice.

Fucking A. He realized that this was what they wanted, for him to talk, for him to get angry, like some goddamned show for somebody's entertainment. Watch the gangbanger be shamed or humiliated. He wasn't talking anymore; he wasn't going to be made a fool.

"How big is your plot against the nation?"

He remained quiet. He wasn't gonna be baited anymore. There was movement to his left as a shadow moved behind him and shoved a needle in his neck. He quickly faded out again.

Dammit, he still didn't know where the fucking hell he was or what was going on. But he knew they were playing some game he didn't like.

"… good first session, maybe one or two more … "

He stored what was happening inside him, because when he got loose, he would get even. Thoughts of revenge faded to black.

CHAPTER FIFTY-SIX

Tito

Philadelphia had progressed from some demonstrations and riots to a city under siege. Violence accelerated, and it came from surprising sectors that attacked regularly but who normally were least likely to turn violent. Middle-aged and even more senior white folk were shooting up black places of business, restaurants, and neighborhoods. The death toll was up to one hundred and fifty-nine men, women, and children so far – more than the number killed at the Pentagon during the nine-eleven attacks.

Tito sat at a dark wood table covered with a linen tablecloth in the back of his prized four-star steak house and behind an antique screen, well out of view from the front of the operation and away from curious ears as he conducted a dinner meeting with his five gang managers of the various operating units about the situation.

The restaurant was cherry wood paneled with custom wine-red plush carpets and each fine linen covered dining table had high-backed leather chairs, fine china, and imported silverware. The clientele was high brow and primarily white, so they were safer here than their usual meeting places.

Tito's managers were uncomfortable with the multiple forks, china, and crystal glasses, but Tito enjoyed the civilized beauty.

"I don't know what to do with our street supplier brothas. If you black out there, it's open season. I recruited some white-bread boys to sell product and they're doing well." The lanky drug manager sank back into his yellow leather chair.

"How many of your boys in the hospital now?" Tito had to ask. He took being a leader seriously.

"Five, two may live. They got no insurance or shit. Who knew these middle-class whities could beat a man so brutally."

"Families?" Tito leaned forward.

"Mostly they have mothers depending on them and brothers or sisters. Only one was married." The thin but scrappy manager rubbed his eyes.

"We'll pay the hospital bills, their families sure can't."

Tito scanned each tense face that reflected hardship and hardened eyes. When other teens were having angst over high school peer pressure and dating, these kids were worried about getting shot from stray bullets.

"How about the stables?" Prostitution was like a stable of horses, after all.

"Same, same. White bitches all the rage and keeping the sista bitches off the streets cause I can't protect them right now." The stable manager glared, but he always glared.

"What about legit biz, how we making through?"

Tito had begun some businesses as his personal investments. They were separate from the gang operations, but occasionally he utilized them to aid one another. Thus, it was easier to have them in the same meeting.

"A few changes like everyone, shifting whites to more public jobs and the rest in kitchens or behind doors. Hurting the restaurants and furniture stores since every person had a role and now it's all fucked just to keep some out of sight. I may have to lay off people." Legit biz manager huffed like it was an inconvenience. He was chubby but had a college degree, when he couldn't get hired Tito offered him the job.

"Could be worse, could be like the studio." Tito reminded him.

"True, could be like the studio." Legit biz manager nodded.

The Philadelphia offices of the gang's Rap record label had been bombed with Molotov cocktails and were closed until it was safe to repair and reopen.

"Keep your people safe, even parents. This is when we take care of our own, no matter what. That's what gangs are supposed to be about." Most gangs acted like mean junkyard dogs that had marked their territory and reacted more out of whose cock was bigger.

The Black Apostles had nothing to prove, they were in business to make money and fucking with that would get a reaction. Of course, then there was Apache and Shark-tooth who were more about proving theirs was bigger and blacker.

"That's a big order." Stables manager ran a hand through his hair.

"I'm not suggesting, I'm telling you. If I hear one of yours was hurt or suffers when you could've helped them, you'll answer to me. Clear!"

The five sitting around him swallowed. *Clear.*

Mario, his assistant, had quietly approached and whispered in his ear, "News from L.A." He stood waiting for any orders.

"Listen up fuckheads, we got news." He motioned for Mario to tell them all.

"Apache made a move against the Nuestra Familia – a car bomb right outside one of their nightclubs before opening." Nobody spoke. Mario cleared his throat and continued. "Killed twenty, seriously injured more. Nuestra struck back, but Apache must've expected it and ambushed them. National Guard is being called in." Mario barely made it without stuttering.

"God damn the mother fucking asshole. His orders were to wait." Tito slammed a fist against the white tablecloth, causing the china to rattle. "He just started a goddamn war for no real reason."

"Maybe he knows something we don't?"

"That's what the meeting in Chicago was for. He had nothin' but some trash talkin'. He's proving his is bigger than Nuestra's, that's all. Stupid fuck." He took a deep breath and counted to ten.

"I need to talk with Mario, we're done for today. Stay close to your phones." Tito and Mario watched them file out the back of the restaurant.

"Well?" Tito raised an eyebrow.

"I haven't gotten through to Cenisa, she doesn't answer her phone, I don't dare leave a message." Mario looked at the floor.

"We've got to get her away from Apache before he finds out about us. I know he'll take our rivalry out on her." He never expected to care about another as he cared for her, and especially not with Apache's sister.

He cared about her, and didn't want to think what Apache would do to her if he found out she had been passing info on him, let alone to his rival. Both Apache and Tito wanted to be the next in line to head up national business for the gang.

He would have Cenisa by his side as he worked his way up the gang's hierarchy. He'd still fuck any piece of ass he wanted, but they would be good as a team. If Frank and Claire Underwood on the television show could work as a team in their power grab, so could he and Cenisa.

"I'll keep trying her cell, but what should I do if she doesn't answer?"

"Give her to the end of the day, if she doesn't answer we'll send somebody out there. Somebody Apache doesn't know." He wanted to punch somebody, anybody, even a wall. But he pushed the rage down. They hadn't killed that family, and they didn't break Hunter out of prison. It was like the world was spinning out of control.

CHAPTER FIFTY-SEVEN

Malcom Alexander

The one-room cabin was sparse but had everything necessary, including plumbing and a kitchen. Against the opposite wall of the kitchen were two twin beds and the couch that looked to be a pull-out bed. The couch and bedspreads were a yellow and black plaid; even the kitchen towel was the same plaid. As hunting cabins went, it was sufficient, as a safe house it was isolated but lacked high ground. They were surrounded by trees, which he didn't like, but it had only one road in or out that made it easier to defend, unless Elizabeth's attackers walked in through the woods.

Malcom could make it work, but he didn't trust the Sheriff's offering this cabin to them. He would rather nobody knew where he and Elizabeth were. But he was pushing his luck to hide her out since he was a stranger. Asking her to camp out would have been pushing his luck. She was surprisingly agreeable to staying hidden away in the woods with him.

Elizabeth shuffled in and sat on the couch, listless. Malcom suspected she was dealing with the emotional aftermath of the abduction since the drugs were supposed to be out of her system and she received a green light from the clinic.

"This is just temporary, but you'll be safe." He tried for a reassuring tone, which wasn't his usual. Hard-nosed had become his norm since joining the Bureau.

"I know I've been through a trauma, probably even have shock or PTSD. But, it worries me I feel so safe with a complete stranger based on a *vision*, even if you rescued me," she stated matter-of-factly.

He sat down next to her.

"How much do you understand about your gift?" He kept his voice even.

She released a sigh. "Gift? Madame Antoinette called it that too." They hadn't spoken about her death yet, and she didn't want to either. "I know next to nothing about it and I don't think it's a gift. More like a curse."

"Why a curse?"

"I thought I was crazy or maybe had a brain tumor. Grandfather thought I needed a demon exorcised, but I don't believe in that... anymore. My Uncle sent me to a shrink. I just know it makes no sense and has made me doubt myself since it began."

"There are people who would pay any amount to have your abilities, who work hard to develop their talents to have even a fraction of what you don't believe in or fear."

"People believe in little green aliens, doesn't make it true. I prefer proof, measurable solid facts rather than fantasy or superstition." He noted her voice displayed no passion in the statement. He couldn't fault her. Her family and her own worry had hurt her deeply, but it might make her stronger in the long run. He chose to believe the latter.

"I sense a 'but' in what you're sayin'." He waited as she glanced around the cabin, showing no real interest. When she didn't reply he continued, "But... you've seen things you can't just dismiss. But it doesn't seem bad or wrong—just unexplainable?" He helped her out, a little nudge to get her talking to him.

"But... I like seeing Loralie. I miss her so much. But it scares the hell out of me. What if it's just my imagination and I'm delusional?"

"Seems to me delusional people are happy in their delusions. You aren't happy with this. What if it's real?"

She swallowed and her worried eyes studied him. "You deal with hard reality as an FBI agent every day. You see crimes, deal with criminals, solve how they did the crimes, and even why. Yet, you believe in visions? How is that possible?"

"Madame Antoinette, my Aunt Netty, was immersed in that world of visions, miracles, oracle cards, herbs, crystals, and spells while being practical and rational. I grew up witnessing unexplained events almost every day. The two can exist side-by-side."

He reached over and patted her hand that was twisting the hem of her tee shirt into a knot.

"I have a feelin' you aren't always practical or rational." He smiled his little-used mischievous smile. "I bet you've done crazy things a time or two when the rational you was against it." He winked.

Geez, he hadn't winked at a woman since he joined the Bureau. He was out of practice. It didn't hurt that she was lovely in that wholesome, fresh-faced way. If it were under any other circumstances … well, it wasn't. Not to brag, but he was in shape and didn't spend a night alone if he didn't want to, so if a little charm and flirting could get him a step closer to Netty's killer then he would use it.

She smiled a lopsided, shy smirk. "It's called the college experience. And it wasn't that crazy." She scoffed, dismissing whatever memory had sprung to mind.

"Let me be the judge of that young lady. After all, I have the experience with the weird and wild. It's called the FBI experience." He smiled brighter. She was relaxing with him, and he needed that.

"It was just a party… you know college parties."

"Must've been some party. Strippers? Togas? No Frat boys, I hope." That's the last thing she needed was the rape merry-go-round of frat parties.

"It was nothing, just a little Goth party."

"Oh, I see. You liked all the black leather, chains, and dog collars. Did you assume a persona? Black highheeled boots, maybe a whip!" She was turning bright red as he chuckled. "Did you drink alcohol and let a bad boy vampire bite your neck, maybe even more?" Her hand shielded her eyes for a moment.

"I just wanted to forget everything for a while, so I went where nobody I knew would be. For a few hours I was in another reality."

She was too easy to read. He now understood this young woman was in way over her head with something and Aunt Netty tried to help her and it got her killed. His smile dimmed only slightly. He didn't sense any subterfuge or evasion. Fear and confusion in abundance, though.

She finally let her hand drop. "It must seem silly, a Goth party or being afraid of ghosts when you've probably seen far worse."

"I've seen plenty. Did a stint as Green Beret in hostile areas, helped capture a serial killer and a few bank robbers with the Bureau." His smile vanished. "I think you're somehow in the middle of why somebody killed my Aunt Netty and I'm here to find who did it."

"Me? Involved in her death!" Her eyes flashed anger, and a dose of pain.

"Let me explain a few things. My aunt sent me a letter about you. How she hoped to help you and felt you were in such danger that she would be killed. She saw her own death, okay. She had *the sight*. But she tried to help you, anyway. So you need to tell me everythin' you know about your abduction and why they took you."

Her mouth fell open, "She knew …?" Her shoulders seemed to cave in around her heart. "She warned me, told me I was in danger and should leave. I thought she was kind but – I thought it was crazy talk. Why would she drive all that way knowing it would kill her?" Her eyes were swimming in unshed tears as she shook her head.

"Because that's who she was. She'd never have forgiven herself if she didn't help you, and she was uniquely qualified to give you guidance on your gift." His eyes were getting misty. He thrust his shoulders back and cleared his throat. "Now, what're you involved in?"

"You were there, you heard the guys who grabbed me. I don't have a clue what they were talking about. I know next to nothing about your aunt. She came to visit me and it was the first time I ever laid eyes on her." Her voice was stronger. She assumed he was blaming her, and that was okay for now.

"What did she say to you?"

"She said, she said my missing best friend is dead and worried about me. That I'm in danger, which I thought was… Well I thought it was flat ludicrous." She folded her arms and glared.

"She drove hours just to tell you that? Really!" He was pushing her, but he didn't have time to be nice. Netty's touch he had experienced at the funeral was nothing compared to the slap to his head he felt now. *Not stopping 'til I get some answers,* he mentally shouted.

"She wanted me to leave, to go home. *Me, in danger.*" Her voice lost its volume, deflating. "Did your warning me really get you killed?" She spoke to a spot just over his right shoulder, around the direction his invisible head slap had come from.

"She knew it was dangerous and it would lead to her death, but she didn't know what it was about. You know something, saw something, have something," he stated. He wanted to turn and look for Netty, but he'd never had that talent himself.

She avoided his eyes, looking anywhere but directly at him.

"You're not going anywhere, and I don't have time to build a rapport or swap childhood memories. Those guys who grabbed you were likely locals and now you're a big problem 'cause a police report has been filed. They'll be lookin' for you." At least he thought there was a report. He still didn't trust the Sheriff, even if this was his cabin. There was something more to him, more about Elizabeth and the Sheriff.

"I found Loralie's old diary in the treehouse we played in as kids." She cleared her throat and twisted the hem of her tee shirt again. "It seems insignificant, I know. Thing is, there was a small notebook tucked into the diary that belonged to some guy." She glanced at him, but looked down again. "I read in the old papers at the library dated the summer Loralie went missing that the same guy was shot in the head… execution style, out by the train tracks. I don't know why his stuff is in her diary."

She grew quiet and avoided looking at him again.

"You'd make a terrible liar. I can tell there's more, so just get on with it." He gave his voice an edge.

She grabbed her purse and took out a new notebook that couldn't be the dead guy's, flipped to a page and continued. "Loralie's boyfriend from that summer just told me this morning she was supposed to give that notebook to somebody when she went to Jackson for her class at the university."

Oh hell, she had been asking questions and keeping a record. She probably hadn't been very discreet about it either. Could this all be over a teen girl's disappearance, or more likely her well-hidden murder? Netty got killed because she helped with an unofficial cold case?

"Where's the notebook and diary now?" This might be something, or it might not. But so far, it was all he had.

"I hid it at Gran's house before I left for the library."

"Tell me where exactly you hid them. I need to see them for myself if they're even still there." He held out his hand. "House keys, please."

"While I'm telling you everything, I had a dream about that gang member who broke out of prison. You were in the dream too." She stared at him.

Nothing in his growing up with Aunt Netty, his time with the Green Berets, or working in the Bureau had prepared him for that revelation.

CHAPTER FIFTY-EIGHT

The General

"How in hellfire did this happen?" The person in charge of surveillance of Elizabeth, good ole neighbor Hollis Picket and former Sheriff, was just now telling him of the events in the past several hours.

"Whose shit-for-brains idea was it to abduct her? Do you have any idea how this just blew up in your faces!" He had to stop and take several breaths before his head exploded. How could anybody be so stupid to tip their hand?

"Now hold your horses. It would've worked if that stranger hadn't played hero. She would've talked, told us where it is, what she knew." Hollis Picket's defensive voice only irritated the General more over the phone.

"Did it ever occur to you that until now she may not have realized she had somethin' important, that she may have thought it insignificant?" This was a perfect example of why micro-managers existed. *Jesus, they can't think strategically or consider the bigger picture.* He let out a long-suffering sigh. None of what he said was true. Noah's notes were hidden, and you didn't hide things that were nothing.

"Who's the hero that came to her rescue?"

"Black guy, says he's related to a friend of hers who died and just came to break the news to her. I'm tryin' to get more on him." That's all he had?

Oh, the incompetence. Hollis didn't even get the information from Elizabeth's little nigger friend before he killed her. And he lived right next door to Elizabeth's grandma's house. How hard was it to just watch and report?

"I'll be comin' down personally, with Hunter's part in our plan nearly completed I can't afford any more cluster fucks. I'll deal with you when I arrive." He got up and paced his home office, his feet cushioned by the thick Oriental rug.

He wasn't sure how he would punish this imbecile member. He had proven to be invaluable in the past, tipping them off about Noah Aarons slippin' something to that dumb girl. They wouldn't have known where to look for the leak if this member hadn't been so paranoid and followed the turncoat.

He grabbed his serpentine bladed dagger and threw it at the picture of the President on the wall. The thud as it penetrated the President's right eye and twang of the wiggling handle never got old.

It occurred to him that all these years he had been waiting and watching every aspect of little Elizabeth Grant's life, waiting to grab Noah's evidence, but perhaps now he was liberated from all that. This botched interrogation may have pushed the issue so he could just kill her. Be done with it.

Even if she had Noah's information and had even a clue what it all meant, she hadn't done anything with it all these years. Chances were good she didn't think it was real, maybe thought a delusional person wrote it. After all, who would believe a small town yokel had uncovered a plot to take over the government? He *saw it as taking the country back, restoring its glory and greatness. This work had begun over a century ago by his predecessors, and he was about to usher it in. So why did he still hesitate to kill her?*

CHAPTER FIFTY-NINE

Juanita Alvarez

Juanita hung up from Tito. She wasn't happy with him. But this was what happened when you played ball with a gang. *Damn it, why must she save his freaking girlfriend for him? Wasn't that his job?*

"So, we're leaving to check out that address where the payments are coming from?" Heath turned from his laptop to face her. "What's wrong?" His brows furrowed. He could read her moods and inner turmoil too well.

She let out a sigh, "Sure, absolutely. After we pick up Tito's girlfriend and give her a ride on the plane to safety."

"I don't like the sound of that. Where is his girlfriend that she needs safety with us?" He stared at Juanita and she felt like a bug being scrutinized.

"Where is the last place on the West Coast either of us wants to be? That's right, we get an all expenses paid trip to rioting Los Angeles." She scrubbed her hands over her face. "If all goes as planned, we'll pick up Cenisa at a designated meet and we all drive to the plane at a small airport and fly out of the ticking-time-bomb of a city."

"I don't suppose we have any choice in the matter?"

"Nope, not really. The car with driver will pick us up tonight to drive us to LA so we'll be arriving in the early morning hours to gather Cenisa."

"I thought my life was complicated. You think the guy could pick a girlfriend closer to home?" He shook his head in jest, but his jaw was clenched tight.

She made no comment on that remark. She didn't want to tell geek boy that Cenisa was the sister of Tito's biggest enemy in the Apostles. She wished she didn't know.

CHAPTER SIXTY

Elizabeth Grant

lizabeth had dozed off while sitting in the dining chair, her head rested against her arms on the table. She was startled awake by a voice. His voice. They had snuck into Gran's house through the back to retrieve Loralie's diary and Noah's notebook, putting the cherry on top of the worst day of her life. It beat out the day Loralie disappeared even.

She wasn't sure about this guy. Yeah, he saved her from kidnappers, but he had also taken over her life. Sure, she wanted to be safe, but not hidden away in the middle of the woods. She felt even more isolated and alone than ever before in her life.

She openly studied him. She was beyond pleasantries and manners, just like he was. He was handsome, still boyish in looks, and had that charm she glimpsed that he turned on when it served him. She bet he probably did well in the FBI. People would open up to his baby face and criminals would underestimate him. He was probably younger than he appeared too.

"How did you get this?" He repeated, indicating Noah's notebook. The glimpse of charm, along with his smile, had disappeared hours ago, replaced by the agent... with a capital "A."

She told him the story of climbing up to the old tree house and finding it with Loralie's Diary in their old hiding place. She caressed Loralie's diary, her emotions still close to the surface after her abduction ordeal.

"If I'm right, I think this guy Noah became an FBI informant from inside some organization." He looked up from the yellowed notebook and studied her. She blinked her watery eyes.

"But you know nothin' about this guy other than he was killed? Why do you think this has anythin' to do with you?" He was digging again. He was relentless, and she was so tired.

"This is the only thing I've discovered that might explain what's happening. I... I keep thinking this is part of Loralie's disappearance, it's more than a coincidence finding it with her diary and his murder."

"My aunt thought you were in danger, what else did she say to you? Think back, what were her first words to you?"

She thought back to that early morning knock on the door. "She said she'd driven through the night to see me, and she had to talk to me about Loralie. Loralie believed I was in danger and she wanted me to go back to Denver." She waited while he stared at her, his eyes narrowed.

He then glanced around the room as if looking for something and said "Well Netty, can I get a confirmation her kidnappin' is connected to Loralie or not?" He waited a few seconds.

Elizabeth could see Madame Antoinette slap the back of his head. "Well, I guess that is one lead, we know this has somethin' to do with your missin' Loralie." He smiled and rubbed the back of his head. He could actually feel her. That was unsettling. She didn't want to feel the touch of dead hands; it was bad enough seeing them.

"Do you see her too?" It flew out.

"I sense her only, a touch or sensation mostly, which is probably why she keeps smackin' me." He flipped through the pages of Noah's notebook, distracted. "I understand Loralie isn't just missin', but dead and you see her as well."

She looked behind his shoulder where Madame Antoinette stood and then over by the door to Loralie pacing. Since the drugging, she could see them both more clearly. When she asked at the hospital if the drugs could cause her to hallucinate they had said no. So, instead of this "gift" going away it was getting stronger.

She rubbed her eyes and yawned. Was this his interview technique, keep the person awake and exhausted so they spill their guts? She had endured one of the roughest days she could remember in terms of sheer physical and emotional stress. Her nerves were frayed and she could tell she needed down time. She wanted sleep, desperately.

"I will answer your questions if you cut to the chase of what you really want to know and I can get uninterrupted sleep. Deal?"

"Were you and Loralie involved in anythin', even on a small scale, that got out of hand? Sell any drugs, even just weed maybe... maybe she got involved with a guy sellin' who started to snitch?" Loralie materialized next to Malcom and yelled in his ear. He swatted at it like a mosquito buzzing him.

She couldn't contain her laughter, and even knowing it was her tension finding a release, she kept laughing until tears came down her face. Seeing Madame Antoinette slap him on the back of the head and Loralie yell in his ear didn't help. She wiped her tears and shook her head.

"No. Hell no. Maybe that made both of us unpopular. Loralie had too much at stake. She had the weight of her family on her shoulders. She was going to get them all a better life, and she always knew it would be hard work. By high school, she was focused. I didn't have the drive she did, but then I didn't have others depending on me." She stood up with the assistance of the table to steady herself. She didn't mention Jeremiah's dabbling in weed. That wasn't the right trail to follow.

"She was one of those people that knew exactly what she wanted, what she had to do to achieve it, and was committed to making it happen. Nothing was getting in her way... until somebody killed her." There, she said it. It made it so final to say the words.

She stumbled over to one of the twin beds and flopped on it, not even bothering with her shoes. She glimpsed Malcom beginning to read Loralie's diary as she faded into sleep.

CHAPTER SIXTY-ONE

Juanita Alvarez

The sun was just lighting the sky in Los Angeles. The stretch limousine stopped. Juanita was vaguely aware of the change, but she had finally fallen asleep. She didn't even care that Heath was holding her as they slept.

The driver rapped on the window divider. She sat upright and opened her eyes enough to use the intercom.

"Yeah?" Her eyes felt like the sands of the Mohave had pummeled her eyeballs.

"The meet location is down the street. It looks quiet."

She looked behind them and in the distance was evidence of a burnt-out shell of a car and some smashed windows next to a string of shops with broken display windows. But looking forward was entirely different.

Several tall, expensive looking hotel buildings and a sprinkling of palm trees lined the clean street in front of her. It felt like vacation dreams and business deals in the making, a heady combination. The armed guards in front of the hotels were off-putting.

Los Angeles covered more land than even New York City, which had built up not out, so some areas of LA might survive unscathed from the violence. Plus, the violence was between Apostles and

Nuestra so far. She hoped to be long gone before it spread like a plague throughout the city.

She glanced at her watch. Five minutes to the scheduled meet. Juanita was hoping this would be fast. Drive up to Cenisa, open the door, she gets in, and we all drive to the airport. No problem.

A black gal walked out to the sidewalk a block down from them. She had a loud suitcase with zebra print and red trim. She wore a zebra print jump suit with a halter-top barely keeping the goods tucked inside. Her auburn slick bob-cut hair was more pulp fiction than gang chic.

"That must be her. Let's get this over with." Heath's husky morning voice spoke next to her. She asked the chauffeur to drive to the zebra print parade waiting for them. The car had just stopped when a black man with tattooed muscles appeared, grabbed the zebra print woman's arm and took his fist to her face. She crumpled to the sidewalk. *That must be Tito's enemy, Apache.*

She immediately hated him. Not because he was Tito's rival, she had no loyalty to any gang member. But he had hit a woman with his fist. That was never acceptable behavior. He was a brute who assaulted a woman who couldn't protect herself or even run; she had platform shoes adding a good five inches to her skinny height. There was no running in those.

Juanita was out the door before Heath or the driver knew what she was doing. She had her cell phone and was taking pictures while screaming at him.

"You fucking Neanderthal, I got video of you attacking this woman." Maybe he wouldn't notice her hand quaking.

The driver jumped out his door and hustled around to the sidewalk while Heath was climbing out of the vehicle.

"Bitch, watch who you talkin' to 'fore I put you in your place. Believe me, cunt. I'll make you regret you're alive when I'm done." He looked at the driver, a good six-foot tall and nearly as wide with his arms hanging out like a bodybuilder, then the lanky blond Heath scrambling out of the car. "You can get back in the car and drive away while I deal with my property here."

His *property* took her ring-covered fist and socked him in the balls. Hmmm, the zebra-woman wasn't entirely defenseless. His breath rushed out, but he didn't show any pain. Uh oh, she had just swatted the bear in his sensitive bits and from his face turning red and his eyes practically bulging out, rage was his next stop.

Juanita guessed they would be lucky to be alive when this was all over. *Damn, she should've kissed Heath at least once before this story killed them both.*

The driver withdrew two black handguns, one gun for each hand. Apache had drawn a gun too. Juanita stood still, and the scene went into slow motion. She could feel sweat dripping from her forehead.

"You can't out-shoot me and you're dead in a micro-second." The driver called out, emotionless and lethal, as if he was at a shooting competition and he couldn't lose.

Juanita slowly helped Cenisa to stand. Her nose was bloody, but that could wait. She wobbled but stayed upright and considering the heels she was perched atop that was a miracle in itself. They inched to the open car door, every second feeling like an hour, moving around behind the driver with care to not get between him and Apache.

Heath followed with the garish luggage and flung the bag, Cenisa jumped in after the bag. Both Juanita and Heath blocked the door and watched.

The driver decided he was done with the standoff and shot Apache in the arm holding the gun, then ran around and jumped behind the wheel. Heath shoved Juanita in and jumped in to shield her. The door slammed shut from the power of the car jumping from standstill to sixty in five seconds.

"What in the hell were you doing? He could've killed you, Nita!" Heath yelled, then held her face in his hands and kissed her. A full contact, toe-curling kiss she would remember as long as she lived. It changed everything, and yet it changed nothing.

"Get a room." They both stopped and glared at zebra print woman.

"What? You can't wait until I'm done with my near-death experience." She was quaking and held her face where he took his fist to her while staring at the floor.

CHAPTER SIXTY-TWO

Malcom Alexander

Malcom was making coffee, his battle-ready dark bitter coffee. The summer sun was just coming up and the woods around the cabin were full of birds singing. Best damn alarm system around, they would stop if an intruder came near. He watched the sunrise through the trees and even saw a family of deer wandering past.

He had stayed up all night going through Noah's notebook and Loralie's diary, broken by random patrols around the outside. The picture he had pieced together from the two written records was disturbing.

He wasn't looking forward to waking Elizabeth and breaking this to her. He was still grappling with the last entry Loralie had made; it had knocked him for a loop that he was still wrestling with even now.

He also knew Netty was frustrated with him. After Elizabeth had fallen into a deep sleep, he finally found release for his grief and cried. He missed her with every breath. He hadn't embellished when he called her his bonus mom. He wished he could just hug her and talk with her one more time.

He could tell those head slaps were her telling him she believed in Elizabeth was innocent and didn't appreciate his needling or questioning her. But Elizabeth could see Netty, and he wanted to see her smile and hear her voice like she could.

He had opened cupboards until he found a cooking pan to cook up a hearty breakfast with all the fixings. He had pushed Elizabeth yesterday. She needed more sleep, and they both needed solid nourishment for the day ahead of them. He sensed it would be another long-ass day.

He made pancake batter from a mix. Maybe his time in Army Special Forces and the Bureau had jaded him. Time was he would have accepted Netty's instincts on a person without question. That was before witnessing seemingly innocent girls and women deceive or manipulate, before witnessing children gun somebody down, and before Netty was murdered. But, he was accepting that Elizabeth Grant really was swept up in something she knew nothing about while trying to understand her gift.

Malcom sighed as he broke eggs with one hand into a bowl and whisked them, diced onions and tomatoes for the eggs, then started the bacon on the griddle pan. He was making enough for three; he suspected the Sheriff would come by this morning. That was another puzzle. He knew there was something about the sheriff and Elizabeth, but she seemed oblivious. He had a few suspicions and hoped to confront the law man about them.

He set the bacon on a plate lined with paper towels and began the pancakes while he drank more coffee. He moved efficiently, used to cooking for himself. Something his mother had insisted he learn and told him often as a teen that a woman would appreciate his cooking someday. He was still waiting for that woman and that day. Cooking skills didn't make up for the demands of his job.

The stove was on low to keep the pancakes and bacon warm while he quickly set the small table and cooked the scrambled eggs and made toast. Everything was ready and waking the near comatose Elizabeth couldn't wait any longer.

Sure, he could be nicer about it, but he needed to be focused on Netty's murder – not some girl, even if she appealed to his damsel-in-distress weak spot. Oh, he was aware he had the penchant to save distressed damsels. Both his mother and Netty had chided him regularly over it.

He bent down next to Elizabeth's ear and tried calling her name, no response. The birds quieted, and a car approached on the dirt trail. Malcom raced to the window and verified it was the sheriff, alone.

Malcom went over to the triangle dinner bell that hung next to a window and rang the bell. Even with the loud din of the triangle, Elizabeth barely cracked her eyes and looked over at him.

"Sheriff's here and breakfast is ready. Figured you'd want to clean up and get some food before it's all gone. I guarantee we can eat all this ourselves." He meant to be pleasant, but it wasn't coming out of his mouth that way.

She shuffled into the one-and-only compact bathroom and water ran.

The sheriff knocked and entered without waiting to be let in. =His place – his rules, Malcom figured. Jake Craig looked around the room and noticed only one bed had been slept in. He turned his gaze to Malcom and raised a questioning eyebrow. *Should have figured that's what he's worried about.*

Elizabeth came out of the bathroom with her rumpled clothes and bleary eyes.

"Elizabeth, please tell your local law officer why only one bed has been slept in, not two."

She looked at the sheriff and then at the other bed.

"You," pointing to the sheriff, "nothing happened between us. Not that it's any of your business." Then she turned and pointed at Malcom. "And you, I take it you didn't even try to get some sleep. Just how safe will I be when you fall over from exhaustion?" She crossed her arms and stared.

"I don't plan to make it a habit, okay?" She had a valid point, so he had no real defense.

"You take after your mother when you're mad, ya know that?" The hint of a smile tugged at the corners of Sheriff Craig's mouth.

"Guess I never really thought that you probably knew my mom. She doesn't talk much about growing up here, other than she had a good childhood, but she didn't want to live here anymore." Elizabeth shrugged, then sat down and piled food on her plate.

Apparently, she didn't believe in small amounts of food for appearance's sake. Malcom smiled at her honest hunger for the food he had cooked. The sheriff's eyes were downcast. So, the sheriff grew up with her mother, *interesting.*

"Damn, this is good." She marveled after a bite of bacon and pancake. She surveyed him openly and nodded. "I don't see a ring. How can a good-looking guy like you, who cooks to boot, not be snatched up?"

"That's inappropriate talk from a lady," the sheriff huffed. His comment was more interesting than his own embarrassment over the comment. Malcom's theory about the connection between the Sheriff and Elizabeth was looking more likely with each passing moment. Maybe he should just confront this local lawman and see if he had figured this out right.

Elizabeth answered easily, oblivious to the sheriff's awkwardness. "He saved my life and has taken to guarding me, whether I like it or not. So, I guess I get to abuse the situation a bit. Besides, not enough coffee yet," she said before a forkful of eggs followed with a swallow of coffee.

"Sheriff, I made plenty, so sit and dish some up." He redirected the conversation, hoping to avoid answering her original question. His mother kept harping on the same topic of his lack of a special woman in his life.

"Seeing as how you've made plenty, I'll accept the offer. Thank ya." You didn't have to ask the sheriff twice. He rested his hat on a side table and loaded up a plate.

After a few silent moments, Sheriff Craig waded into the conversation pool again, "Good to see you eating more than some yogurt and fruit, Miss Elizabeth."

"I barely ate anything yesterday, and it's caught up with me. I'm famished."

They ate in silence, surveying each other. The sheriff mostly watched Elizabeth when she wouldn't notice. Occasionally her eyes would look around as if she needed an escape route. He finished and continued to observe their discomfort.

Malcom had to mention the ground rules again, "The plan is still the same. Stay inside and out of sight unless I'm with you. No solitary walks until we know you're safe." At this, the sheriff bristled.

"Just how long are ya plannin' on playin' bodyguard? Surely ya got a job waiting for you back at the Bureau. I'm plenty capable of ensurin' her safety." His jaw was set.

Elizabeth leaned in a bit for his reply, eyebrows crinkled.

"Sheriff, how bout we discuss this outside." He looked the man in the eyes, daring him to talk in front of Elizabeth.

"Sure, I'm as full as a tick' anyway."

They stood up from the table as one and met each other just outside the cabin. Door closed.

"She doesn't know, does she?" He decided to get it over with. "You claimed her mother decided not to tell her about her father."

"No, she doesn't know. And it's gonna stay that way, too."

CHAPTER SIXTY-THREE

Elizabeth Grant

Elizabeth watched Malcom and the sheriff go outside and let her breath out. It was like a couple of dogs circling each other. *How the hell did she end up in the middle of this?*

She didn't trust the sheriff; something wasn't on the level with that guy. She didn't know Malcom enough to trust him completely either, unless she accepted the recommendation of a ghost. That was still hard to go along with.

She cleared the dishes and washed them in the sink, glancing out the window behind her at them talking. They were stiff-backed and the sheriff's arms were crossed. *Was this what bantam roosters sizing each other up were like?*

She let out a sigh. She hadn't processed everything that had happened to her. Since she had been abducted and drugged, she could see not only Loralie and Madame Antoinette clearly, but others too wherever she went. The hospital had been the worst, with scores of people who died in accidents or nasty fights.

This cabin only had one resident apparition, a thirty-something guy with a beard, ball cap, an orange hunter's vest, and a gunshot through his gut. No blood. *Thank God for that small mercy.*

Finished with the few dishes, she looked around for the diary and notebook. They were tucked in her purse where Malcom must have put them. She didn't want to lose that diary. Even though she could see Loralie's spirit regularly at the moment, having her handwritten record of her last months made her feel closer. After this was over, she would turn it over to Loralie's mom.

She left the diary where it was, not ready to have the sheriff ask about it. Maybe she was wrong, but she couldn't stop thinking that everything tied back to Loralie's last summer and death, like a persistent whisper in the recesses of her mind.

Still digging up bones.

Malcom returned, softly shutting the door, but the sheriff drove off.

"So, what do I do now? I can't keep hiding, you know," she ventured as he sat at the table.

"We have to talk now." He was scowling, and she wondered if she had caused it. "I found somethin' in your friend's diary that… well, it concerns me."

"You're kinda scaring me." She sat at the table with the remains of breakfast.

"Well now, it could be nothin'. But, I figure its best if we tackle this together since you're already in danger without even understandin' why." He watched her, probably waiting for a reaction.

"Sure, okay. I'd like to understand what the hell is happening. Mostly I want it to stop. I suppose we have to figure this out to know how to stop it." What she really wanted to say was, "isn't it enough I'm never alone anymore, what with seeing Loralie and his aunt plus any other spirit in the vicinity, shouldn't that be enough to handle in a lifetime?" But she couldn't say that. She still owed Loralie. But, after the kidnapping yesterday, she wondered when she would feel she had paid that debt. Maybe when Loralie's killer got justice, she would be relieved of the debt.

"Have you tried to just ask Loralie what happened to her?" His voice was soft for the first time since she met him.

"It's only been while they drugged me during the kidnapping that I could even hear them at all, and not since the drug wore off. If Loralie didn't tell your aunt, then I don't know if she understands what happened to her." She leaned back into the wooden chair and pushed away from the table.

Netty and Loralie had listened carefully, Loralie nodded and lifted one shoulder in a *sorry* gesture.

"Here's the thing," he took a deep breath and placed his palms down on the table as if he was laying his cards out. "I think you may be right about everythin' – Netty's death and your kidnappin' – tyin' back to Loralie's disappearance... er, death. But I need to know how you're involved in this besides seeing her spirit." He stared her in the eyes until she looked away.

"I... um... I've never really told anyone the whole story. My family didn't know what to do with me, I guess." That came out all wrong. His brows shot up at that, but he remained quiet.

"It all began seven years ago... " She shared what she had been through since seeing Loralie's spirit the first time that summer. It took an hour and then he asked questions, clarifying points. They finished the rest of the coffee laying bare all her long held secrets about her gift and seeing Loralie over the years.

After the first few minutes, both Loralie and Madame Antoinette gave their thumbs up and faded out. Even though seeing them made her nervous, she felt uneasy to be truly alone while confessing all to this man.

She felt a burden, like a heavy backpack full of rocks, removed when she was done. He didn't react like she had come to expect over the years.

"Look, I certainly understand why you've hidden this all these years. I think we're past your runnin' back to Denver as a safe alternative. Whoever is behind this doesn't seem likely to stop now." The determination she saw in his eyes and the clench of his jaw told her he was going to hunt down who killed his aunt no matter what. Hopefully, that would also include Loralie's killer.

"I never thought seriously about turning tail and leaving... until getting kidnapped." She shivered at the memory of being drugged, completely incapacitated and vulnerable.

"Well, I found somethin' in her diary that shook me a fair bit." He left the table and stood at the front window before continuing.

"Her boyfriend was correct; she was supposed to take Noah's notebook to an FBI agent." He took several breaths before coming to some decision and continuing. "She even mentions the agent's name, Siesbolt, Agent Siesbolt of the Jackson office. Who now happens to be a Special Supervisory Agent and my boss."

He turned from the window and watched her.

"That's a good thing, right? He'll believe you and maybe this can be handled by the FBI." He chewed on his lip while she spoke.

"Except, I think he may be involved in whatever this is. She says in the diary she went to meet him, even spoke to him but didn't feel right about him so she said Noah would meet him another time rather than hand it over. But she told him her name. That's the only way I can see anybody would have suspected she had his notes." He continued to tell Elizabeth about an odd phone call from his boss, SSA Siesbolt and the agents appearing at Netty's funeral.

"But, why would he…?"

"Noah's notes tell of a white supremacist secret society that bragged they had members in positions of power and he was makin' some headway networkin' to find out who some of them were. Seems he wasn't extreme enough or grew a conscience and was goin' to be an informant to the Bureau."

"I don't get why you think your boss, this Siesbolt, is involved in what happened to Loralie. He's an agent, right?" She felt she didn't have all the pieces yet.

"Because he should've reported he was fosterin' a potential asset in a dangerous organization. There should've been a paper trail. When Noah turned up dead, the Bureau would've worked hard to identify this group and its members. I've worked these cases and we've no record of any such organization as Noah describes existin'. Siesbolt never reported it. Which makes me think he must've covered it up."

He turned to look out the window again. She could see his jaw muscles clenching from where she sat.

She shook her head. *An FBI agent was involved with Loralie's death?* Then this group wasn't just bragging about the caliber of their members, it was a fact. Who do you turn to when you can't trust the premier law enforcement agency in the nation? *Surely there was another explanation.*

CHAPTER SIXTY-FOUR

The General

The General of The Society for a Restored America sat in one of his leather reclining chairs in his office's little seating area for more intimate conversations when he had visitors. He was alone and celebrating a milestone today.

He snipped the end of the Gurkha His Majesty's Reserve cigar and ran it under his nose. *Magnificent.* The tobacco was aged for eighteen years and soaked in Louis XIII de Rémy Martin cognac for a superlative taste. He touched a flame to it and puffed to get it lit. This cigar cost about seven hundred and fifty dollars and was well worth it for celebrations such as this. He sipped on his thirty-year-old Glenfiddich Scotch Whiskey that was only a mere seven hundred dollars a bottle, but he enjoyed it immensely.

Bret Howard's manufactured interview with Rance Hunter had aired, and it was a masterpiece of propaganda. He knew it was all computer wizardry, but he couldn't detect any glitches as he had watched the Special Breaking News Bulletin. It seemed so real; he was amazed at what computers could accomplish. Hunter appeared to be a homegrown Muslim radical calling for his black brothers to join him in jihad against the white oppressors.

His plan was working, the masses accepted the lie, and the nation was increasingly divided and turning on one another.

He had spoken to his media coordinator, Chuck, as soon as the interview aired. Chuck assured him that the other media outlets were picking up on the interview and repeated the story without questioning its authenticity at all.

Hell, nobody fact-checked anymore, sure as hell not the person sitting at home, and the reporters were told what to report and how by their owners... like him. Hand them a press release with everything already written, and they were happy, particularly when their network heads were telling them to run with the story.

He had recorded it and used a remote to play the interview again. As the Breaking News report started for his third viewing, he had his cigar in one hand and his Scotch in his other hand.

When Operation Cancer Eradication was complete, and they had the President and both House and Senate under The Society's direction, he would celebrate with an even better Gurkha Black Dragon cigar and Dom Perignon Plenitude Brut Champagne.

CHAPTER SIXTY-FIVE

Juanita Alvarez

It took several hours to fly from the west coast all the way to Philadelphia to drop off Cenisa. You might think it would be a great time to sleep on the large comfy leather couch, but Cenisa traipsed around the Gulfstream interior of gray leather upholstery with brushed silver touches and high gloss walnut veneer accents.

Juanita opted for sleep to avoid Heath. She didn't want to talk about their kiss, or have him attempt to pick up where they left off. Sleep was a great avoidance technique when trapped on a plane. If it weren't for the zebra-print pacing.

Cenisa walked from the front club section with four leather chairs back through the mid-cabin area with the smaller four-person couch and two club chairs on back to the conference area where Juanita stretched out on the larger leather couch and Heath sat in one of the four club chairs droopy eyed facing her, all the way back to the full-service galley and spacious restroom. Then she whirled around and walked back to make the circuit again.

On one of the back-and-forth trips Heath finally said something. "Why don't you try to relax a little, I'd bet there's booze in the bar there."

"You've no idea what hell will rain down on Tito for taking me like that. What were you two thinking? And you, little chica, threatening Apache. Tito is a goddamn fucking dead man, and he'll getting me shot with him." There was a string of cursing for a minute after that. The girl had a mouth on her all right.

"And here I thought Tito was trying to bring his lady love to the safety of his urban empire," Juanita let slip, "How silly of me to think you might have an ounce of love for the guy." She was grumpy and fed up with Cenisa's lack of gratitude for the risks taken to save her from her Neanderthal brother.

Cenisa stopped on her way to the front of the plane and backed up to look down at Juanita lying down. "You really think Tito's risking a war in the ranks because of love, bitch? Oh hell no, this is all about who has the bigger set and I ended up in the middle. Don't get me wrong, my man grabbing me and shoving those guns in my brother's face was strategy." She tapped her head and nodded. "Tito always thinking several moves ahead. I only wish the prick would have given me more time to work a quiet escape from the house."

Cenisa seemed to have the mistaken idea she was a crime boss's woman-behind-the-man. She was too self-centered to be the influence behind Tito, but then why was she so important to him?

Juanita's interactions with Tito showed a calculating mind that could strategize for the Apostles long term. She respected and feared Tito equally for those qualities. Maybe it really was all strategy with Tito and nothing to do with affection or love. If these events were all manipulated, gang status and positioning was the very last thing any of the Black Apostles would worry about soon enough.

Juanita was relieved when Cenisa finally left the plane in Philadelphia. Neither she nor Health disembarked. They preferred to get the plane fueled, the safety check ran through, and back in the air as fast as possible. They anticipated getting to Jackson, Mississippi in several more hours, then renting a car to drive into the backwoods and rural areas to find one address.

The address of the payments to the dirty Philly cops and to the suspicious guards at the prison was the same. It was a very curious address with not much more information that Heath could discover.

She feared it might be late in the night before they reached their destination and might have to wait until morning. But she was eager to see what was at the address; whatever they found was the next part of her investigation.

Heath walked over and plopped down next to her on the plane's larger couch. She stiffened. Here we go. What was she going to tell him? She didn't mean to kiss him back when she most certainly did and if it hadn't been for Cenisa, she wouldn't have stopped.

"We haven't eaten and our personal flight attendant can prepare us something." He handed her a short, typed menu. "I need to get me one of these." That's what she was afraid of, an identity thief getting spoiled by the veneer of a rich lifestyle. He held his hands up, "I didn't say I would steal it or anything so just quit looking at me like that." But she couldn't help it.

She selected from the menu and he left to let the attendant know their food choices. She sighed, she had hurt his feelings. Maybe it was for the best.

CHAPTER SIXTY-SIX

Elizabeth Grant

Malcom insisted Loralie share her death with them by walking through what happened. Elizabeth sharing her recurring dream hadn't satisfied him, he had to find the actual spot where she died. Thus, Malcom and Elizabeth were walking in the woods where Loralie had led them.

It was hard enough accepting Loralie was dead and then dealing with the visions being some irrational psychic gift, but now she had to stand where Loralie was killed. She didn't know how she would handle it.

It was only midday, and they had started at the tree house. Loralie indicated this was where the men had found her, probably after hiding the Noah's notes. She led them through the woods from there. It felt like miles following Loralie in the humid heat, stopping only for a few water breaks and a small snack Malcom had packed in his olive-drab nylon backpack.

They stopped briefly at a tiny shack with its roof sagging and about to collapse on the one-room structure. Elizabeth saw a brief memory, maybe a minute, of men brutally beating Loralie to force out of her where she hid Noah's information. She had somehow escaped the men, so Elizabeth and Malcom continued following where Loralie led. That short glimpse would no doubt plague Elizabeth for the rest of her life.

Great, she would need to visit a psychologist over experiences that weren't even hers. That would go over well.

Loralie had slowed until she stopped at the trunk of a large dead oak. The massive skeleton dark and twisted against the greenery surrounding it. A slight breeze provided minuscule relief from the sticky, sweaty heat and pungent smell of ragweed.

Elizabeth shivered as fleeting images raced through her mind, like her dream only more real. For a moment it was the middle of a moonlit night seven years ago with a dog barking and she watched as Loralie broke free from a man's arm-hold around her neck only to be tripped and fall on the dead tree's protruding fallen limb. A stake through the heart.

"Well?" Malcom leaned against the tree that had staked her friend.

"You're at the spot where she died." Her voice was rough with choked emotion. Her nightmares were real now.

"So? Details, please."

She explained what little she knew and pointed to the general area where it happened. The years had affected the tree, and it wasn't exactly like her dream. Close enough.

"Where's her body?" Malcom said as he looked around the tree.

"Is this really necessary? You wanted to see where she died."

"No evidence likely here after this long, but her remains..." He stopped as she glared at him.

"Now look, we need evidence and you wanted to give her mother and brother some closure. Don't you think givin' her remains the respect they deserve would do that?" He sounded so reasonable.

She knew better; he was after evidence, and that meant her remains being scrutinized. But at some point, she could have a proper funeral and burial. Was that worth the painful process to find the body? It sounded so easy back at the cabin.

Loralie touched her elbow, and she jumped. The contact was clammy and seemed to reach inside her. Loralie waved to follow her, apparently fine with showing them where her body had been all these years.

Oh good, more walking. Her memories of summers never included the heat.

"Any idea where we are?" She asked Malcom.

"Yes, in a general sense, don't worry."

She was getting a queasy feeling and Loralie was moving faster, as if being drawn like a magnet to where her body was hidden.

Elizabeth jogged a bit to keep up, sweat dripping into her eyes. They reached a clearing with weathered wooden crosses, some with the wood split apart, peppering the area among tall weeds and wild grass. Loralie picked her way through them and stopped, pointing.

"That one, there." She pointed to where Loralie stood. Her stomach was churning at the proximity to Loralie's body. She couldn't explain why.

"So, they buried her in an old grave. That'll confuse things."

"Not just any old graveyard. I think this is Whispering Oaks plantation's slave burial yard." She swallowed. There were the spirits of two ancient looking male slaves in ragged clothes standing beside Loralie, staring back at her. *Nope, still not used to it.*

"That's a hell of a statement." He looked around at the ancient burial ground, then took out a rough map of the town.

"We must be about here," he pointed on the map. "Where is Whispering Oaks then?"

"She looked at the map, then looked around. The plantation house should be through the trees that way." She pointed northwest. "Maybe a half mile or more."

"Yep, guess this is the slave burial ground."

"How do you plan on digging her up? Call forensics people in?"

He huffed at her comment, slid his backpack off and removed a folded olive drab camping shovel, which he extended and stuck the blade in the ground.

"If the FBI really is involved, who would you suggest I call in, even locally, without makin' us huge targets? Plus, we have no proof to justify FBI resources. You and I believe in the information you received, but law enforcement will want hard facts, so it would be a waste of breath. With the local people involved from your kidnapping, I don't feel comfortable callin' the sheriff either and give anybody a chance to compromise the remains."

"Then why did you insist on this?"

"I'm hopin' for some solid evidence. If we have hard evidence and I can get it to an honest Justice Department agent not involved in whatever this is, we just might have a chance." He removed his shirt and dug, slow and steady.

Elizabeth couldn't avert her eyes from his muscular upper body steadily digging. He had an impressive color tattoo on one muscular bicep of a skull topped by a green beret with wings and a knife between its teeth and the Latin words De Oppresso Liber below the skull.

Wasn't there some syndrome where you fall for your rescuer? Sure, that's all this amounted to. He saved her from a traumatic attack. It's a natural response probably, nothing more. She just felt safe with him. Where was Loralie when she needed a distraction?

"You gonna stand in the shade and watch me sweat myself to a puddle the entire time?" He didn't stop digging.

She felt her face grow warm and got water out of the backpack. She looked away as she handed the water to him, which he took without further comment. He could probably tell where her mind had gone if he looked in her eyes.

He had dug down only three feet before finding the first bone.

"This is probably a recent burial since it isn't down deep. If you can take photos, please. We need to be meticulous as we do this." He wiped his forehead with his arm.

After more of the skeleton was revealed, he asked, "You're sure this is your friend's body?"

"Absolutely. I remember those scraps of her clothes. But the beaded necklace and bracelet... we made matching sets one summer." Her voice sounded raw to her own ears.

She swallowed the lump in her throat, then took a deep breath. *No time to think about that now. Just get this done. How had she ended up digging up Loralie's body?*

She retrieved a camera, numbered tent tags, measuring tape, compass, and notebook from his backpack. She began the process of taking photos as he unearthed each bone, putting a tag on it, and recording quick notes and a basic sketch of each bone's position in the grave. Nothing like handling human remains to take your mind off physical attraction.

It was late in the day before he climbed out of the oblong dig site after having documented the position and labeled each bone.

He carefully wrapped the bones up in the clean tarp where she had gently placed them after logging each one, some with tattered material still clinging. He straightened and drained another bottle of water.

"Can you stay here while I jog back to the cabin and bring the truck back? I'll be fast. I still want you out of sight." His eyes scrutinized her face.

She looked at the tarp. *Why did the bones bother her? What was the big deal after seeing her ghost?* It made Loralie's death real and final.

"Yeah, okay. I'm fine. What's the worst that can happen, see her ghost?" She tried for a nonchalant laugh, but it came out strained.

He took the backpack with everything inside, minus a water bottle for her, and took off like lightning through the trees.

"Those Green Beret guys don't dawdle," she said aloud, feeling the trees close in around her now she was without her protective knight.

She glanced over at Loralie's image standing over her makeshift burial site. Her face seemed like some sadness had lifted. That sight eased her nerves and fortified her to wait for Malcom's return.

CHAPTER SIXTY-SEVEN

Elizabeth Grant

Malcom watched the sheriff drive away in the twilight. He closed the solid cabin door and stood there for a moment. He turned and faced her.

"Spit it out. Throughout dinner you were upset, and it's more than your uncle in town wanting to see you." He moved closer. The gas lanterns added a glow to the fading sunlight inside the cabin.

She was silent for several heartbeats before she blurted out, "I'm anxious about sitting here alone while you take Loralie's… remains to Jackson." She had no experience with death, let alone murder. Her granddad's funeral wasn't the same, and even then she couldn't go past his open casket.

His gaze scrutinized her, and she fidgeted. He slowly held his arms out, and she sank into them, drinking in the comfort. Only then did she feel all the pent up frustration, worry, guilt, grief, and fear since Madam Antoinette's visit bubble up and she cried on his shoulder.

He stroked her hair but remained silent. No uttered promises that everything would be okay. Not that she would have believed such assurances for a second if he had. She didn't need empty platitudes, just a safe release.

Eventually, the tears dried up and his shoulder was quite damp.

She hadn't felt able to cry with such abandon for seven years, especially not with another person around. Was it his acceptance of her "gift" or that Loralie appeared to trust him?

Either way, she became more and more aware of the muscles on the arms that held her, the tenderness as he stroked her back, and the smell of the soap he used. *Oh Lord, this was tempting, but she was too emotional to make sound decisions.* She had made questionable choices with men in college, but there was too much at stake now. *Terrible timing.*

With supreme effort, she broke away from the safe harbor of his arms and chided herself for becoming such mush so quickly. It was liberating to be herself around him, visions and all. But, he was only interested in one thing, finding his aunt's killer not having some sappy newbie psychic crushing on him.

Avoiding his eyes, she had to fill the silence. She cleared her throat. "I... um... I needed to cry, I guess." She was still too shaken to say much.

He backed away from her and focused on clearing the few dishes from the table. An uncomfortable air settled around them.

"You've been through a lot in a short time. But, we really must get her remains to a lab and I'm afraid if you came you'd be at risk on the long road to Jackson. The Sheriff'll be back shortly to keep you safe." He talked while sudsing up dishes in the sink, his attention on the task.

Sheriff Craig had to make an appearance at a civic function, but he promised on returning to look after her.

"I don't trust the man and I don't understand why you do." It came out more emphatic than she had intended, but that was how she felt. She surprised herself. In such a short time, a little over twenty-four hours, she got used to being open with this man.

He stopped, hands submerged in suds, and bowed his head. "I can't explain it. Yeah, I trust him to look after you. Please trust me on this."

"I...," she began.

"No, you can't come with me. This is for the best. If we've got a shot at provin' who killed Loralie, it hangs on getting' the remains to a forensic lab. I suspect your kidnappers are tryin' to locate you and watchin' the two roads out of town so it would be easy to ambush us. If you're seen, it could jeopardize your life and the evidence. If I go alone, I'm less likely to be noticed or followed." He finished rinsing, wiped his hands and faced her.

"So far you've dropped out of sight and it appears we've eluded discovery here. We need that to hold."

"Yeah, I know. I understand all that." *Didn't mean she liked it.* She felt like her security, her protection was leaving her exposed and vulnerable again. Getting jumped, drugged, and abducted proved nerve-racking and she wasn't over it yet.

Then her overbearing Uncle Jairus arrived in town. The sheriff assured her uncle she wasn't missing, and she was safe, but he wouldn't like that she wasn't rushing to see him. Even without Malcom discouraging her to meet him – even to have him come to the cabin, she would've avoided seeing him.

"I'll be back around early mornin'. If you go to sleep, you'll hardly notice I'm gone." He gathered some items.

"Take this." He handed her a gun, but she just stared at it, no clue what type or caliber. She didn't trust herself with a weapon, her self-esteem was in tatters. She would just screw things up worse with a loaded gun.

"You've shot before, right?"

"I've only been to a range once." She sucked in a deep breath. "I can manage, I'm sure."

In a few short minutes, he was gone, and she sat alone at the rustic table. She made herself a promise after hearing Malcom's Suburban leave that she would be strong from here on out.

CHAPTER SIXTY-EIGHT

Juanita Alvarez

"Wouldn't you know it, no bars and no GPS out here," Heath spat out. Juanita wasn't happy to hear that as the paper map hadn't helped so far. The problem was all the side roads with no signage. They had been a few hours in the car already. She was grateful that the platinum card got them an automatic upgrade to a more comfortable car for the long drive.

It was twilight, and she suspected they were lost in the middle of rural Mississippi. She was grateful they'd picked up sandwiches in Jackson on the way out of town for their dinner. She'd never driven so long with no sign of civilization in her entire life. Hell, until the last week she hadn't left Philly.

Heath cleared his throat, "Are we gonna talk about it?"

Oh no. She hoped he would never bring it up. She was fine pretending nothing had happened. Really. Why did he want to talk, weren't guys afraid of their feelings?

"It's all awkward now." He shifted in the passenger seat to face her.

"I don't want to talk about it." There, she shared. She couldn't talk about it. She would either hurt his feelings or give him hope of whatever was between them going further. She couldn't do either.

"It's just, well, I thought you were gonna get shot. I didn't stop to think if we were ready for that step. I reacted."

She glanced at him quickly. His face showed earnest openness, and that scared her more than if he lied to her. *Ready for that step?* They weren't dating, so why say it like that?

Her emotions were all in a jumble. She expected bad behavior from him; he was a thief, after all. She couldn't get past that fact. Sure, he had the boyish charm, clean cut looks, playful smile, and a surprisingly caring side. He had hurt people with his identity theft. Sure, he fancied himself a Robin Hood, taking from those with considerable and deep pockets for his poor self.

It was his targets that got the FBI devoting resources to catch him. The little people didn't get that kind of dedication. He hated those who preyed on the elderly, on those just getting by, even those who had worked and saved for a good retirement. He had his standards, or so he said.

"You can't get past my record, can you? No matter how close we're getting? I haven't stolen an identity again. I swear." He swallowed, and Juanita became intensely aware of his breathing.

"I don't know if I can get past it." Her voice was a whisper of disappointment. She wouldn't confirm his comment about getting close. They were finishing each other's sentences; and sometimes she swore he knew what she was thinking. It scared her when she knew what he was feeling and how much it mattered to her.

She wasn't going to acknowledge how she kissed him back and really wished Cenisa hadn't been in the car. He had surprised her on the last leg of the flight after dropping Cenisa off. For dinner he lit candles, played soft music on the sound system, and found wine to share.

He claimed they needed a calming moment, but she knew it was his way of making it a date. He had a romantic side that was on full display at that moment and it touched her. He could be everything she ever wanted if it weren't for his being a thief. That and the fact her family would never accept him.

Also on the plane she resolved to push the kiss and romance aside and focus on the path they were on because all indications were this was a deadly agenda enacted by influential people who get away with murder. So each time the memory of his kiss invaded her thoughts, she ruthlessly stomped it down. It was for the best.

Heath faced forward in his seat again, "I wish you'd try to accept I've changed. Because I think we could have something great." He turned on the radio and found one country music station after another.

All Juanita really knew for sure was the fear gnawing in her core was urging her to be careful and hurry.

CHAPTER SIXTY-NINE

Elizabeth Grant

Elizabeth finished her meditation and felt calmer. For once it was a relaxing visualization alone in the garden she visited. She had missed meditating the last day or two and it was a good escape from all her feelings and thoughts. She stretched, got up from the kitchen chair, and made herself some tea.

The sheriff was taking his time getting back to the cabin, but that was okay with her. He promised he would run interference with Uncle Jairus and get them a day or two longer in hiding and without telling him where to find her. The later Sheriff Craig was, the more she suspected he probably was missing a limb after Uncle Jairus didn't get to exert his authority in her life. Better the sheriff than her.

Her eyes found Loralie's diary and Noah's notebook tucked in her purse. She needed something to occupy her mind, so she didn't worry and fret. She settled in to read more of Noah's journal. She hadn't finished it before her abduction.

Crickets created a cacophony around the cabin. Before long, she was skimming Noah's entries of names and places. Seems he was attending meetings not just in this state, but also in neighboring states. He had gained their trust and was gathering every scrap of information he came across.

He detailed a school curriculum push that was slanted towards their view, claiming whoever headed The Society was successful in getting it used in some school districts throughout the nation. But, members wanted more, they were restless for bolder and bigger moves. She rubbed her bare arms. The fervor Noah described to advance their agenda was stoked with a sense of righteousness that didn't allow for any belief or idea outside their own as valid.

She was towards the last ten pages when she saw a symbol crudely drawn that stopped her with a sense of dread. Noah wrote the symbol was on rings each member wore, but also on some of their businesses to signal other members – sometimes even used discreetly in signs. It was a bricklayer's trowel crossed with a sword to represent their fight to rebuild the nation to greatness.

There was something familiar about it, she could swear she had seen it… recently. She reviewed her activities since being in town. She had walked all over the town and visited different shops, even the diner where she had eaten a few times. She couldn't place it. She closed her eyes and visualized the symbol, just focused on it, like a meditation exercise or something.

Her eyes sprang open. *That was it.* She had seen it at Whispering Oaks when the rude foreman had refused to talk to her about the renovations. That symbol had been on the plaque affixed to a veranda column. It had the bricklayer's trowel crossed with a sword over an outline of the nation on the sign. Was it just a coincidence? Was she getting paranoid?

She sucked in her breath when she remembered the intimidating foreman at the plantation house, and the realization dawned that he was the man who'd abducted and interrogated her. She had thought he seemed familiar, but he had been in shadow on the veranda for the short confrontation. Her mind had been fuzzy from the drug during the abduction, but she was positive now.

She trembled a little at the memory and quickly stood up and paced. She wouldn't cry anymore or succumb to panic. She'd made it through and was fine now. Besides, she had vowed to be strong. She moved to get her cell phone to call Malcom, but stopped. Her cell phone didn't have reception out here, and there wasn't a landline in the cabin.

She would tell Malcom about the Whispering Oaks when he returned. She could be wrong, it could just be a coincidence. Or it could be used, as Noah claimed, as a sign to other Society members. But she didn't want to sound paranoid, grasping at straws and waste time.

She could go to the plantation house and look at the sign again. It would give her something to do rather than let her imagination scare her, and nobody would be around now that it was dark. She grabbed the hand-drawn map the sheriff had initially given them to help find the cabin. She wasn't all that far from the Whispering Oaks if she followed the road and stayed out of sight.

She changed into the only dark clothes she had and that was thanks to the sheriff retrieving her suitcase, so she had a few clean items. She left a note that she would be back shortly in case the Sheriff made it by before she returned. She grabbed the flashlight Malcom had supplied, stuffed some cash in a pocket, and started out at a fast pace. She didn't trust taking the gun.

CHAPTER SEVENTY

Juanita Alvarez

"There, there's a motel." Heath pointed urgently.

"I see it, I see it." They had been driving from Jackson for hours thinking all they had to do was reach Cyprus and they would find a place to stay. Naturally, there was nothing online about hotels or motels in the small town of Cyprus.

They had continued driving through the five blocks of downtown Cyprus with no sign of lodging in sight. Downtown was like stepping back into the 1950s. Even the bank was a small storefront between a barber and a diner. *There were still barbershops?*

Juanita had never been outside of Philadelphia, although Heath had been to other large cities. She didn't count Corcoran since it was a visit to the prison. Cyprus felt restrictive to Juanita, as if she were in another country, or just a strange land where everyone suspected an outsider, or was it her Mexican heritage? People stopped on the sidewalk and stared as they drove past, a few children pointed.

They had hoped if they kept driving, they might find something on the outskirts of town. They thought they would have to circle around and stop for directions, but they wanted to avoid calling any attention to themselves. Then they finally spotted the antiquated motel next to the epitome of a dive bar.

She turned into the entry drive for the motel and parked in front of the small little office. Heath jumped out to get their rooms. She could see two semi-trucks parked towards the back of the motel on one side. She counted six rooms total.

Heath jumped back into the car. "You aren't going to believe this. They only have one room."

Juanita socked him in the arm, "Sure there is. No fooling around, Heath. I'm not sharing a room with you."

"I guess I can sleep in the car then," he said matter-of-factly, without a pitiable tone to get sympathy.

"Let's hope that diner we say back there stays opens and then locate that address so we know where we're going tomorrow. Maybe by the time we return they'll have another room available."

He opened his mouth to say something, but she pointed to the semi-trucks and then over to the sign proclaiming *The Gutter: Quench Your Thirst Headquarters* next door. When she looked at him she raised her eyebrows.

"Ohhhhh. Gotcha. I'm starved. Want to try the bar there?" He pointed his chin toward the bar. "Motel manager says they have decent hamburgers and catfish."

She had driven the entire way from Jackson and she was tired and hungry. It was late enough that the little diner they passed would be closed or about to, anyway.

"Okay, but if they decline me service don't make a scene."

His brows furrowed in question, then rose as the meaning became clear to him. "Oh, I didn't think of that. Well, let's give it a try."

But once she walked in, she knew getting service wouldn't be a problem for this little Mexican senorita. It was practically an old west saloon with the girls working the room. A dark-skinned girl of maybe twenty tops rubbed up against a man and slid a hand down his stomach... and on down to stroke his jeans and growing package. She whispered in his ear and they left out the front door, headed for his car, semi, or the motel next door was Juanita's guess. The bar seemed to quench more than just a thirst for alcohol.

The lights were dim to show off the neon beer signs, and the joint reeked of hamburger grease. They found a semi-clean table tucked away from the majority of patrons. She couldn't help but notice how all the women were staring at Heath. His charming persona, nice pressed jeans and button-down shirt with a Vacheron Constantin watch made him appear like a European prince next to the farmhands and truck drivers around them. Heath was oddly unaware of the attention, and that seemed out of character.

"Let's hurry and eat..." she began.

"...and find that address so we can get some sleep." He finished her sentence.

They were finishing each other's thoughts again, and that worried her almost as much as this trail they were following or as much as his never even looking at the barely clothed girls eyeing him like a bowl of double-dutch chocolate ice cream.

The waitress took their orders and had beers delivered quickly. Laverne, according to her name tag, leaned over to deliver a basket of peanuts, providing Heath a view of all her goods down her unbuttoned top. Heath barely glanced and his neck turned red.

Juanita occasionally glanced at the large flat screen TV situated up high in a corner, right above and to the left of the restroom sign. It had the sound down and captions on so it didn't compete with the country music piped in.

Their hamburgers arrived in record time, as if telling the outsiders to hurry up and move on out of town. A ketchup-soaked French fry stopped halfway to Juanita's mouth as she stared slack-jawed at the screen. Heath noticed her frozen gaze of wonderment and turned to see what the cause was.

There on the screen was Rance Hunter, gang leader and prison escapee, in an interview with VOX reporter Bret Howard. He was claiming he had converted to Islam and then, to Juanita's horror, called for a jihad against their white oppressors. That just made no sense with everything they had found.

She jumped up to call Tito outside where she could yell.

CHAPTER SEVENTY-ONE

Elizabeth Grant

She only used the flashlight a few times and relied on the half moon and clear sky for most of her light. She jogged a few times when a noise spooked her, but she had done better than she thought, nearly turning back only twice until she had convinced herself she was being silly. Loralie had flitted in and out, worrying her hands, and at one point stood in her way with her hand out to stop. Elizabeth sidestepped her best friend's specter.

Elizabeth approached Whispering Oaks from the backside roughly forty-five minutes after starting out from her estimate. The back of the building wasn't as grand, no majestic fluted columns or impressive wide porch. Just a back door centered amid sets of windows.

There were a few cars tucked away among some trees several hundred yards away from the house. Their darkened lights reflected the thin moonlight as she crept forward. Probably some workers had left them because it was quiet and no signs of activity or workers staying late.

An owl hooted, like a foghorn blasting through the cacophony of crickets. It swooped over her and she could hear the whistle of the air over his feathered wings that spanned six feet at least.

She circled around to the front and the sight of the long oak-lined drive gave her chills, as if something evil lurked among all the shifting shadows. *Make this quick and get back to the cabin.*

She stared at the plaque affixed to a white column lit by the moonlight shining down. It was exactly like the drawing in Noah's notebook, just the addition of the national map behind the sword and trowel. *Oh crap, this couldn't be good.* That was more than a coincidence in her mind, a perfectly matched rendition. Using her cell phone's camera, she took a quick photo, the flash a harsh beacon in the night.

She got what she came for and turned to go back the way she'd come when she noticed a sliver of light at one window. Looking around, there was no sign of anybody, so she crept over. The base of the window began at shoulder level, and she could see a slight portion of a room from the gap in the curtain.

She bit her lip. There was a big man with bulging muscled arms and broad shoulders tied to a chair with a large video camera facing him. He appeared unconscious, and the room seemed empty otherwise.

She remembered the cold reception she had received when she visited before and her suspicion that the surly foreman had been one of her abductors. The hair on the back of her neck prickled, and a cold finger ran down her spine despite the hot clinging air. A trickle of sweat began down her cleavage when she felt a whisper of a hand touch her arm.

She jumped, her heart pounding a staccato, and whirled only to look down at a girl's spirit vaguely before her. If not for the moonlight she could have missed the faint image in the dark. She was perhaps ten, twelve tops and looked like she had been shot several times from the dark holes in her dress' bodice.

"He's my brother, please help him." To her ears, the spirit sounded hushed but urgent. She gulped, she hadn't heard Loralie or Madame Antoinette, only seen them, since her kidnapping.

Since the abduction and drugging, she was seeing more spirits and apparently had progressed to random auditory capabilities now. If Malcom hadn't repeatedly assured her it was normal, and she was sane, she would likely have run away in terror. She threw her shoulders back; she was being strong now.

The young girl took hold of her sleeve and tugged her towards the window. "They're going to kill him, I know it."

"Pretty sure it's unlocked. Go on. Please." The girl said.

Elizabeth looked around, but nobody lurked in the shadows that she could discern. She reached up, stretching her height to the cross pane of the window and pushed up.

It opened enough for her to get her fingers under the bottom of the window, and raised it. She held her breath, expecting the window to screech from humidity and swelling, but it opened with only a scratching sound.

What in the hell was she doing? Trespassing now... after excavating bones earlier today. What did she think she could do to help this man? She glanced back, but the young girl's image was gone. Crap. She jumped up to the window and heaved herself up, her feet scrambling for traction, onto the window ledge. She found her face inches away from a table under the window with bloody knives and tools laid out. *Don't think about that now.*

Balanced on her stomach on the ledge, her hands sweating and breathing labored, she looked at the man. He still appeared unconscious, and the young girl's spirit was standing before him with fear emanating around her like an aura. Loralie popped in and flailed her arms, shooing her out the window.

"Hurry. I don't think he'll live through another visit." The young girl's voice was laced with panic. *Good thing nobody else could hear her since she was practically yelling now.*

She swung her legs, so she was sitting on the window ledge and scooted the table aside until she could stand. She crept over to the man.

The closer she got to him she could see his face was bloody, one eye was swollen shut, he had deep cuts on his arms she didn't want to look closely at, and his hands and feet were tied to the chair. This was torture, horrific and inhuman. She felt her stomach turn; she broke out in a cold sweat and held a hand over her mouth. *She couldn't retch now.*

His eyes sprang open, and she saw fear and hatred. She held a finger to her lips in the universal signal.

"Shhhh. Please."

The ropes were tight and she couldn't get the knots to budge. She grabbed a small serrated blade from the table by the window, but he started to squirm, his muscles spasming at the sight. She realized the blade had dried blood on it and understood the cuts on his arms with another wave of nausea.

"No, I have to cut the ropes. There's no other way." She looked at the door. *No damn lock!*

As gently as possible she sawed at the ropes, but his wrists got nasty scrapes by the time she finished. He had passed out while she worked. *How the hell was she going to get him out? He was in bad shape, maybe close to death for all she knew. One thing at a time, one step at a time.* After placing his hands on his thighs so blood could flow to them, she sawed on the ropes binding his ankles to the chair legs.

She heard the voices first, a low murmur, then the footsteps. She placed his hands on the chair arms again and laid the loose rope around his wrists and tucked under. *Maybe they won't notice.* She ran to a door the girl ghost waved her to, slid to a stop, and barely flung herself inside what turned out to be a closet when the other door opened. The closet door was still open a crack when two men entered.

She tried to quiet her breathing. Watching through the sliver of a crack at the door, questions peppered her mind. *Why was this man being tortured? Who was he and what had he done?* She stared at his tattoo on his bicep, artwork that looked like the grim reaper with a circle around it and lettering she couldn't read. She hadn't paid attention to it until now, but it was the most prominent feature in her field of vision. She had seen that tattoo before, but where?

The men were gathering items in the room into a black trash bag.

"When'll he be here?"

"General didn't give an exact time, just be ready for him."

"Why d'ya think he's comin' here?"

"I think he wants to kill this bastard himself, cut his head off to send to his gang. That would get his gang killin' and wake up the complacent white folk. Don't know and don't care why he's comin', he just is."

The General.... like in Noah Aaron's notes? Here? Send this man's head to the gang...? It dawned on her who the tortured man was. *Oh my God, oh shit.* It had to be that gang leader who broke out of jail, and his tattoo had been in the newspaper as an identifying mark. She could visualize the picture in the paper now. She felt her heart skip several beats. *What had she walked into?*

The two men spread out a tarp next to the chair. Elizabeth shivered thinking what it would be used for, disposal of the body seemed likely. One man was definitely the foreman she met when she was hoping for a tour of the renovations, and he was the same guy who had abducted her. She was certain, and the realization made her knees weaken.

A phone rang, not a cell phone but a loud house phone echoing off the walls. Her prior abductor left the room, his heavy booted steps clomping down the hall.

"Yeah. I'll come get ya. We'll have him all ready fur ya....Outside? Nobody'll see nothin' round here. They'll never find his body, guaranteed." He slammed the phone handset down.

"I heard. Wants to do the job outside, huh?"

"Says it's easier for clean up, coverin' up, and gettin' rid of."

"Makes no nevermind to me either way."

"I'll be right back. Have to pick up the General. Have him ready out back."

She heard his clomping footsteps moving away and a door open and close. The remaining man grabbed the tarp and left, then she heard a door opened and the crickets were louder.

Easy cleanup... never find the body. This was the clinch moment. This stranger would be killed while she was hiding in a closet. Sure, he wasn't a good person or a pillar of society. But torture was evil and murder was murder all the same.

Of all the times to be without a purse. Not that she carried much more than a whistle, not even pepper spray. Maybe she should have brought the gun, but she didn't trust she wouldn't shoot her own foot. *Note to self: if you live through this carry pepper spray.*

The table by the window where she came in had a blood-spattered old pipe, an X-Acto knife, and some tool she suspected dentists used to pull teeth, also covered in blood. She couldn't even force herself to use those as a weapon against the remaining man.

It was just her and the tortured gang leader alone with one man and no idea how long before the foreman guy would return with the General. She really didn't want to be here with the head of a hate group and murderer.

She ran out of the closet and the battered captive's eyes flew open.

"You're gonna have to walk, I sure can't carry you. You look far bigger than me." She finished cutting the rope around his ankles. The rope had been a little loose. She prayed he had some circulation in those feet so he could hold himself up.

She jumped around to the side, ignored all the sweat and blood covering his shredded prison uniform, and took an arm over her shoulder to help support him. From the smell, she was certain they hadn't allowed him bathroom privileges either. She gagged before breathing through her mouth.

His first step nearly sent them both tumbling down, but he caught himself and limped to the door. She didn't know if she was any help; he was considerably taller than she was so he couldn't get much support from her.

It felt like hours to reach the door of the room. In the hall, she glanced around and spotted the front door about ten yards away. The back was not an option since she was sure that was the where she heard the man go out a few minutes ago. They limped and lurched to the front door inch by inch, their heavy steps making thuds on the wood floor. She was pulling the front door open when she heard the lone man stomping up the back steps.

Their footsteps became frantic small steps out the door until he could support himself holding onto the outer wall. She spun and yanked the door closed just as the back door slammed shut. *Oh shit, no time! He would go to the torture room and find it empty.*

She grabbed his arm and prayed the veranda boards were in better shape than she feared a few days ago. They shuffled to the four steps, nearly tumbled down them, finally got their feet coordinated and were getting a limping fast walk rhythm on the ground down the lane. They passed the first tree on the right in the long tree-lined driveway when she heard the front door thrown open.

"Let's get to the trees and keep going," she told him. They veered to the tree closest on the right and got off the gravel, onto the lawn, and in the shadows of the trees. She was praying the time it took was worth it in being less exposed.

A bullet whizzed past, taking a chunk of a tree's bark with it. There was just no damn way she could get out of this mess. *What had she been thinking?*

They hobbled past the third tree in the line and he stumbled, physically giving out.

"We're close to the road, come on. Come on." She growled through gritted teeth. He was really heavy now.

She heard running footsteps getting closer. They passed the fourth tree down the lane.

"Stop or I'll plug ya in the back li'l missy."

They stopped, barely standing without falling over.

There was a rustling off to her right, in the dark. *They weren't alone.* Then she heard brief running. She looked around, still holding the tortured man's arm. She followed the sound of running and saw a stranger take a broken-off tree limb and hit their pursuer to the ground with a knock-it-out-of-the-park hit to the head. Then he jumped on top of the man and hit him three times, maybe it was four, with his fist.

"Damn that hurt. Probably broke my hand." The rescuer turned, and she saw a nice-looking young man; clearly a city guy from his tasseled leather shoes.

"Help me get him outta here." Elizabeth's voice was near panic. He grabbed the other arm and took a few shallow breaths from the smell too.

They dragged him; it was faster, to the end of the lane where a car was parked and a young Hispanic woman had the back door open. The tattooed man collapsed across the seat. Elizabeth got in from the opposite side and had to help prop him to a semi-sitting position or she would never have fit inside. Hope they didn't mind cleaning their car because this seat would never be the same.

Elizabeth had just closed her door when... "Holy shit, what is that?" The young woman yelled, pointing out the front window.

The coyote that had followed her during the last visit had his front paws on the hood of the car and let out a howl. He then turned, snarling, to the revived man approaching the car attempting to stop them; apparently, he hadn't remained unconscious for long from the tree limb to the head.

The coyote bared his teeth and stood between the man and the car, snarling so loud Elizabeth heard him inside the car. The hair on her arms stood at attention. The coyote lunged, the man screamed, the gun he held went off wildly into the treetops, and their car backed up in a cloud of dust, turned hard, and roared away. She hoped the coyote was okay.

CHAPTER SEVENTY-TWO

Juanita Alvarez

"What the hell was that?" Juanita let out in a rush as she glanced in the rearview mirror.

"Do you mean the coyote or the man with the gun?" The girl in the backseat asked. "Doesn't matter. If you could take me to the cabin where I'm staying, you can be on your way. You'll come to a turnoff on the left in about three miles."

Juanita hazarded another glance in the rearview at her. This brown-haired chick's eyes were huge and she kept looking out the back window.

The rescued man who collapsed in the car was in shadow. When they heard the shooting, they both leaped to help them escape. Maybe they should have determined what was happening before they rushed to help. First rescuing Cenisa and now this. *Mother Mary, please protect us.*

She never figured Heath for a hero type, so his actions put him in a whole new light. He had been fearless and was the primary reason those two in the back seat were still breathing.

She glanced at Heath. He motioned to the back seat with his head, worry etched deep furrows on his forehead. She spotted the turn and barely slowed to take it. After another hundred yards, she stopped and turned the engine off.

She turned in her seat and faced the back where the two fugitives huddled. "Just who the hell are you two?"

"I could ask the same of you. You're not from around here, that's clear."

"We stuck our necks out for you. You can start by telling us why you were running from that man." Heath turned around in his seat too.

"Thanks for the rescue. Didn't mean to seem ungrateful. I found this man being tortured and overheard the plan to kill him, so I helped. I couldn't walk away knowing they would murder him."

Heath's eyes sought Juanita's, then he reached up and turned on the map light. The light didn't amount to much in the back seat, but it was enough. They both sucked in their breaths at the sight of prison escapee Rance Hunter – bloody and beaten, in their rental car.

"We got to get out of here. Oh shit. shit, shit, shit." Heath ran his hand through his hair. She reached over and took his hand in hers and squeezed.

"Is this cabin safe?"

"As far as I know, and... my boyfriend will be back shortly."

Hmm, hesitation there. Could she be lying? Some cabin tucked away was better than sitting alongside a road waiting for the people who will want Hunter back, or more likely dead. She picked the least of two evils and drove down the road, following the backseat directions.

It took both Heath and the fresh-faced girl to wrestle the barely conscious escapee into the cabin, straining under his weight. They got him on one of the twin beds and got water and rags to clean him up.

Heath found a first aid kit, industrial sized, and offered it up. The prison shirt was in tatters from the cutting on his arms and chest. So they cut off the shirt. Some cuts looked bone-deep and possibly infected. Occasionally he moaned as they tended to him.

Juanita's mind was churning as she helped to bathe the blood and sweat away. Whoever busted Hunter out wasn't his own gang from looking at the abuse.

His rescue from torture and imminent murder cast Hunter's televised "interview" she watched as likely staged and manipulated.

The reporter conducting the interview was a highly regarded broadcast journalist. Why risk your long-standing career and reputation on a falsehood? Maybe even more important, how much did he know about the people behind the breakout and torture? He had to know it wasn't his gang involved. Did the reporter see Hunter being held against his will?

Then a thought presented itself. This wasn't a rival gang either. A coordinated jailbreak and then transported across several state lines to be tortured. Nope, definitely not another gang.

She looked around to find Heath busy icing his knuckles, ready to wrap his rapidly swelling hand. Bare knuckle fighting isn't like in the movies, it hurts like hell and the hand takes a lot of punishment.

The girl they rescued cleared her throat, "I really hate to say this, but several of these cuts will require serious disinfecting and stitches." Her fair complexion turned ghostly pale. Seemed she really hated the idea.

"Going to a lot of trouble for a guy you claim you don't know." Heath had suspicion written all over his face. There was a part of her that worried about how she could read his thoughts. But she shoved that aside. No time for distractions, and he was more and more distracting with each day.

"Look, I'll settle for your name for now." She couldn't keep thinking of her as "the girl."

"Elizabeth Grant. My mom grew up here and I'm house sitting for my grandmother." When she made eye contact, she didn't detect any deception. But she had a look of fear lurking in her eyes, as if this Elizabeth was scared but keeping her shit together through her own determination.

"Juanita Alvarez and Heath Grayson... From Philadelphia." Yeah, she didn't confess upfront she was a reporter, or why they were even here. "Do you know him?" She nodded towards Hunter who was moaning as Elizabeth doused Hydrogen Peroxide on the open wounds.

"We haven't been introduced. We aren't friends or anything." She looked up and locked gazes with her. *She knew. I'll-be-go-to-hell, she knew who he was.*

"You know…"

"Yeah, he's that guy in all the newspapers. I don't know what he's doing here. But I couldn't just let them kill him."

Heath's eyes met Juanita's. They both knew this Elizabeth might have just averted an escalation of gang violence, and whoever was behind this mess would want them all dead now.

"Well, Elizabeth Grant. You may have just saved the nation from self-destructing; now we just have to keep him alive." Heath stated. Juanita silently added, keeping us all alive.

The door burst open and a fine looking black man leveled his gun at them.

"Elizabeth, who're these people and what's going on?" He asked in a level tone.

"Fed." Heath tossed out like identifying a car. He should know after his experience when he was caught.

CHAPTER SEVENTY-THREE

The General

The chair that only a few hours ago held Rance Hunter now held Boone Cofer, who had been guarding Hunter when he miraculously escaped. Boone was securely tied, just as Hunter had been, arms and legs bound with tight knots. Dried blood matted the hair on his head where he had been hit, and one hand was swollen where a coyote had bitten him. He was in sorry shape all right.

Boone was trembling before the General and his voice pleading, "I don't rightly know how the woman got in here. I don't know how it happened at all. He was tied up like a turkey and unconscious. Before I knowed what's up, I see the front door is open, and some woman helping him limp away." He sobbed, tears running down his face.

The General slid a silver knife from its sheath, its whisper ominous as the man continued to whimper. The razor-sharp edges glinted in the dim overhead light. A genuine smile spread across the General's face.

Oh, how he loved what a nice series of cuts could do. No need to cut off fingers joint by joint. If you knew the most sensitive body areas a cut could be far more searing without the retreat of shock that an injury like cutting a joint off would produce. He knew all the most sensitive areas.

Today he would let his talent for blade work make an example of this sorry piece of shit. He bent down so his face was only inches away from Boone's and placed the knife's point against his crotch. He should have had him stripped naked, but cutting his pants to shreds might be fun before he got to his cock.

"A useless woman and a barely walkin' carcass got the better of you?" He tsked and shook his head in sympathy.

Boone wet himself and the smell filled the hot sticky air in the room. The General moved the knife over to the tender inner thigh, stabbed through the denim into the muscle and tendons, and sliced downward into the chair. Boone screamed like in the movies, high and with volume. The foreman of the Whispering Oaks plantation restoration stood in a dark corner with a hand over his face. *Useless at discipline.*

He didn't mind the screaming; he rather enjoyed it. Boone screamed long, just how he liked it. Once he stopped screaming and was only pleading for mercy, he removed the knife from Boone's now useless leg and continued.

"Boone, how did two inferior beings, a woman and a starvin' wounded nigger, get away when you said you were chasin' and shootin' at them? Explain that, Boone."

"They… they… they had help. I was hit from behind. Knocked me cold. I swear. I swear they had help. I swear it."

The General leaned down into his face again, "Boone, listen to me carefully. Who was this woman, what did she look like?" He placed the knife tip against his cock again, just to sober his thoughts.

"The woman? I never saw her 'fore. She… she had aaah… dark hair. Ummmm, she, she ah was I don't know short like 5-4 or some-thin'. Not from 'round here."

"Did she have a little meat on her bones but not too much, and her hair came down to about here?" The General indicated past shoulder length with the blood-drenched knife. Boone nodded, wide eyed, between sobs.

The General had a sneaking suspicion creep up his spine. Why hadn't he killed Elizabeth before now? He had her surrounded all the time; hell, the only boyfriends she had in college had been Society members there to get anything out of her about what she knew. Even Elizabeth's shrink had been a member. It would have been so easy. He should have exterminated her within the first days, then they wouldn't be in this *situation* now. He balled his fist, wanting to sink it into that little bitch's head.

Boone bled on the chair, dripping over the front lip onto the floor. Plop-plop. Plop. The General's breathing raced at the sight of his blood.

"Now this is real important. How did anybody know he was here to rescue him in the first place? I can't send his head to the Black Apostles now and keep the violence fueled for the National Guard to come in and save the decent people from the risin' black tide." Anger rose in his voice.

Boone's already pale face lost all color as he swallowed and looked towards the corner at the other man.

"No, I didn't tell a soul. Not a word. No, I didn't." He repeated the words over and over, shaking his head no.

The General waved the foreman over and instructed him to unzip Boone's pants. Boone began bucking and screaming his innocence. The chair toppled over on its side and the foreman sat him back upright.

"Tie his stomach tight to the chair back to keep his hips down. Now hold the chair down with your foot on a rung so I can cut this man's pecker right off for screwin' up our operation." He planned on shoving his useless manhood down his throat too.

The General grabbed the Boone's withered cock in his hand and raised the knife, "Boone, I don't believe ya. Somebody told, and some-body's gotta pay. I wish I could take my time and cut it piece by piece over a few hours, but I'll have to rush the process."

The bloody knife slashed down.

CHAPTER SEVENTY-FOUR

Elizabeth Grant

"Malcom, we need to talk, please put the gun away. Juanita, think you could work on the big guy's wounds for a little while? I'll stitch him up." Juanita visibly swallowed and looked at the job.

Juanita was a lovely Mexican-American young woman with medium length hair and exotic brown eyes and a full-figure that wasn't overweight but healthy and robust.

"Yeah, I guess." Her reluctance for the job hinted she wasn't as tough as Elizabeth first thought. She couldn't fault her on that score; she didn't know how she would stitch him up without passing out herself.

The cabin was compact and there wasn't much in the way of privacy. Elizabeth motioned to the door, but Malcom shook his head no. At least the gun was in its holster. She met him at the sink.

She told him about her adventure, how she ended up at the plantation, was led to Hunter being tortured, how she hid in the closet, and finally rescued the brutalized gang leader.

He didn't hide his anger at her for taking risks. He ground his teeth and his eyes were hard. He asked several questions when she related how she met Juanita and Heath and their efforts to save both herself and Hunter.

He watched the infamous gang leader throughout her account of events. The gears in his mind whirring and churning.

He stalked over to the bed, shooed the others away and patched up the worst of the wounds. Elizabeth somehow wasn't surprised when he cleaned and sterilized the wounds, neatly sewed up the gaping slices, and bandaged them with the supplies in the first aid kit.

"We've got to get him proper care and contact the FBI. He could have muscles severed from that butcher job, or nerves cut," Malcom proclaimed. His anger had boiled down to a simmer at seeing the torture.

Juanita, who hadn't said a word prior, rushed to speak, "You can't put him in a hospital. He'll be dead within hours. That tortured man is indisputable proof the prison break wasn't his gang. In case you missed it, there was a supposed interview with him that made him appear to be free and encouraging an uprising against the peace-loving white citizens that aired on cable news this evening." She stopped to take a breath only to have Heath jump in.

"She's a reporter, and we started on the massacre of a family in Philadelphia that then led us to the prison after his disappearance." He nodded towards Rance Hunter. "We've got evidence that suggests there is a much bigger plan being orchestrated. We're here following a lead and came upon those two trying to escape and a man shooting at them."

Juanita jumped in again, "He isn't going anywhere on his own and he's no threat to anybody in his shape. He can't go to a hospital without being killed. Technically, he's in a Federal agent's custody." She motioned to Malcom. "So please let us tell you what we've discovered." She visibly held her breath.

At the mention of Hunter being in his custody, Malcom's shoulders relaxed ever so slightly. His eyes continued to study everything in the cabin as his mind turned the information over and considered every angle.

He looked into Elizabeth's eyes with an unspoken question. *What did his aunt think?* She could see Loralie, Netty, and the girl who led her to Rance Hunter. Netty nodded to her and her meditation came back to her where Netty explained her dream. *You will help one and one will help you.* She nodded affirmative back to Malcom.

Heath rubbed a hand over his face, "Look, we're going out on a limb trusting you at all. Our evidence ranges from dirty cops and prison guards involved in breaking him out who all received suspicious payments. For all we know, you could be waiting to kill him off to further the agenda we're uncovering."

Malcom stared at them while Elizabeth observed everything from the sidelines. The spirits surrounded the two strangers who claimed to be a reporter and her backup. The spirits probably contributed to their anxiousness if they could sense the three specters even slightly. They sure as hell made her nervous.

Malcom dug out handcuffs from his duffle bag and cuffed one of Hunter's hands to the bed frame.

Elizabeth's mind recalled the room she had rescued Hunter from and grabbed onto what Juanita had said.

"When I found him, they had a camera in the room. Not your home movie version, but a professional level on a heavy duty tripod." She glanced at Malcom. "Let's find out what brought them here." She nodded her head towards the two newcomers. She couldn't say in front of the two newcomers how they might have information that connected to Netty's murder and her own kidnapping. She wasn't sure how much of their side they should share.

"After what you told me, I think I better check to make sure we haven't been discovered. Do me a favor and cover all the windows with blankets and dim the lights." Malcom ducked out the door before she could answer.

Juanita helped her fasten blankets up to the window with duct tape they found in a drawer.

"Philadelphia, huh? I'm from Denver. My Gran lives in town." Elizabeth was grateful for another woman near her age.

"Never thought I'd be in the Deep South, that's for sure. Do you two live out here?" Juanita asked.

There was no way for Juanita to realize they were in hiding themselves. Sure, she had told them Malcom was her boyfriend when she wasn't entirely sure about trusting them. She still wasn't positive on that score. It felt awkward saying they were a couple, like she was hoping for it. Which she wasn't, at all.

"Temporarily only. I hope." She smiled a tense, tight grimace. "How about you two? How long've you two been together?" Elizabeth wanted to change the topic.

Juanita looked over at Heath, who was using a bucket of water and a sponge to continue cleaning the unconscious gang leader of the caked blood and sweat. Not only would that help his healing by reducing germs, but would help all of them breathe better inside the small cabin.

"It's not like that, we're not a couple. He's assisting me with this story, he's a computer expert." Juanita's voice was low as if she didn't want him to hear. Elizabeth doubted he would mind being called a computer expert, so maybe their status wasn't as clear-cut as Juanita would like. But Juanita's eyes seemed to be evaluating Heath, Elizabeth suspected she was weighing some pro and con list.

Juanita changed the subject. "I'm thirsty; can we have something to drink?"

Elizabeth served bottles of soda to them and tried to dribble water down Hunter's throat in small doses. He likely hadn't been given any water since he was captured. She had to hydrated him and get some nourishment into him. After riffling the kitchen cabinets, she found beef bouillon cubes and made up a batch. She was carefully trickling spoonfuls of bouillon into Hunter, who reflexively swallowed.

She had grown increasingly concerned the longer Malcom was gone. Her shoulders ached with knotted muscles. She briefly wondered when she might be able to relax again. It wasn't looking like anytime soon. Malcom finally returned and she could breathe again.

It would be dawn before long and each of them looked exhausted.

They all converged at the table and Elizabeth sat a cola in front of Malcom expecting he needed the caffeine if not the hydration.

Malcom began, "I'm listenin'. Tell us how you ended up here and don't leave anythin' out. We need to understand your involvement since we're investigatin' a murder ourselves." Elizabeth was glad he told them at least that tidbit.

CHAPTER SEVENTY-FIVE

Elizabeth Grant

The weak sunrise was showing around the doorframe. Another batch of coffee in an old-fashioned percolator was boiling on the stove, wafting the strong and bitter aroma throughout the cabin.

Elizabeth poured four cups and Malcom helped carry mugs to the table. Elizabeth glanced at the mountainous man on the bed. He seemed to sleep deeply rather than knocked unconscious. Or so she hoped. He may have answers to what they had been discussing for the last several hours.

"So, Elizabeth went to Whispering Oaks Plantation because Noah's journal had the same logo depicted, while you two found payments from Restoration America addressed from the Plantation linking to the dirty cops in Philadelphia and payments to prison guards on the take who covered Hunter's breakout." Malcom looked into Elizabeth's eyes.

She knew he was waiting to blast her for going out on her own, for risking everything to see that logo. She had no way to know what Whispering Oaks was hiding.

She could tell he was considering sharing what information they had. Interesting how they already understood each other in such a short time. There is probably some study on extreme danger bonding people. He was probably still grieving, and they were thrown together in a life or death sticky wicket.

"We might be working different angles of the same group of people. We have a murder from seven years ago, and my aunt recently." Elizabeth nodded for him to go ahead.

Elizabeth continued to observe Juanita and Heath. They seemed open in sharing everything except how they got the bank records. No doubt because a federal agent like Malcom would have to act on even the suspicion of hacking a bank.

The three spirits were sporadic in appearing for the last few hours, as if they were keeping a ghostly ear on things but didn't want to sit through all the talk. She was barely staying awake herself and felt removed, like a part of her was sleeping even though her eyes were open and she heard everything. She couldn't drink any more coffee, the acid in her stomach wouldn't tolerate it.

Malcom explained about Noah's notebook in more detail, how Loralie had taken possession of it and what he suspected was a compromised FBI agent who had informed the local men of the notebook. Noah was executed and Loralie disappeared. Until Elizabeth came to town and stirred up a hornet's nest.

"Why would her visit trigger anything? I don't understand." Juanita looked between Malcom and Elizabeth. Malcom looked to her for permission to continue.

Elizabeth sighed, "Juanita, do me a favor. I know this will seem strange, but think of somebody you knew who died. Don't tell me who and let it be somebody close to you so you can really remember them. Mentally call out to that person." Elizabeth had no idea if the spirit would come forward, but she was hoping a demonstration of some sort would cut through all the resistance she expected.

"I don't know what you're doing, but okay." She narrowed her eyes at Elizabeth.

Elizabeth was surprised when a new spirit appeared next to Juanita. Even more surprised, it was a young Hispanic man. It must be this sleepy frame of mind. *Javier, her cousin,* popped into Elizabeth's head rather than hear him actually speak.

"You lost your cousin Javier. He was young to die." She related. *Tell her I'm sorry I argued with her when I last saw her. I didn't believe the drugs would kill me.* Okay, she didn't like this before, and it was getting worse the more she found out how it worked.

"He died from drugs and regrets arguing with you the last time you were together." Juanita made the sign of the cross and swallowed, her eyes wide.

Heath leaned back in his seat and eyed her. Disbelief shone in his eyes. Suddenly a lovely woman appeared by his side, long flowing black hair and gray eyes. *I'm Gloria. We were engaged. Drunk driver killed me. It's okay for him to move on.*

"Heath, Gloria was your fiancée when a drunk driver took her out. She wants you to know it's okay for you to move on." His mouth dropped open. Juanita's head whipped around to stare at him. He turned his head away from her. Elizabeth could see tears forming in his eyes.

Malcom relieved the awkward moment and resumed explaining their involvement. "So, Elizabeth saw the spirit of Loralie at the moment she died. She was frightened, and she insisted on talking to Loralie on the phone. That raised awareness fast that Loralie had disappeared without a trace." He took a big swallow of coffee before resuming.

"I have a theory that the White Supremacist organization that Noah Aarons was documentin' killed Loralie and they thought Elizabeth had been in contact, maybe knew all about them. How else would you explain her knowin' somethin' happened to Loralie if you didn't know she was gifted?" He shrugged his shoulders to Elizabeth, a rushed apology for voicing his theory without warning.

Heath blurted out, all trace of tears gone, "Wait a minute, are you saying this racist group is the same ones behind the massacre in Philadelphia and this elaborate kidnapping of a black gang leader? Because they're both connected to that plantation?"

Malcom answered swiftly, "The military grade helicopter isn't somethin' you acquire last minute and takes some top brass to swing. That break out took plannin' at high levels too, just like Noah's notes warned they had highly influential members. You said the hooker divulged the one cop involved talked like a racist and spoke of action needed, just the same as Noah's notebook explains. Noah seems to have been close to discoverin' names of the influential members and perhaps even somethin' of what they were plannin'."

"But that was, what – seven years ago? They'd be on somebody's radar before now or given up on their plans in that time," Juanita asserted.

Heath jumped in, "Not if you're playing the long game, like a long con that takes time to set up for a bigger payoff."

Malcom finished with, "And if you have FBI agents in your ranks, the same agency that's tasked with protectin' civil rights since the sixties, investigatin', and prosecutin' groups like the KKK for criminal and violent activities. If you've infiltrated the Bureau that's tasked with stopping such activity, well…"

He then shared how his own boss was the man Loralie met with but didn't hand over Noah's notes. How Siesbolt never documented his contact with Noah or a possible hate group. More of the story was revealed and hashed out.

"Even if we're working the same problem, what's the endgame? We've spitballed plenty of theories, but what the hell does this all amount to?" Juanita huffed in frustration.

Malcom had shared more than she ever expected, but she still saw suspicion in his eyes. Silence had settled as everyone considered the information shared.

Malcom looked Juanita in the eyes. "It occurs to me you are rather young for such a story. You said you started in Philadelphia and then followed leads out to California and now, here. Seems you have some vast resources for a freelancer. You even have a *computer expert* along. So how did you get the first lead about the cops in Philadelphia? You aren't a local reporter to get a tip." He went from amiable listener to FBI interrogator in just seconds. But Elizabeth thought he had an excellent point.

Heath glanced at Juanita quickly and shifted in his chair. Juanita took a few moments before answering. "I told you about the video of the cops. None of the local police would even look at it when the neighborhood man tried to give it to them, then he started being harassed by the cops." She grew silent.

"I'm waitin' miss Alvarez."

"That working-class man had a family member in the Black Apostles gang, so he asked for protection from the police and turned over the video." Her eyes were focused on the tabletop.

Malcom seemed to pounce on that information. "Now are you telling me you are a mouthpiece for the gang?"

Juanita's head snapped up and her eyes were fierce, "NO! I took the tip and investigated on my own. That's when I went to Heath."

"I checked all the metadata, GPS location, and all associated files to the video. I checked for tampering of the file. I know what phone number originally took the video. It's the real deal," Heath provided.

Juanita continued, "But before I could continue on the dirty cop involvement, Hunter was broke from jail. The tipster contacted me and swore the gang had nothing to do with it, and they wanted to know which gang was involved so they could do a strategic retaliation rather than striking any or all of their competing gangs."

Malcom had jumped up and paced, three steps and turn, three steps and turn. "You're their patsy. We can't trust anythin' you say." His voice was clipped.

"Let me show you something." She grabbed a soft leather laptop bag and took out some papers that she handed to Malcom. "That is the legal contract with the Apostles. I am to report what I find with no pressure on results other than to show what evidence I dig up. I am free to use my results for my own freelancing under no obligation to them." She remained standing and planted her hands on her hips and eyes followed Malcom.

After glancing through the contract, he wasn't so agitated. "You can't seriously think this contract means they won't pressure you to make Hunter and the Apostles innocent?"

Juanita let out a harsh laugh and went nose-to-nose with him, "I'm not the one who dragged him out of the lair of clearly non-gang members. Men who were going to kill him after they manufactured an interview – maybe like a terrorist's hostage he was forced to say what they wanted. He's your proof, and you sewed up the evidence of his torture yourself. All my evidence so far is documented paper trails, and no gang influenced that." Now Juanita stalked back and worth.

She continued ranting, "I left corporate media so I could follow true investigative stories, so I could uphold the public trust, to report ethically and inform the public, to uphold the press as the critical fourth estate. You should be protecting us. We've put our lives on the line, too. We secured a minor who saw the helicopter and would be killed if he had gone to any of the local police or those corporate dweeb reporters having their stories handed to them." Occasionally an arm would thrust and she would point and her voice was getting progressively louder.

Heath walked over and faced her, stopping her pacing. He placed a hand on her shoulder, "We're in hiding, I don't think the yelling is particularly covert. Nita, we know we've dug up the truth. Far more than anybody expected. The evidence will speak for itself."

Through Juanita's tirade, Malcom had stood by and watched her. Was that satisfaction in his eyes?

"Thank you for the truth. I believe you've now told me everythin'. If your contact is waitin' to hear from you, will it stop some violence between gangs that's spreading if you tell them Hunter has been found?"

Her eyes still sparked and sizzled when she looked at Malcom, as if he had personally insulted her mother. "It may lessen it. The Los Angeles branch went against the leadership decision, so I don't know how they'll handle that. The catch is, they'll likely want to come and retrieve Hunter."

"As you pointed out a few hours ago, he's in FBI custody and I consider all of us now in witness protection mode. You can safely inform them you've worked a deal to be *embedded* with the agents protectin' Mr. Hunter. You can give them updates on his health and well bein', but not his location or our plans. Is that a deal, Ms. Alvarez?"

She nodded once, "It's a deal, *Agent* Alexander."

Elizabeth asked Juanita. "Tell me about the manufactured interview with Hunter."

"It portrayed him as a homegrown Islamic terrorist advocating an uprising against the peaceful white folk of the nation. A hostile takeover, essentially."

"Seems the attack on that family in Philadelphia that set up Hunter's gang was laying the groundwork for that interview. Then they broke him out and fake an inflammatory call to bloodshed, which allows this group to engineer more violence and push fear to justify... maybe National Guard involvement and the black community is somehow, what? Enslaved? Mass incarceration? Killed in retaliation?" Elizabeth was putting the pieces together. She wouldn't hide away in ignorance. She looked at the cluster of spirits, Loralie and Netty held each other and nodded at her.

Again silence settled as they sank into their own thoughts and conspiracy theories until Elizabeth spoke up. "Okay, now what guys? We've got a fugitive from prison over there and likely powerful people scouting to find all of us and kill us. They have some plan in progress we don't fully understand. What do we do about it?"

"I have an idea. It's an offensive move rather than playin' defense." Malcom had his arms crossed over his chest.

A shot of fear ran through Elizabeth.

CHAPTER SEVENTY-SIX

Elizabeth Grant

Elizabeth and Malcom got their allotted two hours of sleep first. She took the bed, and he took the fold-out couch with a sleeping bag.

After their exhausting discussion and planning session last night, Juanita had made a call to her Black Apostles contact, *Tito*. Malcom had insisted on the call be on speaker after Heath assured him it couldn't be traced. Something he had engineered through voice-over-IP that sounded technical and maybe even illegal from the way Malcom regarded him after that.

Tito's voice filled the small cabin. "Look, reporter girl, what do I tell my boss? I can't give him some scattered ideas on what happened."

"Tell him we rescued Hunter, which wasn't part of the deal, at great risk to ourselves, let me tell you. Tell your boss that we're taking good care of him and that he's in protective custody. Tell him we rescued him from men who aren't gang members of any kind. I'm gathering evidence on their motives for snatching him." She took a breath and held it, waiting for his response.

"You're fucking positive it wasn't a gang trying to flex on us?" Tito's skepticism was on full display.

"Completely positive, if anything they want to stir up gang violence. So please get the LA and Miami branches under control."

"Yeah, wish I could little reporter girl. Apache and Shark-tooth done gone off the reservation and picked fights with Nuestra and Russian mob. I fear those Russkies more than anybody else." Tito paused before continuing, "Why hasn't it been on the news he's in custody or something?"

Juanita looked at Malcom and licked her lips, "Well, he was badly beaten and cut up. Whoever they are, they're no doubt trying to get him back. So we're staying on the down-low to protect him... and us."

"You tell me where you are reporter girl and I can have the best doctors and nurses in private care there for him." It came out as a demand. Juanita swallowed.

"Can't do that Tito, he's in FBI protective custody and no gang-paid anybody is coming near him. But we're taking good care of him." Ultimately Tito had no choice but to accept it with the Bureau being involved.

Elizabeth was prepping a big breakfast of scrambled eggs and pancakes. She was sleep deprived, her eyes felt like coarse rock salt had scrubbed them, and her mind felt like it was in some alternate universe.

"He's awake." The young girl's spirit, Angelique, whispered next to her ear. She flicked her hand to swat at the whispered voice.

She turned from the sink with a smile pasted on to see Hunter glance around, lift his arms to see the bandages and that he was hand-cuffed to the heavy wood bed frame. Although, from the looks of his bulging muscles, she feared he could break the bed frame into match-sticks with little effort.

"We'll get a doctor or nurse to look at your injuries. We patched you up the best we could. We just have to find somebody we can trust."

He looked at her with confusion, as if he was having difficulty remembering who she was, then his eyes looked startled. *Guess he remembered their running in the night.*

"How're we not blown to hell? I could barely run and we were being shot at." He ran his free hand over his face, then shook his head.

"We'd both be dead, if not for those two." She indicated with her chin the next bed where Heath with his bandaged hand and Juanita lay fully clothed getting their few hours of sleep. He had an arm around her waist as they spooned. It seemed clear to Elizabeth, despite Juanita's protests, that they were closer than she admitted from their cuddling.

"They saw us being chased, and he took a fallen tree limb to the man's head who was shooting at us." She sat on the edge of the bed and placed her hand against his forehead. "You're still feverish. I tried to get some fluids down you, but I don't think it was enough. Do you think you can keep food down?"

He struggled to sit upright. "Wait, I don't know you. Why are you helping me? Do you know who I am?" He jangled the handcuffs.

"Yes, Mr. Hunter, I know who you are. We all do. I didn't know when I discovered you and saw what they did to you. But by the time I helped you escape, I'd figured it out."

"You didn't answer my question."

"I helped you because I don't believe in torture. Because they were going to kill you and I don't believe in murder. Because Angelique begged me to." She felt he needed reassurance. Getting him to cooperate with their plan was critical.

"You didn't answer my question either," She said, keeping eye contact. At his questioning look she reiterated, "Do you think you can hold down food?"

He gave a slight smile. "I'm starved."

She nodded. "Okay, we'll take it slow with some eggs and bacon. You need plenty of protein to heal."

He placed a large hand softly on her arm, "How could Angelique beg you to help me? Are you fucking with me?" He spoke in a murderous growl.

"Mr. Hunter, the short answer is I communicate with spirits. Your sister was most insistent I save you."

"You're fucking shitting me? You talk to dead people, really?" He wasn't smiling now, and she didn't want to see him angry – ever. Angelique was next to Elizabeth in the next heartbeat. *He never told anyone that I was caught smoking at school. He laughed at me, called me the normal one in the family. Tell him all that.*

"You never told how she was caught smoking and you said she was the normal member of the family." She watched the surprise strike. "I'm not lying. I don't even like seeing the dead, let alone hearing them."

Malcom walked in and Rance stiffened.

"Mr. Hunter this is FBI Agent Malcom Alexander. You're in protective custody since somebody engineered a prison break using a high-tech helicopter, faked an interview for TV where you claim your gang broke you out and you're calling for an ethnic war, and then were about to kill you. Needless to say, we're all likely targets for helping you." She blurted out to stop the men from posturing.

"Nothing like breaking it to him slowly, Liza," Malcom huffed. Startled by the use of her nickname, she was slightly flustered and could feel her face grow warm, but continued.

"We don't have time for nice and gentle." She crossed her arms, "I get the impression he likes the situation straight up." She left Hunter and worked on breakfast in earnest for everyone.

Getting Hunter to participate willingly in Malcom's idea was key. It was their only plan of how to stop the violence and growing resentment between white and black citizens. The radio station she had listened to for only a few minutes reported interracial violence spreading faster than the riots in Los Angeles.

Malcom explained that we all must get out of town to survive. Then he covered how Apache bombed the Nuestra Familia and the resulting gang violence spreading in L.A. He covered the riots in Philadelphia. He assured Hunter that they had contacted Tito and informed him of the situation, hoping to stop any further attacks.

"As long as you're with me we'll keep you safe and expose how you were used. Clear your name of the breakout, but I can't stress enough how it is in your best interest to cooperate in my custody."

"I'm not afraid to fight, not even afraid of dying. But I ain't stupid and I don't like being played. This violence all seems to hand whoever did this to me exactly what they want." Rance Hunter hesitated for a few moments. "Give me one good reason I shouldn't just run and try to save me and mine in this whole mess."

Elizabeth slammed a biscuit pan on the kitchen counter and spun around. "Really? How about stepping up to prove people wrong about you and your gang? How about for the sake of this country? How about for the memory of Angelique? No wonder she's still here worrying about you. You may have grown large and muscular, but you sure as hell haven't grown to be a man." She tried to control her anger with little luck. "Let me show you something."

Juanita and Heath had jumped awake at the slam of pan and sat on the bed with wide eyes taking in Elizabeth yelling.

She went to her purse and took out a picture of Loralie taken the last summer they spent together. They were arm in arm with big smiles. She held it out with shaking hands.

"This is the first casualty we know of from this Restoration America or whatever they're called. That is my best friend in the world, although we were more like sisters. One year after that photo, she was hunted down with dogs and brutally beaten. She died that night to keep evidence of that *organization* from being destroyed. She died a hero and you want to just walk away from her." She was being strong, and she was paying her debt to Loralie. Seven years worth of pent-up emotions were coming out in a fireball at Hunter.

She stood next to Malcom, "His beloved aunt was killed trying to get me to safety from this *organization*. She's another hero. She was a lovely woman I wish I could've spent more time with. She helped raise him, and he's trying to bring the people who took her life to justice. But you, you just want to turn tail like a whipped dog and hide with your gang while the nation potentially burns around you." Tears were racing down her cheeks.

He tried to jump up, but the handcuff on his one arm held him. "Bitch, you..." But she walked up to Rance Hunter, the leader of a violent gang, and put her face right in his.

He reached up with his free hand and wrapped it around her neck.

The spirits of Aunt Netty, Loralie, and Angelique were all pulling on his arm. Angelique was begging him. Malcom took his gun out and pointed it at Hunter's head.

Elizabeth stared into his eyes and whispered, "Am I wrong? What would Angelique think?" Thank the powers that be he was so weak, but she might still have bruising from his hand at her throat.

At those words, he removed his hand and seemed to slump into himself. Angelique's name had stopped him, or maybe her spirit got through to him. There was a heart in there behind the murderous rage. Or maybe it was the gun ready to blow his head clean off.

After several heartbeats in which nobody moved, he finally said, "What do you want from me, woman?" He looked at her with a shadow of fear lurking in his eyes.

Juanita cleared her throat as if reluctant to call attention to herself, "We have a plan of how we can counter the fake interview where you called for a race war and hopefully short circuit the growing violence and animosity to stop whatever agenda is in play." She took a breath and squared her shoulders, "But first we have to get out of here and to a television news channel studio in Jackson. Getting out of this town alive is our next hurdle."

We had decided Hunter shouldn't know it was Malcom's idea. Rance Hunter sat and listened to the plan. He asked a few questions but seemed to have resigned himself to participating. Elizabeth was quiet, shocked that she had provoked a man she knew was a murderer.

They finished eating the breakfast Elizabeth and Malcom prepared when the sheriff pulled up. They both went outside to prevent him from entering. The fewer people who knew about their special guest the better. Besides, she had to explain her absence last night, and they had to convince him to help in their escape. Oh crap, then there was her demanding uncle.

CHAPTER SEVENTY-SEVEN

Heath Grayson

I t was go time, Juanita and Heath had gone by their hotel, ruffled the bed to look slept in, showered, and threw their luggage in the rental car. After paying their bill, they drove out of town to make sure anybody watching would think they had left. They turned around and drove back, taking a logging road that wound through trees with no sign of people. The road ended at a small lake, or more of a large pond depending on your definition of a lake.

Heath released the trunk and got out to stand next to it. He smoothed the blanket he placed inside it. He surveyed the surroundings. The late morning warmth, fragrant pines, and shimmering lake were wasted on him. All the trees made him nervous, too many spots for a person to hide. Finally, he heard a vehicle coming through the trees, off-road. That would be the FBI Agent.

Heath saw Malcom as a necessary evil in this endeavor. If they came through this alive, his involvement would cover a multitude of sins. Or so he hoped. Actually, Malcom seemed like a reasonable enough guy. Who was he kidding? The instant Malcom found out he did jail time for white collar crime, he wouldn't be so semi-pleasant. He's sure protective of that Elizabeth gal. Could there be more between them than they let on? He sensed some sexual tension between them, but this was more than that.

He didn't know what to think about Elizabeth. She was pretty in that girl-next-door way, but he hated wondering what all she knew. When she pulled that stuff about Juanita's cousin out of her ass he thought it was a con. Somehow.

Then his mind went to Gloria without intending to. He couldn't help but think of her and how he missed her when Elizabeth was saying to think of somebody who died. Then, as if by some witchcraft, that Elizabeth was speaking for Gloria. It was more than unnerving. It was scary.

That woman scared him – that she could see his most vulnerable scar and just laid it bare for everybody to see. The only good aspect of her being in the car was that Juanita wasn't likely to ask him about Gloria when Elizabeth could hear them talk.

He felt guilty for not sharing about Gloria, but Juanita was so damned defensive about what they had. She resisted and fought the growing feelings between them. Besides, they hadn't really had a good time to discuss his prior fiancé. He wasn't afraid or anything. He sure as hell wasn't waiting for some sign it was okay to move on. If anything, it was more Juanita who had the problem.

His thoughts were interrupted by a four-wheel drive Suburban that crept between trees with the sheriff walking in front and guiding Elizabeth as she drove. The plan was for Rance Hunter to be lying down in the back, covered and out of sight. So far, the sheriff remained unaware of Hunter's presence in his town. Malcom followed on foot behind the Suburban.

The Suburban stopped a few feet from the car and Elizabeth climbed out.

"I don't feel good about this, Miss Elizabeth. You going off with these men, it ain't right."

"Sheriff Craig, this isn't the 1800s and I don't need a chaperone. Malcom is a respected federal agent." She gave the crusty lawman her hand to shake, "I'll let you know once we stop for the night, ok?"

He must have said or done something because she rolled her eyes,

"Don't go making more of it than there is. This isn't some romantic vacation." After how she went off yelling at Hunter, he wouldn't want to push that gal too far.

Elizabeth walked over to Heath. "I put a thick blanket down to cushion it a little and there is a pillow for you. I have the backseat propped open so you can get air and we can talk back and forth. I don't think anybody can tell."

She flashed him a tired smile, "Let's do this." She climbed in and he made sure she was safely away from the latch, then closed the trunk on her.

He watched as Malcom climbed into the backseat of the Suburban while the sheriff got behind the steering wheel. The Sheriff was to drive Malcom, and a hidden Hunter until they were halfway to Jackson, where the sheriff had arranged for a trucker friend to give him a ride back. After that, they could risk Malcom and Elizabeth driving in the Suburban. Hunter would have to stay out of sight for the entire trip.

Heath figured the gang leader would likely sleep most of the way. He was still rather weak from his ordeal and keeping solid food down was iffy.

They were on the one and only road out of town, headed west with the rental car first and the Suburban following. He didn't find it amusing that they had driven into town on this road less than twenty-four hours ago. The daylight didn't provide no comfort since he imagined all the hiding places among the trees on each side concealing an ambush. Thoughts assailed him of stealth helicopters chasing them, making him even jumpier. *Geez, just stay cool. You're on your way to the next stage.*

They had gone a few miles, not far enough to think they had gotten away without notice, when a rusty green truck swung in behind the rental car. The sheriff had dropped back and this truck now split their little caravan in two.

The two-way radio crackled and Sheriff Craig's voice boomed, "I don't like this truck between us. Slow down and see if he'll go around."

Heath initially scoffed at the long-range radios, but revised his opinion now. He was grateful to have them. He eased his foot up from the gas and the rental sedan slowed. The truck stayed right behind them.

Elizabeth's voice reached him, "What kind of truck?"

"Old rusty thing."

"Color?" She persisted.

"Some kind of pea green. Why?"

"That truck has followed me before. I've got a bad feeling about this." Elizabeth's voice shook.

CHAPTER SEVENTY-EIGHT

Sheriff Jake Craig

J ake Craig had a bad feeling too. Anybody else would have gone around the slow-poke car. Heath had even moved over in the lane, stuck his arm out the window and waved for the truck to pass. Nothing.

He knew most of the vehicles in town, but he couldn't place this truck's owner. That bothered him even more. He wished he had some of those portable flashing light bubbles. He would have pulled his weight as sheriff. Sadly, neither the department nor he owned one.

The next instant, the passenger in the truck leaned out the window and shot at the tires. *Elizabeth was in the trunk.* A ricochet or miss could hit the trunk and Elizabeth. This would never do. He couldn't sit by and watch that.

"Malcom, we got trouble. This truck is shootin' at the car." He figured Malcom staying hidden was a moot point now. His hands were suddenly sweaty. He had to make sure Elizabeth got away alive. No god damn wonder her mother left town and never looked back. If anything happened to her... well, he already was blaming himself for not being the father she needed.

Malcom threw off the blanket and sat upright in the backseat. Jake could see him grab his duffle bag with his weapons stash. "I'm on it. I can return fire from their flank." He loaded bullets into a stainless steel revolver, "Ah, my trusty M1911 from my Ranger days." Jake approved silently since he had used the same gun in his military service days, but any gun might hit the car with Elizabeth hidden in the trunk.

Malcom rolled the window down and leaned halfway-out, took aim and shot twice. The truck swerved and his shots went wild, missing. The truck shooter returned fire and Malcom ducked back into the Suburban.

Malcom leaned out again and got off another shot. Probably aiming for the tires, but it wasn't as easy to do as the television shows made it out to be, fighting the vehicle jostling and the wind from driving and other factors you don't notice until you attempt a shot. Jake noticed liquid trails from the truck. He had hit something.

"I think you got their gas tank somehow, don't think you could've got their radiator."

Malcom leaned forward to get a look. "I'm betting gas. If we're lucky they'll be out before long."

The truck sped up and pulled next to the car, then drifted into their lane trying to run them off the road.

A string of cursing exploded from his mouth.

Malcom leaned out the opposite window for a clear shot. He let off two more shots and one tire blew, sending the truck swerving wildly and Jake had to avoid hitting them. As he was passing the truck, the shooter got off a few more shots. He felt a thwack and jerk in his arm, then a burning like a few dozen yellow jacket stings.

He sucked in a breath through his teeth. Then the metallic scent of blood reached him.

He held on tight to the steering wheel with his good arm. His left hand was going numb. It wasn't the first time he'd been shot; a stupid hunter friend had clipped him one year after guzzling too much damn beer.

The green truck had swerved off the road and into the ditch, but gunfire still sounded for a while until they were out of range.

"Malcom, got a problem here." He wouldn't be able to drive for much longer. Malcom leaned forward into the front. "I'm shot in the left arm. Numb and bleeding."

"Damn it all to hell," Malcom grabbed the two-way radio from the front passenger seat. "Craig's shot. Drive for another mile and pull over. We gotta change drivers and try to stop the bleedin.'"

"Ask about Elizabeth." He had to know.

"Everybody okay on your end?" Malcom asked.

"Barely." Heath's controlled panic was clear.

Jake gritted his teeth; he had to drive the next few miles no matter what.

CHAPTER SEVENTY-NINE
Elizabeth Grant

Heath kept driving for several miles, the minutes ticking by. Elizabeth's nerves were strung tighter than a guitar string about to snap, and she wanted to slap Heath. The Sheriff was shot, and they needed to take care of him.

"I don't like pulling over. What if more of them show up? We should keep going." Heath's voice was hitting a higher register.

Juanita's voice held a tinge of terror, "We can't risk both Hunter and the sheriff. I see Malcom driving from behind the front seat. He can't keep that up. We have to pull over or he may lose control of the car."

She held back from saying anything, Heath had been avoiding her ever since she had done her demonstration and mentioned Gloria. She was sorry for that, but she was trying to get past their resistance and distrust. She hadn't had time to tread gently. He wouldn't like it if she burst forth from the trunk with demands they stop. Malcom was the only one she trusted, and he was in trouble.

"Okay! Okay! I'm pulling over. But I'm taking off if they show up." He gradually eased the rental car onto the edge of the road.

Elizabeth had crawled out of the trunk into the backseat and as soon as the car came to a stop she was out of the car on the opposite side from the road.

The Suburban didn't seem to be stopping and was coming right towards them. She could see Malcom reaching from the backseat around the sheriff, but he had no control over the gas or brake pedals. She could tell he was yelling for the Sheriff to stop.

Finally, the Suburban jerked to a stop a few feet short of their car. Elizabeth ran and jumped in the passenger side. She grabbed the emergency brake and wrenched it back hard, then turned the engine off. Heath and Juanita opened the driver's door, and the sheriff slumped into Heath's arms.

His eyes bulged at the blood, "Guys, some help here. He is not a feather-weight, guys."

The sheriff moaned.

Malcom was by his side in a second taking an arm, "Let's get him stretched out on the backseat."

They had barely wedged him in, working from both sides of the vehicle when Sheriff Craig opened his eyes to slits.

"Where's Elizabeth? Is she all right? I have to see her, where is she?" His voice was a strong whisper, but that was the limit of his strength.

"I'm right here sheriff, now just let Malcom help you out." She had reached over the front seat and held his meaty hand in hers. "Malcom will get you bandaged and help stop the bleeding." Why he was so concerned about her right now was puzzling.

Malcom caught her eyes and shook his head. "Sir, I'm not gonna lie. The bullet is in there and I don't know how bad it is. I'm gonna try to get the bullet out if it isn't lodged too far in. I'm not a paramedic, so tell me if you don't want me to try."

Rance Hunter sat up from the very back of the vehicle and tossed his blanket off. "I've dug out plenty of bullets from my guys. If I can get the bullet out fast, and you do the bandaging, then we can get the fucking hell out of here pronto." He leaned over the seat and surveyed the wound in the arm.

Great, they hadn't told the sheriff about Hunter and now he would dig a bullet from his arm. Maybe he was in shock and wouldn't realize who the hulking, stitched up, and swollen-eyed man was. Elizabeth was torn about trusting Hunter. She became protective of the Sheriff who she suspected at times.

"I've lost a lot of blood, so in case I don't make it… I got to tell you somethin'…" He was struggling to speak.

Malcom was running a lighter flame over his knife blade, "Really, you got to tell her now! Can't it wait?" His voice was like a drill sergeant's with an immature recruit. He rolled his eyes and glanced out the back window.

No sign of a vehicle.

Sheriff Jake Craig cleared his throat, "Elizabeth, I grew up with your mother and we… well, we dated all through high school…"

Elizabeth's eyebrows drew together, what the hell was this about? She was aware they knew each other, maybe not the dating thing.

Heath, standing at the door of the Suburban, rolled his eyes and threw his arms up. Juanita's eyes grew big, and she covered her mouth.

"I had just joined the army when she told me she was… in the family way." He was struggling to get each word out.

Elizabeth went numb. No way. It couldn't be *him*. All those times she and Loralie imagined who their father was, she never would have thought it was him. Not that there was anything wrong with him per se. *Where the hell had he been all her life? Why had she been robbed of knowing him? Did he not want her?*

"I wanted to get married at the Justice of the Peace before I left for Boot Camp, but your momma wouldn't hear of it. See, I only ever wanted to live right here. She wanted nothin' more to do with small towns and especially the attitudes of some here about. She chose not to tell you and I was madder than a wet hen about that. But I said I'd respect her wishes. I went to both your graduations though. Your grandma keeps me informed on how you're doing. I'm prouda ya." He went limp as if his confession had taken all his strength.

Elizabeth whipped a tear from her face. Her eyes were swimming, and she blinked to wash the unshed tears away. Her throat had a lump obstructing swallowing, let alone speech. She was in shock, just one more thing to add to the growing list of secrets she had stumbled into. But why had her mother kept it a secret? There was a bubble of anger for her being deprived a father all these years that was rising up.

"He's out." Malcom handed the knife to Hunter, "Don't mess this up just cause he's law enforcement."

"I wasn't gonna, but now that I know he's her father, wouldn't dream of it." He nodded his head toward Elizabeth and took the knife to the bloody hole in Sheriff Craig's shoulder. She suspected he thought she was a witch or something and right now she was okay with him believing that.

Malcom gritted his teeth and looked from Hunter to Elizabeth then out the back window. *Geez, what was his deal now?* She couldn't afford to be dazed and confused right now. She had the rest of the drive to try to untangle her feelings and sort through the anger welling up.

CHAPTER EIGHTY

Christine Roberts

They arrived at the news station's back door in the early evening. Only two people knew about guests for a special broadcast. The arrangements were made by phone that morning and included a doctor, sworn to secrecy to treat some medical need, and food for five hungry people.

The National Gazette had been the point of introduction for this reporter, a Juanita somebody or other that the studio never heard of before. But National Gazette was known, so everything was set into motion.

Christine Roberts had been the point person to coordinate this special broadcast, but she had absolutely no idea what to expect. Her information was limited to a special report needing the utmost secrecy for a special guest who would need medical attention upon arrival. No hint of what or who was involved.

She stood by the back door in the alley behind the station when the dirty and road-weary Suburban pulled up followed by a nice sedan. All five people, three men and two women, congregated at the back of the Suburban. One man had a shoulder bandage made of what looked like a spare shirt that had a patch of dried blood. *Was he the man who needed the doctor?*

A massive figure covered by a blanket climbed out of the back of the Suburban and slowly stood. It was a man from the sheer bulk and the muscle on the legs, but weak, he took assistance from one of the women. Maybe he was the special guest who needed medical attention. There were a total of six instead of the five she was told and it seemed to Christine two of them needed a doctor.

She escorted them to the Green Room, a waiting room for guests, where the food and doctor were waiting. It wasn't until they were all locked inside that the man removed the blanket.

He had bandages over his arms and his face was swollen from some serious beatings, one eye swollen shut. But it was the tattoo on the massive arm that made her heart skip a beat. It was the escaped gang leader, and he looked to be in bad shape. She wouldn't have recognized him if it weren't for his infamous tattoo. Did he have a falling out with his gang, maybe a power struggle and he was removed as the leader? Was that what this was about, they would break the story on the air? That could give their ratings a much-needed boost.

The Hispanic young woman spoke first, "I'm the reporter, Juanita Alvarez." They shook hands and Christine looked around at the others.

The fresh-faced white woman cleared her throat, "Call me Beth." She noted the wording used, *call me Beth*. So, it wasn't her real name.

The sandy-blond guy next to Juanita didn't offer a name. Curious. The handsome and athletic black man nodded to her and tossed out, "I'm Alexander."

Christine nodded toward the escaped convict, "And Rance Hunter." She looked at the man with the make-shift bandage on his arm, easily the oldest person in the room, and raised her eyebrows in question but nobody offered a name for him either.

The doctor helped the elder of the group to sit down. After a few minutes of examining, cleaning, and bandaging with heavy gauze, he proclaimed, "You should be fine, nice job fishing the bullet out, mostly fatty tissue. Sit upright and apply pressure for a while to lessen the bleeding." *Beth* sat by him and applied pressure. They seemed awkward around each other.

The doctor then checked Rance Hunter's multiple wounds. Hunter grunted a few times at the prodding. She would have been screaming bloody murder at the prodding examination.

"Not damn bad work young man." The Doctor said to Alexander who volunteered he had tended the injuries. "One area looks infected, so I'll remove the stitches and clean it out and stitch it back up. I'll administer an antibiotic shot to ward off infection for both of you gents. But that eye needs looked at by a specialist. I'm afraid it might have serious damage."

"I was worried that nerves or major muscles could have been severed." Alexander replied.

"Full x-rays and an MRI are in order to know the extent of the damage. May I ask how these injuries were obtained?"

All six looked at each other. Without speaking they seemed to defer to Alexander as their spokesman. "He was repeatedly tortured and about to be killed when he was rescued."

The fresh-faced Beth added, "They used crude short saws and X-acto knives, he had been tied to a chair for a while, too."

"I can talk for myself. That's true for these injuries, they turned to the knives and then to the small saws, but they started with the beatings like I was a punching bag to get out all their hate. I don't know how long I was tied up." Hunter looked at Beth and Alexander bristled at the look.

Well, well, well. Maybe the gang leader had taken to Beth and the good-looking Alexander didn't like it. But, Hunter didn't look at her with lust or affection, more like he was careful around her. Either way, it wasn't her problem unless it impacted the special report.

The reporter gal, Juanita, spoke up "He was tortured for several days before he was rescued, but that'll be covered in the interview."

She did some quick thinking and calculating. "That predates the televised interview yesterday; he wasn't hurt or tied up for that."

Juanita turned to her, "Are you a hundred percent sure of that? Did you see his hands, arms, or legs at all during the interview?"

That's ridiculous, how stupid could this cub reporter be?

Christine turned but was stopped at the door by the sandy blond man, "Where're you going?"

"I don't want to sit here during all the patching up. There's an intercom I'll answer if you need me before I return."

Alexander turned, "Please don't tell anybody else about this." He took out an FBI badge. *Special Agent Alexander, surprise, surprise.* "He's in protective custody and utmost secrecy on this interview is beyond critical."

She smiled her best reassuring smile and swallowed. This had to be a bigger story than Hunter's gang cutting him out of the gang or his capture by the authorities. *Protective custody? From what?* People would typically need protection from him. This would bolster their ratings if it didn't bite them in the ass.

She left the Green Room that had seemed a good size until a gang leader and a handful of people filled it up. She went directly to her desk and pulled up the first interview with Rance Hunter. She watched it a dozen times.

Fucking hell, he could've been tied up, you never see his hands and once she was looking for it, it seemed unnatural. What's worse, on slow motion she noticed a slight, like a millisecond, lag from the video and his words. She didn't know what to believe, but she figured this second broadcast would be explosive.

She checked on the readiness of the crew to broadcast whenever their guests was ready. It would be simulcast over their syndicated network and to National Gazette's website.

She returned to the Green Room just as the doctor finished stitching up Hunter's wound and gave the promised shot. Forget makeup for Hunter, let the horror of his injuries shock the viewers, that's always good for ratings.

Juanita approached her, "We haven't discussed the broadcast. I'll interview Mr. Hunter and Beth. She wishes to remain anonymous for the moment."

First, this upstart challenged her on the validity of the prior interview, and now she was acting like she was in charge. The little cub reporter didn't even work for the network. It felt personal, like she was being squeezed out of her job by this little punk nobody girl.

The others looked at Christine.

"Our producers don't like surprises. This is television, not a newspaper. We're not about stories that might offend our viewers. This is a numbers and ratings game, it's not about heroic reporting." This cub reporter might as well get a lesson in the real world.

Juanita stiffened at her words. *Tough, it was the reality of modern television news, just keep the people tuning in and entertained, not necessarily informed.*

Agent Alexander spoke up, "We really must insist that Miss Alvarez do the interview." His smile was meant to soften the blow, but it didn't.

Rance Hunter stood up, dwarfing the others. The intensity of his presence, even beaten and cut up, felt deadly. "This ain't your story to tell bitch. Juanita interviews me and Beth will be by my side. Now, do we have a problem?"

"I see, you're trying to clean up your reputation and damage done by bombing the Nuestra Familia..." Christine began. Having a Hispanic girl interview him and a white girl lending support was good damage control.

Agent Alexander weighed in too. "There's far more at stake than his personal story. We know the details and what needs exposed. Are we clear?" If Hunter gave off a deadly aura, the FBI agent radiated unquestioning authority.

Maybe it was time for her to find another career. This wasn't journalism any longer and now she had to take orders from nobodies or wet-behind-the-ears children. *Just remain calm and get this interview in the rear view.*

"Crystal. Clear. I still take offense at being elbowed out at my station." She had to add that last part. She had learned to not be walked on by voicing her feelings.

It was another fifteen minutes getting Hunter, Juanita, and Beth wired with lapel microphones and onto the morning show set with living room chairs around a coffee table. FBI Agent Alexander was always near Beth's side on set. There was more here than Hunter's apparent torture and capture. Hell, she didn't think Beth was even the chic's real name.

The man with the bum arm stayed in the Green Room reclining on a couch and watched the room's monitor. Hunter was looking more and more grayish cast as time passed, he really wasn't doing well. They needed to get this interview going before he passed out.

Christine had settled into the control booth when the blond man entered. He nodded to her, but remained silent. She ignored him.

The lead-in graphic of a special report ran and Christine spoke into the live microphone, "We are interrupting normal programming for a special News Channel 12 report. We join special guest reporter Juanita Alvarez of the National Gazette in the studio." She motioned for the studio camera to go live and her microphone was muted. She pointed through the glass at Juanita indicating she was on the air-live.

"I am here with Mr. Rance Hunter and his rescuer who will remain anonymous. Mr. Hunter, we can't help but see you don't look the same as in the prior interview you gave. Can you please explain that to the viewing audience?"

His voice came out strong but deceptively cordial, "I just saw the interview you're talking about. Those ain't my words, I never called for an uprising in any form. I was recorded while I was tied up in a chair and asked questions by my captors. But, I didn't say those things, so I leave it to… experts to figure out how my voice was used."

Christine folded her arms. *Where was this going?* Maybe the studio shouldn't have agreed to this, it could backfire, and this was a volatile enough time. Most importantly, this could be offend their target demographic. The prime directive was not to upset their target audience with facts they don't want to hear.

Beth spoke up then, as if this had been rehearsed, "When I discovered him being held captive, he was in and out of consciousness, he had been tortured with a small knife and a hand-held saw. Many of his cuts were down to the bone and his blood was everywhere. I hid while a few men discussed killing him."

Christine sucked in her breath, no wonder the woman didn't want her name splashed about... if it was true. She didn't know what to believe, Brett Howard was a well-recognized reporter, and this girl was a nobody contradicting a veteran reporter.

The blond dude was suddenly by her side and handed her a thumb drive. "You'll need these graphics for this next part that Juanita will cover in a minute."

She ground her teeth but handed the drive to her technician. For the next twenty minutes, far longer than the studio had expected this special report to last, they were given financial records of the police who were first on the scene at the Philadelphia family massacre attributed to Hunter's gang, then a video of the cops sitting in their car down the street while the murders took place and the killers leaving from the back – clearly white men.

The evidence kept coming; Juanita covered how one of the responding cops was known as a racist. Then, the financials of two prison guards who had been shot during Hunter's prison break showed they received payments for schooling from the same Restoration America. Juanita then showed the affidavit of a witness (name withheld) to the prison break describing in detail a high-tech helicopter with Caucasian men killing the guards.

Christine understood now why the interview had to be done by this nobody reporter. This was an exposé, and she knew the material backwards and forwards.

The next part was more speculative with a "would-be informant" from years ago who was killed who claimed a white supremacist society was thriving and boasted of their highly placed and influential members.

Beth believed this linked to the same Restoration America that made the suspicious payments and she proposed such a high-tech helicopter suggested the involvement of a federal agency or perhaps even military. Then she explained about being kidnapped and interrogated about what she knew of some organization.

"What was the name your kidnappers used?" Juanita asked Hunter.

"They called it The Society for a Restored America, the same as the informant and whistle-blower exposed."

Then Beth continued, "The man who made those notes was supposed to hand them over to an FBI agent, but he was somehow discovered. He gave those notes to another to deliver, but that intermediary person didn't trust the FBI agent. Within hours, the intermediary went missing. But, the remains have since been discovered, exhumed, and are undergoing forensic testing to identify the killers."

Photos of the bones with close-ups of a bracelet and scraps of clothing were shown, then newspaper clippings of Noah's murder were shown.

"What is next for you Mr. Hunter?"

"I'm in federal protective custody. I'll eventually return to prison when it's safe. But, I'd like to send a special message out..."

Christine jumped on it, "Get me a close-up of him, don't shy away from the swollen eye."

"I'm no saint, but I never called for any violence or uprising and I never converted to Islam or any such BS. To the Apostles, stop the killing, stop blaming a rival gang."

Beth finished with, "Some secretive group of people has manipulated this situation and we fell for it. We all bought into the fear and hatred. Demand a widespread investigation of this Society for a Restored America and the group Restoration America. Demand that our officials on federal and local levels be investigated for any connections, too."

There were some closing remarks and Juanita thanked the unnamed computer experts who assisted in her research.

Christine gave the cease recording signal. Her head was swimming. Without experts to dissect all the supposed evidence, she didn't know what to think. None of it was corroborated by two sources like she was taught. But, the two sources rule was old-school and rarely the standard in television news where sensationalism was more important for ratings than accuracy or truth.

The silent blond guy extended his hand, and the technician handed his thumb drive back. She still didn't know his name, another anonymous person involved.

They all met back in the Green Room.

Christine meant to let it all fall on this novice reporter but couldn't help saying something. "You've no sources to back up any of this. It was a sensational *story* with a thug convicted on RICO charges as your main witness. What were you thinking?"

Agent Alexander walked up and into her personal space. "We were out to stop the widespread violence in the quickest way possible. We got the news of a white supremacist organization with ties to police, prison guards, and maybe even the FBI, broadcast to the populace where it can't be quietly swept under a rug and delegated to a short ten-second headline. That's for starters."

He turned his head, "Did you get that website up and the trap in place?"

The blond guy had set up two laptops and some other equipment in the Green Room. "Yeah, it's live, and the trap was sprung as soon as Hunter's face was on camera. That video I set up successfully downloaded the cookies too. I'm getting data back." He turned to Juanita and high-fived.

CHAPTER EIGHTY-ONE

The General

The General was livid. Back home, he had to watch a video replay of the interview with that bitch Elizabeth trying to tear down all his hard work. Not just his work, but the prior Generals of The Society too.

He had raged at first, broke a lamp and slashed the President's picture. He was calmer now. He realized they didn't have actual proof of membership, let alone the high-level members. So, The Society would be fine, he was sure. They would survive.

But he was concerned about this operation underway to flip the presidency and bring the nation under his; or rather, The Society's control to restore the nation to greatness. But all was not lost.

They were looking into the wetback reporter filth. Hell, she's got a website like she's some hotshot reporter.

He knew where Elizabeth lived. Eventually she would go home. He would kill her himself. No more pissing around about it. He would take his time about her death, use a knife again, and make her know pain intimately. That's what low life nigger lovers deserved.

He ordered the hit on the two brainless wonders who kidnapped Elizabeth and even blabbed The Society's name to her. Sheriff Craig would find their bodies dumped at his door. It was time to clean up the loose ends and rally the members to close ranks and stay calm.

The interview confirmed Noah took notes and that teen black bitch had gotten them to Elizabeth. It no longer mattered where she had kept them over the years. The Society had searched every place she was connected with or had lived since Loralie had the gall to die before revealing her secrets. She kept Noah's notes from The Society shrink and the arranged boyfriends.

It was no matter. So far, his network was still in place. Sure, the interview had been sensational, but nobody was jumping to do a fucking thing about it. He would have heard about it. He would exert all his influence to ensure no substantial actions were taken to find The Society.

After several phone calls, he had set in motion the counterattack against the damaging report.

He turned on his office television. His blond on-air "news" personalities on his multiple channels were feeding the public his counter message and people would believe all of it.

His media outlets continued to air the first interview with Hunter and viciously discredited this latest interview as he instructed them. He gave them their script: Hunter was a black thug you couldn't trust, his appearing beaten up was probably at the hands of his own gang to fool people, his pleas to stop violence were likely a disguised message to blacks everywhere to rise up, like sleeper cells.

Now it was time to locate that ape, Rance Hunter, and blow his brains out for alligator bait. They were looking at hospitals in the Jackson area. If he'd been admitted, his members would report back to The Society. Hunter's hours were numbered.

He finally rested back into his leather chair. Nobody could take The Society down that easily.

CHAPTER EIGHTY-TWO

Juanita Alvarez

She was in the hospital outside Hunter's room, down the hall in the waiting lounge. Although, calling it a lounge was very optimistic for the eight hard chairs and three side tables against the walls just outside the secondary elevators. Even "seating area" wasn't accurate since nobody sat there longer than their butts could take the uncomfortable plastic chairs. It actually provided a level of privacy if you didn't mind standing. At least it had large windows with sunlight streaming in.

Juanita answered her phone. She'd been screening calls since the interview, but she recognized this number. Suddenly everybody wanted to talk to her. She answered only calls from the National Gazette and family. Lots of calls from family yelling at her for getting involved, no matter how she tried to explain. Her parents were now afraid of being deported because of her.

She may have broken the single most important story in the nation's history since Watergate, but she felt like a failure as a daughter. Her parents would never understand or forgive her for the developing thing between herself and Heath. Her shoulders slumped, as she wanted to hide, just escape. But she couldn't, she had come too far now.

The voice on the other line was her editor, Karyn, at National Gazette and the only contact there she dealt with anymore. "Listen Juanita, I have the Justice Department breathing down my neck to talk to you. I have an agent here and you're on speaker." Karyn spoke, rushed and clipped.

She whispered to Heath, who was gazing out the window, "Get Malcom fast." He took off at a trot down the hall.

She needed to stall for a moment. "I suppose the Justice Department wants to talk about the interview. Okay, I'm listening."

Malcom and Heath came running back and skidded to a halt. Juanita placed her cell phone on speaker. They crowded around the phone.

"Miss Alvarez, we need to investigate the evidence you briefly showed during the interview. We need to determine if it's actionable. We don't want to have to issue a BOLO to bring you in, but we will." They wouldn't put out a notice to police to be looking for her unless it was to stop her. Freedom of the press after all.

They had discussed the eventuality of this and the issue remained they didn't know who they could trust.

"Who am I speaking with, please?"

"Well, this is Agent Kascinsky. You understand what you presented must be investigated. Who has Rance Hunter in protective custody? He said he was in custody, but we don't show any record of that." Agent Kascinsky was gruff, worse than a snarling junk yard dog. Malcom, Heath, and Juanita stared at each other in their tight huddle.

"Agent Kascinsky, the last person who met with an FBI agent to turn over evidence on this organization went missing. The informant who compiled a few notes was executed. You understand how I might be afraid for my life in turning over anything to you. You can also understand why Hunter's life is in danger to be in your system right now. He is in custody by law enforcement, just not on your books for his own safety. That would be the protective part."

This was what they had rehearsed, but it terrified her. She was actually sparring with a federal official. Her stomach threatened dry heaves and her hand holding the phone began to shake. Heath placed his hand on hers.

"That's a serious accusation, but from what you presented..."

"I'll speak to DOJ Supervisor Hiram Auerbach and nobody else. If you give me his phone number now, I will call him directly and coordinate with him." All part of their plan.

Before waiting to hear a reply, Malcom ran down the hall to Hunter's room. They had to leave. Fast.

"I don't have a roster of phone numbers with me. If you give me your cell number, I can have him call you." Heath and Juanita looked deep into each other's eyes. He wanted to trace their location like they suspected. Probably already had. She had gotten Heath into this and she felt guilty for that too.

"I'll call him myself then. Karyn, I'll be in touch about my assignments." That last part was a prearranged code to let her know this phone was no longer good to contact her.

She hung up, slid the back off the cell phone, took out the battery, and tossed it all in the trash can in the corner.

In Hunter's room, Rance wore the jeans and T-shirt Heath had purchased for him before the interview. He couldn't reach his sport shoes to lace them up with all the cuts and stitches. Malcom assisted. The four hours on IV had him looking less gray and his eyes seemed brighter.

Elizabeth ducked in the door, holding the fast food bags for their late dinner. They hadn't been able to eat much at the studio. She suspected neither Elizabeth nor herself would have eaten much, anyway. Elizabeth hadn't eaten since this morning and looked ill most of the time now. She also kept looking around at empty space. For the first time in her life, she felt bad for somebody with her *gift*. A hospital had to be chock full of spirits for her to deal with.

"DOJ forced National Gazette to call and I suspect they only wanted to trace her location. We're on the move again," Malcom blurted out.

Juanita had to hand it to Elizabeth. She dropped the bags of food, turned, and cracked the door open to watch the hallway without a word. Sure, she had paled a little, but she didn't question or panic.

This would be another long night. If they lived, that is.

CHAPTER EIGHTY-THREE

Elizabeth Grant

"We're out of time. I think two goons just stopped at the nurse's station." Elizabeth hissed over her shoulder.

She didn't belong in the middle of some conspiracy and eminent death around each door. Yet, here she was. At least Sheriff Craig... Jake... umm, her father had been treated and released. His friend drove to Jackson to take him home, no questions asked. She would have to get used to him as her father. They had a few short conversations since this morning, but they needed to take more time.

She was exhausted, angry, and overloaded on high alert status to where every spirit made her want to run screaming out of the hospital. Many spirits were trying to talk to her, often all at once. Something had to give, and soon.

She kept her eyes on the goons through the crack in the door. As much as she hated being around the scores of spirits walking the halls and popping in and out of the room, she didn't want to join them. She knew her mood was obvious to the others when Malcom hugged her earlier for a few minutes.

She hadn't had time to wrap her head around the enormity of blowing the news wide open on The Society. The news networks were mixed, some had picked up the story and poured over the interview while others tore it apart and replayed the fake interview.

"The nurses don't know enough to share and they understand this patient is highly sensitive. We have to use the back elevators by the visitor waitin' area," Malcom informed them. She heard movement behind her but kept watching the goons arguing with the nurse.

"Get in the wheelchair. It'll hide your bulk a bit with us around you." He didn't even try to make it sound like anything other than an order. The chair creaked in protest. *Damn, Hunter was a mountain.*

The men had stopped arguing with the nurse and seemed to go back to the main elevator bank.

"Now, I think they're waiting for an elevator." She advised.

"Heath get the Suburban to the back entrance. Juanita, bring the car there, too. We might be runnin', so face out and be ready to bolt. Send the elevator back up for us."

Elizabeth stepped aside for Juanita and Heath to duck out and speed walk down the hall to the back elevator.

She faced Hunter and Malcom. "Well, here we go again. Ready for another escape?"

Hunter nodded, "You saved me once, let's see if our luck holds black magic woman."

She listened and heard the elevator ding, meaning it returned and was waiting for them. She glanced out the door again. Clear.

She opened the door wide and Malcom pushed the wheelchair out at a fast pace. Elizabeth walked next to the chair with one hand on Hunter's shoulder and the other on Malcom's hand.

Footsteps. Coming fast down the hall. Please let it be nurses. She glanced back. Goons were coming at them.

"Run." Her whisper was gravel.

Hunter jumped out of the wheelchair. Malcom swung the chair and launched it at the goons. He grabbed her hand, and they ran. Skidding around the corner to the waiting area and the elevator, Hunter held the doors, and they ran full on into the elevator's back wall.

Hunter punched the close door button repeatedly. Malcom had his service revolver out. The goons slid around the corner. Malcom shot twice as the doors closed.

"Did you get them?" Elizabeth asked.

"Couldn't tell. Didn't stop 'em if I did."

They watched the floor indicator slowly creep down. She felt like jumping out of her skin. *Too slow. Come on.*

Ding. The doors slithered open. A married couple stood waiting for the elevator. They ran out, barely missing the couple and Malcom took the lead. He had memorized escape routes as soon as Hunter was admitted.

Down corridors, turns, and pushing past hospital staff, they emerged into a hall with glass doors at the end and cars outside. Malcom glanced back, Elizabeth and Hunter were keeping up with him. They poured on the speed. She didn't know how Hunter could manage with his injuries.

They burst through the doors and charged down the wheelchair ramp. Malcom stopped for a second to look around, then pointed to the Suburban and a car a hundred yards away.

"Just a little further." She said to Hunter. He had that gray cast to his skin again.

Heath jumped out of the Suburban with the engine running and dived into the rental sedan with Juanita. Malcom opened the back door of the Suburban and Hunter clambered in, his energy spent. Elizabeth threw herself into the passenger seat and Malcom burned rubber following Heath, who was disappearing in front of them at the street.

They had chosen a pre-arranged location to meet up. Malcom turned in the opposite direction from the one Juanita and Heath took. Studying the traffic out the back window, she glanced at Hunter sprawled on the back seat. He was unconscious. *Damn it.*

"Car pursuing us. Tan, about a block back." She bit out.

No response from Malcom. All his attention was on the road. He made a series of turns, circling back onto the street they were just on. She didn't see anybody following, so she faced front. She could see the goon's tan car a distance ahead of them now. Elizabeth glanced back at Hunter again. He better not die, was all she could think. But then a wave of doubt hit. *What would happen if he died in their care?*

The tan car turned to follow their long cold trail, so Malcom turned the other way. It was instructional to observe what a circuitous route Malcom used, with several double-backs. No further tail as far as she could determine.

A half-hour later they rendezvoused with Juanita and Heath at a dilapidated old motel.

"I'll get our rooms, I know the owner and he'll help us." Malcom explained.

Juanita handed him a credit card. "Use that, the Apostles will foot the bill."

He held it out for her to take back. "I can't take money from a gang," his voice was rigid.

"Oh, that's right – go ahead and use your personal cash. Don't have enough, by all means, use your personal credit card that can be traced and get us all killed. Seems like you live in town, so why don't we go to your house? Or we could stay undetected by using the card." She refused to take the card.

"I don't like it, but for the interests of safety, I'll concede your point." He walked into the teeny-tiny office and returned with room keys.

"Ladies stay in one room, gentlemen in the other."

Heath and Juanita looked at each other, not so much with disappointment but uncertainty.

"Are they adjoining rooms?" Elizabeth asked. Perhaps everyone would feel better that way. She would feel better knowing she could throw a door open or scream and Malcom would be right there.

"As a matter of fact, yes. The rooms are adjoining." The ghost of a smile haunted his lips.

CHAPTER EIGHTY-FOUR

Elizabeth Grant

The hotel looked like it was barely standing on the outside, but the rooms had been maintained well over the years. The carpet was maybe six years old in an industrial beige, and it looked recently painted in a crisp white. The drapes and matching bedspread looked home-made on close inspection and were clean and cheery. The beds seemed to be the splurge item; she sat on one and they were like clouds. The bathrooms were small but spic and span clean. The rooms smelled of bleach and industrial cleaner, which she found comforting at the moment. It was normal.

Hunter was conscious again, but looked drained. He had torn some stitches in the escape from the hospital. The doctor at the television news studio had provided some medical supplies, so Malcom used them. He removed the old stitches, cleaned the wounds, stitched them up, and bandaged them again. Then he took the used bandages outside to the asphalt and set them on fire. No traces left behind.

They ordered Chinese since the fast food she had brought to the hospital was left behind in their mad dash to leave. The man in the office called in the order for them. Seems he was a long-time friend and informant. She figured if Malcom trusted him, that was good enough for her.

They sat around eating, no chitchat, and listened for any vehicles. A car horn blared, and they all jumped. Her sesame chicken and egg rolls tasted like a five-star gourmet meal. The wontons were divine. She had been hungry most of the day, it seemed. She had a helping of the orange chicken too. Her fortune cookie said, *The greatest risk is not taking one.* She crumpled it and tossed it in the trash. At least she could breathe in this motel. There was a spirit that walked back and forth outside their doors, but he didn't enter either of their rooms.

Heath had set up computers and was monitoring… something, she wasn't sure. Anytime she wondered close to his domain in the corner, he closed the lid on the laptops. She sighed.

What good had all their efforts amounted to, really? They risked their lives to get to that television studio, believing that airing the truth and exposing The Society for a Restored America would turn things around, investigations begun, arrests made. So far lies were generated, twisting the truth. There was no telling if the violence had eased even a little.

"You're quieter than usual." Malcom sat down on the bed next to her. They were all congregated in the guy's room so Hunter could stay in bed.

Watching Heath and Juanita talk in the corner with the computers, they seemed to trust only each other. She answered. "I'm wondering if there is any way out of this that doesn't involve our deaths. Seems worse than ever."

Special Agent Malcom Alexander leaned in and smoothed a stray lock of hair out of her face. "I don't know, even in the midst of runnin' for our lives there are positives. We met, I think that's decidedly pleasant." A slight smile appeared on his lips. "I know Aunt Netty's killer is part of this white supremacist group. I took hair samples from your kidnappers and the lab I went to last night called. One of them was a match to a hair I found at Aunt Netty's home."

"How's that a positive?" Seemed it would be blood boiling.

"I know she didn't die in vain, she died a hero in my book. I hope to shout that far and wide soon, along with Loralie's story."

"Maybe you could write a book?" Her smile broke out. For this moment it was calm and she could relax just a smidgen.

"I think she could do justice to both their experiences, don't you?" He nudged his chin in Juanita's direction.

"True, she probably could," she confirmed. "You always so positive?" It slipped out. After all, he was grieving his aunt's murder, and it had only been a few days since the funeral. He had to be hurting, yet he was taking the situation rather well.

"No, but I make an effort to look forward and only bring what is good from the past with me."

"I need to do better at that." Basking in the close and comfortable air between them, she leaned into him and placed her head on his shoulder.

"I said I make the effort, I'm not always good at it." He smiled.

For a moment she felt safe. The realization that she had felt anxious and tense in Cyprus and never really welcome or safe dawned on her. There was only a veneer of small-town southern charm, she had felt the undercurrent – a clear mistrust of her since she was considered a city person and an outsider, not like them. But, although now she felt danger, there was comfort, nevertheless. It wasn't a false sense of assurance; she knew they couldn't stay long here either, and this was far from over.

CHAPTER EIGHTY-FIVE

Juanita Alvarez

Juanita was thankful for the motel rooms and even more for the chance to regroup. The motel was luxury compared to the rattletrap rooms they had in Corcoran. There were only two other rooms in the motel being rented, which meant minimal traffic and noise. That made it easier to listen for somebody who didn't belong, at least in theory.

Heath was digging into who had the authority to start an investigation of the magnitude suggested by what they knew so far. The Inspector General in the Justice Department investigates FBI corruption or criminal activities. Every federal office has a different Oversight and Internal Affairs. The Office of Professional Responsibility investigates Department of Justice Attorneys. Who could investigate widespread corruption other than the FBI? They were coming up empty.

"Wish we could just go to the President. He could initiate a wide sweeping investigation. I don't think anybody else can," Heath said.

"You have a point there. How could we talk to the President, even just a phone call?" Juanita wondered aloud. There was no single third party who had authority to investigate so many state and federal agencies for members tied to The Society.

Heath brought up the message board where he first contacted the hacktivist *Betty* and communicated with the other hacker volunteers.

"Incidentally, you have several messages saying thanks for the shout out to them after the interview. They're elated their work got results, and you thanked them."

He was tired, yet he still thought of her. They worked well together, too. She trusted him before anybody else. They had started down this road together and they would make it through together. They never said it in words, but it was clear. He hadn't stolen anybody's money or identity that she knew of either. All the hacking was outside the law, but even Bernstein and Woodward would probably bend some laws with so much at stake.

He glanced up and winked at her and flashed that boyish grin. She admitted to herself that she liked him. But he must never know because he would find her weakness and chip away at her resolve. Giving in to him, even after this crisis was over, wasn't a good idea. Ever.

His fingers seemed to glide and flow over the keyboard. "Let's see if anyone has suggestions of how to get the information to the President or a message to him." He glanced up from the laptop and blew her a kiss. "The goodwill you built may really pay off."

"I'm going to write an article for National Gazette on the interview and detail out the implications. I think a three- or four-part series of articles should do it justice." She was blabbering. Who blew kisses as an adult, anyway? He knew she was susceptible to such romantic nonsense. How did he know when she didn't even realize it until now?

"Excellent idea. We have to keep the pressure up and if the National Gazette is still behind you, go for it." He stopped typing and his face was serious. "Just tell me they are paying you top dollar for this because you totally deserve it?"

CHAPTER EIGHTY-SIX

The General

He felt surrounded by incompetent idiots. That was the only explanation the General of The Society for a Restored America could devise to explain Elizabeth or Hunter still breathing. Sure, that small-town Sheriff aided them in escaping Cyprus alive. But there was no excuse after they traced that phone call for any of them to walk out of that hospital. That the nigger thug was walking galled him.

He was back in his Louisiana restored Greek Revival home, in his office again to regroup. He had The Battle Hymn of the Republic playing as he drank 21 year old Glenfiddich Scotch to calm down. He bought the house because it was an antebellum home from the Old South. He loved that fact. Ah, the Old South, when a man could run his business however he saw fit without regulations or anybody sticking their nose in. Plantation economy was a shining example of capitalism the way it should be with cheap labor.

The railroads were built by the servitude of Chinese. The cotton, rice, indigo, and tobacco industries flourished and made America shine on the world stage because of cheap labor. The high-and-mighty North, particularly New York, built their tall testaments to the wealthy on cheap labor in steel mills and workhouses.

Servitude is what built America, made it great, but now we have to worry about labor rights and pay for time off. Then there's the ridiculous notion of overtime pay and maternity leave, and even cheaper children can't learn about hard work anymore. These laws have weakened the nation, but The Society will turn it around.

Ah, those were the glory years of America.

He stood tall and pushed out his chest before the sepia-toned portrait of The Society's founder. It was up to The Society to bring the nation back to its glory, take back America. Overturn the Amendments to the Constitution after the Twelfth Amendment. Other people have publicly floated that idea without much recrimination, so it's time would be ripe.

Once The Society had the Vice President installed as President, they could tear down and rebuild the nation properly. The first order of business would be turning all prisons into for-profit labor camps and filling them with all the inferior ethnic groups that weakened the nation.

All was not lost. His media campaign of discrediting the exposé interview was working as more and more people believed it was lies and followed his news channel as they continued to play Hunter's fake interview. His man had talked several news channels into following suit. It looked like revealing The Society, and its agenda wasn't so hard to sweep under the rug after all. No investigation had begun either. Of course, he had his well-placed members downplaying the need to follow up on lies.

But he had to take care of the business at hand. The little snag of Hunter getting on the air and The Society's name blasted to the world convinced him speed was of the essence. All was not lost, but decisive action was needed quickly. He picked up the phone to call the President personally; after all, they were friends. If you wanted something done right, you had to do it yourself.

CHAPTER EIGHTY-SEVEN

Elizabeth Grant

Elizabeth and Juanita were in their room with the door between rooms left cracked open. Malcom was still protective of her, which she was okay with. They each got a separate bed, although they were close together in the small room. The guys tossed a coin over who slept on the floor. It was Heath this time.

"So, what's the story with you and Heath? I want a few minutes to just be two professional women talking. No impending doom." Yep, she went there. She hadn't had a woman to talk to for a few weeks, and she wanted to just be normal for a few minutes.

Juanita studied her for a minute before answering, "It's strange. He has a *past* that I don't approve of, but he swears he's changed. Maybe he's changed, but not completely."

Didn't approve of his past, hmmm. "Something to do with his prowess with computers, or with women?" Heath seemed like the type to be popular with women.

She let out a huff, "A little of both, I guess. What was that about an old girlfriend or something who died? He won't talk about it. You'd think it was a federal offense and he couldn't confess."

How much to tell? Even new to embracing this seeing-the-dead gig she realized she had private information that Heath seemed to want to keep private. "I don't feel comfortable sharing what I know. You'd want me to keep anything I knew about you that was very personal confidential, too."

Juanita nodded.

"He makes these suggestive propositions ever since I met him reporting on a story. It always seemed like his crutch, like some people use humor. But that all changed when he helped me on this story. The innuendo is less, and the propositions are more sentimental."

"He treats you good. That's the first thing my mother said to look for. He thinks of you in big and small ways. But I get it. If he has a shady past, it's scary."

"What about you two? Fancy that fine black man even though he has a dangerous job?"

She blew out a breath, "That's a hard question. I mean, sure, he's easy on the eyes. I trust him since he saved my life and we've made friends in the last few days. But I honestly don't know him. He could be a completely different man outside this situation."

"I hear you on that score. That's why I stopped dating. You can't tell if what they present is the real guy. Under these extreme conditions you can't tell if he's a workaholic that would ignore you or only wants a wife to have his babies."

They talked about their jobs and the mutual obstacles of moving up the ladder. Juanita was a lady she could become good friends with given less stressful circumstances. They had much in common.

They said good night with a little less anxiety over what the next day would bring. Having one more friend was always comforting.

CHAPTER EIGHTY-EIGHT

Malcom Alexander

Malcom was adjusted to only a few hours of sleep when in action from his Green Beret days. So he was up before any of the others. He had walked the perimeter first and checked the other guests in the motel.

He stepped outside to call and check in with Sheriff Craig without disturbing the others. The seventy-degree weather was a pleasant break from the nineties during the day, and the rose and coral colored sunrise renewed his spirit.

"Elizabeth's fine, she's still sleepin' as a matter of fact. We had to make a run for it from the hospital, but we lost them and got a good night's rest. How's your arm?"

Craig's gravelly voice was intensified by the early hour, "Arm's fine, but I'm gettin' hell from Elizabeth's uncle. He's madder than a wet hen that I'm keepin' him from his kin, and it's somehow my fault she's with a convict. I also have her momma and grandmomma tearin' me a new one after seein' the news broadcast."

"You tellin' me you can't handle them?" He didn't know what else to do but get the man out of his own head. Malcom felt for the guy. He was catching all the fire for events that swept Elizabeth up, and none of it was either of their faults. At least he didn't ask about the sleeping arrangements, like he knew the man was aching to.

"Your momma never teach you to respect your elders son?" he tossed back. "But that isn't the real news." He hesitated and took a few breaths before he added, "We had a double homicide dumped at the sheriff department's door yesterday evenin'. They'd been severely cut like Hunter, only so badly and so much they bled to death." His voice was solemn.

Malcom shivered at how gruesome and painful their deaths were. "Sounds like this Society isn't very forgivin' of mistakes or losin' a prisoner."

"Also, when I got home, I found my house had been trashed, furniture slashed, everythin' tossed around."

"Think they were lookin' for a clue to where you took Elizabeth and Hunter?" Malcom held his breath.

"Naw, it was more a warnin' that I had just pissed them off for helpin' you all escape." Malcom promised to keep him informed, and Craig asked for Elizabeth to call her family before they hung up.

Malcom brewed coffee in the room's coffee maker. It was a wonderful convenience since he could practically live on coffee during times like this.

Heath woke up once the coffee aromas filled the room and immediately huddled over his computers. Malcom had to threaten him with bodily harm to get him to leave his laptop long enough to shower. Hunter slept late, and that was probably for the best. He would have to check his wounds for infection and apply dry bandages after he showered.

Malcom waited until he heard the shower run twice on the girl's side and gave them time to finish enjoying their morning before he knocked on the adjoining door. It was the first night Elizabeth got a full night's sleep since her kidnapping, and she needed it. Heath and Juanita hadn't gotten much sleep either, but Elizabeth was his responsibility.

Netty had entrusted him to ensure her safety, and Elizabeth wasn't fighting him on that score. He wasn't sure about the fondness that was growing between them. Sexual attraction was just pheromones and hormones that were a dangerous luxury right now, but they trusted each other and he found he liked her.

Elizabeth and Juanita knocked and then entered. They both looked better from a full night's sleep. The dark circles were gone from around Elizabeth's eyes and she had some color to her cheeks. Juanita had a little more energy in her step.

Once the ladies had joined them, Heath, his hair still wet, couldn't contain his update any longer.

"Our *computer experts* have rallied troops. Overnight the internet is full of demands to investigate The Society for a Restored America on both twitter and Facebook. Instagram has photos of people with signs saying the same. It's gone viral. Independent news has picked up on the phenomenon and are pressuring the President to begin a widespread investigation that covers all of the Department of Justice and local law enforcement." He was beaming like a kid who got the impossible-to-obtain gift under the tree.

"So, what does that do? Who cares?" Malcom had to voice his skepticism over such insignificant news.

Juanita answered, "Before, even the Indy news outlets were skeptical of our interview because the big media conglomerates were ripping our interview to shreds. Now, they're paying attention and shining a spotlight because of the demands for investigation by the people."

Still, so what? "What'll that really amount to in the long run?" He didn't see how some tweets and Facebook rants would help beyond the two seconds to post something and forget about it.

Hunter sat on his bed, taking it all in. Should he be worried at his silence?

Heath had been reading something on his screen and he got excited, "Turn on the news, hurry."

The President was about to speak. The Press Secretary, an average guy in a suit who looked like he'd had little sleep, announced the President would give prepared comments and then leave. No question-and-answer period would follow.

As the President, tall and lanky, entered the racket of cameras clicking and feet shuffling took over. Eventually the room of reporters quieted. He gave opening comments of his anger over the violence in Philadelphia, Los Angeles, and Miami and reports of smaller outbreaks in Minneapolis and Orlando overnight. He admonished those involved on all sides to cease for the sake of the nation's cohesiveness. He spoke for ten minutes before dropping a bombshell.

"I am extending an invitation to the reporter of the recent interview with Rance Hunter and those involved in her efforts to sit down with me and my advisors." He made a few more statements of admonition and the need to pull together as a nation.

Malcom turned off the television, and they all looked at each other.

Heath's laptop began buzzing, and they all jumped. "It's the untraceable Voice-Over-IP phone I set up for Juanita."

"Must be the National Gazette editor. She's the only one who knows to use it." Juanita explained.

"Federal authorities can trace most VoIP, even Skype and such." Malcom felt he had to warn them.

"This is through, shall we say, specialized and not commonly available software to keep it untraceable." Heath wouldn't look him in the eye. That was one more indication that he was on the shady side of computer expertise. Malcom suspected these other *experts* that had assisted with *research* were serious hackers and their aide was on the illegal side.

There was a side of him that felt the cards were stacked against stopping this Society, let alone just expose them without resorting to such extraordinary measures. The Society's membership could be anywhere from military, judges, local and federal law enforcement, to even reporters. If his supervisor in the FBI was a member, then who could he trust or turn to?

Radical times required radical measures. But he was supposed to be upholding the very laws he was positive Heath and Juanita had violated. On the other side, the corruption and financial tracks would likely have vanished if they went through proper channels. Was the system broken or was he out-of-line and making excuses?

Even Department of Justice Supervisor Hiram Auerbach wasn't a hundred percent safe bet, although he had told Juanita not to talk to anybody else. Now they had to figure out how to get to the President when there would likely be Society members flooding to DC to stop the meeting. Announcing the invitation over the air made sure The Society knew where they would be headed.

Juanita was ready, and she answered the internet call so everyone could hear. "Hello, calling because of the press conference?" She jumped right in.

"Yes, of course. The President has been in contact with me, or I should say his representative. Anyway, we're talking about safe places for you to meet."

"Wouldn't the White House be the safest place in the nation?" Juanita's eyebrows knitted together.

"I think there is a perception problem in having a convicted and escaped felon invited to the White House." The National Gazette's editor's voice was strained.

Malcom snorted, the President's opposing party would attempt to paint him as disgracing the White House or some such thing, you could bet on it.

"Ummm, okay." Juanita shrugged her shoulders.

Malcom whispered, "The Eisenhower Executive Office Building?"

Juanita asked about the Executive Office Building.

"Good idea, next to the White House, so the POTUS could potentially make it over without drawing attention and security will be easy to set up since it has many staffers and VIPs working there. I'll run it by them. Give me the names of everybody for security."

Juanita and Heath looked at Malcom, panic showing. So far Heath, Elizabeth, and Malcom's names had been withheld.

"Hold on just a minute please," Juanita said and Heath muted her.

"I get they have security protocols and can't let just anybody walk in, but I don't feel good about this," Heath said.

"I know. But let's think about it, Heath is probably a known entity by The Society because you traveled with Juanita and checked into the hotel under your name. They already know about Elizabeth, evidenced by the kidnappin'. I'm the only one that may not be on their radar by name. I think we can risk it."

"Um, they don't exactly know about me." Heath said while averting his eyes again.

"Spit it out."

"I used a false ID when I checked in, actually since we left Philadelphia." He still didn't look up.

"False, not stolen." Juanita clarified.

Malcom studied them. *False, not stolen,* was a tipoff. That is probably why Heath was uncomfortable around a federal agent. Stolen identities were the territory of the Bureau and the Secret Service. But, it's gotten so commonplace and resources are so tight, the high-dollar amount ID thefts are the ones that get investigated.

He tucked that away for the moment. When he could look into Heath and his recent activity, he would think about it. For now, there were significantly bigger concerns at hand.

"Still, give our names. They'll likely do basic background checks, although that is rather moot at this point." Rance was about as bad as it could get, other than escorting a foreign government representative.

Once the call was completed, Malcom shared his biggest concern.

"We can be sure The Society knows of the invite to see the President, so they'll be on full alert to keep us from the meetin'."

"We have the use of the private plane, we just call Tito."

"All airports, includin' those for private and charter flights, bus lines, and trains are standard to monitor, especially here in Jackson since they know we're in town. We might never make it out of the airport or terminals alive."

Heath jumped up like a child going to an amusement park, "Road trip! We rent a big camper and even avoid restaurants by cooking in the RV. Over night is the only sticky point and we keep to ourselves in campgrounds. Minimal exposure all the way around."

"Oh hell. I've been stuck in tiny motel rooms and a one-room shack with you guys, now I'm going to be squeezed into a miniature home on wheels with all of you!" Hunter shook his head.

Elizabeth ignored him, "I don't know that Heath's name is that safe if he gave it at the hotel in Cyprus. We need to rent the camper under a name they don't know, even yours." She indicated Malcom with her hand.

All eyes turned to Heath. "Wow, I don't have unlimited fake IDs to use. But we can see about withdrawing enough cash on the gang's credit card to rent the RV and expenses along the way."

"They'll still require identification to rent," Malcom rubbed his chin. "Hold on, at any time since you left Philadelphia have you used your actual name? Can't you use that?"

"No. Umm my name kinda gets flagged, so we didn't use it."

"Caught at identity theft, huh? Convicted?"

"Did a year. I've been clean from theft since." His voice was small, and he studied the carpet and didn't look up.

Juanita's jaw was clenched and lips pressed together. That explained her holding back in spite of the glaring attraction between them.

"You going to arrest me for my electronic snooping the last week or so on this investigation?"

That was an excellent question that he had to face now. He needed Heath, even though he was questionable in his use of those computer skills. If this was going to work at all, Heath's suspected recent illegal computer activity was small potatoes in the bigger picture.

"I don't know what you're talkin' about. I don't personally have knowledge of any criminal activity other than a fake identification as a self-defense move. Now, about rentin' the RV, a cash withdrawal of enough for the rental and trip expenses is good. Use your real name to rent it since it's unconnected to any of us in The Society's view. Even if your name gets flagged, it won't be in association with Hunter or Juanita's interview with him."

That was their best shot of making it to the capitol and the Eisenhower Executive Office Building undetected, and hopefully alive to meet the President.

CHAPTER EIGHTY-NINE

Tito/Doberman

Tito had been flown to Chicago in Daniel Baker's personal plane. All he had been told was that the acting head of The Black Apostles needed to discuss business with him. During the plane and limousine rides, his mind raced through what the meeting could be about. As far as he knew, he was the only person invited to meet with Baker, or Icepick as he was also called.

As the limo pulled up to the house and the wrought-iron gates opened, he had concluded that the obvious topic for discussion, Apache's disobeying his orders to hold off on making any moves, was likely what he wanted to discuss.

When the thought struck him how unlikely it was for Baker to discuss the situation in Los Angeles with him, his hands began sweating as he was ushered through the front door of the mansion. What if his snatching Cenisa out from under Apache was about to bite him in the ass?

"In here Doberman," Baker's voice came from the same huge living room decorated in primarily white with red and gold accents that the city heads had met in only a few days ago.

Baker, in a silk button-down shirt and matching silk slacks, handed him a glass with straight up Vodka from the smell and motioned for him to sit in one of the white raw silk couches or chairs. His hand shook only slightly as he took the glass and sat. Baker sat opposite him and sank back into the couch, a large glass-top coffee table between them. Traces of cocaine powder, a favorite drug of the Wall Street set, and a few rolled hundred-dollar bills for snorting were left in plain sight. Tito couldn't lean back. Hhe sat on the edge of his seat holding the full glass of Vodka.

"Relax brother. I just want to talk, we're good." Baker took a sip of his drink, his diamond rings glinting in the light.

"Yeah, okay. I'm listenin', brother." He scooted back an inch.

"I got three things I want to discuss and they aren't for the phone where somebody could listen in, you feel me?"

"Yeah, I gotcha. I'm happy to visit." He licked his lips. Three important things that couldn't be said on the phone. *Oh shit, what was happening. Just stay cool, man.*

"First item of discussion is Apache. He lit a raging fire when he attacked Nuestra Familia. I don't...," Baker paused a second for effect, "*appreciate* the blatant spitting in my face by dissing my command."

Tito shook his head in agreement but kept his mouth shut. He didn't know where this was going, so it was best to let Baker talk. But at least it didn't seem to be his dick on the chopping block.

"I simply can't let his disrespecting me slide. That isn't good leadership. Now, in the business world, there'd be a verbal or written reprimand that would go on file, perhaps a punishment of having to take a shit job, or be terminated. Our business is a little different, or methods a little more... painful, distasteful." He paused and studied Tito across the glass-top coffee table. He poured himself more Vodka.

"I'm guessing you want me to take care of your... response to Apache's disrespecting you." He ventured. This was unexpected. He shifted; he could feel the sip of Vodka he took hit his stomach and churn.

"You guess right. He'll be terminated, and you need to handle it personally. I want Kodiak to take over immediately. Do you think you can do this?" *Was this a test?* He would need backup, of course. He could use the freelancer who drove reporter girl to get Cenisa.

"It shouldn't be a problem. I can take care of it when I leave here if you don't mind giving me a ride in your plane?" He was asking him to be his enforcer. Would he still have his own territory?

"Then it's settled." He took another sip of Vodka and studied Tito. He twirled a large jeweled ring on one finger. He seemed to make up his mind and sat forward. "The second item to discuss is a tall order." He stood and looked out his floor to ceiling windows at the pool in back.

"I said we'd deal with whoever kidnapped Hunter. It was worse than we could've ever imagined, this group... gang using us and torturing Hunter. If they really have people in high places, influential people, untouchable members... if they can't be brought to justice, I want you to deal with them. You'd report only to me and have any funds and resources you need." He turned from the window and crossed his arms, his gaze drilling into Tito. He walked slowly, purposefully, almost gracefully toward him and stopped to look down at him.

Understanding dawned on him, he was the new enforcer for the bigger problems where it would take patience, not a hot head, planning for a hit when the system failed *them*.

Never saw that coming, no way. He nodded absently. What Baker wasn't saying was how he needed to get all the information possible on the people in this racist Society somehow and then make sure they faced justice at his hand if they didn't do jail time – all without getting caught. He would have to use the reporter girl, squeeze her for more information. But not getting caught was perhaps the most difficult aspect. This could involve a lot of people, important people, guarded and protected people.

He took a breath to steady himself. He couldn't believe he was going to do this. He stood up and faced Baker, "I'll deal with it. It'll be done, one way or another." Mother. Fucking. Hell. He might end up getting the needle or taking several bullets for this one.

"You're a lot like me, Doberman. We like to learn, let somebody else take the punches and bullets to the head and we get their lessons. I'd recommend studying how the Israeli Mossad handled their Nazi problems, how they ran down the Nazi members who disappeared after the war, their Kidon and small team tactics specifically."

He got the message loud and clear. Get trained, get tactical, and lead a small team. "Understood. Any recommendations of an operative I might consult?"

Baker dug a slip of paper from his back pocket and handed it over. Tito immediately memorized it, then leaned over to the coffee table, took a lighter, set the paper on fire, then dropped it in the gold-plated ashtray.

Tito straightened and faced Baker, squared his shoulders and waited for the final thing. After those two surprise requests, what could be next.

"Depending upon your success with these two tasks, I'll need a right-hand man to help me manage in Hunter's absence. Naturally, if we should get Hunter's sentence reduced, he'll resume his position."

Tito could barely believe his ears. He was the youngest of the city gang bosses. They shook hands. There was nothing to say. It was a very big IF all around.

CHAPTER NINETY

Juanita Alvarez

She had never been in an RV and found the experience both fun and nerve-racking. If it weren't for the circumstances of Hunter recuperating and handcuffed on the pullout couch the entire time, Malcom always watching for an attempted escape, and all of them leery to show their faces outside the vehicle, she might have loved the trip.

The camper was compact but could sleep five people in a pinch with the couch made into a bed. It had a tiny kitchen with a small double sink, microwave, and a propane stove top and oven. But most important to Juanita was the bathroom that included a shower. Even a tiny one with five people in the middle of summer was essential. That and the air conditioning made the jostling and tight quarters bearable.

Heath seemed oddly suited to the experience. He explained he grew up with camping trips in lesser models, so he knew the ins and outs of stocking and driving the all-in-one rig.

Heath and Malcom did the grocery shopping with a list they all compiled for food. They only stopped for gas, paying with cash, or at rest stops to cook a meal. The beast used a lot of gas.

Heath and Malcom took turns driving the fifteen and half hours. They wanted to take the most direct route, but that was the most risky, so they took the next best with scenic routes that more tourists and other RVs would be using. They lost a few hours, but it was another precaution.

Juanita sat at the miniature dining table and watched the scenery roll past the window in a daze at the different vistas. She felt a spark of wanderlust bloom inside her. There was such beauty across the land and she wanted to experience it.

The over-cab bed for the guys and queen bed in the back for the ladies were used on and off the entire time as they each caught some sleep here and there. The tension and stress seemed to drain all of their energy even though most had gotten good sleep at the motel. Except Malcom, who she suspected was too wary of Hunter escaping.

She was still amazed Malcom let Heath's suspicious computer snooping slide. She felt she understood why he did it, but it must have been hard for him to overlook. Or could he see that where it counted Heath had rehabilitated?

Elizabeth was more relaxed. It seemed there were no spirits attached to the camper and she only occasionally looked at empty space, which Juanita recognized as the sign she saw an apparition.

Their first evening in the cramped quarters, Heath cooked several prime steaks on an open grill at a rest stop while the rest stayed out of sight in the camper. Heath proved to be a grill master, and the steaks were mouth watering and juicy with a hint of seasoning that made the flavor burst.

She would never forget Heath joining her at the small kitchen space as she got the pre-made potato salad, coleslaw, and salad ready buffet style. He placed a warm hand on her lower back and spoke in soft tones.

"I'd love for us to do a cross-country trek with a camper. We could go back out to see the Sequoias and take our time and enjoy the trip." His warm gaze and words made her heart clench. Had he really changed? Could she trust him to not use his technical knowledge to steal? She wanted to believe in him. She could really enjoy the image he painted.

He snuck a kiss on her cheek and began setting paper plates and plastic-ware on the small table. It was over twenty-four hours of Hunter recuperating, and he was looking considerably stronger. His appetite sure kicked in. She never saw anybody pack away the food like he did. He devoured two of those steaks and all the extras with it.

"Do you think the President will really take action and start a widespread investigation?" Heath voiced what they were all silently pondering the closer they got to D.C.

"Not a clue. It could go either way," Malcom said with a solemn look on his face.

"Are we all walking into a trap?" Hunter blurted out.

They just stared at one another. Nobody could offer reassurance it wasn't. They finished the meal with the radio on, listening to the news, hoping for any sign investigations had begun or the violence had lessened. Nothing.

That night Malcom drove through the inky dark. Driving long distances at night scared her and she couldn't sleep, so she sat in the passenger seat and made small talk with Malcom to keep him awake. He was an okay guy. Maybe he and Elizabeth would be good for each other.

They entered Washington D.C. around midnight and checked into the RV park they had agreed upon before they left Jackson. Juanita was relieved they had a spot open. It was popular with a swimming pool, several small cabins, miniature golf and amenities to attract families. For their purposes, it had a local bus stop so Heath could go into town and rent a car to get them to the Executive Building in the morning.

Now that they were so close to the meeting location and time, she tossed and turned with various scary scenarios playing in her head, none of which had any survivors from their group when it was all said and done. Elizabeth was just as restless next to her in the queen bed.

CHAPTER NINETY-ONE

Elizabeth Grant

E lizabeth had been ghost-free while in the camper, except for the occasional visit by Loralie and Netty, and the campground seemed free of spirits as well. But she was on full alert, her nerves on overdrive. Everybody was jumpy.

Malcom went jogging early to deal with his nerves, and to scope out the other campers. Juanita wrote an article to publish after their meeting. She said it helped her to center and focus. Hunter tried some Tai Chi in the confines of the camper. Heath sat outside and meditated, so she joined him with her hair tucked up in a hat and sunglasses, holding the CD player Netty gave her. The refreshing morning air was a caress and the smells of lush greenery including ferns mixed with the astringent scent of pine trees.

She listened to Netty's voice and slipped into a deep meditation where she returned to the garden and sat with animals gathered around her. She was finally able to relax for a few minutes. No revelations or spirits, as if even on this plane of existence the universe held its breath.

She finished her meditation and stretched. Heath was gone, and the campground was coming to life with a few campers moving about their defined spaces. How long had she lost herself in the meditation?

Heath pulled up in a rented Hummer with dark windows, of all things. Sure they needed something big enough for all of them plus Hunter's hulking form, but a Hummer? They wouldn't be very stealthy in that.

After a few minutes, they piled into the camper with copies of all their evidence gathered so far, including a scan of Noah's notebook. Heath locked up the camper and set the alarm.

Each of them were disguised with glasses, sun hats, or similar garb. Juanita had cut her hair fairly short. Elizabeth pinned her hair up in a bun and donned a tennis visor with glasses, the summer tourist look.

Malcom addressed them all, "How're we goin' to handle the parkin' and entry? Our most vulnerable time will be walkin' from the car to the buildin'."

Juanita blew out a breath, "Right. There is no easy access parking. I arranged for us to pull up at the Pennsylvania Avenue entrance and the valet parking will take the vehicle. We are to enter through that side of the building away from the public access. That leaves about two hundred and fifty yards to cover to get to the steps. Should we just flat-out run for it?"

"We have to expect they will use any opportunity to stop us – such as a distance to cover. Yes, we run like our lives depend upon it," He bluntly said.

Because our lives do actually depend on it. He didn't say it, but we all sure as hell thought it.

She heard about the nightmare traffic in D.C., but she was still amazed at the slow progress, major roads under construction, ambiguous detours, and a confusing city layout. Even the dashboard GPS had to recalculate a few times.

Heath parked the Hummer in front of the Eisenhower Executive Office Building along Pennsylvania Avenue and laid his head on the steering wheel. *Was he praying?* Fear hung thick as smog in the air.

Elizabeth looked out the window and exclaimed, "Wow, French Second Empire style, impressive. I never thought I'd see an example of it until I went to France. It's in great condition." Her voice filled with wonder at the sight of the large building overshadowing the White House next door.

"I forgot you're an architect. Don't stop to gawk at it until you're inside. Okay?" Malcom cautioned her.

A man walked toward the Hummer, clearly the valet.

"Okay, let's do this, folks. Grab everythin' you need and let's run."

They exploded out of the Hummer like horses out of a race gate. She noticed Heath toss the keys to the valet parking guy. Before them lay a wide sidewalk, then a fence enclosing the building, but a gate with a bronze sign was open for them. Inside the six foot wrought-iron fence was a wide promenade of white and red stone squares leading to the stairway.

Malcom would likely be the fastest, but he was beside Hunter, maintaining Hunter's protective custody. Juanita was in the lead hand-in-hand with Heath then Elizabeth closely following. The final stretch was running up the stairs. Long legged Heath took them two at a time, pulling Juanita with him. Elizabeth jogged up each step. Behind them were Malcom and Hunter.

They didn't slow down until they were through the doors and skidded to a stop in the expansive and dim entry hall with black and white tile floor. They were panting or bent over huffing. She looked around and Malcom was standing tall, barely breathing heavy. Hunter didn't fair as well, but markedly better than after the sprint from the hospital.

Five men in dark suits, white shirts with dark ties, and ear buds surrounded them. Secret Service was in the house. They removed their hats and shades. "We're expected," she rushed to say before any guns were drawn.

Their identification was scrutinized and their names checked off a list.

"This way," the suit with graying temples said. They followed up the stairs to the second floor. In the middle of the southern hall they entered what a plaque stated was the Vice President's Ceremonial Office. The halls were empty at the moment, except for a few spirits.

One apparition had a bullet hole in his head and walked on without noticing the group.

She soaked in the ornamental stenciling and gold gilt on the walls and ceiling, the mahogany, white maple, and cherry woods on the floor. Old-fashioned chandeliers lighted the room and reflected in the enormous ornate gold gilt mirrors. Everything smelled of importance, history, and furniture polish. But it was the rich wood conference table for eighteen in the center of the room with the President of the United States that commanded attention.

CHAPTER NINETY-TWO

Elizabeth Grant

The President of the United States stood and shook their hands with both of his, cupping their one. Then he came to Hunter, and she was surprised to witness no hesitation. Rather, a wag of his head at the damage to Rance's face, which had improved since she first saw him. The President moved with an athlete's assurance. He smiled, a reserved quirk of the lips on an otherwise serious face.

"Please be seated. I watched your interview and heard the outcry for an official and extensive investigation. I felt it prudent to meet you and go over what you've found. I need to hear your story before taking action." He waved and meat, cheese, and fruit trays were sat on the table and water glasses were placed with coasters before them.

They looked to one another for who should start and Malcom nodded to Juanita. She began to tell how she started out investigating the Philadelphia massacre of an innocent family.

Elizabeth sat back. They were going to be here for a while from the looks of it.

But she had barely popped some meat and cheese in her mouth when the Secret Service approached the President.

"Excuse the interruption, ladies and gentlemen, but we have an additional guest to join us." The President waved a hand, and a man was escorted into the room.

It was... her uncle. *What was her uncle doing here?*

Uncle Jairus walked directly towards her, but Malcom and Hunter both stood and blocked his path.

"Elizabeth, I've been worried sick and had to see you." He looked at the two men between them, "I'm her uncle, gentlemen."

Malcom locked eyes with her, hard and suspicious. Hell, she was suspicious of the timing. Netty's spirit popped in, followed by Loralie. They scrutinized Uncle Jairus.

The President made introductions, "Ladies and gentlemen, this is Jairus Grant, CEO of one of the largest broadcasting conglomerates in the nation, and Elizabeth's uncle. He needed to see me and was ecstatic to hear his elusive niece would be visiting with me." He extended his arms, "Please, let's sit."

Uncle Jairus took a seat on the other side of Elizabeth from Malcom and gave the agent a glacial look. "We need to have a serious talk young lady, your disrespectful treatment of me was inexcusable." His whisper held venom. Then he gave a murderous look at Hunter.

Uncle Jairus seemed to radiate fury as he sat next to her. It had been a mistake to not contact him at all when he came to Cyprus. She would probably be mad if she were in his shoes too. But she had told him not to visit, and he refused to listen.

"We were listening to the evidence that they have collected. Please continue Miss Alvarez." The President nodded to Juanita.

Juanita took the interruption in stride and backed up a little in her presentation.

There was a current buzzing under the polite meeting. Netty and Loralie felt it too. They twisted their hands and watched each of them while pacing. The President was absorbed in looking over documents. He replayed the video of the police on the night of the massacre several times and asked questions about its origin.

She was concerned at the tense presence of Netty and Loralie. They watched Uncle Jairus and seemed agitated. Something wasn't right with this picture, and they sensed it. Loralie had never met her uncle. He had left Cyprus and never looked back, even married the daughter of the media company mogul he worked for beginning in his late teens. The owner had taken him under his wing and taught him the business. But Elizabeth and her mother were still shocked when the man left his entire business to Uncle Jairus in his will, even if he was the son-in-law.

After the tragic summer when Loralie went missing, Uncle Jairus had spent more time and resources to help. He paid for the psychologist to get her over the *hallucination* they decided she had. He was never particularly warm or nurturing, but he made an effort over the last few years to *provide a positive male influence,* as he put it, which had made her mother feel like a failure.

Juanita passed out the copies of the bank statements for the Philadelphia cops and the California prison guards. Elizabeth's focus was on Netty and Loralie's spirits. They were shaking their heads and wringing their hands. She wished she could get past whatever block she had and hear them like she did other spirits now.

Her attention wandered. She was jumpy and anxious. Other spirits were popping in and out of the room now, they too seemed anxious. She stared at Uncle Jairus's signet ring, gold with a red stone. It was the same ring he was always rapping on tables. It had some design in the center. The realization of what the symbol on his ring was sent chills of dread through her being. She looked up at Netty and Juanita in shock.

Malcom nudged her with an elbow and raised an eyebrow. Surely she was wrong. Her uncle couldn't be involved in The Society. She noticed Uncle Jairus look at the agent beside the President. *Was that a slight nod to the man?*

The agent then whispered into the President's ear again.

Another agent began directing them, "We have a viable threat and must get the President to safety."

"They can all come with me. I want to finish this. Bring them."

The agent talked in the President's ear again.

"No, I want them along with me. That's final."

Juanita and Heath were grabbing their materials and his laptop.

In an organized rush out the door, agents herded them through the halls, down the stairs to the basement, and past a small bowling alley.

As they were rushed along, she whispered in Malcom' ear, "Something's not right, I think my Uncle may be involved with The Society." His eyebrows shot up and he scrutinized Uncle Jairus from behind. He looked back at her and nodded.

They were then hurried through a heavy reinforced metal door with a proximity card reader and shifting key login pad. The door slammed shut behind them with a BOOM that echoed. Elizabeth felt like the door on a mausoleum had just closed, sealing their fate.

A concrete tunnel stretched before them with hanging lights illuminating the claustrophobic way ahead. The light left dim pools of light every twelve feet or so and she felt like she was inside NORAD back home where they had a military facility inside Cheyenne Mountain. Malcom was right behind her with Hunter and she sensed both were tense, ready to spring.

She dropped back so she could talk to Malcom.

"Remember the symbol in Noah's notes?" She asked in low tones.

"Yeah, it led you back to Whispering Oaks Plantation House to discover Hunter."

"I noticed my uncle's signet ring that he's had for years, he's always tapping it on tables and such. I swear it has that symbol," she said as they followed behind the others.

He sucked in his breath. "Are you positive?"

"I'm pretty sure. Your aunt and Loralie have been upset since he arrived too." She kept her eyes on the tunnel ahead.

"You realize what you're sayin'. He's your family. Wouldn't you all know somethin' like that?"

Before she could reply they came to a stop in a widened circular space and stood around in an oval to hear what was happening. The President was calm, as if this was just part of the job or a drill.

They were down to three Secret Service agents that accompanied them into the tunnel. One of the Secret Service men tossed a gun to Uncle Jairus. She couldn't believe her eyes.

"What's happening? What threat warrants giving your gun to a civilian?" The President demanded, his eyes blazing.

"Uncle Jairus, what's going on?" She felt she had to intervene.

"Don't act like you don't know. Immediately after that bitch died you were raisin the alarm, you come back to town and immediately have a visitor in the night. Don't play innocent."

She couldn't speak. He grew up alongside her mother. How could he be involved with this?

"I have to hand it to you. Wherever you hid Noah's traitorous notes I wasn't able to find them. And everywhere you lived was searched, I even arranged for boyfriends to get close and find whatever Noah had gathered. Hell, even your therapist and your college roommate were Society members. But it all resulted in nothin', until now."

She could only stand there, processing his long involvement with The Society and apparently in Loralie's death. How could he be involved with that murderous group?

No wonder he came to Cyprus to see her after the failed kidnapping. He needed to finish what the goons had messed up. It also explained his glaring at Malcom, the man who rescued her from the kidnappers. He wouldn't actually hurt her, would he? He kept his gun pointed directly at the President.

"Why're you just standin' there?" Malcom asked another Secret Service man. "Stop him!"

Uncle Jairus chuckled, "Don't bother, they're all Society men. We have a job to do. When this is all over, Hunter and Mr. FBI will have killed the President plus all of you and these loyal agents will have shot them."

The President was stunned, "Jairus, you're a trusted industry advisor, welcome at the White House. Why are you doing this? This is madness."

"Why? To save this nation, restore it to its former glory. All the concern over rights and tiptoeing around the truth has ruined the country. You animals," he waved the gun at Malcom and Hunter, "don't know your place anymore. This nation needs to cut out the cancer growin' to save the body."

His eyes shone too bright and his jaw clenched. She glanced around for help. The agents had guns on the group, so the one agent must have carried two.

Juanita had her phone tilted funny. A cell phone wouldn't have any reception down in these concrete lined tunnels. She must be recording what was happening. If it was found after they died the real story might survive. Juanita was a reporter to the bone, ensuring the truth would be told.

"Uncle Jairus, whatever this Society has convinced you about current affairs, you can't do this. You can't murder anyone. This isn't you, it would kill Gran." She tried to get past his hate and prejudice.

Uncle Jairus pounced and struck her in the face. She couldn't see and stumbled backward. Arms caught her, but white fog swirled in her eyes. Not the proverbial stars. That answered her question; he would definitely hurt her without a second thought.

She heard a vicious growl deep in a chest rumbling. It was only slightly surprising to realize it was Hunter. Malcom had caught her, like she knew he would.

"Oh yes, sweet old mother. The brainwashed idiot that let you associate with that nigger girl, have sleepovers and such. She's part of the problem that must be exterminated. No, Elijah Wiltshire was more my family. He showed me how to be a man, to rule a house, and keep the women in line. He taught me the truth about the nation's direction and how we must take decisive action to restore this nation." His shoulders were back, and she swore his chest was thrust out.

Elizabeth removed the gris-gris bag hanging around her neck from under her top and held onto it. *If there was ever a time for extra protection, it was now.*

He stood a little taller, as if posing for a portrait. "What I've built won't be stopped. The large membership I've recruited, the teachins in schools I've fostered, the exposin' of inferior races, placin' my people all over the nation in important jobs, all my efforts will be rewarded. Even if by some miracle you stop me today, the army I've amassed will rise up in my wake and take back this nation if I should somehow fail. With force if necessary, they'll kill anyone standin' in the way of makin' this nation great again." He smiled, proud of his hate-filled seditious accomplishment.

Blood dripped down the side of her face. His ring had cut her cheekbone. She understood now that she didn't know her uncle at all; he was a stranger to her. He was a stranger to her mother and grandmother too. The impact of who he truly was made her heart grieve. She stood on her own and Malcom's arms released her. A quick glance confirmed that Juanita had caught it all on her phone's camera.

She glanced behind her, Malcom, like the well-trained Special Ops Ranger he was, watched every move of the men with guns.

They all needed to be ready to intervene. She sensed both men behind her tense. Later, she would have nightmares of what followed, all in slow motion as if time slowed, but in the moment it happened quickly.

Uncle Jairus faced the President, extended his arm, and aimed his gun. At only a few short feet away, there would be no missing. The President didn't shrink. That image fused in her brain. He faced the gun without flinching. "History bears out that hate never rules for long," the President said.

In seconds Heath was standing between the gun and the President. Hunter tackled Uncle Jairus in a football tackle leap, Malcom whirled toward the agent behind him with a bone crunching fist to the nose, Juanita swung her purse at the gun hand of the agent closest to her – the man who supplied Uncle Jairus with the gun, and Elizabeth swung her leg out successfully knocking the third agent off his feet. Shots went wild. Heath was slammed backward with the force of a bullet hitting him, knocking the President down with him.

Juanita's agent recovered first and covered us all with his gun while the other agents and Uncle Jairus stood. Hunter received several punches to the face from Jairus, which he took without showing any reaction but a maniacal look in his eyes revealing he had killed before and would again before this was done.

Heath was on the floor bleeding from his stomach and the President had his hands on the wound trying to stanch the blood.

The agent who had brought two guns took charge. He held his gun out and shot the other two agents in the head. He didn't even wait for their bodies to fall before he turned his gun on Uncle Jairus.

Her uncle scoffed at the gun, "What do you think you're doin', pointin' a gun at the General of The Society? You've made a huge mistake if you think you can take over."

Elizabeth sucked in a breath. Her uncle was more than just a member of The Society. He was the General, the man behind The Society, leader of a bunch of white supremacists filled with hate and self-righteousness, traitors to the nation. How had her family not known his very heart had turned to stone?

"I'm not taking over. I'm loyal to another organization that's watched you since you became General of The Society and increased the membership so drastically. Not that we don't have similar agendas, because we do. But you're not one of us. We simply can't have that."

Uncle Jairus had to have the last word, "I've changed this nation and its future by raisin' an army who will shed blood. Someday soon someone just like me will rule this nation…"

He shot Uncle Jairus between the eyes and her uncle fell backward. His body hit the cement floor with a whomp and his head made a loud cracking sound.

Juanita had inched her way over to the President and Elizabeth had done the same. She would process everything about her uncle later. The President was still in danger. When the gun turned toward her, she grabbed Juanita's hand and they blocked Heath and the President from the rogue double agent.

His attention was on them, the two women who stood up to his gun, and didn't see the mountain of muscle behind him.

Hunter moved as fast as a rattlesnake striking, grabbed the man's head from behind with massive cuffed hands and twisted it. He tossed the body aside like a rag doll.

She would never get that image and the sound of the man's neck snapping out of her mind. Her stomach threatened to upchuck, but she managed to keep herself together.

Malcom was by Hunter's side in seconds, "We really needed him alive to find out what organization he was with. There's still a threat out there to the President. I just wish there'd been a way to stop him without ending him." He nodded to Hunter, then turned.

"Mr. President, the threat has been eliminated." Malcom had stepped in as the only remaining Federal Agent. "We must get you out of these tunnels and to safety."

"This man must have medical attention immediately, I'm not leaving him."

Malcom turned to Hunter, "Get one of their earwigs and see if they were just turned off."

Hunter searched the man he killed with rough hands, jerked the earwig loose and gathered the transmitter and receiver unit secured on the belt. He handed it to Malcom, who put the earwig in his ear and fiddled with the controls.

"Testin', can you hear me? Hello, we're in the tunnel to the Executive Building. There's a man in need of an ambulance immediately. Send the medical examiner and forensic techs too. We have bodies of three men who attempted to assassinate the President."

Then she saw the spirits of the Secret Service men looking down at their bodies. Without thinking, she walked up to one of them and yelled, "Leave here, you aren't welcome and we sure don't want your hate hanging around. Isn't hell waiting for you?" Her emotions got the best of her. She probably looked crazy in front of the President, yelling at nothing any of them could see.

She turned and faced the other spirits, only to find Juanita standing with her again.

Juanita held out a pendant from around her neck and began praying, "Saint Michael the Archangel, send these violent and murderous spirits where they belong, I ask."

The spirits were gone in an instant. Whether they left on their own or were confronted by a non-nonsense Archangel, Elizabeth didn't know and didn't care.

"They gone?" Juanita asked.

"Yeah, but the damage they've done is still with us."

She looked around at Heath on the floor with the President's bloody hands holding his stomach and at all the bodies on the floor. What a waste. She felt sick to her stomach.

The President eyed her. Apparently he witnessed her momentary slip. He nodded at her and turned back to Heath.

Malcom gathered her in his arms while they waited for the ambulance.

CHAPTER NINETY-THREE

2 Months Later - Elizabeth

It was an overcast Mississippi morning with a steady drizzle soaking everything since the early hours. Loralie's remains had been released for burial, finally. All possible forensic evidence collected. Cyprus was a bad memory, so Elizabeth was relieved her friend was being laid to rest in Meridian where her mother and brother could visit her.

The memorial service was held graveside under a canopy because of the rain. The President and his family attended. Rance Hunter had politely requested Tito and Daniel Baker be permitted to attend the service to pay his respects to the family.

Juanita was the only reporter Mrs. Carter would allow to cover the funeral, which she insisted be a small affair. Heath, still frail but regaining strength daily, attended in a wheelchair. Juanita had stayed by his side through his emergency surgery and the touch-and-go first forty-eight hours. Juanita was now Elizabeth's closest female friend, so she rejoiced in her finding some resolution on her relationship with Heath.

Elizabeth's mother and grandmother were beside her and hadn't quite forgiven her for keeping them in the dark through her entanglement in the affair, although Uncle Jairus's assassination attempt outweighed her transgression. Her mother and grandmother were in shock still, wondering why they didn't realize what had happened to him and even questioning if they could have prevented any of it.

Elizabeth and her mother hadn't worked through their issues concerning her father's identity being kept from her even as an adult. To say family relations were strained was an understatement. She had spent a weekend with her father in Denver, just talking and getting to know him.

Before Elizabeth was the rectangular hole in the ground waiting for Loralie's body, like mother earth's womb taking her remains to a refuge after her sacrifice. The white satin deluxe casket and the profusion of lavish funeral flowers were Rance Hunter's contribution in honor of her sacrifice. He was in a Supermax prison in Florence, Colorado, under protective watch. She still couldn't forget his killing that man without the slightest hesitation. It kept her from forgetting he was a killer in maximum security for a reason.

Malcom, dressed in men-in-black standard issue suit and Ray-Bans, stood next to her. He looked good, and she naturally gravitated toward him. They had managed a few dinners together since the events in the underground tunnel. She remained cautious even as they grew closer, but he was often pulled away on an assignment, which didn't bode well for much of a relationship.

In particular, he was assigned to lead a task force to clean the Bureau of any Society members and to coordinate with the Department of Justice for the same objective. Rooting out The Society members in powerful positions was a top priority of the President and dangerous work.

Now that the financial records could be scoured from the main Society bank accounts and Uncle Jairus's computer and phone records were scrutinized, the Bureau was exposing shocking leaders as members of The Society. When the Vice President was arrested for his participation, the nation reeled at how close The Society for a Restored America came to succeeding at taking over the government and how it had sparked the level of violence among common citizens.

Uncle Jairus's last words still haunted her, *I've changed this nation and its future. Someday soon someone just like me will rule this nation.* A shiver ran down her spine.

Elizabeth pulled her mind back to the funeral. Standing in the rain, the President gave a short but moving eulogy, calling Loralie a heroine for the nation to learn from as healing began. That seemed optimistic; prejudices had been inflamed and fanned and healing felt like a distant hope.

A black college professor had been beaten to death by middle class white men and vice versa. Reports of violence against Black and Hispanics still occurred regularly. But the horror of a man assaulting an inner city school and gunning down thirty-two innocent black second and third graders had slapped many awake.

Elizabeth said a few words sharing how Loralie was her *gifted* sister, the sister that the universe had sent her. She choked up every other line because she was saying them directly to Loralie's spirit standing next to her own casket.

She finished with Mary Elizabeth Frye's poem "Do Not Stand at my Grave and Weep." The words were laden with double meaning for her.

Elizabeth and Loralie's family all cried. It wasn't grief, after this long they had already grieved her loss; it was a release of the long-buried worry and questions. The closure brought tears to cleanse all their hearts.

After the funeral, Elizabeth and Mrs. Carter clung to each other, crying softly.

"Thank you for bringing my baby girl home. I don't know how you did it, I only know you've always been good to us. You are my *gifted* daughter." That brought more tears. Jeremiah joined the hug.

She left Jeremiah and Mrs. Carter, promising to come by her home for refreshments.

Malcom stood among the Secret Service with the President. Before she could walk over to him, Juanita wheeled Heath over. Elizabeth bent over and gave him a big hug and a kiss on the cheek.

"How is our hero doing?"

"Every day I'm a little stronger. I'm glad to have work to do."

Elizabeth raised her eyebrows at the pair.

Juanita lowered her voice, "Besides funneling everything we gathered from Heath's website traps and cookies to the special investigation task force, Tito demanded all the proof we had too. Now we've been going through the information for my ongoing exposé articles. So we're busy."

"What do you think Tito is going to do with all that information?" She could speculate, but maybe Juanita knew.

"He won't tell me anything more than to say it's best I don't know. I had to give him the information according to our contract. I don't even want to make a guess what the gang might do with that knowledge."

"Did you guys know Hunter, through the Black Apostles, set up a college scholarship for young black women in honor of Loralie?" Of course, it was officially through their rap and hip hop recording label with a separate foundation set up to administer the money. But it was unexpected all the same.

"We were taken completely by surprise, I suspect Hunter was behind it after you yelled at him that morning about Loralie being the first casualty." Heath chuckled. He looked up at Juanita with happiness and unveiled love.

"Think you might get a Pulitzer?" She sure hoped so. She deserved it.

"Wouldn't that be a hoot, first generation Mexican American wins Pulitzer for exposing White Supremacist plot?" She shrugged a shoulder, "It could happen I guess, but that's not why I do the work. It's always been about the Fourth Estate and journalism's role in the checks and balances of the nation for me." She lowered her eyes, still adjusting to the instant attention she had garnered after the shooting was made public and her articles were syndicated.

A Secret Service Agent trotted over and asked for Elizabeth to join the President for a word.

Under black umbrellas, because any other color today would have somehow been a slap in the face, she joined the canopy of umbrellas sheltering the first family along with Malcom. After formal introductions to the first lady and their three children, they ducked into the waiting stretch car with blackened windows and she was left with the President and agents under the umbrellas.

"I'm going to cut to the meat of the matter Ms. Grant. Malcom has apprised me of your special talent that aided you in this entire affair. Your talent saved Hunter's life, and that in turn saved the nation." He paused and took a thoughtful breath. "I have a job offer for you. Occasionally, such a unique talent could be of special assistance to me and the Office of the President." His eyes bore into hers and there was no mistaking the full weight of such an offer.

"You wouldn't work alone. Malcom would be assigned to assist you, and your reporter and *computer expert* could be called in when needed as well." He broke eye contact with her and swept his gaze around the dreary water logged cemetery.

"I'm honored... and gobsmacked. I can't imagine how I could... I mean to say I don't know what circumstance could present itself where *I* could possibly help *you*."

"May I, sir?" Malcom asked, and the President nodded. "You'd be behind the scenes, nothin' official. I'd help, and it would be similar to our recent work, completely off book."

Her mouth made a big "O". What could she say? How could she possibly ever turn the President down? He had been the stalwart and calm factor, providing a steady hand and stabilizing influence the nation needed these past months.

"Ms. Grant... Elizabeth, let me be honest. There are forces at work, even within our leadership and elected officials, who'd lead this nation down an alternate path. A path that compromises the democratic republic that has been carefully built and precariously maintained, such as we recently witnessed. For me to take action, even to suggest a quiet investigation of a suspected influence would be all over the halls of power and the individuals involved alerted. With you and your unique talent, any exploration would be far more covert or easily dismissed."

"I can't say no, sir. But that doesn't mean that I'm confident I can be of any service at all."

"Malcom has unending faith in your abilities and after hearing from your friends on how you've communicated with their deceased loved ones, I have come to believe." He eyed her as if to will his confidence into her being.

"I'm giving you a month to further recover from this ordeal and then your first assignment will be the agent who shot your Uncle. He said he worked for another organization who felt Jairus Grant couldn't be controlled." He scanned the cemetery again from under the umbrella.

"This hidden danger of another group could have their own agenda for the nation and the White House. I've lost considerable sleep over that man and the words he uttered. In about a month, Malcom will be in touch and you'll utilize your talents toward what that man was involved with, perhaps be able to query the man's spirit even."

The President got into the waiting car and the caravan of his protection detail drove away.

Malcom spoke after a few moments of silence, "Are you goin' back to Denver? Where will I find you in a month?"

"Your Aunt Netty has forcefully directed me to a teacher to train me in my gift. I'll be on the Southern Ute Indian Reservation in Southwest Colorado. At this point I only know of Ignacio as the closest town." And Ignacio was small, real small. She wasn't sure about this training; a part of her was terrified.

She'd been resistant to such an arrangement and away from home with some stranger. But, Madam Antoinette insisted she couldn't move on until she knew Elizabeth would be trained properly on her gift.

"That's just like her, find somebody in a remote place. Can I still call you, stay in touch in the meantime?"

Elizabeth closed the distance between them. She pivoted up on her toes and kissed him full on the mouth. He kissed back eagerly. When she pulled back, she whispered in his ear, "You better, mister."

AUTHOR NOTES

A few notes for clarification will follow. Cyprus Mississippi is completely fictional, although the nearby town of Meridian does actually exist and some of the other landmarks mentioned.

Whitmore plantation ruins where Elizabeth is rescued are inspired by the Windsor Plantation ruins in Port Gibson, with several modifications for the story line.

Whispering Oaks is inspired by the hauntingly beautiful Oak Alley in Louisiana, which is now a Bed & Breakfast. It is a well-preserved example of the plantation architecture style, Greek Revival, and reputedly has a resident ghost or two. It has been used over the years for movies, most notably Hush, Hush, Sweet Charlotte staring Betty Davis, one of my favorite scary movies.

Corcoran, California and the prison I reference are indeed real. The prison in Corcoran housed serial killer Charles Manson until his death. It has many gang members imprisoned there. The Brunswich bar I mentioned in Corcoran is from the town's past and no longer exists.

Delaware, as I mention in the story, is known as a state-side tax haven and the state's incredibly relaxed regulations are used for money laundering by many including international interests.

Delaware's system also provides a cover for other nations to donate money to candidates in our elections, allowing foreign powers to influence our elections.

I also mention one address being used by multiple businesses as a tax evasion technique and shell company tactic. 1209 North Orange Street in Delaware is the business address for 285,000 separate business entities. I also mention a Russian arms dealer who is connected with this whole Delaware issue which you can read more about in this article in the New York Times about the whole problem: http://tinyurl.com/bnesfhn.

I briefly mention the private prison system and their prison labor as a highly profitable servitude system. This has been covered in newspapers and Amy Goodman of Democracy Now! interviewed prisoners in California who fight wildfires for the state, saving the state one hundred million dollars a year because they only get paid $1 an hour. They are the ones placed mere feet from flames digging trenches to create a break line to contain the fires. The book "The New Jim Crow" by Michelle Alexander is another good reference on this issue.

Ripped from the headlines is overused. The plot for this book was conceived and developed before events in Ferguson, or the June 17, 2015 church shooting in South Carolina and controversy over the confederate flag that resulted from the 21 year old shooter's photo. That tells you how long it took me to write this book. But, Ferguson and the S.C. church shooting did confirm in my mind that the story I was writing took a plausible "what if" scenario and brought it to life. In fact, I started this story a good twelve years ago and it remained on a back burner for a long while.

The idea of White Supremacists rising is nothing new, see the non-fiction books "Soldiers of God: White Supremacists and Their Holy War for America" by Myra Barnes, "The Silent Brotherhood: Inside American's Racist Underground" by Kevin Flynn, and the March 2018 article in the Huffington Post, "Florida Public School Teacher Has A White Nationalist Podcast", of a pretty young White Supremacist middle school civics teacher in Florida spreading her message to her students. In the Southern Poverty Law Center's article about the same teacher, she discusses how she spreads her message covertly under the administrator's nose.

Let's not forget the White pride movement, White Nationalists that are still growing, and individuals such as KKK prior Grand Wizard David Duke who run for public office while being very vocal about their views. These people win elections here and there. The Southern Poverty Law Center lists (at the time of this writing) 72 KKK groups, 121 Neo-Nazi groups, 100 White Nationalist groups, 71 racist Skinhead groups, and 20 Christian Identity (highly racist hate group) all active in the United States currently.

Let's not forget that such radical racist groups now use direct mail campaigns to recruit followers, have dedicated podcasts and talk radio shows, their own newsletters and news outlets. They are growing in numbers with their revisionist history and blatant rewriting of historical facts. According to RacismReview.com, a survey of 200 teachers shows 60% of middle and high school students are using White Supremacist (aka White Nationalist or Alt-Right) websites for their research for homework papers.

This book was conceived well before the KKK would openly endorse a presidential candidate and it didn't destroy the candidate's chances, but rather helped get him elected. I mention these only to illustrate that the concept of White Supremacists (secret or not) making inroads into our government is not outside the realm of possibility; perhaps not in the same manner I portray it taking place in this story. A writer takes the "What if" and runs with it, which is what I did.

The concept of The Society for a Restored America as portrayed in the novel isn't very farfetched I wager. It's probably too tame, if anything. One of my Beta readers was shocked at the rhetoric I bring to life in the book, feeling it was too far "out there." I actually tamed some of their actual views down a bit in my narrative – but I felt I still needed to show their true views and agendas because it is too easy to dismiss such extremism as farfetched. What will vary from White

Supremacist (aka White Nationalist or Alt-Right) group to group is their magic fix to the perceived "problem."

There is a scene where I have a Pastor pray for the White Supremacist leader's success in the book. That may seem unimaginable to many, but the Methodist pastor William Joseph Simmons on Oct 16, 1915 on Stone Mountain Georgia along with sixteen or so men resurrected the KKK from the ashes. At the altar they had constructed, they staged a U.S. Flag, a Bible, and a sword. They took an oath and burned a cross for their revival of the KKK. The burning cross they claimed was to symbolize "the Light of Christ." DeNeen L. Brown, *The Preacher who used Christianity to Revive the KKK,* The Washington Post, April 10, 2018, online. There are many instances of White Supremacist pastors today, and many arguments used by such groups are interspersed with Bible references. The book "Noah's Curse" by Stephen R. Haynes with the subtitle "The Biblical Justification of American Slavery" details how scripture is used to justify their views.

Stone Mountain now has a Confederate Memorial Carving depicting Civil War generals Stonewall Jackson and Robert E. Lee, plus Confederate President Jefferson Davis that has 4,000,000 visitors a year. Coincidence?

The symbol I use for The Society for a Restored America is a trowel and sword with the U.S. Map in the background. The sword symbolizes the willingness to shed blood in their fight and the trowel symbolizes how they wish to rebuild the nation in their image. This is similar to the symbols used on Stone Mountain during that 1915 ritual, but I wasn't thinking of that when I developed it for my fictional group.

I based the idea of Noah Aarons becoming an informant against The Society on the story of Dave Hall who was part of the militant Aryan Nations and was an FBI informant. It is an extremely dangerous avenue to go down. You can read about him in the book "Into the Devil's Den: How an FBI Informant Got Inside the Aryan Nations and a Special Agent Got Him Out Alive" by Dave Hall and Tym Burkey. My version has Noah Aarons already a member of The

Society and becomes an informant, although I never explain why he changes his mind. I would like to believe Noah found he didn't agree with the extremism of The Society.

I briefly mention what has become known as The Lost Cause which sprang up shortly after the South was defeated. To learn more about this mythology that was created, read the book "The Myth of the Lost Cause" by Edward Bonekemper. Part of the Lost Cause is the concept that the Civil War (that I call the war of Northern Aggression as many in the South do) was really over economics and greed which I mention in the book. This alternate history has been steadily gaining acceptance as fact. But, the Confederate Vice President Alexander Stephens said in his 1861 "Cornerstone Speech" that the Confederacy was dedicated to keeping black Americans in bondage as human property for all time. The book "Alexander H. Stephens of Georgia: A Biography" by historian Thomas Schott helps to clear up that issue. I think the words of the Confederate Vice President sets the record straight, as he of all people would know what the Confederacy represented and what they were fighting for.

Allison Dubois, whose experiences were the basis of the television series Medium, inspired the idea of Elizabeth. Elizabeth may communicate with the dead differently than reputed mediums such as Ms. Dubois, which is my creative license for the sake of the story.

I hope you enjoyed The Society and these notes give you more to dig into.

ABOUT THE AUTHOR

C.G. Abbot was born and raised in Colorado, graduated from college with a degree in business administration, and has worked in fortune 500 companies and Department of Defense most of her life.

She lives in Colorado with two cats as her spirited companions. She volunteers for a cat shelter, enjoys scrapbooking and card making, photography, and painting in watercolor and acrylic. She inherited a love for reading and history from her mother and grandmother and grew up talking about books and historical events at the dinner table.

Website: cgabbot.yolasite.com
Signup for my newsletter: http://eepurl.com/gaE1wf